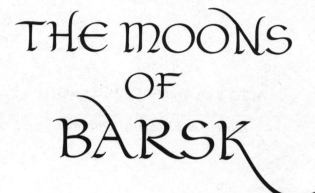

THE MOONS OF BARSK

THE MOONS
OF
BARSK

LAWRENCE M. SCHOEN

TOR

A TOM DOHERTY ASSOCIATES BOOK
NEW YORK

THE MOONS OF BARSK

Copyright © 2018 by Lawrence M. Schoen

A Tor Book
Published by Tom Doherty Associates
175 Fifth Avenue
New York, NY 10010

www.tor-forge.com

Tor® is a registered trademark of Macmillan Publishing Group, LLC.

The Library of Congress Cataloging-in-Publication Data
is available upon request.

ISBN 978-0-7653-9463-7 (hardcover)
ISBN 978-0-7653-9464-4 (ebook)

Our books may be purchased in bulk for promotional, educational, or business use.
Please contact your local bookseller or the Macmillan Corporate and Premium
Sales Department at 1-800-221-7945, extension 5442, or by email at
MacmillanSpecialMarkets@macmillan.com.

First Edition: August 2018

Printed in the United States of America

0 9 8 7 6 5 4 3 2 1

For Joel & Tobie,
Adrienne & Steven,
We gaze up at the same moon.

ACKNOWLEDGMENTS

The chaos of writing a book includes a paradox of solitude and community. Like sitting in a restaurant, surrounded by people and yet all the same isolated in one's own authorial bubble (and trust me, much of this book was written in just such a setting). The words are mine, their inspiration and form were shaped by many influences, friends and colleagues without whose support there would be no book. With the understanding that I'm surely forgetting someone, I need to thank them.

For this and other projects over the years, I have received the generous insights and advice of the members of NobleFusion: Tim Burke, Arthur (Buck) Dorrance, Sally Grotta, Barbara Hill, and Cathy Petrini. A draft of the first act of this novel benefited from the feedback of my beta readers: Paula Billig, Mike Higgins, Michael Oetting, Diane Osborne, and Robert D. Ryne. My sincere gratitude to the members of the Furry Writers Guild who have welcomed me into the ranks and shared so much. Appreciation as well to composer Sydney Faulkner, who somehow takes my words and pulls breathtaking music from them. Thanks, too, to Oz Drummond for the occasional quiet, late-night talks that linger even still in my head, and likewise to Chuck Gannon for his friendship and generosity of spirit.

I am thankful for the continued support of my agent, John Silbersack, and I hope he likes the sailing in this book. I am in awe of the talent of Victo Ngai and humbled to have received another breathtaking cover by her. Thank you to my copyeditor, Elektra Hammond, who believes that I left all those typos for her so she wouldn't get bored. To the many people at Tor who have given of their time and talents to make this book possible, Irene Gallo and Patty Garcia and Linda Quinton, and doubtless more I've never met, I am in your debt. And of course, my editor, Marco Palmieri, who despite being busier than anyone should have to be, has the patience of ten men and the tolerance of still more, a true and supportive friend who believes in talking elephants, mere thanks will never be sufficient.

And always and forever, Valerie, who puts up with all my foolishness, points out where I've gotten things wrong, and always delights in hearing the next story. As I say to you every year on the morning of our wedding anniversary, thank you for not killing me in my sleep.

PART 1

UNDERSTANDING HOME

ONE

NOTHING BUT LIES

A MIDST torrents of rain and blasts of lightning, Ryne stepped from his boat onto the shore of the last island, the place where his life ended. The mental beacon that had guided him across the open water faded away. Clarity replaced certainty, composed of equal parts confusion and anger. Flapping his ears against the downpour he muttered a phrase heard by his students at least once a tenday for the past six decades. "The math is all wrong!"

He stumbled into the surf, limbs weary after too many days spent bailing just to keep afloat. His left hand grasped wildly before finding the gunnel and he went down on one knee, submerged in water halfway up that thigh.

"How did I miss it? How does everyone miss it?" Despite his aches and fatigue, he heaved himself forward, leaving the water and struggling up onto the sand. His head turned left and right, taking in what he could see of the beach through the curtain of rain. Behind him, a shaft of lightning struck his boat and set it aflame despite the storm. Ryne sniffed at the scent of ozone, acknowledged the sizzle of burning wood, then ignored both as he focused on the math once more. His muttering continued.

"Five and a half million Fant on Barsk . . . birth rate of half a percent . . . mortality rate not significantly more as to matter . . . at least three quarters—conservatively—of whom sail away when they sense their life's ending . . . that's more than twenty thousand people showing up here, year after year, for centuries. . . ."

But that wasn't math, that was just arithmetic. Still, it provided a starting point. The bulk of the actual math he shaped into the questions that had assailed his mind, once his need to be here had been slaked by completing the journey and arriving at his destination. Why had he never examined that need? Or its sudden onset? Or how it was simply accepted as part of the natural order of things by everyone on the planet? Or that no Fant on any world in the galaxy prior to the Alliance shoving them all on Barsk—not a single one of them—had ever woken up one morning with the certain knowledge of their coming death and the compulsion to travel to meet it? The slowest of first-year students should have been able to see the incongruities present, and yet . . . no Fant did. No Fant had, at least, not prior to sailing away. How many million Dying Fant had walked this same stretch of sand, dazed and bewildered as he was now, expecting . . . something. Something other than just another expanse of shoreline.

He strode further up the beach until the edge of the island's forest became visible through the rain. Turning slowly, he took in everything that the storm allowed. For a moment it was as if the years fell away and he stood as at the height of his professorial power, poised once more behind a lectern at the front of a classroom. Beating his trunk against one outstretched hand for emphasis he asked his questions, genuinely wanting answers but knowing in his heart they were rhetorical. "Where are all the boats? The fragments of so many journeys? Where are the *bones* of all the people?" He bellowed into the wind and rain with the last strength remaining to him.

The weather offered no reply. The beach remained merely a beach. Ryne's trunk drooped lax upon his chest. His upraised arm fell to his side. The years weighed heavily upon him again. It was over. He'd arrived at the last island, done with living.

And then a voice spoke from behind him.

"Really, Ryne, you might ask the same question of any other island. Or do the people of Taylr leave their possessions strewn upon their beaches? Do they eschew the proper rites and fail to bury such citizens as pass before their time? Surely you don't find debris when you travel the points of either archipelago."

He spun, swiftly, nearly falling but with a skip kept his feet. There at the forest's edge, like an actor stepping onto a stage, a figure emerged from shadow and approached through the rain. It resolved into a person. A woman. An old woman. An Eleph. Here, on this island that existed on no map, that only the Dying could find, that made no sense when you thought about it and which no one ever thought about, here was someone walking toward him as nonchalantly as an aunt at a family gathering. And she'd called him by name.

"Ryne of Taylr," she said, her voice hoarse with years but musical all the same. "I bid you welcome. I am Bernath, my mother's name was Layne."

His ears dropped at the wonder of it, questions of math falling away for the moment. She wore a simple dress of pale brown with a slightly darker vest over it, both clung to her body as the rain soaked them. As she drew closer, he caught a faint floral scent, a perfume that had been popular decades ago. Her eyes locked on his face, her arms opened wide in greeting. The simple familiarity of the ritual provided a touchstone and he shook off his confusion, stammering the traditional reply as he had at other introductions, thousands of times over too many decades. "Perhaps our mothers knew one another." The absurdity of his words hit him. *Knew* one another? It would require a Speaker, assuming one could be found who was old enough to have known either an Eleph named Layne or his own mother before they had sailed away and arrived here themselves. The framing of that puzzle brought the impossibility of the math back to his mind, now compounded. This was the final island. No one lived here. Each Fant sought it some few days after awaking to the knowledge that their death lay at hand and then strove to arrive on its shores. Nothing of the living world belonged here, least of all a . . . hostess.

Ryne sucked air hard as his mind raced with probability functions. Assuming the island's perimeter contained an average span of usable beaches for bringing a boat to shore, arriving on the same day as another Dying Fant had better odds than the annual archipelago lottery. But this Bernath, she had called him by name, spoken of his home, and that unlikelihood exceeded all the stars beyond the clouded sky. He gawked at her as the words fell from his mouth. "You . . . you know me?"

"I feel as though I do, though I know we've never actually met. But in time, you and I will come to know one another far better. In time, I hope you'll entertain some questions I have, questions about magnetic optics and the dynamics of charged particles on electromagnetic fields."

His ears flapped back and down as he lowered the odds of his initial estimate, taking into account the thousands of students he'd had over a lifetime spent in academia, the many papers he'd presented and published. Even so, the math was still impossible. Cut the nearly infinite in half and one still had half an infinity. And yet the Eleph woman's questions reflected some of his most recent work and unpublished theories, research that had never been a part of his classroom, calling into doubt his calculations once more. "You know my work?"

She closed the distance between them and, without inquiry or invitation, slipped her arm around his. "Indeed, yes. It has occupied much of my time in the last few years. You were so close to a breakthrough before you left, weren't you?" She began leading him back toward the forest from which she'd come.

"I . . . I think I was. One can never be certain of course. The simulations were quite promising, but I needed funding to take things to the next level and—"

She patted his hand. "Funding won't be a problem for you any longer. I promise."

He snorted, a piercing trumpet of disbelief. "No matter how small the budget item—and the needs for my work were anything but small—in all my years at the university on Zlorka, funding physics research has *always* been a problem."

"Look around, Ryne, revered scholar. Do you have any doubt that this island is *not* Zlorka? The limitations you endured at the university will not hamper you here."

"You mean . . . I . . . I can continue my work? But I've . . . I thought I'd left that all behind, with my life. I'm dead now, aren't I? Isn't that why I'm here?"

"That life is dead, yes. Everything involving the people you knew, the bonds you forged with friends and colleagues, all the relationships you built, the vast family you have known—all that is gone. But I think you have a few years left to you. Don't you agree? And wouldn't you like to finish what you started? Surely you have some suspicion where it all leads. Now that life is behind you, what else is left but to follow the ideas of your mind's creation down avenues no other being has ever conceived?"

"Of course, but—"

She guided him deeper into the trees, moving slowly in acknowledgment of his still labored breathing but without drawing attention to it. "I imagined as such. One does not settle for only a glimpse of how the universe works, not when there's the chance to see so much more. By the way, I have to tell you, I had to argue with a number of the others to be the one to greet and welcome you."

"Others?" Ryne paused, and Bernath patiently stopped as well. His gaze lifted, as if he could see through the dense forest, up ever higher, perhaps all the way to the canopy. "You've an entire, populated, Civilized Wood here?"

She laughed, a strange sound in his ears after days of deluge and constant bailing. "Of course. It wouldn't be much of a city if we didn't."

"But—"

"Hush, Ryne. All these questions are natural enough, and you're not the first to arrive here and ask them. I promise you, there's a full and informative briefing in your near future and you'll find the answers perfectly satisfying. Now come, let's get you settled. No doubt you can use a hot meal, and a roof over your head, and an opportunity to put on some dry clothes."

"That all sounds quite wonderful," he admitted, though he never expected to experience any of that again. "If . . . if you think there's time."

"There's plenty of time, now that you're here. A couple nights of solid sleep in a comfortable bed will have you good as new. When you're ready—and not before—there are more than a few people eager to meet you, students of a caliber you've never experienced, all waiting to discuss your work."

He nodded, following along as in a dream, a part of him already crafting the next stages of his research, spinning off from the last notes he'd scrawled and left behind for his most promising students. After only a few steps deeper into the Shadow Dwell of this, the final island as he'd always understood it to be, he caught Bernath's eye and asked, "So, is everyone wrong then? This isn't where we come to die?"

"Technically, I suppose it is," she said, as they left the last shore farther behind. "Death comes for all of us eventually. No one's discovered any way to avoid that. But just because you've arrived here doesn't mean you need to be in any rush to expire."

"But then, if it's not the end of the final voyage as we've all been taught, what is this place?"

Bernath laughed again and Ryne realized he could get used to the sound of such delight. She patted his arm as she replied, "I like to think of it as the best kept secret on all of Barsk."

TWO

ONE FACE IN A THOUSAND

THERE was little that Pizlo needed from others. He wore the same thing every day, a pair of shorts with pockets front and back and a set of bandoliers with more places to hold whatever he might find or need at a moment's notice. He'd built various cubbies and sleeping nooks throughout the island, both in the interstitial spaces of the Civilized Wood and down in the Shadow Dwell far below. As for food, the rainforest of the island of Keslo offered an abundance of fruits and leaves and grasses. If in the course of preparing a meal or snack he sometimes sampled from the carefully tended crops of another Fant, well, it wasn't as though anyone would complain. With only a handful of exceptions, all of Barsk society denied his very existence. Pizlo should never have been born.

It was an absolute truth of Fant physiology that unbonded females were not fertile. But Nature abhors absolutes and tosses up the occasional exception. His people called such unintended births "abominations." Nature likewise seeks to correct its own errors and each anomalous, one-in-a-million conception usually carried such a host of genetic abnormalities that if the infant wasn't stillborn it died of its own weakness within a season. At fourteen years of age, Pizlo had defied such probabilities, an abomination's abomination.

Often if he needed something he could simply ask one of the few people who acknowledged his existence. To this day, Tolta, his mother, would welcome him in her home without hesitation, mend his clothes, prepare his meals. Jorl provided paper and ink bamboo, as well as access to his personal library. And while Jorl's wife, Dabni, rarely allowed him in her bookshop for fear of driving away customers, she nonetheless left new books out for him to borrow. The arrangement covered most of his needs but not all. Four years ago he'd become a Speaker, and while Jorl had originally been happy to purchase koph at his request, as Pizlo moved from childhood to adolescence he wanted to stop relying on others. Even if it meant reaching back into the world that denied him.

Pizlo sat on a branch just off a lesser boardway in the heart of the Civilized Wood, no more than an ear's width of dense, living green camouflaged him from the notice of passersby. He peered through the boundary between them to study the apothecary that lay on the opposite side. He kept a tally of the shop's patrons as they came and went. When the shop was free of customers he dropped from his perch, tumbled through the foliage, and rushed within. A wooden bell above the door murmured his arrival. Behind a counter near the entrance, a clerk filled shelves and fronted stock. At the far back end behind a second counter, a chemist compounded remedies and dispensed advice.

The clerk at the front stood facing away from the entrance. She turned at the bell, but Pizlo had already dartted unseen down an aisle of over-the-counter analgesic powders and topical unguents for fireleaf rashes. As he arrived at the back the chemist there had also looked up. She paled—though not so pale as his own albinism—and her eyes desperately sought something else to focus upon even as she searched for an avenue of escape. No such options existed. Her workspace offered only well-stocked shelves, no exits, nor even any place to hide. She made do by backing away into the farthest corner and faced into it like a young child being punished for some misdeed at gymnasium.

Pizlo clambered over the counter. He ignored the chemist and sorted through her pharmaceutical supply bins with purpose until he found his prize—packets of koph-laced wafers. He carried these back to the counter, divided them into several stacks, and carefully wrapped each in squares of waxy paper kept on hand for that purpose. The stiff paper made a slight sound as he folded it into envelopes for the koph. In self defense, the chemist began humming to herself. Pizlo didn't even sigh.

"I know you can't acknowledge me," he said, raising his voice to be heard above the humming. "But I've reduced your inventory and it's not fair for you to bear the cost. I don't have any money . . . how could I? Anyway, the day before yesterday a cove on the far side of Keslo called to me. I know that doesn't make sense to you, but it happened. It happens a lot. So I went there."

He paused, slipping the packets into separate sections of the bandolier across his torso. Pizlo glanced over to the corner. The chemist still faced away, her ears pressed flat to either wall. She continued humming, presumably to block out his words. He needed to finish this quickly and pressed on.

"It's a tiny place, not good for swimming or fishing and hard to reach if you don't have the knack of dropping through the Shadow Dwell and arriving in just the right spot. I found a tidal pool there with some funny-looking anemones. I also found a carving. It was weathered by years in the salt, the wood of it cracked in places from its travels. It told me it was among the last pieces carved by Rüsul of Maxx in the eastern chain, a distraction, I guess, while he sailed away."

Pizlo dug in a pocket of his shorts and removed a parcel, an object wrapped up in a broad leaf and tied with a bit of vine. He set it on the counter. "It's here now, where you'll find it after I've gone. You never saw me touch it, so you can honestly say you don't know for sure that it came from me. You can say you just found it here and that'd be true. Keep it or sell it—it's probably worth quite a bit to a collector—and it's worth many times what I've taken from your shelves." He paused. People were complicated; it wasn't enough that he'd offered a generous exchange. Best to provide the framework for other motivations as well, so when the woman altered and embellished today's events, she could justify her own actions.

He rapped his knuckles on the counter. "Selling it might be best, because I'll be back. I'm going to need other supplies, and your apothecary looks to be the best place for me to come where I'll upset the fewest people. I'm sorry for the stress my being here causes you. I hope this makes up for it. Thanks."

The transaction completed, Pizlo vaulted back over the counter and exited the shop, hearing a surprised gasp as he sped past the clerk at the front. He rushed across the boardway and threw himself into the surrounding growth that provided a barrier to ordinary citizens of Keslo though not one he'd ever agreed to. He scrambled through, bits of branches scraping his body, calling forth thin lines of blood on his pale skin without eliciting any pain as he plunged deeper. Soon he reached broader limbs that allowed him to climb up and up, brachiating his way ever higher until he achieved one of his hidden places at the top of the canopy.

He'd stashed food here, and a couple books, and at various times other things his conversations with the world told him he might need. Alongside a cutting stone he knew he'd need in three days and a folio of maps of the eastern archipelago that he'd meant to return to Jorl last season, he prepared to stash one of the envelopes of koph he'd just obtained. But first he opened it and unwrapped a wafer, placing it in his mouth. A nearby gourd contained water. He took a long drink, swallowed the koph, lay back and waited for the drug to work on him. The ethereal scent of spiral mint filled his sinuses.

Jorl no longer needed koph. He'd told Pizlo as much but not the why or how of his special case. Instead, when they'd discovered Pizlo possessed the gift to be a Speaker, he'd focused on explaining the possibilities open to him and the rules that had to be followed. Becoming a Speaker had changed everything and nothing. He could see nefshons; the subatomic particles of memory and personality would come at his call. If he summoned enough of them that had belonged to a dead person he could even talk to them. But Speaking to the dead required knowledge of their lives, and who did he know? And even if he somehow learned enough personal details to attempt a summoning, any Fant he tried to chat with would be horrified, posthumously confronted by an abomination.

But despite those limitations, practicing with the drug had given him new skills of imagery, sharpened his thinking, and changed how he saw the world. Jorl chose to do his Speaking in a replica of his office, imagining a space filled with familiar scents and textures, beloved objects, comfortable furniture. Pizlo understood that every piece helped anchor him to the physical world and in turn granted greater solidity to the mindscape by settling his mentor's mood and shaping what his conversants experienced.

Pizlo, lacking both an office and potential conversants, had instead learned to use the mindscape as a tool in its own right. Since earliest childhood he'd collected bugs and stored them in his mother's home where housekeeping always warred with organization. Koph provided a better way to keep track of the collection. He had recalled each specimen, hanging them one by one in a mindspace he manufactured just for them. It had taken many sessions and a lot of koph, but at the end he had a vast catalog, a wall comprising tens of thousands of insects each pinned in space a handspan away from those to right and left, above and below. Every detail of each physical specimen existed there in his memory. Having set it up once, he could summon it any time he ingested the Speaker's drug.

When he'd finished, Pizlo had shown the catalog to Jorl. His mentor had been impressed by his ingenuity and in turn had come up with an idea for someone with whom Pizlo might actually Speak, an artificial but sapient mind that had been destroyed years before. Introductions were made, and over that first conversation he'd acquired enough familiarity to summon those same nefshons on his own. From then on, Pizlo met regularly with his new friend. It made him feel a little more normal, but really there was nothing normal about dialogues that occurred only in his mind with a conversant who had been built like a machine many millennia ago.

In the four years since, Pizlo had followed Jorl's example and conjured a place for his summonings, a spot beyond the forest of his home but instead out under the clouded sky. He imagined himself in a relentless downpour regardless of the actual season. A therapist would have found the choice significant, but no mental health professional anywhere on Barsk would willingly observe an abomination's state of mind, let alone extend any treatment or therapy to help him.

Back when Pizlo's father had died, Jorl had become a major part of his life, filling an emotional void that at five years of age he hadn't understood existed. Jorl had tutored him in all things, including the ways of Fant society and other topics that neither expected would ever matter to him. And yet, his mentor had insisted. The world might not acknowledge him, but to be a Fant meant learning the ways of the people who rejected him. The history of Speakers had been among those things, even before he'd manifested the ability that defined them.

"I never expected it would lead to anything." Pizlo spoke within his mind, revisiting the inner scene he'd constructed years before. The rains in his mindscape drenched him. He turned his head to the sky, weak eyes peering up through the rain at the clouds, feeling a connection to the world despite his imaginary surroundings.

"It seemed so . . . what's the word? Ironic? All at once I could see the particles of people, living and dead, people who would never ever talk to me."

A voice replied through the rain, "I'm pleased Jorl introduced us and that you choose to visit with me."

Pizlo's invented surroundings were impossible. He stood upon a massive cube that hung high in the sky. Each side was easily three times his height, composed of grey metal, plastic, and smoky glass. Indistinct shapes swirled inside the cube in response to his voice. Pizlo spoke to the weather all the time, but only in the mindscape could he talk to this cube.

"Me, too. Jorl doesn't have as much time anymore, not like when I was just a kid. And the time we do have, it's more precious. I don't need him for lessons like I did before. Instead we discuss the stuff I've learned from the books he gives me. But the things you tell me, they're different from any of that."

"I was created to tell stories. I am the Archetype of Man. It is my purpose. I am the repository of the hero's lore."

The teen Fant sat there, knees bent, legs crossed at the calf, feet under knees. Jorl had called it "Tailor style," and as his mentor's father had been a tailor, Pizlo accepted it without comment. He unfolded and stood now, as much to stretch as to pace—another habit he'd picked up from Jorl. He stepped to the edge of the cube, peering over the side, willing the pelting rain not to pitch him off the edge. In the real world where he'd left his body high in the canopy, a faint smattering of rain likewise fell upon him. By the time he returned, he'd be soaked through. None of that mattered though.

"Most of your stories follow the same kind of pattern. The people may differ and the things they do might change, but they all kind of work the same way, don't they? Aren't there other kinds of stories?"

"There are, but they are not mine to tell."

"Because you only tell the hero stories?"

"Yes."

"So . . . back when you were made, were there others? Other . . . repositories?"

"That is my understanding, but the details of their making or appearance or content were not entrusted to me."

"None of it?"

"No. I am sorry, Pizlo."

"It's okay. I was just asking because . . . well, if you knew *any-thing* about them, maybe one of them could be summoned, too. Probably not by me, but certainly by Jorl. And once he'd done it that first time, I'd be able to do it any time after, and you could have someone else to talk to. Maybe."

"It is a generous intention, but it would be a wasted effort."

"Why?"

"While you do not match the physiological definition of mankind as defined by my makers, still you are a biological being. You have a sense of your own existence and an awareness of your own mortality. I do not truly possess either of these attributes. Your race exists in uncertainty, without definite knowledge of your purpose in the universe. In contrast, my kind were clearly defined. We existed to share our stories with humanity. Our reason for being was to preserve the best of these, and as opportunity allowed, to teach them. That purpose does not allow for one repository to instruct another. Nor even to interact."

"I guess that makes sense. I am grateful to have you teaching me. Your stories are fun. After listening to them I can think of things that have never existed on Barsk or maybe anywhere in any of the worlds of the Alliance. But . . . can we take a step back?"

"How back?" inquired the Archetype of Man.

"Can you tell me a story about why so many of your stories feel the same?"

Although it lacked anything like a face, Pizlo heard a smile in the machine's voice when it replied.

"Indeed, I can. You are seeking a meta-discussion of story. It is the very definition of my uniqueness. The archetype which defines me."

Pizlo leaned further out, taunting the illusion by manufacturing a wind to keep him from tumbling over the edge. He didn't want to actually fall, but liked the idea of braving such a fall.

"Which is what?" he asked.

"The hero's journey. The structure of nearly all my tales."

"Structure. Like order? The way things are put together?"

"Precisely."

"Like the way I organize your nefshons when I want to summon you?"

"Perhaps. I don't understand how you or Jorl do this thing, but I would not be surprised that it requires the imposition of structure on the particles you have described. I don't believe they were known in my time. Certainly I have no stories of them."

The Archetype rarely spoke of its own creation or time, and under other circumstances Pizlo would have welcomed following his teacher down such a path, but he didn't want to let this current idea go. And uncommon as tales of itself might be, this other thing was completely new.

"You've been telling me stories for years now. Why haven't you mentioned this structure before?"

The machine did not pause, and if there was irony in its response, Pizlo could not detect it. "You never asked."

The wind increased, a reflection of the Fant's sudden sullenness. He stumbled backwards from the edge, arrived near the middle of the square and sat back down. "Fine. I'm asking now. What is the hero's journey?"

"It is composed of three components. These are the Departure, the Initiation, and the Return."

"And all heroes travel through these parts?"

"No, but of all the stories I possess, those that share in all three pieces have been shown to resonate the most with the spirit of humanity. Those heroes inspire and instruct. Those stories reveal and remind the hearer of the greatness that exists within all of mankind."

Pizlo nodded. "We use those words differently, I think. *Mankind* and *humanity*. It's confusing."

"As is the state of the galaxy as you have explained it to me," responded the Archetype. "These terms have become more inclusive since the time of my creation. But I was given contingencies for encountering alien beings so that by hearing my stories they, too, could come to understand my creators. Jorl has explained you are not aliens but rather descendants of other creations. We are, in that sense, distant cousins."

"But that still doesn't explain the difference. How can we have different meanings for the same words?"

"For me, humanity only encompasses the sapient beings that existed when I was made. For you, it refers to the eighty-seven different types of your fellow sapients. Thus, what you and I mean by *mankind* reflect different frames of reference."

Rising again, Pizlo considered this. He returned to his pacing, navigating the perimeter of the rain slick square several times. He stopped at the middle of another edge and lifted his head, speaking up into the sky again. "But . . . all the stories you've told me over these years, they're good stories. I feel them. It doesn't matter that they're about people I've never met, or even that the people aren't like any people I would recognize. You've shared their stories and I've laughed and cried. I've cheered their victories and suffered their defeats. They were *good* stories."

"Indeed. They resonate for you. The stories elicit these reactions in humanity."

"So, does that make me, and probably everyone else in my time, a part of your definition of the word?"

The Archetype fell silent, leaving only the unending sound of the rain striking the cube face beneath the Fant's feet. Then, "The evidence would suggest you are correct. I will adjust my parameters. Thank you, Pizlo. This meta-discussion has been insightful for both of us."

He grinned and stepped away from the edge. "Right. So let's go back to the other thing. Explain to me about the parts of this hero's journey. . . ."

THREE

DEAD SPEAKERS

~~~~~~~~~~~~

ORL rose late in the morning, the tip of his trunk pulled back to press the nubs against his forehead in a gentle massage. He smacked his lips and considered the possibility of just lying in bed a while, or better, going back to sleep completely. The rolling rap of knuckles on his front door tore such thoughts from his mind. Begrudgingly, he sat up. The sound repeated, paused after what he guessed might have been their fifth iteration, only to knock again as he stumbled from his bedroom. Bleary with the shreds of a dream involving a third-century Speaker he'd summoned many days earlier, it was the pinnacle of conscious thought to pull on a robe and wrap the sides closed with a sash before opening the door. As he'd expected from the distinctive knock, his landlady stood on the other side, clothed in a sleeveless dress of dark green fibers, one arm raised as if prepared to keep rapping on his door until the end of time if necessary.

"Good morning, Kentl. What brings you by today?"

"Morning is for songbirds, Jorl. Do I sound like I'm singing? It's nearly noon!"

As if a partially opened door were an invitation, she pushed past him to enter the spacious apartment's vestibule. Jorl turned in place. He followed the intrusive Eleph with his eyes, ensuring she didn't plunge any further into his home. He muttered under his breath at the way she acted, as if ownership gave her the rights of an aleph to go whither she pleased. Not for the first time, he wished his actual aleph worked in reverse and could bar people as he chose. Instead, he counted to twelve, found he still possessed too much irritation and counted again before replying. "Which is still too early to bid you a good afternoon." Jorl'd long since learned not to trade barbs with Kentl; the woman had the sharpest tongue in a dozen islands.

She spun, frowning as her eyes ran over him, cataloging the details of his disheveled appearance. "Did I interrupt your nap? You're supposedly a busy professional; were you intending to sleep the day away?"

"It's the sartha buds outside my bedroom window. I wrote to you about them last season." He yawned, spread his ears wide, and tried to wake up. "For lack of pruning they're propagating wildly. Isn't maintenance of that garden patch part of what I'm paying rent for?"

She dismissed the argument with a wave of her trunk. "Pay someone to cut them back, and send me the bill. I'm sure you can find some neighbor child to do it."

The irritation won out that time. He nodded and said, "Fine. I'll ask Pizlo the next time he's by."

Kentl froze. A quiver of her trunk's nubs was the only sign that she understood Jorl's intention to have a boy that Fant culture insisted didn't exist and couldn't be acknowledged tend the garden of one of her properties. An instant later she slapped those same nubs against her thigh and continued as if he hadn't spoken. "Or your daughter—what's her name, Rina? Task her with it. Some-one in your family should work."

Jorl fought to suppress a smile as he imagined unleashing Rina on the sartha. Give her a pair of clippers and the afternoon and she'd raze his garden. Dabni, Jorl's beloved wife, had assured him of their child's great potential, but despite being raised in Arlo's former home, the girl's talents and interests did not fall toward pharming.

Still, his landlady had a point, he had no shortage of tasks wait-ing for him and he'd already lost most of the morning. Best not to lose what remained. He flapped his ears to clear his head and focused on the immediate problem. "Why are you here, Kentl?"

"I'm here to show you a new property, as I promised. One better suited to your status." She drew a sheaf of papers from a hidden pocket within the folds of her dress, thrusting them at him like a child holding forth a glowing report card. Jorl ignored them.

"I declined that appointment," he said. "I have no desire to move. I'm comfortable here."

"You'll be more comfortable in the new apartment."

"No, thank you."

She let the hand with the papers drop to her side, fanned her ears once, and changed tactics. "Look, Jorl, I didn't want to go this route, but your continued presence here is costing me money. You're bringing down the value of all my surrounding properties."

He shrugged. "Which is it, Kentl? I need to move to better accommodations because you think my social status has improved, but at the same time I'm a blight on your real estate? No, don't answer. I don't care. I'm happy here and I don't want to move."

"Your wants won't matter if I bring suit before Keslo's housing board."

"Bring all the suits you like. I have a lease, a lease which *you* wrote. It stipulates all the reasons why you can evict me, all the fees and damages you can assess for irresponsible or negligent treatment of your property. But it also clearly specifies that as long as I pay my rent on time—and I've already arranged that you get prepaid a season in advance—my lease renews automatically until such time as I give you notice of my intention to vacate."

Kentl scowled and stuffed the papers away. "It's unnatural."

"Hardly. Uncommon, perhaps, but in either case, there's nothing in the lease that speaks to your opinions on how I choose to live. Have I violated any of your provisions? No? Have I expressed a desire to move? Also no? Well then, that matter is settled. Now, was there anything else? Because I actually am busy."

The landlady replied with an abrupt trumpet of disgust and rushed past him as if the winds of the entire season shoved at her backside. Jorl closed and latched the door, feeling almost sorry for her. Kentl did have a point. The norm on Barsk was for men to wander, rarely maintaining the same dwelling for more than a season or two. Bachelors traveled the most, often skipping from island to island, sometimes even jumping across to the opposite archipelago. Even bonded males grew weary of the same walls and regularly sought out new housing, albeit within an ever-changing proximity to the larger home that supported their spouses and off-spring.

Jorl had bonded with Dabni more than six years ago. Every other husband he knew throughout Barsk had lived in multiple different apartments, lodges, and boarding houses in that same span. But not him.

Since returning from the Patrol, Jorl had maintained the same simple apartment, year after year. He'd experienced his share of life-changing events—becoming a Speaker, being marked with an aleph, achieving tenure, acquiring a seat in the Alliance senate,

marrying Dabni, siring a child—Kentl had shown up at his door
soon after each of these, attempting to roust him out of his familiar
rooms and lock him into a more profitable lease, one appropriate
to new beginnings. Then, as today, he'd declined. Initially, he'd
told himself it was so he could remain near Tolta, the widow of
his best friend who had likewise defied custom and lived on her
own. Not that a grown and independent woman needed anyone,
least of all him, to keep an eye on her. Then he rationalized that
he stayed put for the convenience of Pizlo, his deceased friend's
son, providing some stability for the wild child denied by the rest
of Barsk society. After that, he'd been courting Dabni, who worked
in a nearby bookshop and it made sense to stay put. Once they'd
bonded and he'd fathered a child with her, Tolta had graciously
opened her own home to his new wife, and again it seemed the best
of sense to just remain where he was, at least for a few seasons.
More years had passed and, far from succumbing to the wanderlust
that claimed nearly all men, he had become more complacent with
where he lived.

Unlike any other Fant alive on Barsk, Jorl had served in the Patrol. He'd visited the edge of the galaxy, and in the process traveled many times further than every man, woman, and child on
Barsk combined. He suspected that experience had long since extinguished any need to move from apartment to apartment. Indeed, having resolved never to leave the planet again, he'd be
content to purchase his current home outright and live out his days
there, not that Kentl would ever sell.

⁓

HAVING lost the morning, Jorl didn't bother with proper clothing,
and even opted to forego breakfast. Keeping his robe he settled
at the desk in his study and began by reviewing the letter that had

arrived the night before by special courier. As a member of the
Alliance senate, the Committee of Information had insisted he
equip his office with state of the art communication gear, the better to weigh in on petitions and projects they vetted or rejected.
But with rarely an exception, the people of Barsk eschewed technology of such caliber. Only two other comparable sets existed
on the planet. His allowed him to send a coded message to the
Alliance satellite in orbit, and from there to the nearest portal at
the edge of the solar system where an automated repeater would
transfer it via connecting portals from star system to star system
until it reached halfway across the galaxy to Dawn in less than a
day. Locally though, a note from the university on Zlorka took at
least that long.

More than a tenyear before, he'd been one of a small group of
new, tenure-track junior faculty with hopes of making a name for
himself as a historian. He'd taken a break from that—the university generously pausing his academic clock—to join the Patrol.
When he'd returned, his position had been waiting for him even
if most of his original cohort hadn't. Few measured up to the ex-
acting standards of the finest university on Barsk, but even a year
there ensured employment at lesser schools on other islands.
Zlorka was the gold standard for academic careers.

He'd worked hard but, despite some critical articles in the better
journals, the Provost estimated his chances as, at best, one in
three. Then the traveling council had arrived and marked Jorl with
the aleph, a singular event that had not happened to anyone at a
university in hundreds of years. The trustees, eager to claim him
as faculty, not only granted him tenure but named him a "historian at large" as well. In exchange for a modest stipend, he taught
a seminar on Keslo every three seasons and otherwise pursued his
own research interests. The arrangement suited him, and once he

became a member of the Committee of Information his fellow senators expedited the peer-review turnover time for his journal submissions. That was just another benefit the university enjoyed from his affiliation.

Last night's courier had brought a letter from the university, specifically from Mickl, his department head, inquiring as to the status of an overdue monograph. Worse still, the monograph was actually only the opening chapter of a larger work. For the last few years, Jorl had been building a secret history of Speakers based on direct interviews going back eight centuries. Though anyone capable of manipulating nefshons could summon a simulacrum of any decedent they could personally identify, the Speaker's Edict forbade summoning another Speaker. Margda had been the first Speaker, the founder of their order, and her training as well as her rules had influenced all who had followed. Thus all previous direct accounts of Speakers had been limited to interviews with living subjects and perforce failed to capture the full scope and shape of the thing.

But Jorl had learned Margda's true reason for crafting the trio of laws that made up the Speaker's Edict. And, as she had intended centuries before, he had broken all three. It only made sense then that he should set one of them aside now for his current project. Since Margda's time, Barsk had produced one hundred thousand Speakers! The planet supplied koph, the Speaker's drug, to the rest of the Alliance's eighty-five other races, who in turn had managed about half again as many of their own Speakers spread across four thousand worlds. Jorl limited his research to Speakers on Barsk, and had randomly sampled his interview pool from all successive generations, allowing every island a chance for inclusion. Even that had left him with more than thirty Fant to summon. His project manager contained an elaborate timeline of their names, with stacks of pages for those he'd already interviewed. He had started the task with enthusiasm, but the excitement of summoning other Speakers had waned. Everyone he'd summoned had been horrified to be on the receiving end of the experience, despite their intimate knowledge of it from the other side. Over and over, his violation of the Edict had created a nearly insurmountable affront in his conversants.

Fascinating and heretofore unrecognized patterns had emerged after the first few interviews, developing color and complexity as the number of Speakers increased. Jorl had finished twenty-eight interviews. He already had more than enough material for the promised monograph and most of the book beyond, but he'd been putting off the few remaining summonings to complete the span of years. Mickl's letter was just what he needed to dive back in and he resolved to resume at once.

His stomach growled as he finished reading the letter and he allowed that in the long run he'd be better served if he paused. Sustenance first, and then work. He snatched up a bowl of fruit and munched through a plel to quiet his belly's immediate complaints, then continued grazing on some berries as he consulted his notes and scanned the biographical specifics he'd already researched, familiarizing himself with sufficient details to accomplish the summoning of one of the remaining Speakers on his list. He settled back into his hammock chair and performed the familiar mental exercises to access nefshons. The koph variant that forever lived in his blood responded to his will and Jorl found himself in the mental space of a summoning, an imagining that left him seemingly seated in the same room, as he pulled the infinitesimal particles of another Fant's life to him.

As always, his self-construct included the glowing aleph on his forehead. This allowed him to do what none before him could have when talking to the dead. Every past Speaker that he interviewed had met their summoning with outrage for violating their laws. And each time he had patiently explained that, just as Margda had set forth the Speaker's Edict, so too had she been responsible for the creation of the aleph, and thus implicitly established an exception to her own rules. The logic of his argument—as well as the invocation of the discoverer of the drug that made summoning possible— eventually mollified each of his conversants, at least enough to tease, albeit grudgingly, a meaningful interview out of them.

He'd prepared for today's Speaker for much of the past three tendays before becoming distracted by other things, but reviewing his notes brought it all back to him. Fisco had joined the ranks of the Dying and sailed off two hundred and thirty years ago at the ripe age of ninety-seven. In her day, she had been the most re- nowned and respected Speaker of the eastern archipelago. Eleph and Lox who manifested the talent to use koph had traveled to her home in Belp to learn their craft at her feet. Thirteen separate bi- ographies had been written about her, and Jorl had read them all—as well as countless journal and diary entries from her con- temporaries and students discussing her technique—to the point where he felt he knew her as well as his great-great-grandmother, a woman who'd sailed off well before his birth but lived on in end- less stories told by the generations that remained in the family house she'd bequeathed to her daughters and their daughters' daughters.

It required little effort to call Fisco's nefshons to him and pull together sufficient quantity to cause her to take form for him. An ancient Lox glared at him with squinty eyes. She wore a robe of pale yellow and a series of three decorative wooden studs pierced the upper edge of her left ear. From the biographies, Jorl knew them to represent the three husbands she'd outlived.

"Fisco of Belp," he addressed her. "Your time in life has ended; you are now as you were in life, but not alive. In this, a world of my own making, I welcome you." The ritual of establishment complete, Jorl braced himself for some variant of the withering retort that all previous Speakers had delivered when he'd summoned them.

Fisco had other plans.

"What's going on? I was in the middle of a seminar. Why did you pull me out?"

"I . . . I . . . ," Jorl stammered with surprise.

"And what are you playing at with a ritualized summoning? If I never have to hear that nonsense again it will be too soon. Well? Is your tongue lost up your trunk? You still haven't answered. What was so important that's worth more than the time of ten of my best students?"

"I'm researching a history of Speakers. I chose you to be part of the survey."

"Oh for the love of . . . Thousands of Speakers to choose from between the island, the moon, and six new worlds, and you had to bother me? What's your name, oaf?"

"I'm Jorl. Jorl ben Tral. Of Keslo."

"Keslo? The island, Keslo? This is making less and less sense. By what right does a field agent pull me out of my seminar?"

"Field agent?" Jorl's ears flapped with confusion.

Fisco's face paled and her own ears dropped. She extended her trunk and snapped her nubs in front of his face. "No, of course not. Not with an aleph. Tree and leaf, you're not of the Caudex, are you? You haven't a clue what I'm talking about."

"I . . . I don't. What did you mean I pulled you from away from something? And what is the . . . Caudex, you said?"

She slashed her trunk left and right and her construct stepped away from him. "Never you mind. It's not for you to know."

"But . . . hold on. What was that about new worlds?"

"None of that matters. Forget we spoke, Jorl ben Tral. This was all a dream."

"I don't think so," he said.

"Trust me, it's better if you do."

Fisco closed her eyes and to his amazement took control of the nefshons he'd gathered. Before he could stop her, she dissipated her own construct and left him alone in the mental space of the summoning.

With the ease of power and long practice Jorl relinquished his perception of nefshons and sat once more within his actual study, staring at the notes he'd prepared for his conversation with Fisco. Nothing he'd read had made mention of agents of any kind, field or otherwise. What was that nonsense about her teaching a seminar? He'd intentionally gathered nefshons from the end of her life, a point shortly after she'd sailed away and her students were a part of her past. So, what island had she meant, and *which* of the seven moons was she invoking? And new worlds? Was that some kind of metaphor? And why, most importantly, why hadn't she balked at being summoned, as every other Speaker he'd interviewed had?

Jorl had been a historian and a researcher for longer than he'd been a Speaker. He opened a drawer in his desk, withdrew the compact data terminal his senate colleagues had insisted he needed though he seldom bothered to use it. Activating it, he began the protocols for a mega-query across all library channels. Probably most of them would time out without encountering any hits. Some would return useless, false positives. But with luck a few might provide some clues, clues that would allow for still further queries, which would in turn generate hypotheses that he could test. Such was the way of research. One way or another, he'd eventually have answers. He finished keying in the parameters of his search and leaned closer to speak directly into the terminal's pick-up. "Caudex," he said. "Begin search."

FOUR

COMBATTING ENTROPY

ERNATH had been true to her word. After a warm bath and light meal, Ryne had been shown to a luxurious bed and slept well into the next day. Clean clothes awaited him upon his awaking, as well as an impressive assortment of morning foods. Midway through breaking his fast, he'd looked up to find Bernath waiting for him, smiling to see his appetite in such good form. They chatted a while and others joined them, asking questions about Ryne's work, his theories, the kind of schedule he liked to keep, what equipment he saw himself needing overall and which bits sooner rather than later. Some of the people who came and went clearly couldn't follow any of the math and seemed more interested in details of what he liked to eat or how he preferred to dress. A few of the others, Bernath among them, scribbled furious notes and listened with slack trunks as he walked them through the physics that had been living mostly unspoken in his head for the last few years. She and one or two others would ask an innocuous question that had bubbled up in them in response to something he'd said, and he'd go barreling off on a tangent that set them all to scribbling ever faster. He smiled to himself. Hadn't she promised him there'd be people who wanted his ideas? He continued like that, holding court, describing the math, until others came with the evening meal. Ryne found himself eating and drinking like a much younger man, despite keeping up a running commentary on his theories and responding to the endless questions of his hosts.

In the morning, Bernath escorted him to a large office—*his* office, she insisted—replete with a massive desk and slate walls and a pitifully inadequate supply of chalk. His new routine began in earnest. Over the next several days he covered the walls with endless formulae written in a specialized subset of the ëgul used for mathematics. Two assistants had been assigned to him, an impressive Lox woman—young even for a graduate student—and a middle-aged male Eleph who spent half his time as faculty at the island's own university. They introduced themselves as Gari and Krokel. Both had been among the scholars in attendance the previous day, but neither had managed the nerve to ask any questions.

Now they glommed onto him, taking turns to ensure one was always on hand. They carried themselves with a blend of pride over assignment to his project and diffidence at being in the same room with him.

The two states combined in an emotion he'd seen in the eyes of past assistants, particularly in the early days of his career. Both were fantasizing about seducing him, as if sex would somehow make them better physicists. Ryne did his best to ignore it, much as he'd ignored his own libido for years. And while yes, Gari was attractive and bright, he'd never cared to frolic with any women of her race. What if such a one turned out to be the person he wanted to have a child with? Biology assured that Lox and Eleph could not reproduce. A lifetime of habit—even at this point in his life where offspring weren't an issue—meant he couldn't imagine looking at her that way. And as for Krokel, while Ryne had enjoyed the pleasures of other males now and then as he wandered the islands, he'd never felt fully satisfied by those liaisons. No point pursuing one now. Better for both of them if he ignored the signals and focused on the work. That's why he was here. The math called to him with an allure that no bedmate had ever come close to matching.

At the beginning and end of each day his assistants took turns photographing and transcribing his walls with equipment that Ryne had known existed but not bothered to obtain. That first day, they had demonstrated what they called a "smart wall" in an adjacent room. He'd dismissed it. Three separate times they implored him to try it, and when he finally relented he found himself too self-conscious using the wall's stylus to relax into the mindset that freed his best thinking. He didn't need technology to express himself. Chalk and slate had always served him in the classroom and the lab, or a stick and a stretch of sand when he had over the years felt a need for greater solitude than the Civilized Wood afforded and strolled along one beach or another working through the math of an equation. Computers could do the blunt work of calculation and simulation far faster than his trunk could write, but the underlying ideas required a living mind, and he'd not suffered over the limited availability of technology during his long academic career.

His new hosts had scrambled to provide him with blackboards and chalk, showing genuine surprise in response to his stated preference for such crude tools. In fact, Ryne had even eschewed the simple digital tablets they'd offered after showing him his lab. "Chalk and slate," he'd said. "Keep your world simple and save the complex things for the math." He knew he'd been heard when the next morning a crate of chalk had been delivered to supplement the initial supply. The fresh clean smell when he'd opened the lid had brought him a memory of the best years of his life and left him with a smile of ease.

After those first restorative nights, they'd also supplied him with an elaborate apartment, better quarters he suspected than the provost on Zlorka enjoyed. It included the same kind of bed he'd once enjoyed at a resort on Kemtal, a traditional mattress and frame fashioned of local wood with a loosely woven tick that kept bundles of sartha leaves from escaping but allowed their soporific fragrance to be released when he lay upon it. That first night, body weary from days at sea and mind numb from so many revelations, it had been like being embraced by paradise. Still not dead, he'd slept like one who had no intention of ever waking. The rest of the apartment was just as splendid, but also far more than he either needed or wanted, especially when his lab turned out to be part of a suite of rooms larger than the apartment, with separate living spaces for the assistants, an eating area, group shower and sanitary facilities, and several other rooms not yet designated. It all seemed too much, but Gari assured him all of the space was his to use as he saw fit, waiting to be equipped with whatsoever he requisitioned.

Disbelief gave way to acceptance and Ryne requested a small cot for the empty room nearest his lab. As wondrous as that bed was, he needed to work not sleep. He had no intention of dreaming away this opportunity. To the distress of his assistants, he sent a note to Bernath thanking her for the apartment but declining its use. From that point on he slept in the lab—for that brief span of each day that he needed to close his eyes and rest. To be fair, he spent a portion of each day in meditative trance, running thought experiments the way normal people mused on what to have for lunch. On Taylr, his graduate students would often find him wandering the boardways of the Civilized Wood, oblivious to his surroundings or the passage of others around him, though some part of his mind kept track of the mundane details and his feet had always carried him back to the university's cafeteria in time for the evening meal.

By the fifth day after his arrival on this nameless island, Ryne could be seen meandering throughout their Wood, always followed by either Krokel or Gari and always from a discreet distance. And again a portion of his awareness noted what he saw, cataloged the frequency of other labs and libraries and manufacturing facilities, the profusion of metal and plastic, the ready availability of technology both complex and ordinary. Most amazing and unexpected of all were the others like himself, Eleph and Lox of extreme age who wandered deep in thought. When Ryne met such a one on his first stroll it jolted him from his reverie, a glimmer of recognition of a pharmer several years his junior whom he'd met decades before at a conference on Myer. Her name surfaced in his mind along with the recollection that he'd read in a journal of her presumed death, having sailed off more than a year ago. She nodded his way, not slowing her own step but treating him to smiling eyes and a slight nod of her head before passing him and soon after vanishing around a curve in the boardway, leaving him to wonder if Bernath had been the one to greet her on a beach when she'd arrived.

His walks took him past many others, young and middle-aged adults who had clearly been born to this island, whose lives had apparently not been tainted nor their souls corrupted despite ready access to the kind of plentiful technology the rest of the Alliance enjoyed. Occasionally he passed herds of school children stampeding noisily, laughing and pointing and tumbling as children do, on their way to some destination, chaperones and teachers meeting his glance with sheepish expressions of apology or animated trunks of amusement as they passed. In addition to the oddities, he also saw traditional and familiar shops, much like he'd known on Taylr, fewer perhaps, but that could be a consequence of a smaller population—he hadn't thought to ask about their last census and neither Bernath nor any of the others he'd spoken to had offered the information—or an efficient side effect of the technology they enjoyed.

Soon enough that trickled through to his awareness. Technology was what they desired. Advances in science and engineering and mathematics sought with a gusto unmatched on any island of either archipelago. Concentrated in this one spot, somehow having access to all the gifts of the Alliance and building on those designs, questioning those theories, thought experiments enfleshed, hypotheses challenged every day. And for those experts and academics with enough flexibility to their thinking to embrace rather than resist dramatic shifts in paradigms, a new life at an age when death should otherwise have claimed them. Or at least, a reprieve for a brief while.

In the afternoon of the eighth day in his lab, Krokel had shyly begged Jorl's pardon and asked his presence in an adjacent room. Following him there he found a physician, a female Lox half his age garbed in the traditional spotless lab coat that was all form and no part function of the profession. So intent was she on unpacking an assortment of medical diagnostic devices that she failed to notice their arrival until Krokel coughed softly, tip of his trunk in his mouth.

"Ryne, please allow me to introduce Lolte, one of the finest systems biologists we have and, with your consent, your new doctor."

"Doctor?" he'd said. "I'm an old man and I'm still recovering from the rigors of my journey here, but I'm not otherwise ill. Why do I need a doctor?"

Lolte finished laying out her equipment and regarded him with a smile. "In part, that's what I'm here to determine. Please, have a seat on the desk and we'll begin."

The rest of the day involved so many tests that Ryne found himself nearly as exhausted as the day he'd arrived. Through it all, as was his nature, he asked questions about every bit of technology and each procedure. In response, Lolte maintained a running commentary, explaining the provenance of her devices and their diagnostic purpose, but always stopped short of mentioning the results she obtained as she moved through the examination.

She had almost reached Ryne's limit, when the physician declared the exam portion of her visit complete. In response to the question of what other portion remained, she had escorted him out of the lab and walked him to one of the better restaurants the physicist had ever experienced. Their arrival had been expected and a maître d' led them to a private booth and provided menus. Ryne found half of the items available unfamiliar. When the server arrived he'd simply asked the young man to bring him whatever he himself liked best. As he surrendered the menu, he wondered how he would pay for the meal. The question must have shone on his face and his dinner companion laughed.

"The Dying who join us take a while to adjust," she said, her eyes shining with amusement though perhaps not completely at his expense. "You were told that your old life has indeed ended. That includes thinking of yourself as someone who has accepted his death. Here, not only are you reborn, you're an honored guest. Anything you need or want will be provided."

Ryne had laughed. "Easy for you to say, with your whole life ahead of you. I may not be dead as I expected to be, but how many years do you think I have left?'"

The merriment faded from her eyes. "That depends on whether you follow your doctor's advice."

"I don't understand."

"There are three kinds of Dying, Ryne. Only two that reach the shores of this island. Most are simply old, their lives having reached the natural limits of their bodies. We make them welcome, document their lives, ease their passing. Others, like yourself, are summoned a few years prior to when we estimate natural death would occur. They get another life, a chance to make a difference, to contribute to what we're building here."

"Doctor, I'm grateful for the opportunity to continue my work, but that doesn't change the fact that I'm an old man."

She smiled again. "Indeed not, but we can do a thing or two to convince your body from further aging. And perhaps even reverse some of the effects of time." From a pocket of her lab coat she drew a vial, popping its stopper with her trunk and offering it to him. "Drink this, please."

"What is it?" he asked, holding the glass up to the light. The liquid was a pale blue but that told him nothing. It could have been colored water or cleaning fluid or a miracle drug for all he knew.

"A suspension of biological machines that begin to arrest your body's aging process. This is a crude version, just to get you started. It will begin removing unwanted plaque from blood vessels, lessen the traditional inflammations of aging, and curate the flora in your gut. You'll likely start to notice some positive changes to flexibility and general movement within a few days, as well as some improvement to your vision and digestion."

"I've heard of this technology. It's nothing new. The Alliance has had it for more than a thousand years and banned the use long since. It's a temporary fix at best. A body knows how old it is, and even if you clean it up its tendency is to go back to what it is."

"That's true enough, but as I said it's just to get you started. I'll brew a more precise batch once I've had time to work with the biological samples I took from you today. And that dose will be unlike anything the Alliance has ever seen. Just one of the discoveries we've made here, and available only to Fant."

He frowned, a part of him doing the math. "Youth in a vial? What next, will you tell me you've discovered immortality?"

"Hardly. As you say, Ryne, you're an old man. You've enjoyed more than eighty years, and kept yourself in good health through them all. You have a good constitution, your parents were of good stock and passed that along to you." She gestured to the vial he held and still hadn't consumed. "That and the treatments that follow it won't make you young again, but conservatively should allow you another twenty to fifty years of continued good health."

He shook his head. "And you give this to all the Dying?"

"No, as I said, there are three kinds. The first never make it to our shores. Some significant number perish in the journey, having reached the end of their lives in their attempt to arrive here. I've told you what becomes of the second kind. That just leaves the third group."

"The ones you've summoned."

"Just so. But only a small subset of the last group receive this drug. It's still fiendishly expensive to produce. Some day perhaps it will be as plentiful as the rain, but for now its distribution is limited."

"Then why me?"

"Before I answer that, I need to explain something else. As a scientist, Ryne, you possess an analytical view of the world. Surely the questions must have begun pouring down on you from the moment you stepped ashore, not least of them being why you hadn't thought them before then."

Speechless, he nodded, uncertain if she was somehow reading his mind or acting out a part she'd played many times in the past with other new arrivals. Summoned arrivals.

"You're familiar with Speakers," she said.

"Of course, what of them?"

"Ours are not like the ones found throughout the rest of Barsk. Ours do more than reconstruct and converse with the dead. They create . . . memes."

"Memes?"

"Concepts. Simple ideas that over time take root and grow, shaped by Speakers who monitor their development and others who, working in tandem can stimulate them, stir them such that they transform from thoughts to behaviors. We have Speakers on every island and beyond, and one of the memes they foster is the understanding that near the end of each Fant's life an awareness will bloom in the mind. A time and place to be. A certainty. You've felt it or you wouldn't be here now."

"The compulsion to sail away . . . that's artificial?"

She spread her hands. "It's a lot to accept, I know. Take as long as you need."

Memes. Ideas placed in the heads of millions of people. Driving them to their deaths. For centuries. The math sang to him with grim outcomes of cruel manipulation.

"You've taken the lives of untold generations."

"No, Ryne. I can tell you precisely how many generations and so could you if you think it through. But more importantly, we've taken no lives. The meme is placed in every one of us in childhood but in most cases it's not triggered until natural death is close at hand. That way, instead of a heart attack or a brain aneurysm or simply passing in one's sleep, the sudden awareness that there is a destination awaiting every Fant creates a sense of purpose, a clean and satisfying end to life."

"But . . . why? What's the point of it all?"

"To save us."

"Save us from what? What could possibly justify the manipulation of a planetary population? Let alone the expenditure of the resources necessary to accomplish it for all this time?"

"Save us from the Alliance. You're not the only one who runs simulations, Ryne. The Alliance is made up of eighty-seven distinct races spread out across more than four thousand inhabited planets. The Fant are just two of those races. A millennium ago we had communities on eighty worlds, living and working and creating right alongside the other members of the Alliance. Complex beings of different cultures and physiologies called us friend and neighbor, mingled their lives with ours. Two centuries later and all of that vanished. Suddenly those eighty planets were reduced to only this one. And for the past eighty-three tenyears the Alliance has been systematically imposing more and more restrictions on us."

"But the Compact guarantees that our—"

"The Compact cannot last forever. The Alliance didn't bargain with us in good faith, they allowed us to do all of their work and keep only the smallest result of our efforts. And there are factions within the Alliance rumbling that even that tiny piece is too much."

Ryne waved her arguments away with his trunk. "Even if all of that is true, what does it have to do with these memes?"

"The memes made this island possible. It gave the Caudex a place to begin and a home where we could build. Our founders were among the first generation born on Barsk and they sacrificed everything they had to create a dream of future prosperity for all Fant. Each generation that followed has worked tirelessly in pursuit of turning the impossible into the possible. This island? It was just the very beginning. A range of miracles has sprung forth from it. That vial in your hand is one example; there are thousands of others. Literally thousands. And if the Alliance knew about any of them it would be sufficient cause for them to shred the Compact that has kept them away from us for more than eight hundred years. But there will come a time—possibly in our lifetime—when they come back to this world they promised was ours and ours alone, and take it for themselves. And then where will we be?"

Lolte paused, propped her elbows on the table of their booth, and lowered her head into her hands. Her trunk flailed listlessly at the vial Ryne had restoppered but still held.

"I'm not convinced," he said. "You haven't explained what purpose all of this serves."

"The Caudex's ultimate purpose is to preserve us, our race and ways, our identity, in a galaxy of billions of people who experienced no moral dilemma taking us from our homes and dropping us here, locked away from the rest of space, from art and culture and science."

"But we have all of that."

"Barely. Only because the dispirited Eleph and Lox that first arrived here stumbled upon secrets in the rain forests that provided riches in such profusion, substances not available elsewhere. That's the Compact that you hang all your hopes on. It bought us some concessions, little enough for what we gave—what we continue to give—away. But how long can that last, Ryne? Did you know that two thirds of what once could be obtained only on Barsk is now grown on other Alliance worlds, or has been replaced by other goods from more reliable and readily accessible sources than Barsk?"

"But—"

She cut him off, again, any glimmer of humor long gone from her voice. "Here we prepare for the day when a majority of the Alliance tires of the Compact. When they no longer need us or choose to honor that treaty. Poor Barsk, a rainy world where the locals reject technology in favor of a life closer to nature. That wasn't who we were when we lived on other worlds. We adopted that path out of necessity. Such a meek notion fills the rest of the Alliance with a sense of superiority. It fuels their entitlement and their contempt but also makes us appear safe. How could we possibly be a threat? They have vessels that traverse space while we sail between our islands. They possess weapons that can pacify entire colonies should they step out of line, while we pick our plants by hand and send them up to an orbital space station where no Fant is permitted to even visit. We're quiet, harmless, and even the best of them see us as repugnant. But one day, all too soon, they'll tire of putting up with us and just take what they want. When that day comes, what's to keep them from eliminating us as well? Nothing, Ryne. Nothing except this island. Nothing except brilliant men and women like you who are given a second chance at life and a second opportunity to serve our people."

"You really believe the situation is that dire? Or that my work can make a difference?"

"As to the first, it's why this island is here. As for the second, yes, Ryne, it's why you're here. Now drink what's in that vial. The waiter is coming with our dinner and the biologics will work better on a full stomach."

He'd been running the math while she spoke, assigning values to each of the variables as she defined them. He'd need to flesh them out—he'd never bothered with Alliance politics before—but even the little he knew suggested she was right. Maybe he'd be able to improve on the Caudex's models and give them more accurate projections. Either way, his course was clear. Ryne again pulled the stopper free and upended the slender tube, drinking it down. It tasted like licorice and wind and hope.

Lolte nodded her approval. "You'll doubtless start to feel drowsy before we get to dessert, and your assistants will arrive to help put you to bed. You'll sleep away most of tomorrow as your body accepts the changes that are coming, and the next morning you'll begin the work that we believe is your destiny and the reason we summoned you here so you can do your part to save us all."

Moments later, the waiter came by and placed a plate in front of him, a mix of familiar and unfamiliar foods, all of it delicious. But the doctor proved to be wrong. He didn't make it to dessert but rather slumped in his seat halfway through his meal, lost to a deep and dreamless sleep.

FIVE

BEDTIME STORIES

OST women's homes in Keslo were enormous and tended to get bigger as generations of women and children branched and expanded. Rooms were added, porches enclosed, neighboring dwellings annexed and connected by inventive and oddly constructed temporary hallways that acquired permanence and extensions of their own. Back yards became internal patios, became parlors, became bedrooms and kitchens and even bathrooms depending on need and whim and available materials. This was the pattern in every Civilized Wood throughout both archipelagos, expansion and adaptation rather than contraction. Rina knew this from conversations with the other children in her extracurriculars. Twice each tenday she took lessons in painting, and three days after each of those she had rhetoric. Eight others of her age, both boys and girls, Eleph and Lox, learned brushstroke and color theory and regularly came home with garishly bright sheets for mothers and aunts to exclaim over. In addition, she took classes with four other Fant, all girls and all Eleph and all at least two years older, acquiring techniques of verbal sparring and persuasion on topics as weighty as technology versus simplicity and as frivolous as the best time of day to eat fruit. Every fourth session the five students engaged in formal debate, each in turn holding the orator's spot on one of Keslo's public performance spaces. Family members flocked to these forensic events, and each girl had at least ten guests from their overcrowded homes occupying the benches in the audience.

All except for Rina.

Other households overflowed with mothers and aunts, siblings and cousins, sometimes to triple digits. The house Rina occupied had originally been a rarity on Barsk, a single-family dwelling. In the beginning, Tolta had lived there with her husband, the pharmer Arlo, and occasionally—when the mood struck him—their son, Pizlo. But Arlo was dead, had died well before Rina had been born, and Pizlo didn't really exist to almost everyone on the planet. Often as not he lived outside of the normal spaces of the Civilized Wood, and only sometimes remembered to visit his mom. Tolta had invited Rina's own mother, Dabni, to move in after she'd bonded with Jorl and become pregnant. Tolta wasn't kin—though Rina had called her "aunt" all her life—but as Dabni had no other ties in Keslo, all of her family being back on Taylr far to the east edge of the eastern archipelago, that circumstance had been sufficient to expand a widow's household to include a pregnant friend. Though not unprecedented, it was uncommon, and as Pizlo didn't officially exist, Rina was the only child in the household.

Because her mother operated a small bookshop, and because her house lacked the usual mob of sibs and cousins to provide daily distractions, Rina spent most of her free time in a corner of the store, reading through the stock in a random and serendipitous order. Other times she took supplemental lessons in history and governance with her father, Jorl, drilling down into levels of detail that the coursework at her gymnasium never came close to. Sometimes he took her for walks throughout Keslo and spoke of dead people, both Fant and not, and the conversations he'd had with them in recent days. Rina followed much of the formal lessons and her young mind grew keen from them, benefiting not just from her father's expertise as a historian but also as Barsk's first senator to the Alliance. At least as applied to the material on civics.

Her father's tales of the dead though, these landed on her like fables whose true meanings lay just beyond her reach, wisdom that she couldn't quite grasp when he told them, but which would burst in on her without warning to illuminate something else that was happening around her. Though no one had taught her the words, she'd acquired an indirect understanding of simile and metaphor and it colored everything in her life. It gave her a greater appreciation of her father than most girls her age. Her mother was wonderful and together her parents seemed perfect, but taken on his own the range of her father seemed vaster to her than anything else in the world.

That awe for him could have grown worshipful, but Dabni dealt it a stunning blow each season by dropping Rina off to spend a few days at the vast house where Jorl's own mother lived. That woman, aided by an unending supply of sisters and cousins, told tales of her father's youth that stripped away his status as scholar and senator and Aleph-Bearer. In that place he was repainted as a boy who got into enough trouble to become the subject of other people's stories, often as not in the company of Arlo, the boy who would grow up to become Tolta's husband.

But of all the people in Rina's life, the one who came to her late at night and woke her from her sleep with his quiet conversations was whom she loved the best. Each evening, after finishing her supper and laying out her things for the next morning, after her mother and Tolta had both come to her room to kiss her good night and bid her sweet dreams, Rina would close her eyes and pretend to be asleep. And wait. Pretense often gave way to reality, waiting to dreaming.

That's when Pizlo would come.

He visited most nights for as long as she could remember. Sometimes he also stopped to see his own mother, sometimes not, but always he came to sit on the floor by her bed and tell her a story until her eyelids grew heavy again and she had to finish the tale in her dreams.

Rina knew that her bedroom had once belonged to Pizlo, that his mother had repurposed and redecorated it after Dabni moved in a season before she'd been born. Pizlo had to have known, too, but he never mentioned it, nor gazed wistfully about at this lamp or that wall hanging as Rina imagined she would surely do if their situations were reversed.

That night she had dozed off and didn't see him as he'd arrived.

"I met a Panda once," Pizlo said, his voice soft as new leaves but the rhythm of it pulled her to wakefulness and caused her eyes to flutter open. It couldn't have been more than seconds since her mother had kissed her forehead and slipped away and yet Pizlo had crept in and taken a seat by her bed. Or perhaps he'd been in the room all along, hidden away and silent, moving to sit there only after she'd settled. Or maybe she'd just fallen asleep and lost track of wakefulness and he'd arrived with plenty of time to get situated and watch her sleep while he decided on a story to tell.

"You didn't," she replied, though in fact she knew he had because he'd told her at least part of the story before. She reached under her pillow and found her doll, Kokab, and set it up on her shoulder to listen to Pizlo's story too.

"I did. It was the same day that Jorl became a senator. The day up on the station when he'd saved all of us, everyone on Barsk, and no one knew it."

Rina crinkled the nubs of her trunk. Of all of Pizlo's stories, the ones featuring her father made her happiest. "I thought he saved everyone by beating that Yak, the one no one remembers. Not a Panda."

Pizlo fell silent, and for a moment Rina feared she'd done something to cut story time short. But then he whispered, "I remember him," and shook himself, his pale ears flapping and wrapping closely about himself. "The Yak didn't live on the station, he was just there to cause trouble. But Pandas lived there. The station doesn't need a lot of people, machines do most of the work. And I don't know why, but everyone who did live there when I visited was an Ailuros. I didn't think about it at the time, but it was kind of funny."

"Funny how?"

"The station had no color. Nothing grew. Everything was dull plastic and ceramic and metal. And now I wonder if the Ailuros were there because, being all black and white themselves, living in that kind of a world didn't feel like a hardship to them, or if whoever assigned them there thought it was a joke. Monochromatic humor."

He smiled at her and she smiled back and tapped his wrist with the tip of her trunk. "Now you're the one making a joke."

"Maybe." He smiled with his voice, something she didn't understand how to do but delighted in when he displayed his skill at it. "Anyway, the Panda I met helped me settle into the yacht that

Jorl had just acquired. Or inherited. Depends on whom you ask. But that's not important. Anyway, your father had a lot to do that last day, talking to the forgotten Yak, and to a bunch of senators who'd gotten mixed up when everyone forgot the Yak. And also some dead people, because Jorl is always talking to dead people. And also, a lot of this time he was working things out with his new Brady assistant."

"Druz!" exclaimed Rina. She'd never met her father's senatorial aide but had heard about her, and now Pizlo was talking about the first time, when the Sloth had forgotten the Yak and in that gap of memory deduced that she worked for Jorl.

"That's right, Druz. And because I wasn't much older than you, when neither she nor Jorl could spare the moment to keep watch on me, Druz assigned an Ailuros to the job."

"Did you mind? Being treated like that? Like you would get in trouble without a minder?"

"I might have," said Pizlo, his lips working around something he'd just shoved into his mouth. He'd produced another handful of succulent leaves from one of the pouches on his bandolier, gave her a guilty glance as he remembered his manners and offered her some. She shook her head and he happily ate them himself, chewing and swallowing before continuing. "I already had marked myself with several moons by then . . ." He gestured at his bare chest and the ink from his latest redrawing of the seven dark circles he'd painted upon it. "But no . . . so few people ever talked to me, even fewer then than now, that just really being seen by someone was incredible. And that it was someone who I could never expect to ever meet on Barsk just made it more so. In the moment, it never occurred to me that really Druz was assigning me a babysitter."

Rina responded with a scowl of understanding. Although nothing like the wildling upbringing that Pizlo had enjoyed, she'd grown up inventing much of her own structure, free of the socializing and rules of age mates in a large house, lured instead into flights of imagination courtesy of the books in her mother's shop. Those few occasions when Dabni or Tolta felt compelled to hire some local teen to watch her for an evening still bristled and burned. But yes, being minded by someone from another world would take away all the sting.

"So what was he like?"

"The Panda? Well, you've read up on them in your studies, right?"

Rina nodded. "Uh huh. They're big, taller than Fant but not as thick. And furry of course. And I think their ears are cute." She giggled and then covered her mouth with both hands, embarrassed.

"Cute? Those tiny things? Well, I guess. Anyway, this Ailuros was all that, like all of them are. Except, he also wasn't. He talked to me, a bit. I could see he didn't want to, I think he really disliked having to even be on the same space station as Jorl or me, let alone the same room, but once he and I started talking that changed."

"Changed how?"

"He started out by calling me a 'tiny monster' as soon as Druz left me with him. I thought he meant on account of my being different, the way everyone on Barsk treats me—"

"Not everyone!" Rina trumpeted and then blushed and gripped her offending trunk with both hands.

"Well, no, not everyone. That's true." The smile had returned to his voice making Rina smile in turn. "But anyway, he meant because I was a Fant. He thought Barsk was a planet full of monsters. He admitted he'd never really thought about it though, and as we talked he realized it didn't make any sense and he apologized for calling me a monster."

"A tiny monster."

"Right, he was sorry about that, and he started calling me 'tiny Fant' instead."

Rina giggled. "Not 'tiny Lox'?"

"Nope. I think because both Eleph and Lox look so different from all the other people in the Alliance, and so much like one another, that no one but us really understands we're different races."

"But that's . . . that's just dumb."

Pizlo nodded, shrugged, and continued. "I told him my name, and asked him for his. I'd never done that before, asked someone for their name. I mean, when would I have? Anyway, he told me. Ciochon. Not like any name I'd heard before. So I said, 'Hullo, Ciochon. My name is Pizlo.' And he scowled at me."

"Why would he do that?"

"That's what I asked him. And he said if he called me by name, then I'd stop being a Fant."

"That's dumb, too," said Rina. "What else could you be?"

"No, see, he didn't mean it like that. Like before, when I asked you what you knew about Ailuros. Everything you said was true, but none of it really told you anything about Ciochon, about his life and his family, about his hobbies and his favorite foods, or his hopes and plans. It was like that. He said that if he called me by name that I'd become a real person to him, that he couldn't see me as a monster any more."

"What's wrong with that?"

"It bothered him. He said that when you live on a space station you spend a lot of time in your own head, thinking about the same stuff over and over. And that if he came to see that the one Fant he'd actually met wasn't a monster, than what did that say about all the other monsters on our planet? Because he'd roll it all around in his head and eventually have to accept that an entire planet was a lot of people to be wrong about. And not just that, but it called into doubt other things that he knew to be absolutely true, taught to him by the same teachers and leaders who explained about us being monsters. It's like talking to me, admitting I was real, would end up breaking everything he knew. He started rocking and sniffling. I mean, he was thinking real hard, but it was making him feel pretty upset, not like when Jorl causes me to think about stuff."

"What did you do?"

"Well, it looked like he was having some kind of panic attack, winding himself up tighter and tighter, more and more unhappy. Only back then—remember I was about your age now—I didn't know what that was. All I could do was watch it happen. It made me feel so helpless. I wanted to help him but I didn't know what to do. But then one of the hundreds of thousands of things Telko had said to me earlier that day popped up in my thoughts—"

"Telko the moon, right?"

He grinned at her. "That's the only Telko I've met. Anyway, Telko had told me something that I didn't understand, with names that made no sense, but I just repeated it to the Panda, because I knew that Telko knew it was what Ciochon needed to hear at that moment."

Rina gasped and clutched her doll with excitement. "What did you say?"

Pizlo's voice dropped as he spoke in a monotone. "I know where Su and Lin sleep. I know where they play. Every moment of every day, I know."

"I don't understand. Who are Su and Lin?"

"They're Ciochon's daughters."

"Ewwww! Why would you say that? That's creepy."

He nodded. "Yeah. The Panda fell out of his chair and scrambled away from me. He had a weapon on his belt and he reached for it but didn't draw it, only kept a hand there. And he was shaking and asking 'How do you know my daughters' names? How could you know anything about them?'"

"And what did you say?"

"What Telko had told me to say. What Ciochon needed to hear. I said, 'It's because I'm a monster. Just like everyone on Barsk.'"

Rina frowned and shrunk back against her pillow, clutching Kokab to her. "Pizlo! That's terrible. Why would you do that? You said he was seeing that Fant weren't monsters, that you were a real person and that all those bad stories were wrong. You threw all that away. Why?"

Pizlo rubbed at his face. He looked away and fiddled with a scab on his elbow and said nothing.

"You can't end a story like that," said Rina. "And you never do anything without a reason. So why did you do that?"

He looked up at her and sighed. "It's . . . it was what he needed. I didn't see it clearly for a long time, which I guess is why Telko helped me with it. But see, he had to make a choice: if I was real, then that meant maybe everything he knew was wrong, that his life was a lie and maybe nothing else was as he understood it to be. Or, if he could see that maybe I'd tricked him—cuz monsters are tricky—and fooled him about not being a monster for just a short while, then his life could go on as before and everything would be fine again."

"But—"

"Jorl had just caused everyone but me to forget someone. The entire galaxy forgot him, and there was a hole in everyone's memory. And now here was this Panda who had never done anything to any Fant, and just by talking to him I might have broken his life. Can you imagine? Like everything you know, in your whole life, suddenly becomes wrong? That was no good. I wouldn't ever want to do that to someone on purpose, and here I'd done it by accident. Telko's words let me fix that. Besides, nearly everyone on Barsk calls me an abomination, so being a monster for one Ailuros wasn't much of a burden."

Rina climbed out of her bed to wrap her arms and trunk around Pizlo and hugged him. "You did it so the Panda could be happy."

"Well, yeah, that's one way to end the story," he said.

"You're *not* a monster, Pizlo."

He laughed. "No, that's what I learned from the Panda. It's part of the moral of the story."

"What's that?"

"None of us are monsters."

"None?"

"Nope."

She let go of him then, chewing on her lip as she climbed back into bed and processed what he'd told her.

"You said that was only part of the moral. What was the rest?"

"The other part? Oh, just that all of us *are* monsters. Not just Lox and Eleph, everyone, in all the galaxy."

"But you just said—"

He was grinning at her. "I know, right? See, I told you monsters were tricky."

SIX

HIDDEN IN PLAIN SIGHT

~~~~~~~~~

THE portion of the firstborn generation of Barsk that established the Caudex based their entire existence on a single
core belief: the Alliance wanted every last Eleph and Lox—every
man, woman, and child—dead and gone. They believed the bu-
reaucracy responsible for transporting all the galaxy's Fant to
Barsk had only enacted the beginning of a plan, putting them all
in one spot to facilitate their eventual annihilation. Margda's Compact had forged a truce of sorts, but it was at best a stopgap; it
bought some time for the Fant, but not safety. The Caudex resolved
to use that time to best advantage, to develop plans to ensure they
survived at any cost.

Sometimes the Alliance's contempt for anything and everything
touched by Eleph or Lox worked to the advantage of the Fant.
Eight hundred years earlier, when the first waves of resettlement
had begun—before the tone of the relocation had grown darker—
among the many ships ferrying Fant to their new home on Barsk
were commercial spacecraft owned and operated by Fant concerns
on Marbalarma and Kensington, Venango and Slon, Dramblys

and Passyunk. In the rush to be done with the unwanted Fant, these vessels slipped off the grid, ostensibly kept in active service to transport latecomers, which went on for most of a decade. When the planet's pharmaceutical treasure trove opened, these same ships provided some support for building Barsk's space elevator and orbiting satellite. But then, under the guise of "business as usual," various agents of the new forming Caudex purchased every Fant ship and began hiding them throughout the system, powering down all nonessential energies and limiting personnel to the barest of crews. Alliance licensing databases showed all of them as decommissioned, sold to other concerns, or crashed on the surface of one of the moons of Barsk and destroyed.

Instead they merely waited.

After two hundred years, everyone had forgotten the ships even existed. By then, other projects had begun to bear fruit and the Caudex found themselves in preparation to return Fant to the larger galaxy in a way no one expected. One by one the sleeping ships powered up, took on cargo and passengers from Barsk, and vanished.

∼∼∼

KLARCE sat in the Speaker's chair on the bridge of *Cerulean,* formerly *Oberon's Treat,* a refurbished shipping vessel now serving the Caudex as an emergency transport. It had docked with *Cahill's Absence,* a seeming derelict of a private vessel, the sort traditionally associated with corporate directors of world-spanning financial concerns. A search of Alliance records would reveal the craft had been stolen six hundred years earlier, reported as lost and destroyed. Instead it wound up here, floating on the edge of a solar system seemingly devoid of life. More than a thousand years earlier an Alliance Patrol craft surveyed this section of space and found it wanting. It held no useable planets, just a lone gas giant with several unpromising moons. The Patrol ship traversed the system from one end to the other, filed their report, and kept going in search of more welcoming worlds. Standard Patrol procedure involved always looking outward and never so much as glancing back.

The policy suited the Caudex just fine.

Though *Cahill's Absence* was dead in space, it was also large enough to contain a much smaller vessel, once assorted bulkheads had been cut away and all equipment removed. The ship wasn't so much a derelict as an empty husk. Inside its dead skin hung an unmarked two-man scout ship that was very much alive.

A tenday ago it looked doubtful the same could be said about one of the scout ship's crew. A routine bit of repair work in the gap between the ship's surface and the *Cahill's Absence*'s inner hull had gone horribly wrong, all but crushing Damace, the Fant handling the repair. He survived, but required medical attention beyond both the equipment of the scout ship and the expertise of his crewmate. The specifics had passed quickly through channels all the way to the Quick Council on Barsk back in its distant star system. As protocol dictated, a rescue vessel had been dispatched. Owing to the injured ethernaut being one of Klarce's younger brothers, she had set another protocol aside and insisted she be part of the rescue crew.

No signal, no electromagnetic energy of any kind, had come from *Cahill's Absence* or the small ship it contained, and the *Cerulean* had transmitted none. After docking with the derelict, it affixed a transfer umbilicus to the long-blown hatch, and transferred a five-person team—three medical personnel, an engineering specialist, and a replacement crew member who brought up the rear towing four crates of supplies. They swam into the space between the ship in a ship, aware of the irony of their location, and then boarded through the inner vessel's airlock. It was snug for a while, then the medicos brought Klarce's brother back to the umbilicus in an emergency capsule. The engineer disconnected the umbilicus, waved a go-ahead to *Cerulean*, and remained behind with the replacement ethernaut as the transfer tunnel retracted. Back onboard their ship, the medical team secured their patient in a bare bones infirmary far superior to what had existed on his original ship.

Klarce had no medical training. Her only assistance would have been to hover over the team and glower inspirationally. Instead, she remained in the Speaker's chair and along with the captain watched the video feed as the experts she'd brought attempted to stabilize Damace for transport. She'd taken koph once her brother's capsule came over and when the captain signaled she reached out for the nefshons of her brother's recent crewmate, connected to him as easily as she might greet someone walking down the boardway.

"Hello, Porlie. *Cerulean*'s captain informs me Damace looks as ready for transport as he's going to be."

In her mind, Klarce sat in the all-purpose room of a two-man scout ship hanging on the edge of space, all its systems shut down save passive sensors mounted on the surface of the derelict around it, for all the world like a little fish wriggling in the belly of a larger one that had swallowed it and died of the action. She shook her head, dismissing thoughts of dying, and instead looked at the person sitting next to her. Porlie was a male, twenty-something Lox, whom she'd known for most of his life. He faced her in an identical hammock chair.

"Thank you for coming so quickly, Klarce, I'm so sorry—"

She waved him to silence and his ears fell back and stilled. "The

Caudex looks after their own, whether back home on Barsk or out in space. You know that."

"Yes, of course, but . . . thank you for coming yourself." He cleared his throat, sat up straighter. "Councilor, if you'll hold, I'll reach for the operator on the other side."

"I'd appreciate it. We all want to get Damace home."

"Understood, Councilor. Quick as I can."

She watched as Porlie's eyes unfocused, as he spoke to Damace's replacement and authorized the transmission of a coded signal. Back on her own bridge, the captain's eyes would be watching for the result, as the pieces of a disassembled portal came together and powered up. The code changed daily. Four people in the entire galaxy knew it and one of them was unconscious in the infirmary. She could force her way onto this ship, but even a member of the Quick Council couldn't violate the security protocols necessary to keep them all safe.

Porlie looked up to her. "Portal diagnostic comes back green on all lights. Hold, please. Reaching for the operator."

His eyes closed again and somewhat ironically the nefshon construct of his body slumped. Like her, Porlie was a Speaker. Every Caudex vessel possessed at least one, along with sufficient supplies of koph to ensure that untraceable, point-to-point communication could take place instantly across the vast distances between stars. The Alliance's Patrol built and established massive and permanent portals throughout the galaxy as the means of allowing their ships to skip the space between inhabited solar systems. The Caudex had created their own, considerably smaller, gateways. They then quietly spent centuries moving these new portals into position, and once arrived, they deactivated and disassembled them until need dictated otherwise. Without a working portal, anyone seeking to enter this system would spend many years doing so and provide plenty of warning to the Fant here.

Klarce waited. It was an odd thing to watch another Speaker in mindspace reach out to connect with a third. The moment dragged on and then Porlie was back. A third Fant joined them in the shared illusion of mindspace, an older Eleph who had probably requested the duty for the relief the lack of gravity brought to her aging body.

"Hello, Councilor Klarce. Porlie. Nice to see you both. Right on schedule. The portal on this end has been activated and is standing by. There are no other vessels insystem at this time, and according to the agent on the other side of our Alliance portal no one is within three days of coming through. We're ready for your return at your convenience."

"Thank you, Jenna. I'll inform the captain here. A moment."

Klarce shook her awareness free of the nefshon venue and lifted her head. *Cerulean*'s captain sat at the command station, watching her.

"We have clearance to proceed, Captain."

She nodded. Klarce glanced at the instrument panel showing a newly opened portal on this end. Unlike an Alliance portal which never shut down, *Cerulean* had awaited Klarce's confirmation there was an open gateway on the other end. The captain snapped her trunk at the Eleph sitting at helm. "You heard the councilor. Thread the needle and take us through."

As the vessel hurtled toward the portal, Klarce slipped back into conversation with the agents guarding either side of it. "We're on our way now. Porlie, standard procedure. When Jenna tells you we've successfully cleared her side, power yours down and disassemble until you get the next call."

"Yes, ma'am."

"Jenna, same deal. After we've come through, shut it down."

"Klarce," said Porlie. "Take care of Damace."

She blinked back a tear. "Like you have to ask."

~~~~~

KLARCE allowed herself a sigh of satisfaction as the ship entered the edge of their home star system on the opposite end from the Alliance portal that provided access for the ships that docked at the station above Barsk. Under the watchful eye of her primary assistant she'd taken an extra dose of her meds—reasonable given the stress of the trip—and then allowed Temmel to guide her through *Cerulean*'s labyrinth of corridors to the infirmary. They joined the medical team and together headed to the bay where they transferred her brother's capsule to a shuttle. Moments later, with Temmel in the pilot's seat and after receiving permission from the ship's captain, they slipped from the larger vessel and dove unobtrusively deeper into the system. In only a couple of days she would have Damace back on Barsk and the unnamed island's best physicians would restore him to full health. That was the plan. Nothing in the rescue mission had required her presence. It was all sentimentality, and now it was time to set such thoughts aside. She slid into the empty copilot's seat and nodded to her assistant.

While she'd been on the bridge of the *Cerulean*, Temmel had himself made use of koph to get in touch with other members of her team back on the island and prepare a schedule for her review. She glanced through it now, the usual endless list of tasks, organized into sections showing which she could delegate, delay, or ignore, and which demanded her immediate attention. The life of a member of the Full Council.

Taking an unscheduled trip on a rescue run had put her well behind, and placed a burden on the rest of the Quick Council. They'd grumble, Sind worse than all the rest, but they also understood her motivations and it would pass. She'd have done the same for any of them.

"None of these can wait upon landfall?" She scowled at her assistant's list of critical items. Just because she had to wait days to get home didn't mean she wanted to bore herself with trivial makework. She handed the list back to him. "Summarize!"

Temmel flipped through the document, unperturbed by her petulance. "The early projections from the physicist's work are promising though the power required to operate the prototype-in-progress appears daunting. He's been informed of the problem and insists there's a trivial fix. Also, his handler is requesting authorization to begin longevity treatments on him. She believes his potential contributions will more than justify the expense."

Klarce snorted. "Does she now? Hasn't he only just arrived?"

"Yes, but she's been tracking his work for a tenyear and believes he'd have made a breakthrough long since if he'd had funds and a proper engineering team to turn his theories into a working prototype."

"Huh. And does she have any inkling what kind of argument I'll receive from the Full Council over this? Every person we add to that program is another enormous drain on our resources. What is she thinking?"

Temmel pressed his lips together, eventually nodding when he realized her question hadn't been rhetorical. "Perhaps . . . she's considering the loss if he expires before finishing the work after so much effort to bring him along to this point."

"No, she's right. It's just . . . his theories are extreme. Anyone qualified to evaluate them acknowledges he's out there beyond the edge of the understandable. If he's right, then our security takes a vast leap forward. But what if he's not?"

"Surely then we're not worse off than we are at present. Still secure, and simply out those resources we invested in the attempt."

"You think I should authorize the treatment?"

"Ma'am, with respect, I'm not qualified to have an opinion."

She snorted again. "My grandmother's snot you're not. What have I been training you for if not to assume my seat on the Quick Council one day. Not only do you have an opinion, you have the luxury of it not carrying any responsibility, yet. So out with it. What do you believe I'm missing here?"

Clearing his throat, Temmel let his ears drop back in earnest. "Have you met him?"

"Met him? What? No, of course not. You've pored over every moment of my schedule for years now. When was I supposed to meet him?"

"You should. I'll try and make some time in your schedule. Perhaps you can attend a lecture, or I should ask him to do one, a colloquium or some such. I heard him, years ago when I was on assignment on Taylr. Hearing him talk about his work, it was unlike anything I'd experienced."

"So he's a charismatic lecturer."

"No, ma'am. He's a physicist whose skills and insights have allowed him to glimpse something beyond our universe and bring the sense of it back with him. Assuming he's a suitable candidate for longevity, I can't imagine anyone who would benefit the Caudex more by another few decades of productivity."

Klarce's snort turned to a smirk. "More than me? My name will be up for consideration in a few years. Do you think his work constitutes a greater contribution than my own?"

Temmel embraced the temerity she'd suspected lurked within

him and said, "It's not for me to say, ma'am, but the physicist is unique and as you've observed, you expect to be replaced. By me."

"Fine. I look forward to stepping down after a long and triumphant career. Maybe I'll retire to Wella or Nita, sit on my porch and spoil grandchildren with before-dinner sweets until my years catch up with me, while this physicist lives on and on. Approve the request, but tell his handler I want to see some preliminary findings. I'll need them when I have to beat back the noise of the other councilors about this."

She watched him make a note of the decision.

"What's next on your list?"

"The Aleph, Margda's chosen."

"What about him?"

"He's been researching societal patterns on mixed worlds where Fant lived prior to the transportation to Barsk."

"And we know this how?"

"Our field agent put a trace on his terminal. It's as sophisticated a piece of hardware as exists on Barsk, the same model as in your office both at home and in Ulmazh. And as a member of the Committee of Information he has access to any and all data in the Alliance."

Klarce waved the remark away with a sweep of her trunk. "As an an Aleph-Bearer he theoretically has access anyway, but what's your point?"

"He's compiling lists of races which Fant successfully lived among in the past. He published several 'thought pieces' in academic journals, hypothesizing ways in which we might find ourselves commingled with various combinations of other races, taking up rational or at least plausible reasons why they might be resistant to the idea and offering up potential solutions. He's advocating ending our isolation and independence."

"He's been out there, you know."

"Ma'am?"

"He's left Barsk. It was one of the *accomplishments* that earned him his aleph. He's been out there and returned. For more than a full turning of the seasons, Jorl ben Tral lived and worked among several handfuls of other races. No doubt the experience has given him an extremely special perspective on the matter. He might even be right, how would we know?"

"Ma'am? You can't be serious. What he's advocating would constitute a potential risk to the security of everything we've built!"

Klarce nodded. She held up a hand to forestall anything further; this discussion was one that would only escalate her assistant's concern. "It's something the Full Council has discussed as well. But tell me, how have his peers responded to these journal articles? Has he garnered any support among the intellectual elite at Zlorka or elsewhere?"

"Quite the opposite. The most positive reaction has been resistance. At the other extreme, several of his previously close colleagues have denounced him for his reactionary ideas, and a petition had even been circulated demanding the revocation of his tenure on the grounds of moral turpitude."

"Moral turpitude? That's not a justification that gets invoked much." She smiled briefly. "Did the petition gain much traction?"

"Not really." Temmel consulted his notes. "Ah, a past provost—who had published a brief response of his own, strongly hinted Jorl ben Tral would be better served focusing his talents in other avenues of research—invalidated the petition on the grounds that even though the most, and I'm quoting now, 'bizarre and wrongheaded direction of inquiry might be construed as demonstrating poor judgment, such a thing is qualitatively different from a reflection of morality, but rather an expression of academic freedom, which should be recognized and protected by all scholars.' That appears to have been the end of the matter."

Klarce settled back, lacing her fingers together and bringing her trunk up to rest curled behind one ear. Was Temmel paying attention? It was precisely the things he learned during these conversations that would allow him to grow into a councilor rather than remain a personal assistant. "Here's the thing about this Jorl ben Tral. He came to our attention when he left the planet, though of course we couldn't keep a watch on him then. Upon his return—honorable discharge resulting from a personal obligation back on Barsk—he went back under routine passive observation; we labeled him as a special case, someone worth checking up on now and then. His status was later upgraded to active and an agent assigned to him after he'd been marked with an aleph and identified as the Lox whom Margda had mentioned in one of her prophecies. But like most Bearers, his life has been unremarkable, albeit with a few notable exceptions. He returned to his work as a historian and we expected him to remain a quiet academician. The first blip we observed was his decision to associate with and even tutor an abomination. A few years later he was somehow involved with an incident on the space station—which I will note has yielded neither official nor unofficial reports—the upshot of which led to his designation as an Alliance senator."

"Ma'am, how does a Fant become a senator? I realize we're technically a part of the Alliance, but Barsk has never sought nor been offered participation in the government."

"If you're expecting me to make sense of this for you, I can't. The whole thing is absurd, not least because this historian has never shown any political leanings at all. Someone is hiding something here, but we've found no trace of who or what. And in the years since his appointment there's been nothing unusual to report. And believe me, we've expended considerable resources in the investigation but it proved futile. As a senator, Jorl ben Tral is an excellent academic, which surprises no one. This latest thing you've brought me is the first hint of anything subversive from him. He's been completely apolitical till now."

"So you're recommending the council take some action?"

She brought her trunk down and waggled it at her assistant. "These essays of his, they aren't a concern yet. But they do justify why we assigned a field agent to keep him under observation. Margda singled him out for a purpose, and not knowing why is reason enough for us to watch him. But seriously, do you imagine his idea of reuniting us with even one other race of the Alliance is going to gain any traction?"

Temmel had the good sense to blush. "No, ma'am."

"Right. What's next on the list?"

SEVEN

KNOWLEDGE, QUESTIONS, AND CHOICE

FOR the past several seasons, Pizlo had pondered the flaw in his devotion to Jorl as his mentor. To be sure, there wasn't a living soul in the galaxy who cared more for him, had been more generous with time and teaching, and believed in his potential. But for all that, no matter how he tried not to, Pizlo had at last come to the understanding that he could never do what Jorl did. Yes, he had followed him along one path, becoming a Speaker, but that was biology not intention. The choices Jorl had made were choices he wanted for himself. Pizlo, on the other hand, had no interest in history, nor could he envision a future in which he was either a husband or a father. And the thought of serving in the Alliance senate recalled to mind the nightmares he still had of Bish and how Jorl had caused everyone in the galaxy to forget him.

If Pizlo's studies with the Archetype of Man meant anything, then Jorl had already fulfilled his responsibilities as mentor. Today, Pizlo stood on the edge of acknowledging—and thereby moving past—his own reluctance to take the next step. He'd grown up,

mostly, which meant he had to reassign Jorl to a new role, that of
friend and advisor.

It was part of a larger picture. Change was coming. Events that
others would see as random held intention and meaning for him.
The connections did more than talk to him, they suggested a call
to action that he couldn't resist much longer. The individual pieces
had been building for nearly a year, little more than dust motes of
possibilities in the beginning, but they'd since grown into solider
forms. Leaves spoke to him of it, stones in the Shadow Dwell called
to him. The signs made themselves known in the most routine of
things. Portents fell like rain.

An outsider to Fant society, Pizlo nonetheless hungered for it,
to know it vicariously if not directly. From earliest childhood he
had built himself blinds that allowed him to observe people going
about their day, hidden forts tucked into public walls of foliage that
looked out upon busy boardways, camouflaged nooks providing
access to parks and amphitheaters. From these spots he had
watched and listened and witnessed the public lives of the citizens
of Keslo, coming to know the names and ways and details of many
in a city where everyone knew of him but never spoke his name.
In recent years, he'd sometimes take koph while watching them,
to see each of them cloaked all around in the golden fabric of their
nefshons, burning their gleaming images into his brain to keep
when the drug wore off. They were all so special, wondrous in ways
he could never be, freely chatting and laughing and joking with
so many others. He had so few. And yet, numbered among his
handful was a person unlike any the people of Keslo would ever
know, someone who was neither Eleph nor Lox, someone from
another world.

The fourth person in all the galaxy ever to speak to Pizlo had been a Brady. She'd introduced herself as Druz, and in a time that no longer existed she'd been the personal assistant to Senator Bish. When Jorl took the Yak's place her loyalties and responsibilities transferred to him. Under the terms of the Compact, Druz could not set foot upon the planet, she visited twice each year. She'd pilot her employer's personal spacecraft to a water landing not far from Keslo's shore, pretending the vessel was simply a ship for traversing the ocean. Jorl would sail out to meet her—sometimes allowing Pizlo to come along—and when they finished their business she would travel off to another world of the Alliance on some senatorial mission.

Pizlo had last seen Druz two seasons ago. While she spoke with Jorl and completed whatever errands had brought her to Barsk, he'd taken the opportunity to explore the ship that years before he'd actually piloted for a short time. Sitting at the control boards again, he found them a better fit at fourteen than they'd been at six. He reviewed the protocols and procedures for flight, hands moving across the locked-down helm as if at a simulator. The pilot's seat seemed to whisper approval to him; soon, soon he'd fly this vessel again. He didn't know why or when, but that didn't change the certainty of it. Soon.

As a mental exercise, he ran through the checklist for shutdown, arriving at the configuration that the boards were actually in, then hopped off his chair, suddenly possessed of the knowledge that Jorl and Druz had concluded their business. Any moment now they'd call for him. He went to them instead, finding them in the cargo hold. The ship's outer hatch stood open, water flooding the space. Jorl's boat lay tied to a gantry, right where they'd left it after sailing into the spacecraft. Jorl, having finished his senatorial business, was in the midst of carrying some small crates onto the boat. He waved his trunk in a combination of greeting and summoning, but as Pizlo went to join him, Druz pulled him aside. She bowed to him and placed a small package in his hands.

"The senator informs me you have a birthday coming soon, Little Prince."

She'd named him that on their first meeting and though it made him blush now that he was no longer a boy, he endured it as a sign of her affection. And, too, because Jorl had said it was so striking to see him blush given his albinism.

"It's nearly a season away," he'd responded. Birthdays weren't something he tended to think about. Nor the passage of time in general. The future didn't flow out before him as it did other people.

The Sloth had continued. "My research suggests that our people share a custom of bestowing gifts at such a time. As I will be far away on the actual day, please accept this token in advance."

He'd taken the gift, hugged and thanked her, leaving unspoken the fact that he'd received few such presents. Though the people in his life loved him, he'd only had cause to learn about birthday gifts a few years ago when Rina began receiving them. Fant society didn't acknowledge the birth of abominations like him, and it simply hadn't occurred to anyone to celebrate the anniversary of his entrance into the world, let alone mark it with a gift. Druz, not being raised to Fant custom, had seen him initially only as a precocious child, then later as a boy who enjoyed the kind regard of her employer, and finally as a young friend. What need of birthday presents when she already gave him so much?

As he stepped from the gantry and onto the powered boat floating as if at dock, he'd slipped the present into a pocket on his bandolier and forgot it amidst waving farewell and watching as Druz convinced the vessel to slip away from them on the water before rising up through the rain and vanishing in the cloud cover. Then he and Jorl had guided their own craft back to shore. It had been a short journey; Druz had "parked" her craft just beyond the island's shallows and thus they'd returned quickly to the dock where Jorl maintained a slip. Pizlo knew the harbor well and frequently visited the boat while Jorl was busy elsewhere, raiding the craft's galley or just enjoying the gentle rocking motion of being on the water.

Under the carefully averted gaze of the harbormaster they'd returned through the Shadow Dwell and back up to the Civilized Wood, chatting all the while about Pizlo's studies, his conversations with the Archetype of Man, and what bits of senate business Jorl could share. After they parted, Pizlo slipped from the regular boardways used by other Fant and settled into one of the wild spaces he'd created for himself over the years, just another niche that he could find but which to the uninvited appeared to be a solid and uninhabitable space within the forest that defined the city. Only once he'd settled in did he remove the gift from his pocket and examine it.

At first Pizlo mistook the present for the box it came in. Druz had wrapped it in paper decorated with a colorful fractal pattern of shades of green. He appreciated the gesture; anything wrapped in such paper blended in instantly and vanished within his nook. That would have been present enough, but there was more. The box under the paper was a dark, burnished grey metal. It fit in the palm of his hand, a third as tall as it was wide or deep. Druz knew of the Barsk-wide aversion to polymers, machined items, and obvious signs of technology, but the simplicity of the metal box slipped past such prejudice and was a thing of beauty on its own. He didn't know what he could use such a box for, but he had no doubt he'd keep it.

The issue was resolved upon opening it, discovering it had its own purpose as a home for its contents. Nestled snuggly in a bit of black cloth lay a circular amulet made up of inlaid woods in a swirling design, the whole thing hanging from a chain of tiny links of metal as pale as ash that nearly blended in with his own skin color. Pizlo fiddled with the chain until with a twist a magnetic clasp clicked apart and he was able to refasten it around his neck. The amulet itself rested at the base of his throat.

He ran a finger over both its sides at the same time, feeling a faint depression in the back. And then it talked.

"Happy birthday, Little Prince," the amulet spoke in Druz's voice, buzzing against his neck. "I hope you like your gift. It's a personal recording device that will respond to your touch. Pressing against the spot in the middle of its back will let it know you want to use it. At the same time, tap the top front once to record and again to stop. Tap twice to begin recording a new item. Tap the bottom front to play back, and the sides to move from item to item. It's easier than it sounds and you'll learn the knack of it readily I have no doubt. You're very special, Pizlo, and you witness things others do not. I thought you might find it helpful to be able to keep a record. If you ever wish to transfer the recordings to another device or other media, Jorl can show you how. Enjoy."

Pizlo removed the amulet and stared at it a long while, agog at a message recorded just for him, at having Druz's voice available at any time. He studied the gift, cataloging the look and shape and weight of the thing in his hand. He put it back in its box, wrapped the paper back around it and tucked it away in a nook. Making a record of his own observations in turn confused and excited him. But who would listen to him? Surely no one, if they realized the source was an abomination. Had Druz realized what a complicated gift she'd given him?

He drew a wafer of koph from his bandolier and slipped it under his tongue as he set off to another wild space higher up, midway between the Civilized Wood and the canopy. It was one thing to sit in a nook where he could watch the nefshons of Keslo's inhabitants, but for actual summoning he preferred less accessible spaces. He had an urge to chat with the Archetype of Man, to include his new amulet as part of the nefshon construct of himself, and discuss with the long dead storyteller how he might make best use of it. Plenty of stories he'd heard had no witnesses other than the hero, which suggested that the hero had to be responsible for either writing down the tale or telling it to someone who did. Perhaps it was time for Pizlo to consider telling his own story, or at least recording some of its pieces.

~~~~~

AS a general rule, Pizlo liked abstract things. While concrete objects had the advantage that you could touch them or taste them, hold them in your hand or hide them under a stone or in a stream deep in the Shadow Dwell, they contained within themselves a lie. A book he borrowed from Jorl existed not only on the shelf in his advisor's home, but also as a memory, a recollection of the emotions and thoughts it had sparked in him. The memory of a thing was different. An image in his mind owed nothing to the physical world, and presumably could exist within him even if the concrete source of it was lost or destroyed. Jorl had called this the "permanence of idea" and at first Pizlo thought his friend had it wrong. How could ideas be permanent when every time he rolled one around in his thoughts it changed? That was before he'd come up with the idea of building a catalog of his insect collection in his mindspace. The bugs in that memory were static. Yes, each specimen led to a more elaborate memory of how and when and where he'd acquired it, but they didn't roil in his brain like abstractions did.

So, maybe Jorl was half right, at least when it came to ideas about things. But thinking ideas about ideas still felt like an endless cycle of rain that was always the same but always different. It made his ears twitch, as if holding such a thought in his head meant he knew something that not even the moons above had realized yet. That didn't happen very often. After talking with the Archetype, he'd spent the next day and night and most of another day wandering through interstitial spaces of the Civilized Wood, ostensibly restocking his various hideaways, but really using the physical motion as an analog of profound cogitation. By the end of it, he had things to share with the moons.

He sought out the deepest darkness that existed only in the Shadow Dwell. Any artificial light from the inhabitants of the Civilized Wood lay far above and behind him, blocked by impenetrable layers of branch and leaf. Pizlo nestled amid the roots of a massive meta-tree, sorting out what he wanted to say and waiting for the right time to say it. There was life all around him, the tiny bugs and animals that made their home in the rocks and muck and soil of the place. Parasites and symbionts lived in bark and leaves, spores and pollens and things too minuscule to see floated on the air with opportunistic hope, fungi grew in colors that no one ever saw, molds rippled with alkaloids that would produce visions to rival anything imagined while under koph.

But his thoughts tonight were not for the living. He walked a weaving path through blackness until he stood upon a tiny patch of sand on one of the island's innumerable minor coves—this one not so different from where he'd found the statue he'd used to pay back the chemist—emerging from rainforest into rain and a slightly lesser darkness in the clouds far above. He sat in the sand, a trunk's

length above the wet line where gentle waves climbed the meager
beach. Water lapped at his feet. Druz's gift rested against his
throat. He brought a hand up to it and began recording.

"I liked you better when I was just a kid," he said, speaking to
the world around him, beach and ocean and sky. All seven of
Bark's moons were shining down on him that night, though the
clouds blocked any sign of them. Pizlo looked up, moving his gaze
from one part of sky to another, acknowledging where each hung.
He felt their yearning to speak to him, which in turn gave him
strength to talk to them instead.

"It was easier. Everything simply . . . was. Nowadays all of it
requires thinking, and then more thinking about the thinking.
Everything is a question that demands an explanation that suggests a theory, and most people can't even agree on any one of
those for anything at all." He paused, applying some of that same
thought to what he'd just said. "Or maybe they do, I'm not sure.
I only know six people, and one of them's even younger than me,
and one doesn't much like me, and one's a Sloth and so maybe
doesn't think like a Fant at all, and one's never had flesh or blood
and besides is already dead. So . . . yeah, I don't have a lot of experience to draw on here. And when you think about it, that really
begs the question of why I got picked to have these conversations
with you, to carry the knowledge you give to me, to just *know*
things."

He drove a fist into the sand at his side and brought up a handful of coarse grains as several tiny crabs scampered free of his
grasp, fell to the sand, and burrowed deep again. He rolled the
sand between his fingers and as he focused, each solitary grain
spoke to him, expressing delight in being part of this patch of
beach, of the endless waters they had known, of how they were both
like and yet utterly unique from the other grains. Not a single one

of them asked questions or posed hypotheses or would probably ever feel a need to.

Ignoring the moons, he asked the sand, "Can you explain it to me?"

Ideas of waves in infinite variety seemed to come from them, and for an instant he perceived the solidity of the beach as an ever-changing configuration across a span of time. It made him gasp. The sand had a lot to say, but none of it spoke of life or purpose. It happily shared with him, provided no insight beyond the simple metaphor of the endurance of granular existence.

As had been happening more and more lately, Pizlo found these sorts of conversation deeply unsatisfying, not least of all because no one else could hear them. Years in the past, he'd tried to share some of them with Jorl. Far from being a mentor in that moment, he had instead suggested that perhaps Druz was better equipped to advise him, and had made a point of giving them time to discuss the matter during her next visit. In hindsight—as was often the case—it had been a wasted effort born out of false optimism. Like most adults in his limited experience, she'd heard what she thought he was asking and not what he was saying. This had led to her explaining his experiences as a projection of his talents, that the whispers of moonlight and waves and wind were not real, despite his obvious experience of them.

"All of it comes from within you, Little Prince," she'd said, even while the world around them refuted her words and rolled its eyes for his observation alone. "I have met no few beings with similar precognitive talents, though never so powerful nor in one so young. What you think to be conversations with bits of the world are really glimpses of the future."

When she'd said it, he'd wanted to believe her, less because she might actually be right than from honoring that he had such a person in his life, someone who wasn't a Fant and hadn't been taught to shun him or turn away just because. He'd been newly turned ten when they'd had that talk, feeling proud and mature to be in double digits, he'd been especially open to the notion that childish ignorance had caused him to attribute his experiences to the world around him and not some talent that lived in his own mind. More, Druz had been so certain, wrapped in the confidence that adults could possess about the world. Except . . . the world itself constantly reminded him that this Sloth possessed only a piece of the puzzle, nor should he expect her to understand things she'd never experienced. Doing so would be like asking a fish how it felt to live without breathing the air.

Similes. He'd come to hate similes. Too often that's how the world spoke to him, not in simple and clean language, but talking about one thing as another, and frequently before either had yet come to pass. And metaphors were even worse. He'd grown up immersed in both blends of figurative language long before he had words or concepts for the things. That alone might explain the odd way he saw things. Well, no, maybe, but probably not.

Whether in response to a change in the rain, an unspoken word, or some nudge of his talent, Pizlo set aside these recollections. It was time. The thing he'd been waiting for came to pass, as he knew it would. He slipped some koph under his tongue and lay down on his back in the sand. A tiny patch broke in the cloud cover in just the spot for someone seated right there to catch a glimpse of a portion of Telko where it held court amongst the other unseen six. This was the largest and wisest of Barsk's moons. He had once seen it in all its glory, when he'd snuck aboard the space station. It had filled his field of vision and flooded him with its light and knowledge. Since that experience, Telko had appeared to him more often than to any other Fant on Barsk. But this once it did not pour its wisdom into him. This time it waited upon him, the master ready at last to hear the student speak.

"I think I'm like a tree." He spoke softly, knowing Telko could hear him despite the distance and vacuum that lay between them. "Everything on Barsk, and you and your fellow moons, you're like the soil that I grow in, providing the nutrients and water and light that I need to grow tall and strong, to become something that you're not. You give me knowledge, explain what is, and often that includes things that haven't happened yet. But it's like the stories the Archetype tells me. It's not just stuff to know. I'm starting see that now, everything you offer me, all of it is actually tools. In the beginning, when I first started hearing you, you just told me things. But then, as I learned more, I realized that you told me those things so I would start asking questions. And I know that made you happy."

Though it still hadn't spoken, Telko's radiance projected approval.

"Yeah, but it's not about the questions. I get that now. It's about choices. Knowing can be a path to asking. And asking creates the possibility of choosing. And that's scary, because at one level it means that everything—absolutely everything!—that you've taught me can be undone by choice. Because in that sense, nothing is fixed. When you showed me Jorl becoming many, that wasn't inevitable. When he unleashed the Silence and destroyed that Yak, it could have gone differently. This is what Druz means when she talks about me being a precognitive. She didn't get all of it right, but she led me to find the heart of it. Knowing a thing isn't the same as choosing a thing. And that's hard. There're millions of people on this planet who would cringe at the sight of me, owing to knowledge and not from their own decision. And there's only four people here who can see me as me, and act from choice. I'm only fourteen, and you're as old as the world, and it's mean of you to ask me to think about these kinds of things. And you know that, and you do it anyway, which makes you cruel. And I don't think it's right that moons should be cruel. Ever. But I talked it over with the Archetype, and it helped me to understand that all this time you've probably been preparing me to go on that Hero's Journey, and it's time for me to cross some kind of threshold. Only, before I do, in case I fail, I want you to have something. I want you to know me."

He closed his eyes. The koph had had time to work and when he looked around again it was to see himself in a space created within his own mind. He floated above the clouds, above even the atmosphere, hovering at the same height as Barsk's space station hung above Zlorka, the archipelago's northernmost and only equatorial island. To left and right at varying distances hung the other six moons, Nita and Ulmazh, and all the rest. Telko, much closer to hand, shone upon him in all its brilliant glory, its imagined light bearable here in his imagination. It regarded him silently, waiting.

"Jorl can do things other Speakers can't. I know that. I don't know how or why, but I've seen him choose to do it. And I also know that there are laws that all Speakers follow. That's knowledge too, but it's false. They're not laws, they're only rules. He's chosen to break them, and I can, too." He focused on his own nefshons then, bringing back into awareness the golden weave of particles so dense and close that Speakers always dismissed from their perceptions before attempting a summoning. Instead, he made them the object of his concentration.

All of his memories lay before him, the nefshon warp and weft of his life. Everything he'd experienced, everyone he'd ever met. Here were particles dedicated to time spent with Arlo, the one dead person he might have summoned but Jorl had told him not to, that his father had asked to be allowed to rest. He had many many particles from talks with Jorl. Other particles were memories of Tolta, going back to his earliest thoughts. More recent were those of Rina and her mother Dabni. Different but vivid were particles from the stories told to him by the Archetype of Man. Others linked him to Druz. The chemist was there, the Ailuros from the station, the Yak that had so frightened him half a lifetime ago. Everyone he'd ever met lived on in these nefshons.

But there were no nefshons from the forest or the beaches that had whispered to him all his life, nothing from the rain that had chatted with him every day, nor anything from the ocean. He had knowledge from each of the moons he'd seen, but not a single one of those experiences tied him to them, not even the epiphanies that Telko had shared. In every instance where he had learned things from the world around and above him, the only living source that shone in the nefshons of those events had been himself.

"It's just me," he whispered. "It's always just been me. I made you up and set you outside of myself, but that was just another metaphor. None of you actually exist. You're only real because I needed you to be real."

Staring into the writhing cocoon of his own nefshons, Pizlo lost himself. It was as if he stumbled and fell into it. The swath of golden fabric that he routinely dismissed as soon as koph made it perceivable now gripped him and would not let go, would not be banished. It swallowed and engulfed him. Pizlo struggled and found himself drowning in it, drowning in himself. And even that experience was a new memory that added to the whole. There was no way out because he couldn't stop being him. There were no moons, no world, no sand, no water. Only Pizlo, for ever and ever. No escape.

"Okay, so this is why Speakers have rules."

He flailed, but it was like being helplessly deep in water, trapped in another stupid simile. But maybe that was the solution, that none of this was literal. To save himself he had to be figurative. He reached out, grasping the nefshons around him instead of trying to wrench free of them. They defined him, leaving them behind was an impossibility. Instead, he focused on that definition, on the idea of seeing every particle as a piece of who he was, sorting them in infinite combinations, to produce his entire existence.

Suddenly he was free, floating once more in space above Telko. And floating not an ear's length away was a golden, gleaming simulacrum of himself. Not a simple construct like any Speaker might make of a conversant. This was him. All of him. Every particle of his existence duplicated and assembled before him and gawking right back at him. Pizlo reached out his trunk and his doppelgänger did the same. They touched and his creation dwindled and shrank, lost shape as it compacted tightly upon itself, collapsing into a single golden grain, bringing to mind the beach he'd been on.

He rolled his eyes. "Another metaphor," he said, even as he clutched the grain and turned to address Telko once more.

"This is me. Kind of. It's me as of this moment. Everything I am, but it's not who I can be because there's no choice in it, no agency. It's an echo of me. An echo of what it is to *be* me."

All seven moons shone upon him where he hung in space. Serious, listening. Just as he needed them to be.

"I'm going to leave soon. I don't want you or anyone else to tell me what might be just ahead. This is my journey to take, my choice. And maybe it won't go well. So, because you've given me so much, I want to give you something back before I leave. You're

not a Speaker, and when I die you can't summon me. But in case
I don't come back, this is how you can always know me."

He hauled back his trunk and then let fly, hurling his echo at
Telko. It fell toward the moon, taking its time, instantly lost to view
but still visible in his imagination. Pizlo waited and watched. In
the real world, far below on the tiny cove, delicate waves had
climbed Pizlo's legs, the rain fell upon him, and the clouds had long
since closed to again hide any glimpse of what lay beyond them.
Eventually, Pizlo returned to his body, sat up, and ran off into the
forest, ready to begin his quest.

EIGHT

GENIES AND BOTTLES

~~~~~~~

CHALK dust covered Ryne's hands to their knuckles. Broad slabs of slate had been bolted to three walls of the lab and he'd spent the morning filling them with tightly scrawled formulae that defined and described the manipulation of forces in ways no other mind had imagined let alone tried. Over the span of several days, Gari and Krokel had fed his earlier equations into the computer model, which in turn had offered up half answers and more questions, glitches, and hints. He had pondered all of them during a particularly lengthy walk last night, and arose this morning to write out the answers that his brain had sorted out while he'd slept.

The chalk slipped from his fingers and he stared at what he'd wrought, panting and grinning.

Krokel stepped into the periphery of his vision, lifting his trunk in inquiry and Ryne nodded permission. His assistant began transcribing the contents of the chalkboards.

"Your last simulation went well?"

Ryne turned to regard Lolte. She'd dropped by his lab earlier—shortly after he'd arrived but before he'd lost himself in the fugue of chalk and equations—to give him an injection of what she laughingly called "Ryne juice." Her business done, she'd invited him to join her for a picnic later that day, Gari having apparently told her that he'd get so caught up in his work that he'd forget to eat. He'd agreed and watched his physician leave before beginning the day's work. He had no idea how long she'd been standing there, a large picnic hamper held before her. The flow of concepts and the song of the math had driven everything else out of his perception. If she'd spoken before now, he hadn't noticed. In reply to her question he just smiled, still too caught up in the math to drop back into mere language. Instead, he took a moment to wash the chalk dust from his hands, and then left the lab with her, walking in a companionable silence to one of the city's public spaces, an oblong park of carefully tended lawns, gaming benches, and minor performance alcoves. The biologist put down a coarse cloth and unpacked the contents of her enormous food basket onto it as Ryne lowered himself to the grass. She'd warned him that occasional joint pain could be a temporary side effect of the longevity treatments, but it was minor and only troubled him when he'd been on his feet all day, which admittedly was every day he worked at the boards. Even so, he already felt better than he had in years. As he made himself comfortable he let the math slip away and found his voice, answering at last the question she'd voiced in his lab.

"Too well. I've gone as far as I can with simulations. The model is solid, the math works. Today's work will correct the last few issues—minor irregularities that could have led to instabilities in the field effects but that weren't otherwise substantive on their own. Krokel and Gari will apply the corrections to the designs I've drawn up for the engineers and they'll implement a prototype to demonstrate the effect." Ryne paused, blushed, and added, "Assuming it works." He accepted an offered bowl of succulent leaves drizzled with an exotic sauce that his assistants had introduced him to.

"Why wouldn't it work?" Lolte prepared her own meal, seemingly focused on the food, but Ryne knew better.

"It should, but how would I know? I'm working from theory. I have no sensitivity to koph. I can't actually *see* the particles that I'm working with."

"Surely that's not a problem. Particularly here."

"I suppose not. Krokel assures me there is a line of qualified engineers with the Speaker talent eager to test the prototype." He munched on his leaves, unable to keep from smiling at the flavor. Something about the new sauce continued to delight him.

"Is that the end of your work then, a device that puts theory into practice?"

"What? Oh my, not even remotely. The prototype is really just a proof-of-concept. It will show Bernath and the others that my theories are sound, that otherwise dispersed and free floating nefshons can be maintained in an organized state, without an active mind or the use of koph."

Lolte frowned around a mouthful. Nearby, a mob of children squealed as they chased one another around the park in some kind of game that involved tripping the leader and then leaping over the victim's prone body before running away. She smirked. "Like you, I don't have the Speaker's gift. My expertise is all in life sciences. I'm afraid I know little more than the basics of nefshon science."

Ryne tried not to drop into lecture mode. Lolte most certainly was not one of his students. She was primarily a systems biologist, with a research program of her own that involved improving the longevity treatments she administered to himself and a handful of formerly Dying Fant that had reached this island. As the physician charged with maintaining his health, she most likely kept tabs on him for Bernath and the others, but more than that she genuinely appeared to want to be his friend, and one did *not* lecture to friends. Still, a lifetime of habit crept into his voice.

"Generally speaking, particles tend to diffuse, from areas of higher concentration to lower. That applies to one of two states of nefshons. Those which are still attached and integrated into a person's memory don't diffuse. Likewise nefshons that are still bound to their source don't either. Dispersion only becomes a thing after their source stops generating them, or when the memory that has received them loses coherence."

"You mean when we die," said Lolte. She passed him a sealed bowl of soup and took one herself.

"Right. But a Speaker can reverse that process and pull a specific individual's nefshons to them. Under that guidance, when the particles reach a critical mass their very nature allows them to organize and a simulacrum forms, but only for so long as the Speaker continues to apply their will. It's very much a quantum phenomenon."

"Meaning that when the Speaker stops, the organization they imposed upon the particles falls away?"

Ryne dipped his trunk into the soup and transferred the bowl's contents to his mouth, nodding all the while. "Just so. Diffusion reoccurs."

"And your prototype reverses this?"

"What? Oh no, not even close. I haven't even begun to approximate the math that allows Speakers to do what they do. I can't summon nefshons, let alone pick out one individual's particles amidst all others, or build a simulacrum. Imposing order on that level of magnitude requires an active mind. But, I can prevent the natural entropic processes that would follow once that mind is removed. At least, according to the simulations."

"So . . . your prototype will maintain a nefshon simulacrum once it's been created?"

"Well, yes. When you stop the diffusion the established organization continues."

"Without a Speaker? Without requiring more koph?"

"The mind and the chemical agent that grants perception and manipulation are only needed to bring the particles together and create the simulacrum. Once that's been done, the state can be continued indefinitely. It still requires energy to operate, but not a living agent. That part's done."

"How long have you been working on this?"

He shrugged. "I had the idea about thirty years ago. I gave a paper on the subject at a conference on Yargo around that time. It stirred a bit of interest, a touch of controversy, but nothing much because it was only an idea. A thought experiment. The math only started falling into place over the last fifteen years or so."

"I think I understand now why the Full Council set Bernath on your trail. They're wild for anything involving nefshons." She waved her trunk in a wide arc. "All of this exists because of that."

Ryne reached into the picnic hamper with his trunk, questing for dessert. "So I've gathered. You explained about the memes. I suspect there are applications far beyond that, perhaps that no one has imagined yet. But that's for the engineers to manage. I've always been a theoretician."

Lolte batted his trunk aside and took a pair of individual fruit pies from the hamper, placing one in front of each of them. The conversation lagged as they enjoyed their dessert. A trio of drummers entered the park, set up as far from the roving children as possible, then began to play. As Lolte finished her pie she looked up and waved at their surroundings with her trunk. "This is why they do it. All of it. The Caudex looks out for all Fant, for all of Barsk. What we have here is a reflection of what they want for everyone. The simplicity of a good life. Children enjoying themselves, musicians expressing their art, and scientists like yourself encouraged and supported in pursuit of new ideas."

He nodded, licking away the last crumbs from his fingers and nubs. "Yes, I understand that larger picture. I just don't see how my work contributes to it."

"Would you like to?"

"How do you mean?"

Lolte was already packing the detritus of their meal into the picnic hamper. "Time for a field trip, Ryne. You've been so focused on the work in your lab, you haven't seen half of the marvels that happen in this place."

～～～～

THE biologist cradled the picnic hamper while Ryne shook out the blanket, scattering crumbs into the grass. She took his arm and they left the machinations of children and musicians behind, strolling along one of the major boardways, transferred to a narrower path and from there ascended several levels higher in the city.

"What was the organizational structure on Taylr?" asked Lolte.

"How do you mean?"

"Did you have a mayor or a city council? Something else? How were decisions made? How did people get heard? Boardways repaired? Local gymnasia funded?"

"Oh, we had a grandmother committee," said Ryne.

"I don't know that term."

"That's not the official name. There probably is one, but I don't know it. Taylr wasn't colonized for more than a century after Fant came to Barsk, and its Civilized Wood took decades more to build. It was very much a 'planned' city, not like some of the first ones. Anyway, Taylr's founders were five women, Four Eleph and a Lox. They each came from a different island, having raised development capital. They pooled resources and came together with the intention to create a new city with twin emphases on stability and innovation. The first thing they built were schools, both gymnasia for the children as well as vocational schools and colleges for young adults. They each laid claim to vast areas of the still largely empty city, marking off where each would build her line's house, both the respective core homes for themselves and their immediate families as well as clear plans for successive expansions. Next they built some of the best bachelor facilities anyone had ever seen, which made the island a draw for young men eager to get an education. The hitch was the housing came with limited-span leases to ensure a good circulation of men."

"What does any of this have to do with a 'grandmother committee'?"

"I'm getting to that. As the city began to attract immigrants, the five women who had started everything were all too busy doing things to be bothered with actually running their city. But they'd each persuaded their grandmothers to come over and run the houses they'd built for themselves. They agreed it was a natural thing to let the grandmothers make the governance decisions for all of Taylr, and that tradition continues."

"And the grandmothers of these five houses still run everything?"

"That's my understanding. There are a lot more than five multigenerational homes now; the original five have long outgrown the grandest of their expansion plans. But yes, the senior-most woman in each of those five family lines are in charge, and they rule by a system of consensus."

"Huh. Well, that's different. But . . . I think you'll find the system here even stranger. We have what we call a 'Full Council,' made up of two parts, and there's nothing like it anywhere else on Barsk."

"In what way?"

"Well, for one thing, membership on the council requires sensitivity to koph and the ability to manipulate nefshons."

"That seems . . . capricious. It's a biological talent and not correlated with leadership or management skills."

"Maybe not, but it's a necessary prerequisite."

Ryne twitched his ears in irritation. "How so?"

"Half of the council is dead."

He stopped, dragging Lolte to a halt. "Wait, what? Dead? How can half of your governing council be dead?"

She smiled and pulled him forward "Because the other half, the living half we call the 'Quick Council,' is made up of Speakers. This way we get a balance, the benefit of the best minds that ever existed on Barsk, and the perspective and skills of the brightest of our current public servants. Together, they not only set policy for the island, but help to plan the course for the survival of all Fant going out beyond Barsk."

Again he paused and Lolte stopped with him. "How do you mean, 'beyond Barsk'? We're cut off from the Alliance, deliberately so. What influence does this council have when no other community on the planet even knows of their existence?"

"That's what I want to show you. What your discoveries are going to affect in ways that will do wonders for us all. Come on!"

She led the way, exiting the narrow avenue onto a mall of shops and restaurants, museums and arcades, the main commercial boardway for the unnamed island. They fell in with the flow of foot traffic and turned down a cul-de-sac lined entirely with art galleries, save for a single, simple office building at the far end. They passed beneath the lintel of its double doors and paused in a modest rotunda with ascending staircases to either side.

"This is the council building. The members of the Quick Council have offices upstairs, and the main council chamber is up there as well. Directly in front of us is a hidden door that leads to a series of smaller offices used by the support staff—"

"I don't see any door," interrupted Ryne, "just a portrait gallery along the wall."

"I told you, it's hidden. When people come here, it's for formal pronouncements and the like. The councilors—the living ones at least—stand at the railing of the landing where the staircases meet with the crowd here below. It's very impressive seeing them proclaim and such. The space was built for that. When the public comes, they don't care that there's a team of assistants and adjuncts and the like supporting the councilors, so the access to them is tucked away. Here." She led him toward a painting on the far wall. Her fingers slipped behind the edge of the frame as if she might pull the artwork down. Instead, a portion of the wall fell back and slid to one side, revealing a door-lined corridor behind.

"Come on, there's someone I want you to meet." She stepped through and after a moment he followed. Ryne heard the wall fall back into place behind him but refused to look back. What would be the point?

The alternating doors of the hallway reminded him of similar university spaces, though these doors lacked the personality of individualized notes and images that faculty used to adorn the entrances to the tiny spaces where they met with students and did so much of the work of the mind. His own had borne a humorous cartoon of two Fant arguing over a formula whose meaning changed depending on the interpretation of a smudged glyph in the equation. At least once in every tenday for all the many seasons since an anonymous student had affixed it to his door, that cartoon had brought a smile to his face. In contrast this corridor was all business. Small plaques with tightly printed names hung at eye level to the right of each doorway. Lolte barely glanced at them as she led him along until she stopped and gestured at one. He read the sign.

"Ajax?"

"A cousin. He's my aunt's youngest son. I used to babysit him and some of his sibs back before I went off to school, and during his college days I bailed him out of trouble on more than one occasion. So, he owes me."

"Owes you? Are we not supposed to be here? Lolte, I don't have time for pranks or intrigue. My work is too important."

"More important than you know, which is why we're here. You should see this." She knocked twice on the door, then pushed it open and stepped within without waiting for a response. Ryne followed.

The room beyond was much as he'd expected, a simple office with a desk and matching chair hammock behind it, a pair of comfortable-looking standing chairs for visitors waiting in front. One wall was a vast screen set up to look like a window gazing out onto a scrap of beach and the falling rain of a small bay. The other walls had been painted an institutional green, broken up by another door and a few photos and free-standing shelves with bric-a-brac. A young Lox sat slumped in his hammock, hands folded in his lap, trunk lounging across the bend of his right arm, a stylus lightly gripped in his nubs.

"That's Ajax," said Lolte.

Ryne scoffed. "Does he usually sleep in the middle of the workday?"

"He's not napping, he's working. He's a Speaker. Can't you smell the koph?"

"If he's Speaking, where's his client?"

"You're thinking in terms of the rest of Barsk," said Lolte. "Those Speakers follow the training and rules laid down by Margda, and typically only summon the dead at the behest of someone else. But this island was founded by a different breed of Speakers, and they use nefshons for other purposes. Did you know that a Speaker can summon the particles of someone who's still alive, and communicate with them no matter where they are? Not just on Barsk, but anywhere!"

"What? No, surely not. That would mean . . ." Ryne paused, the common knowledge that every child had about Speaking supplanted by what he understood of the physics of nefshons. The math swam before him and fell into place and his ears lifted in astonishment. "That would mean instantaneous communication, anywhere in the galaxy."

"Yes."

"No lag whatsoever."

"Yes."

"Faster than messages transmitted from portal to portal."

"Exactly."

"Faster than light!"

"That's what I'm saying."

Ryne's jaw dropped open. The implications staggered him. "Does the Alliance know about this?"

"Not a clue. Because all of *their* Speakers were trained by Speakers who, when you go back far enough, were trained by Margda, and all of them embraced her edict with the prohibition of ever summoning the living. They absorbed it as axiomatic, never questioned in eight hundred years."

"Except here."

Lolte smiled. "Have I mentioned how much I admire how quick you are?"

"So . . . if not the dead, then with whom is your cousin Ajax conversing?"

"Ajax is assigned to Councilor Sind's office, which is directly responsible for the sentry posts at each of the portals the Caudex maintains, both within our system and without."

"Portals? What, do you mean interstellar portals? Those only work on the periphery of a star system. Why would the Caudex have any portals on Barsk?"

"They don't. The closest ones hang at the edge of space, several days out from here. And each has a small outpost to maintain it. And each outpost includes a sentry. Ajax here contacts each of them on a daily basis."

"You said . . . you said the closest ones . . . where are the others?"

Lolte's smile broadened. "There are six in our system, and the matched partner of each opens onto the edge of another star system. The nearest of those is more than two hundred light years from us. The Fant aren't just on Barsk, Ryne. Our people are exploring the galaxy."

"You're saying the Caudex has starships out there?"

She nodded. "I grew up on one."

"I don't understand."

"I wasn't born on Barsk. My father was a medical researcher here—in fact he made some of the most significant refinements to our longevity treatments—and my mother was an engineer on a ship. I was something of a surprise, conceived the night before she took a shuttle up to her ship. By the time she realized she was pregnant they were already well under way. I was born in space. At the end of the mission my mother returned a while, long enough to get me settled in the family home. Then she went back out there. After I finished schooling I had the choice to join her, but I opted to stay. I wasn't born here, but Barsk is my home, now."

Ryne stared at her a while before letting his gaze slip back to the slack-faced Ajax. "Astounding. But . . . what does this have to do with my work?"

"The work that my cousin here does is just one of many uses that the Caudex has found for nefshons. And both Speakers and the koph they need are of limited supply. But the prototype our engineers are making from your theories would allow us to place the constructs of past Speakers at these outposts, as well as in places less hospitable to life. They can't completely replace the need for people like Ajax, but they'll extend the reach of them. Any one of them could serve as the bridge or relay to connect two living Speakers, without using a single bit of koph. Your theories will make that possible. That's why the Caudex brought you here. That's why they agreed to the longevity treatments for you despite the scarcity and the expense. You're critical to the next stage of the master plan."

"Which is what, exactly? Where is all of this leading?"

"Departing Barsk entirely."

"What? Why? How?"

"One day, when everything is ready, the plan is for all of us to just slip away, leave this planet behind, with no trace for the Alliance to know where we've gone. Only then will all Fant be safe."

NINE

RIPPLES

A FTER too many days away, and still more days apart due to
the reports and schedules and far too many meetings,
Klarce had at last managed to find time to spend with her lover.
Even within Adolo's mother's home, it often proved impossible
to manage any privacy. Her status as one of the quick councilors
meant that every adult woman in the house, some fifty aunts,
cousins, and sisters—and make no mistake, the sisters were the
worst—wanted to snatch a moment of her time, build a connection, possibly even supplant Adolo's position in her heart, and/or
in her bed, or at a minimum fawn over her when all she wanted
was a chance to take her lover's hand and slip away. She'd finally
managed it, most of the household away attending a music re-
cital involving a good number of the children. Delighted with
their luck, the two women had spent the time bringing one another to a series of satisfying climaxes. They romped like lovers
half their age with all the attendant enthusiasm and noise—further
evidence that the sisters were elsewhere. Eventually, limbs and
trunks entwined, they lay basking in the afterglow somewhere

between bliss and sleep, murmuring shy syllables intended for one another's ears alone.

Regina, Klarce's second assistant, cleared her throat on the other side of the chamber's curtains. "Your pardon, Klarce, your presence is urgently requested in the council chamber."

Adolo murmured something that could have been an endearment or just as easily a swear word of exasperation and propped herself up on one elbow as she used her trunk to caress Klarce's ear in the way that always sent shivers through her, even sated as she was. The abrupt end of such a hard-won encounter could be blamed on nepotism. Regina was a fine second assistant, but she was also Adolo's cousin, the adopted daughter of one of her innumerable aunts, and thus someone who could enter the family home with impunity and seek her here despite the instructions she'd left not to be disturbed.

"Go away, Regina. I am off shift and the rest of the Quick Council knows it. Whatever it is needs doing, pass it on to Sind with my compliments."

"Again, your pardon, but it was Sind who insisted that I fetch you. He says he received word that a Speaker has broken the edict."

Adolo rolled her eyes at this bit of news, a fair reflection of Klarce's own reaction. "What of it?" she called back. "We've been breaking the edict every day since Margda first created the damn thing."

"My apologies. I'm not being clear. This Speaker wasn't one of ours."

Klarce bolted out of bed and was halfway to the curtain before she recalled she was naked. She spun around and there was Adolo handing her the simple, floral one-piece she liked to wear during her personal time. She hadn't known, years earlier, how limited that time would become once she ascended to the Quick Council. Would she have aspired to it all the same? Probably. Klarce snatched the clothing with her trunk, blew her lover a kiss as she turned, stepping into the garment. She slid her arms into it as she plowed through the curtains and nearly bowled into Regina.

"Do we have a name for this renegade Speaker? A location?" Klarce hurried down the corridor toward the main exit from Adolo's family's home, reviewing the best route to get to the council chamber from this location, something she'd never had cause to consider before.

"Yes, ma'am. A Lox. Male. Name of Jorl ben Tral. He lives on the island of—"

"Keslo," finished Klarce. "It's the Aleph."

"Ma'am?"

She sighed. "It's above your clearance, Regina. Though, I suppose Sind will be upgrading it or he wouldn't have sent you with that name. Jorl is one of only two Fant currently alive who bears one of Margda's marks."

"Yes, ma'am. I know what the Aleph is. I thought the name was familiar."

They were out of the house by that point, racing down a boardway of the Civilized Wood. Klarce waved her trunk to indicate her intended direction and Regina hustled along beside her.

"I would assume so. What you probably don't know is that we investigate every recipient of the mark. No doubt Sind will ensure you can rattle off the names and particulars of all fifty-seven of them since Margda invented the damn thing and had herself inked with the first one."

Klarce knew Regina already had a full workload and an ongoing educational track, she'd composed much of both herself, holding the girl to higher standards to offset any claims of impropriety. She may have gotten the initial interview through nepotism, but she'd earned her position time and again. It was only the young woman's naturally diffident nature that obscured a quick mind. Adding a bit more to her studies wouldn't break her, and again if Sind had cleared her for a security promotion now was not the time to coddle her.

"The more recent Aleph is a fishmonger. She's . . . an amusing case, but of no real interest to us. Jorl ben Tral is a different matter. Of all to take the mark, he's the only one that Margda included in her prophecies. Don't look so shocked, girl. Yes, his being a Bearer was foretold, but that's not the half of it. He was an odd leaf even before he came to our attention. Actually petitioned the Alliance to set aside his right of deferment and joined up with the Patrol."

Regina gasped, eyes wide. "He left . . . left Barsk?"

She nodded, puffing as she forced herself to better speed to the council chamber. "He's an odd one. Tested positive for koph upon his return. A nice perk for a historian. That damned council—the one that determines Bearers, not *our* council—marked him soon after. That's when we put him under observation . . . about ten years now. Turns out his academic specialty is the prophecies of the Matriarch. Let me tell you, that set off some alarm bells. It was all just a little convenient, do you see? But, while his work is insightful—and believe me, I've read every word of the six published treatises he wrote on the subject, from his dissertation on down—there's nothing in there to suggest anything other than a talented scholar. Even so, seven years ago we reassigned an agent to his island to cover him specifically."

"An agent for just one person, ma'am? For a historian? That seems . . . excessive. Even if he is a Bearer."

"You're right to think so. And odd as I said he was, he's also been fairly conservative in his views. Or he was. Something happened seven years ago, a hiccough in the Alliance senate. Somehow Jorl got himself named to a seat."

"I don't understand. A seat? You don't mean a senate seat?"

They arrived at the entrance to the council chamber and Klarce pulled up short and leaned against the doorframe, catching her breath and collecting her thoughts. She eyed her second assistant closely, finding doubts in her earlier assessment of the girl's intelligence. "Stay with me, Regina. That's exactly what I mean. Jorl is a member of the Alliance senate. It's not a secret, but it's not bandied about either. The average person on Barsk couldn't care less about the doings of the senate, and the members of the larger Alliance would be aghast if it was brought to their attention. But a senator he most certainly is, the first and only Fant so designated."

"Is this something Margda foresaw?" Regina's ears pulled in closer to her head as her eyes narrowed with concentration.

Klarce nodded her approval as her assistant focused and took in the information. "We don't believe so. There's no indication in any of her prophecies, not the ones she published or those from her private journals that are in the hands of the Caudex. No, our best guess is that Jorl's historical research accidentally discovered dirt on someone of interest to the Alliance government and he brokered a deal."

"So he's an opportunist and an extortionist?"

The councilor smiled even as she shook her head, holding up her trunk in a gainsaying gesture. "That would be a convenient explanation, but no. It doesn't mesh at all with the file we have on him. Everything in his psych profile suggests he's as straight a branch as ever grew. Jorl's no more likely to blackmail someone— even some fuzzy Alliance politician—than you're apt to call yourself Pholo and fly away on a fine wind day. But enough, I'll discuss your additional educational assignments with Sind after I meet with the council. I've allowed myself to be distracted and I need all the information Sind would have passed along before sending you to me. Tell me, which part of the edict did Jorl break?"

"The first. He summoned Fisco, and with sufficient power that he pulled her out of a class."

"How long ago did this happen?"

"Just over two hours ago, ma'am."

Klarce frowned. Regina took a half step back, her ears folding forward defensively.

"This makes no sense. Surely Sind activated a team to scramble the memory before it consolidated fully. We have people in place to layer in some suggestions that it was all a dream. It's reason enough to double our surveillance of him, but not to pull me out of bed or summon me to the council."

"That's just it, ma'am," said Regina. "The scramble didn't take."

"Don't be stupid. It can't *not* take. Memory consolidation and its disruption are well understood at the nefshon level. An individual Speaker can manage it. We only use a team as a precaution in case something goes wrong—with our agents, not with the process."

"Yes, ma'am, only the team couldn't do it. This Jorl fellow still had koph in him."

"Well, of course he did, he'd just summoned Fisco, hadn't he?" Klarce checked herself. Her tone had become strident and now threatened to cross over into outright bellowing. She pinched the bottom corner of her left ear, distracting herself with the stab of pain and paused for the span of several breaths. "Why didn't the team wait for it to flush out of his system?"

Regina swallowed, stared at her feet, dropped her ears, but said nothing.

"By the moons above, show some spine, girl. Out with it. What aren't you telling me?"

"The team waited, ma'am. But it still didn't work. They waited more. But still, no. They'd just tried a third time and failed. That's when Sind instructed me to fetch you."

"I don't understand."

"Jorl ben Tral finished his summoning of Fisco more than two hours past, and he's still showing as having koph in him."

"That's impossible!"

"Yes, ma'am. That's what Sind said, right before he sent me for you."

SIND met her in the vestibule outside the council chamber. He was an Eleph like herself, but that was the extent of their similarity. Klarce had been born into the Caudex, but Sind had arrived on the island's shore thirty-two years earlier, following the siren call of his own death after an impressive career as an administrator across fourteen separate islands. He'd climbed through the ranks until now, at the age of one hundred seventeen, he was the oldest living member of the Quick Council. The other half of their governing body—that comprised the Full Council—was made up of Fant all born long before him, some by as many as seven centuries.

He waved Regina away and instead of stepping back inside with Klarce, guided her down a hallway to his office.

"Thank you for coming."

Klarce dropped into Sind's guest hammock and regarded her former mentor. "Did Regina get it right? Because it's quite frankly impossible."

"I know that. You think I don't know that? And yet . . . it's happened."

"Yeah, well, we'll have to figure that part out. In the meantime, you need to keep a tight lid on this. It's exactly why we have contingency protocols. Who else knows?"

"Just you, me, your second assistant, and two three-member scramble teams. I have the teams on lockdown and in a disturbing bit of irony, once we're done here I'll meet with them and disrupt their own memories of the attempt. They'll sleep it off and in the morning recall none of it. But frankly, I don't have a clue what any of this means."

"You haven't told the rest of the Quick Council? Or summoned any members of the Full Council?"

Sind flapped his ears in barely restrained panic. "It doesn't make sense. Damn it, I wrote some of those protocols. This can't be happening."

Klarce nodded. "That's why you activated a second team? To be sure it wasn't some fluke with the first?"

"Yes, and it's also why I pulled you in. I need your sharp mind here, backing up my own in case I missed something. This is exactly the kind of thing I don't want to distract the council with, either our fellow living members or the rest. Everyone has enough on their plate."

"You haven't missed anything. All the pieces should fit together, but they don't."

"I don't like puzzles," said Sind. "How can he still have the drug in his system?"

She shrugged. "We know he's a researcher. Maybe he's on some kind of deadline, pulling an 'all-nighter' and summoning several different conversants for some project."

"For two hours? I was a damn good Speaker in my day, and I

couldn't maintain that, not and perform multiple summonings. We know he pulled in Fisco, so what did he do after she ended it? Is there anything in his dossier to suggest he has that kind of strength?"

"Nothing," said Klarce. "He tested well within the normal range of talents. Speaking isn't like a muscle. It doesn't improve with practice or over time. Something else is going on here. We don't have a clue what it is, and I don't like not having that kind of control over the situation. And this isn't just any Speaker."

"That was my thought as well. Margda's chosen. But chosen for what?"

She stood and regarded the man who had been her mentor for most of her life. "I don't think we have the luxury of waiting to find out," she said. "I don't like it any more than you do, but we're out of options."

Sind closed his eyes and brought a hand up to massage the bridge of his trunk. She waited. This was the real reason he'd sent for her. Sind had a brilliant mind, but age had banked the fire in him. He could set policy but needed her to follow through with procedure. Or maybe he just wanted plausible deniability if any of this ever came back on them.

After several beats Sind dropped his hand and opened his eyes. Tight-lipped, his reply was a curt nod. That was enough. She turned and left his office to do what he couldn't.

~~~~~

BACK before Arlo's death, the space that now served as Dabni's bedroom had been a supply closet. In fairness, it had been an inordinately large supply closet, and she suspected that before Tolta's husband had done the surprising thing of co-habitating with her, that it had been a luxurious walk-in closet. It was also far more space than she'd had growing up on the last island.

The austerity learned in youth resists the greater opulence that often comes with adulthood. Added to this was Dabni's understanding that as an agent of the Caudex she could be called upon to discard her identity and location literally at a moment's notice. All of which explained why she possessed little in the way of furnishings. Since arriving on Keslo she had acquired a simple chair and secretary desk, a tiny bin in which she folded her spare clothes, a handful of trinket reminders of signature life events, and a cache of koph hidden in a hollowed out book. She'd limited herself with the deliberate understanding that everything but that last handful could be abandoned if the need arose, even including her young daughter.

A new sleeping pallet had been waiting for her when she moved in and Dabni had placed it in the corner farthest from the room's only door. Tolta had not only refused to accept payment for the room, she'd also insisted on repainting it to a color of her new housemate's preference. This was Dabni's only nod toward decoration. Paint was *not* a possession. She'd chosen a midnight blue, a hue that would require many coats to paint over at some future point and not even remotely the fashion for interior rooms anywhere in either archipelago. But Dabni found it soothed her spirit. More, it gave her an empty setting to re-create when she manufactured her mindspace for manipulating nefshons.

She lay asleep on her pallet enjoying a dream of playing with her daughter on a white sandy beach of Peckl—a place that Rina had never visited—when another Speaker gathered sufficient strands of her nefshons to pull her conscious mind to them. Most people saw consciousness as a static state; one was either conscious or not. Mind scholars and Speakers knew this consciousness for a continuum, one which included the normal waking mind, the altered state of dreams, and the unbounded state of existing as a nefshon construct. She found herself in this third consciousness now, neither awake nor asleep, standing in an office back on the last island. An administrator's office. Facing the Fant who had summoned her, she recognized Councilor Klarce, her supervisor's supervisor's supervisor. She'd met the woman only once, upon her graduation nearly ten years before. Klarce had personally attended to award her a commendation for being second in her class. She'd appeared stern back then and the span of years had not changed her.

"You recognize me, Dabni?"

Despite lacking physicality, Dabni's self-image flinched and nervously flapped her ears even as she nodded assessment.

"That is well," said Klarce. "It seems that each time we meet I give you a gift." The councilor opened her hand, revealing the glowing loops and knotted strands of a meme. Dabni gasped as she recognized it from an advanced seminar. As a field agent she had handled and distributed an assortment of different memes, but not this one. Nor had she ever expected to receive it. Klarce held a meme of death.

The concept was simple: reify the memory of a body's response to illness, pass that memory to a healthy person and in the process infect them. The technique had been developed to inoculate large populations quickly, allowing one's own body to do the work of traditional drugs. This was different. This meme had been made by a Speaker in the final stages of a brutal, engineered disease. A swift and fatal disease. But it made no sense; the Caudex fought to preserve the life of all Fant on Barsk. Murder was not among their tools.

"That's a physicality cascade," she said, staring at the circlet of light being offered. She didn't reach for it, swallowed instead, opened her mouth to speak, stopped, and then managed it on the second attempt. "Have I failed in my assignment? Are you needing to kill me?"

A thin parting of her lips was as much of a smile as she'd heard Klarce ever showed to field agents, but the older woman's eyes twinkled. "No, my dear. The meme is not for you. It is for your charge. He has come into possession of knowledge that may lead him to awareness of the Caudex."

"Jorl." Dabni swallowed again.

"Yes."

"Your pardon, but I was taught that this has happened before and contingencies exist to handle such discoveries."

"That's true," replied Klarce. "In this case, though, these traditional measures have failed. Repeatedly. Your Jorl ben Tral was already an anomaly, fulfilling a prophecy of the Matriarch herself. It's why you were assigned to keep watch over him. And no, you haven't failed in your task. I've personally reviewed your reports and they're exemplary. But the fact remains, even with direct observation for most of a decade, we still have no idea as to Margda's intentions for him. For all those years that was sufficient; nothing your target did bore any resemblance to a threat. But this new development has made him a liability. The Caudex cannot afford such an unknown and unknowable variable to exist. Not at this stage of our operations."

Klarce flexed the fingers of her outstretched hand in reminder until Dabni felt she had no choice but to take the meme. Round and around in the knotted strands of its nefshons was a repeating imperative that would turn the recipient's own body against them. It would build from the cellular level, spreading and disrupting critical systems until they faltered and triggered a cascade of organ failure and finally death. The Caudex wanted this for Jorl, her husband, the father of her daughter. Her assignment all these years.

"Your target is in good health and as a Speaker has a more resilient mind than most. The meme's effects vary, and he could require as much as a tenday to expire. Keep him under observation until he dies. After which, you'll continue with your duties managing the index on Keslo until a replacement can be sent. The council will reassess whether to provide you with a new assignment in the identity you've created, or recall you from the field. Rest easy, no decision will be made until the end of the next season, and we will take into consideration your own wishes in the matter."

Klarce paused and then used her trunk to point to the loops of deadly instructions now in Dabni's hand.

"But that's many days away. For now, your only immediate concern is to place this meme into your target's mind. You must kill Jorl ben Tral."

PART 2

LEAVING HOME

TEN

AGENT IN PLACE

A TENDAY before Klarce had reached out to Dabni with the directive to murder her husband, a Caudex field agent—the first she'd seen in years—had limped into her shop. He'd been an elderly Eleph, the sort of fellow who had probably traveled the islands extensively in youth and middle age and come to rest in Keslo to enjoy his retirement. An easy-going smile dominated his face. He wore loose shorts and an open vest, both made from dull brown tapa cloth, more for comfort than style. Covering the crown of his head he affected a bizarre tricorn hat fitted with an enormous feather from a bird that only flew among the islands of the eastern archipelago. He had a slightly fishy odor to him that stopped just short of being unpleasant.

"I wonder if you can help me," he said, after browsing the shelves of the bookshop long enough that the only other customers present that early in the morning had gone and no new ones had arrived to replace them. "I'm looking for a book about the Vulp of Kitsu and their mythical cities on the northern continent of Skennel."

Dabni recognized the phrases from coursework years in the past, but had never heard them spoken aloud. She bit back her surprise and responded with the appropriate counter phrase. "The Vulp never lived on Kitsu, nor does that world possess a continent named Skennel. Perhaps you're thinking of some other imaginary place?"

The Eleph nodded, considering. "Yes . . . perhaps. Perhaps some tea would help me to remember what I thought I knew so well when I came in."

That phrase confirmed that the customer was indeed from the Caudex and a Speaker, knew her for one as well, and wanted them both to ingest some koph for a private exchange. Dabni excused herself, locked the door to her shop and went into a back room to boil water and prepare two cups of drug-infused tea. A short while later she sat with the old man at a small table near the center of the shop, and soon after that they regarded each other on a colorless plane of their shared making, a pair of nefshon constructs that could neither be overheard nor spied upon by others who happened upon them in the shop.

"Hello, Dabni. I am Walto. I knew your late mother, oh so many years ago, long before the Caudex sent me into the world for one mission after another. You look just like her, a delightful surprise." Walto paused as if he'd forgotten why he'd come to speak with her in this way. He shook his head, fanned his ears, and resumed. "I bring you greetings from the Caudex. They are pleased that you've established yourself in Keslo and asked that I pass along their praise."

The façade of simple shopgirl fell away and she responded with more of her natural impatience. "Thank you. But they could have told me that themselves. Surely that's not why you're here."

"No, of course not. I am to pass on to you a secondary assignment. By this time tomorrow you will be responsible for managing the index, or rather, the portion of it that contains everyone on Keslo."

"Index? I'm sorry, but I don't understand."

"Well, you do, but you don't. You've probably not thought about nefshons in this particular way, but I've never met a Speaker who didn't grasp the concept once they held it with their trunk. It's like this: each of us is unique, different from everyone else down to the squiggly bits in our cells that define us. We're all individuals, right?"

Dabni nodded. "I'm with you so far."

"Good. And each of your cells, even though they may differ from one another, they're all still clearly part of you. Not someone else's. All you."

"Still following."

"And the same is true of your nefshons. They're not like anyone else's."

"That's how we summon people. Because having known them while they were alive, we have an unconscious knowledge of their nefshons. It's why a Speaker can't summon a stranger."

"Exactly. That's precisely what every Speaker is taught." He paused and his eyes did that twinkling thing. "It's also wrong."

"What?"

"Right now, as we converse like this, you're effectively holding some of my nefshons. It was an easy thing for you to pull strands from the weave that surrounds me, just as I did for you. And were I to drop dead this instant and that fabric came undone, you'd still be able to summon me. It wouldn't matter that I'm almost a complete stranger to you. Having once perceived my nefshons you know the pattern of them, what you called an unconscious knowledge."

Dabni found herself focusing on the Eleph's nefshons, pulling her attention away from the shared illusion that provided sight and sound, scent and texture. She regarded the nefshon thread of his personality, his identity, that she'd grabbed hold of to have this conversation, and realized in that moment that yes, she could summon him, despite knowing nothing more than his name.

Walto smiled at her and clapped his hands. "That's it. The epiphany shows in your face. Now, let's take it up a branch. Consider that metaphor and make the idea a deliberate and conscious act. But don't stop with just my nefshons. What's to prevent you from doing that with anyone you've spoken to like this?"

She gasped as the realization hit home. She didn't need to actually know the details of a person to summon them, just to have previously accessed their nefshons in the past. Each was unique, and that was sufficient to distinguish one individual's particles from all the rest in the galaxy. She could stand up this very moment, with the koph still heightening her perceptions, step out in front of her shop and pull nefshon threads from passersby and have everything she might need in the future to summon any of them.

"You're right," she said, and then belatedly realized he'd asked her a question. "Nothing's stopping me. I just . . . I never thought of it that way. All I need is a single strand to use as a sample to draw more from the same conversant."

"That's it precisely. But once you let it go, how would you remember it, tomorrow or next season or next year?"

"I'd . . . I wouldn't, I suppose. Not unless I made a point of deliberately holding on to it, created a record of it."

Walto's ears flapped with excitement. "Like a list?" he asked. "Like an inventory?"

"I . . . I guess so. Yes."

He clapped his hands again and intertwined his fingers. "That's the trick of it. Rather than simply letting go of that strand, you spin a duplicate of it and add it to your list. Simple enough. Now imagine taking your list and adding it to mine. There might even be some overlap, but that doesn't matter. The duplicates merge. In the end, everyone you could summon becomes someone I could as well."

"That would . . . that's amazing."

"It is. And of course I could then take our combined lists and share them with some other Speakers who have their own combined lists of all the people they could choose to summon. And you know, that's how it happened, centuries ago. When the first Caudex Speakers thought to do this, pooling their knowledge to create the first index."

He opened his hands and revealed a gleaming gold polyhedral lattice of so many sides she at first mistook it for a sphere. It was knowledge, a dense compacting of information unlike anything she'd seen. That slightest glimpse sparked a yearning in her. She hungered for it more than anything she'd ever wanted before.

"This is the index. Or rather, it's my most recent version of the index. With this, you could summon any Fant going all the way back to the first generation born on Barsk. Your job will be to add to it. To keep the index up to date with respect to the people living here on Keslo. You'll check in with your superiors at least once each season and share your latest version with them, and receive back the updated index that reflects the work of agents throughout both archipelagos and everywhere else Fant exist."

"Everyone? Everyone ever?"

Walto grinned. "Pretty much. Adding to your existing catalog is relatively easy. It's sort of like a structured meditation, well within your abilities or we wouldn't be here having this conversation. I'll walk you through the technique later today."

"Are you leaving Keslo when we're done?"

He nodded. "These old bones aren't good for much down here. It wore me out just making my way to your shop today. I'm leaving gravity behind so I can continue to be of use. Anyone who notices I've left will simply assume I've sailed away."

Dabni swallowed hard, suddenly serious. Leave gravity behind? She looked at Walto with new respect. "You're going to stand sentry on a portal? Protecting all of Barsk?"

"That's the plan. Well, not the 'stand' part. I'll mostly be floating. It's a nice cap to a long life of service."

She'd never been to space, but every Caudex operative knew of the portals. Far from retiring, Walto was taking on some of the Caudex's most important work.

"It's a formality, Dabni, but I need you to say that you accept this assignment before I can share the index with you."

She snapped her mind back from imagining Walto's future and grinned as she held out her hands to take the gift he had come to offer. "Yes, of course, I accept this assignment."

He passed the index to her, pouring it from his hands into hers, both vessel and contents. When he had finished he still held it but so did she, the same one or a copy. It didn't matter which. It was as heavy as a star and as light as a breeze. And just that easily she incorporated the knowledge of a hundred million individual Fant into herself. Her nefshon construct spun, nonexistent as it was, and she had the sudden understanding that she was passing out while in the middle of a nefshon trance.

"Don't worry," said Walto. "It's overwhelming both mentally and physically. You're going to experience a bit of deep sleep. Your body needs a nap to accommodate what you've just received. I'll stay here until you awaken. Then I'll take you out to a nice meal and show you how to add the waitstaff to the index. But for now, rest well."

The plane of their conversation dissolved but Dabni had already dropped into a dreamless sleep.

~~~~~

SHE woke near the end of the day, stiff from sleeping in a chair, and found Walto wandering the aisles of her shop looking through books of eastern archipelagic philosophy. He smiled as she staggered toward him. Her head felt fuzzy and her stomach ravenous, realizing that his suggestion of dinner had been anything but random. In fact, he had made a reservation for them at one of Keslo's most prestigious and expensive restaurants—a place she'd never imagined dining given her cover as a simple shopgirl, and so was only too happy to visit it with him. Over the span of several courses and surreptitious sips of koph-laced liqueur from a small flask he had, Walto guided her through the process of sampling nefshons from a trio of young waiters—a simple matter of drawing a strand from each—and binding their respective uniqueness to the index that now came to her awareness when she called. Dessert consisted of light sweet grasses, and tasted the way she imagined success should taste.

And why not? The Caudex had been pleased with her work and entrusted her with an enormous responsibility. Their paranoid fears over the target of her official assignment had never materialized. Instead, she'd found love with a brilliant scholar who in turn had gifted her with a darling daughter. Life was perfect, a dream come true.

But that was a tenday ago. Now Klarce had passed along a new directive and a meme of death. The dream shattered.

ELEVEN

DISCOVERY

~~~~~~~~~~~

PIZLO was moody. To be fair, if anyone on all of Barsk had a right to stew in his own juices or rail against the injustice of daily life it was Pizlo. But the boy wasn't cranky for his own sake. Never having known fairness, he rarely noticed its absence. Rather, he felt bad for the Archetype of Man, whose nefshons he had just dismissed after the machine had filled his head to bursting. For years, Pizlo had been listening to its stories, thousands upon thousands of them ranging from anecdotes to epics. Most of the stories involved men and women, young and old, but hints here and there throughout the tales had made it clear that those words meant something different to whomever had first told those stories. And some of the stories included beings who were clearly *not* men and women, but animals that weren't animals because they were smart and could speak. Sapient. Animals that were sapient, but still weren't men and so weren't like him. Pizlo had grappled with that for a long while because he couldn't wrap his thoughts around it. People were sapient, not animals. But the heroes in the machine's stories were mostly just one kind of people. Even the

Fant had two kinds of people, Eleph and Lox. But not the people
in the stories. Maybe that's why they were all gone. Maybe that's
why they hadn't recognized what they had made when creating
their Archetype of Man.

That the Archetype had produced nefshons was the only proof
Pizlo needed to see two points as incontrovertible: first that it had
been both alive and sapient. Maybe not from the moment of its
awakening, but certainly during most of the long span of its inor-
ganic machine life. It had spent the majority of that span with its
systems powered down to a dormancy that by comparison made
the paralysis of mortal sleep like running fast enough to walk on
wind. So that was one thing. The other was that it possessed wisdom. Its knowledge outstripped even Jorl, who often seemed like
he'd read and understood *everything*. The Archetype didn't simply know all its lore, it was the embodiment of it. A miracle storyteller and teacher.

It amazed Pizlo that people had created it, and he wondered if
they'd really understood what they'd done, what a miracle to
have built sapience into a machine. And yet, despite that miracle,
its creators had cheated it as well.

The Archetype lacked agency. It had never once initiated any
action. Always it waited upon inquiry. According to Jorl its last
words before being physically destroyed had delineated its pedi-
gree and qualifications, its tone imploring the Patrolers who had
stumbled upon it to use it. Instead, they'd denied it without knowing what they'd extinguished. But even that pointless, willful act
of annihilation didn't upset the boy. Rather it was the cruelty that
the Archetype of Man's long vanished makers chose to imbue
it with so much insight while denying it even a hint of free will.

If knowledge was power—as Jorl had taught Pizlo with endless
examples—how could such power exist without will? How could

will exist without accountability? Accountability without integrity? And so, back again to the fundamental question, how might a person—ancient hero from Before or Fant abomination such as himself—how could any of them even conceive of integrity without agency? More simply, how could the Archetype's makers be capable of such majestic creation and so stupid at the same time?

As often happened when he used koph, Pizlo felt both frantically alert and yawnishly sleepy. In just such a state he'd wandered along the hidden pathways that were his private routes, pausing at a concealed spot above a favored park where he could watch people come and go without being noticed himself. The drug he'd ingested to speak with the Archetype still buzzed in him. The people in the park each shone with their own golden wrapping of particles. This section of the park held one of Keslo's public mazes, a shadow-laced space constructed of winding walkways cunningly separated by translucent screens. Fant making their way through adjacent portions of the maze saw their fellows only as questing shadows on the screens, the sound of their laughter and conversation seeming to come from ever-changing distances. The maze offered little challenge except to the youngest of children, and among its many twists and turns were alcoves with comfortable cushions, pairs of chairs and gaming tables, and the occasional bit of artwork appropriate for a span of contemplation. Pizlo's perch had sufficient elevation that he could see down into the maze. Seniors strolled in unhurried steps, young lovers slipped through for a moment's private caress, and some wandered at ease in a needed break from the demands of the day. He liked to watch people meander along the paths, much as he had always studied the progress of insects about their day, seeking larger patterns of purpose in the actions of individuals. People weren't so different. Sometimes he would guess at the identity of the person beneath a particular nefshon cocoon and banish that individual's particles from his perception to see if he was right.

Muzzy with sleep, moments passed before he recognized one of the gleaming figures in the maze, not just as a resident of Keslo that he'd passively watched for years. Some familiar movement beneath the glowing gold identified her as Dabni. Pizlo dismissed his awareness of the active nefshons blanketing everyone around him, now seeing the men and women in the maze with normal eyes. Was Dabni taking a break from work? But why? Why would anyone want a break from working in a bookstore. That seemed as alien as growing tired of the taste of air or wistful for the ability to fan someone else's ears.

Almost he left his spot, knowing that while Rina's mother didn't like him much, she had been working hard at it for years now. At her daughter's urging, she and Rina had prepared treats for him, and more substantial meals besides, leaving them on the sill of an open window of his own mother's house. Dabni would even chat with him now, albeit grudgingly, and almost always about books he'd read. She sometimes set aside books for him where he might snatch them up when no one was looking. He always took care of them, handling them more delicately than the volumes from Jorl's collection—which were *meant* to show that they'd been read—and returned them within a tenday, nearly pristine and fit to be sold in her shop without anyone knowing they'd been touched, let alone read, by the island's abomination.

It would be easy to scramble to another branch, use a bit of rope to swing into position and drop into her path within the maze. It would surprise her, but there had always been that about Dabni that caused her to recover quickly. If he encountered her in the maze she'd probably make some clever remark or joke about it. That was when he liked her most. He stretched and grinned, shrugging off sleepiness to do this thing when he followed the thought to its end and stopped himself. As fine as it might be to startle Dabni, once in the maze he'd have to run its course to reach an exit. From his vantage point he knew it would require him to startle several other Fant, and in their panic they could well tear through a panel, injuring the maze and possibly themselves. And where was the integrity in that? Right. Instead, he watched Dabni, much as he had been watching the other people enjoying the maze this day, each in their own way, whether or not it all served some larger purpose.

He tracked her progress, around the grand arc that defined the outermost edge to the left of where she'd entered. He watched as she passed four separate chances to slip through openings in the screens and delve deeper into the maze. Instead she stayed her course, completing the arc to where it branched off in three directions, two of which branched again twice more to wend further into the maze. She ignored both of these and instead took the third route. It progressed in an ever narrowing spiral that culminated in a quiet alcove outfitted with a broad cushion. At the precise center of the spiral the maze's designer had placed a simple glass art installation that invited contemplation. It was the nature of the spiral's end that one could see the shadowy forms of other travelers in the maze coming their way through several layers of screens well before they reached them.

The scene caused Pizlo's thoughts to turn again to the Archetype of Man and the shadow shapes that existed beneath its own translucent panes, vague and indistinct, as if the men and women of its stories constantly rose and fell inside its cubical body. Comparing the two images in his mind, he wondered what role mazes played in the hero's journey. There'd been the one about the man with the ball of string that the Archetype had told him years ago.

He'd liked that one because the hero had traveled from island to island, like a Fant on Barsk might. The other details, especially the ending, escaped him though.

He had sufficient koph left in his system that he toyed with the idea of summoning his dead tutor again just to rehear the tale's end. That notion fled his mind in an instant as a very different thought caught his attention.

Dabni had settled herself on the waiting cushion. She held one hand up in front of her face, brought the tip of her trunk a short distance from it, and all at once held aloft a span of golden thread. It ran from her grasp through the walls of the maze some distance to connect with a young Eleph, one of a pair girls, both clad in the fashion of another island. They looked little older than him, teenage sweethearts stealing kisses from one another as they strolled hand in hand.

But though he'd set aside his awareness of either Eleph's nefshon swaddling, there could be no doubt about the thread that ran straight as a trumpet cry from the one Eleph girl to Dabni, piercing the intervening maze panels without effect. The thread was all of nefshons! He could see it.

But . . . how could Dabni do that? Isolate a thread, from a living person? And did that mean she was a Speaker like he was? Like Jorl? He'd never mentioned it, not once. And why would she work in a bookstore if she could summon the dead? Except . . . that wasn't what she was doing, or he'd have seen her conversant, just as anyone receptive to the effects of koph could see the working of another Speaker. And if she wasn't Speaking, then . . . what *was* she doing?

While he watched, Dabni raised her other hand and a glittering spherical lattice of gold appeared. Pizlo gasped at the sight of it. He knew it didn't exist in the real world because the brightness of it didn't hurt his eyes. The thing—like a gleaming fractal puzzle ball—was made of nefshons, and yet even from this distance he could tell its pieces didn't belong together, not like the summoned bits of a conversant's construct all were of a kind. Every piece of this thing felt different from every other. As he watched, Dabni added the thread she'd drawn from one of those girls, somehow both breaking it off from its source and tying it into the structure she held. The thread winked out of existence. It happened so fast that almost, almost Pizlo believed it a trick of the light. Nefshon threads? Constructs made from many different people's particles? Such things couldn't be. But then another thread winked into existence. Again Dabni held one end in her hand, the other stretching through the maze to the other of the pair of girls. Moments later, this too vanished while the construct in her hand gained a minute bit of complexity. Dabni's trunk kept moving, the tip dancing near the hand that had held the threads. And that quickly, she held a third one, this time the other end connected to an elderly Lox a bit further in the maze who sat by a gaming table, pieces arrayed in a complex game that he seemed to be playing both sides of. Then that thread vanished and in the next instant another appeared, running from Dabni to yet another person. And each time she added something of the thread to the object in her hand.

It didn't make any sense, not to be able to do that to nefshons, nor to tie herself, however briefly, to living Fant, nor to do so without their knowledge, and least of all to build something from the collection of them. But judging by the construct, she'd been doing it for a long time. Too long. It hurt to think of it, but whatever she held contained particles from millions and millions of different people, many times the population of the entire planet. Whatever any of it meant, Pizlo knew of no other Speaker on Keslo who did such things. Nor in all of Jorl's books had he read about anyone anywhere else on Barsk that could. And how long had she been able to do it?

It didn't appear to have any effect on the Fant on the other end of the threads. Pizlo rolled his confusion around in his head a while. This wasn't like a new piece of learning that he'd not quite mastered yet, but rather the realization that someone he believed to be solid and constant in his life was not the person he thought he knew. Dabni, who shared his mother's house, who had married his mentor and birthed the first person in the world who had never thought "abomination" when seeing him, that woman had transformed into someone else. As he watched, she dropped her hands and smiled. The fractal ball vanished, like it had never been.

But it had, all of it was real, and that changed everything, didn't it?

TWELVE

IMAGININGS

~~~~~~~~~~

IN the reality that contained his physical being, Jorl slumped in a favorite chair with face slack, hands folded loosely in his lap, and trunk hanging limp. Anyone familiar with Speakers would recognize the signs and conclude that his awareness occupied a very different reality, one of his own making. In a venue crafted of his imagination he had left Barsk far behind and instead stood on the planet Dawn, in a replica of Senator Welv's office, a space of rounded stone walls painted in shades of umber and rust and sand. He wore the same clothing as back on Barsk, an open vest of blue-green atop loose-fitting, black slacks. He'd clothed Welv in the grab he'd found in his colleague's memory, the typical Prairie Dog sleeveless robe he had donned that morning. The robe flowed down to mid-calf, decorated with innumerable pleats as befit both his age and status as senior member of the Committee of Information, its color the same light grey as the senator's fur. Jorl's own wrinkled skin shared the same color, albeit several shades darker.

They had been talking since mid-morning and both were growing hungry for lunch. Much had been discussed, but little re-solved, and they'd come around again to the heart of the matter.

Welv held up a hand. "You have a scholar's imagination, my friend, and I value it at least as much as the unique cultural per-spective you have brought to our committee. But what you pro-pose goes beyond the possibilities of creativity."

"This isn't some idle fancy that I found in a dream," said Jorl. "If the committee will just—"

The senior senator cut him off. "I have not discussed this matter with the other members of our Committee." He skittered from from one side of the nefshon construct of his office to the other, pausing to run his fingers along the frames of various medical di-plomas and certificates from his time as a physician before joining the senate, as if testing the accuracy of Jorl's mindscape. Seem-ingly satisfied, Welv eventually arrived back in front of the Fant and continued as if he hadn't paused at all. "Doing so would only stir up pointless speculation and debate. We have no precedent and no policy for what you propose." He paused, glanced up at the junior senator, and scowled. "Do sit down, Jorl. Or would you give me a stiff neck to go with the indigestion your words have already brought?"

Jorl obliged, making use of his replica of a large wooden chair the Cynomy maintained in his real office for visitors of races as large as Fant. He received an appreciative nod from Welv and lifted his trunk to signal the elderly senator to refrain from further com-ment.

"There *is* precedent," he said. "Or, more accurately, anti-precedent."

Welv waved the objection away. "Irrelevant, the details of the Compact your people formed with the rest of the Alliance explic-itly prevents any non-Fant from setting foot on Barsk."

"And I'm not suggesting that any do so. Rather that Fant set foot upon other worlds. With only a handful of exceptions, we've been absent from the experience of the rest of the Alliance. After eight hundred years we've ceased to be real people and instead become folklore—hideous, hairless monsters used to frighten children. 'Eat your sprouts or a Lox will come for you while you sleep and spirit you away. Behave or a pair of Elephs will run their trunks over your fur every time your eyes close.' We've gone over this before and we both agree that it's past time to reintegrate Fant into the day-to-day events of the Alliance, but that can't happen when the other races barely have any awareness of our existence."

"I don't disagree but—"

Jorl ignored him and plunged on. "A thousand years ago, Fant lived and worked upon dozens of mixed worlds, right alongside everyone else. It was only by action of the senate that they were transported to Barsk. It took two hundred years to build up the political will to banish an entire race, but it was done. That's your precedent, Welv. I'm not suggesting anything quite so drastic, rather—"

The aged Prairie Dog again interrupted his colleague. "All you're suggesting is to create entire neighborhoods upon dozens of worlds where Fant can emigrate, their relocation at the expense of Alliance citizens, taking jobs from non-Fant, their children occupying desks in the same schools as whatever Urs or Nonyx or Lam children attend already, frequent the same restaurants as Brady and Bos, work side by side with Ailuros and Lutr."

"You have a clear grasp on the concept of equality."

Welv replied with a high-pitched chirp and a disapproving glare from old to young that transcended race. Jorl sighed, inclining his head at the rebuke, his ears dipping forward. Neither spoke for a long moment, and then the Cynomy continued on as if the Lox had never resorted to sarcasm.

"I'm right there with you, Jorl, at least in theory. And if I could envision the means to transform such a vision into accepted policies and viable procedures, I would personally argue the merits with every member of the committee. But it remains—what did you deny naming it? An idle fancy? Tell me how we can accomplish this without inciting civil unrest, riots, even acts of violence? For that matter, where do you expect to acquire the hundreds of Fant you would have emigrate?"

Jorl waved his trunk in confusion. "Where else," he said. "Barsk, obviously."

"And have you asked any of your fellow Eleph and Lox if they wish to leave?"

"I left," said Jorl. "I joined the Patrol, lived in close quarters amongst many other races."

"Yes, and other Fant have before you. But no more than a handful in all the years your people have been on Barsk. And have you forgotten what you endured from your comrades? You have a wife now. You have a daughter. Would you subject them to such abuse?"

Jorl paused. Somehow, all his thinking and planning to date had been in the abstract. Welv had just swept that all away. Jorl loved Dabni and she loved him. If he asked her to follow him to another world and live among other races she would come. She would endure anything for him, and he for her. Their bond was that strong. But Rina, little Rina. How could he possibly put his daughter in a situation that would bring her pain, subject her to teasing and insults, fear and loathing, all for just being an innocent child?"

Welv mistook his silence for stubbornness. "Do you truly believe you can gather up enough others who would be willing to expose themselves and their families to the daily intolerance of other races? What is their motivation, Jorl? What possible reason could they have to deliberately embrace that kind of abuse?"

Jorl flapped his ears, switching from thoughts of his family back to the abstract and theoretical, and his doubts faded. "They have to, if we're ever to resolve the situation."

"Again, I don't disagree, but it's one thing to accept the greater good as a thought experiment and something else entirely to ask men and women to throw away everything they know, everything they hold dear, because it will bring about a better galaxy for their children's children."

"Funny," said Jorl, "that argument didn't stop the senate eight hundred years ago from exiling every Fant from the rest of the Alliance."

The Prairie Dog grew silent, lowering his eyes while absently fingering the pleats of his robe. "And it was shameful, but would you have us perform a similar act as correction? And even if you could find sufficient Fant who wished to emigrate, where would they go? How do you propose we convince even a single Alliance world to welcome them, let alone the many you would seed with your people?"

"With small steps," he said, and he willed the addition of a report folder into existence in the illusion of their meeting. "This is a proposal to fund a minor artists traveling consortium. Talented and creative people from several different worlds will travel around to three cities on each of thirty planets and serve as the kernel of a local art festival. Painters, sculptors, musicians, singers. The core group will give lectures and classes while they're there and then the lot of them will move on to the next city or planet. And once one such group is up and running, another one will be created and sent off to visit a different cluster of worlds, and on and on."

Welv quirked an eyebrow. "And how does this proposal serve the Fant?"

Jorl didn't even try to hide his grin. "Barsk is one of the worlds that will contribute artists to the program. One member of each traveling consortium will be an Eleph or Lox."

"You intend to sneak your people onto Alliance worlds under cover of an arts and culture program? Huh. It might work at that, particularly if we pick the initial cities with care, and put the right public relations spin on it so that other worlds begin to feel like they're missing out—as opposed to being spared the visit of Fant. Yes, that has promise. But . . . how will you get your own people, artists from Barsk, to leave their world behind? You have your own eight hundred years of history of isolationism. You've spun the imposition of your population on a world none of you asked for into a virtue of being left alone. They're not going to want to leave, let along bring the fruit of their creative gifts to people they've never imagined visiting. Even if this proposal of yours gains momentum, you still need a plan for convincing even a small handful of talented Fant to leave their home. Do you have such a thing?"

"Not yet. But I'll come up with something. But you're correct, right now I don't know how to do it. I only know it has to happen or it's only a matter of time before we're on the brink of another crisis where the Alliance wants what only Barsk can provide, where you shatter the Compact because it suits your needs. Actions like these become possible when the people on the other side don't matter. The other races of the Alliance don't see Fant as being entitled to rights, or value our feelings, or even see us as people at all."

Welv crossed to Jorl's chair and placed a hand upon the seated Fant's shoulder. "Jorl, we agree in theory. Do not despair. You've served in the senate for barely seven years. It takes time to figure out how to go from theory to practice. Just because I cannot see a way to make this happen does not mean I am abandoning the desire. Let us both reflect on our discussion and meet again in a few days. Perhaps one of us will have gained some new insight that offers fresh possibilities."

Jorl bowed his head. The fact that a Cynomy would speak to him with such candor, would place a hand upon his shoulder, even here in a seeming born of his own mind, promised that his dream of reuniting Fant with the rest of the galaxy was not impossible. "You're right. Thank you, Senator. I will look forward to that conversation. Farewell."

The Prairie Dog nodded. "Until soon."

With a mental twitch, Jorl let the scene in Welv's office dissolve. The nefshon constructs of both person and place unraveled, faded, dispersed.

～～～

HE stood in his kitchen, the doors to several cupboards flung wide. Bins half full of several different kinds of leaves—some fresh and supple, others dry and crisp—lay before him. Holding a large wooden bowl in one hand, he scooped and sampled with his other hand and trunk, adding an assortment of grasses as well. Next, from the pantry, he acquired three different varieties of plels, transferred them to a cutting board, and with a paring knife neatly sliced them into thin wedges before placing them in his bowl. To these he added an assortment of chopped nuts common to the islands of his archipelago, as well as a much smaller sampling of spiced nahlet nuts, imported at considerable expense from Sworrub, a mixed world with a predominantly Marmo population. Satisfied at last with the variety and proportions of ingredients, Jorl took up a pair of broad forks and gave the mixture a vigorous tossing. His lunch prepared, he carried the bowl into his study, settled into his favorite chair, and opened a book he'd been reading earlier. His trunk moved from the bowl to his mouth.

He'd barely begun eating when a trio of swift knocks at his front door made him set his bowl aside. He finished chewing what was in his mouth as he crossed to the door, and swallowed as he flung it wide. On his doorstep stood a young girl, barely five years old, dressed in a simple shift of bright yellow, a crudely fashioned crown of flowers sitting between her ears. With a swift motion he bent, scooped her up, and twirled her around into the air. The little girl squealed with delight and proclaimed, "Daddy!"

"Hello, little twig. I wasn't expecting you today." He did a slow, spinning dance, swinging her by her outstretched arms until he'd spiraled back into the kitchen, and plopped her onto the counter. "Did you come to join me for lunch?"

Rina's laughter filled the kitchen and she whipped her trunk side to side in answer. "Mommy said I was reading too much and needed to get out." She pouted to show her displeasure with the judgment.

A love of the written word was hardly the thing most parents lost sleep over, but in fairness to the child's mother, Rina's knack for literacy had emerged early. And because Dabni lived with Tolta and lacked access to a traditional family home with the attendant playmates and child minders, she'd perforce taken her daughter to her bookshop most days. At an age when Jorl had been playing tag, and seek-me, and capture-the-melon with as many as twenty other youths and running wild throughout his boyhood home,

Rina had a tiny table in a corner of the bookshop where she held tea parties for her rag doll, Kokab, and read to it, initially from picture books but more recently from texts that would have challenged someone twice her age. Now that she was old enough, she took classes and had playdates with other children in the neighborhood, but even so each day would see her in her spot in the shop, a stack of books close at hand.

Jorl snatched a mouthful of salad with his trunk, chewed thoughtfully, and said, "Did you come to see me thinking I would overrule your mother?"

Her eyes widened and then Rina looked away, perhaps startled that her father had seen through her clever plan so quickly. He bit back a smile at the attempted manipulation, confident and dreading that her skill would improve with age and more compelling issues.

"That's not going to happen. Your mother has say when it comes to how you spend your time. No, don't give me that look, we're not ganging up on you. You won't find two people in all of Keslo who are as happy as we are that you like reading so much. But balance is important, too. Your books will be waiting for you when you get back. Okay?"

A mumbled "okay" reached him as he helped himself to more of his lunch. If she wanted to stew, he'd let her. He'd nearly finished the salad when she finally lifted her head and asked, "Daddy? Can you help me find a book?"

"Of course, but your mother has better access. Did you ask her?"

Rina shook her head. "I was going to, but she sent me away before I could. And . . . it's not for me."

"One of your friends from school?"

She shook her head again, exaggerating the gesture so that her ears flapped wildly. "No, it's for Kokab."

"Indeed?" Jorl grinned. "And is Kokab taking a more active interest in reading? I thought he was content to be the audience."

"Daddy!"

Jorl raised both hands and trunk, protesting his innocence. "Sorry, I've never seen him hold up a book, let alone read one."

"You're being silly. Kokab's a doll. He can't read."

"Of course, I'd forgotten.

"So when he wants something specific, he asks me, and I get it, and read it to him."

"Riiiight. And what does Kokab want now?"

Rina scrunched up her mouth and eyes. It was a face she tended to make when she was concentrating or trying to remember something. Jorl hoped she'd outgrow it. "I don't know the word. It's a science-y word. Something about alleys and eels. Does that sound right?"

"Alley eels?"

"Yeah? Maybe?"

Jorl rolled the sounds around in his mouth for something that came close and might be glossed as "science-y" by his daughter. "Did you mean: alleles?"

"Uh huh. That's it. I need a book about al-eels. Alleles."

He frowned. "You're very smart, honey, but that's still a bit out of your reach. Who's been talking to you about genetics?"

"Kokab."

"Right. Anyone else?"

"No, Daddy. Just Kokab. He says it's important stuff that I'll want to know all about someday."

He turned away, pretending to busy himself with cleaning his salad bowl to hide his frown. Many children had imaginary friends at that age; he himself had enjoyed long chats with a magical creature named Frilbo who had generously taken the blame for any number of broken bits of crockery, before he'd met Arlo and the pair took turns blaming each other for their misdeeds. But Arlo had long since died and his son, Pizlo, heard voices that, while perhaps imaginary were nonetheless prescient. And Rina's imaginary friend asking for books on genetics was a bit different than her reporting that he liked his tea without sugar.

"Well . . . Kokab may well be right, but that's a long way off. And I'm sure he didn't just volunteer that opinion out of nowhere. Do you know what prompted it?"

"We heard Mommy talking to a customer about it. He said his brother works at a fish farm, and they're taking some of the kinds of fish that everyone likes and making changes to some of their . . . alleles? Yes, those things, and getting bigger fish that way."

Jorl sighed with relief. His daughter's clever imagination had simply taken something she'd overheard and run away with it, and much like he might have done with Frilbo, she'd made sure to stick Kokab with the blame, should there be any blame to stick. He paused, flashing back on Welv's words about his own idle fancy. For a moment he was tempted to ask his daughter to ask her doll for a solution. The moment passed, leaving behind a wry smile. Rina sat looking at him, waiting for him to speak.

"Do you think you might like a career at a fishery when you grow?"

"No. We had a field trip to a fish farm two seasons ago. I liked it and had fun, but Kokab says I'll study other things."

"That's very very true, your teachers will introduce you to a wide world of topics. And you have plenty of time, don't you?"

"Uh huh!"

"Good. I'm glad you see that. Because we're going to put that book on alleles and all that kind of stuff off for a while." Rina's face began to cloud over with disappointment, and he hurried on. "But . . . your mother's advice about getting out more applies to me, too. I've been cooped up working too much. Why don't we have an outing together?"

"Really?! Where?"

"Well . . . if we hurry, I bet we can get to Suliv's before they run out of toffee. If you think it'll be okay with your mother for you to have some sweets before dinner."

Rina's head bobbled with agreement. "Oh, sure. That's fine. She said I needed air. Suliv's has air, so that's fine."

"Then that's the plan." He scooped her up from the counter, tucking her under one arm like a sack of leaves, which set her to giggling again. He crossed to his apartment's rear door which led more directly to a stair that would in turn take them to Suliv's grocery and sundry shop, setting her on her feet as they stepped outside.

"Daddy?"

"Yes, little twig?"

"Can we get an extra sweet? For Kokab?"

Jorl's grin brought to mind treats he'd wheedled for Frilbo so many years ago. "Of course we can."

THIRTEEN

INSCRIBED IN PAIN

~~~~~~~~~

EIGHT hundred years ago, Margda had tattooed the first aleph on her forehead. Next she created a council to travel from the far end of the eastern archipelago all the way to the most distant end of the western one. Although they never took anything like a direct path, they visited each and every island along the way. The number of councilors changed from time to time, never fewer than three nor more than eight. They were always welcomed when they entered the harbor of any island, always housed in luxury guest quarters in every Civilized Wood. The precise timing of their arrival was likewise always secret, but once they docked word of their presence quickly spread. How could it not? Still, the residents prided themselves on not letting the news leave their shores until the council themselves did, and in this way people only knew where they'd been, and never where they were or where they were going.

The pattern of such a visit remained unchanged since the first. The councilors met with each island's leaders, scholars, scientists, and artists, usually over a huge feast that moved from home to home and featured local dishes and local intoxicants. The following day, the councilors split up and went to speak and drink with the three oldest male Lox and three oldest male Eleph on each island. Next they went in two groups to the oldest female household and the largest. The topic of conversation was always the same: was there someone worthy of the aleph among them?

Every Fant knew what the council sought, not the best or most skilled, but the combination of three unusual abilities, talents, and experiences. Rarity defined such individuals. Only fifty-seven other Fant had been marked, two in Pizlo's own meager lifetime, Jorl soon after he'd returned to assist in burying Pizlo's father, and three seasons ago a fishwife from nearby Gumti. She had been ranked as a grandmaster in seventeen different boardgames since childhood, had improved on what had been universally acknowledged as the perfect recipe for cribble wine, and could recognize the prophetic dreams of others when they occurred.

Common sense decried the likelihood of another choice so soon, but the leaders of each Civilized Wood took the council's visit with optimistic sincerity. History indicated and every iteration of the council confirmed that if potential existed it would emerge by consensus of the island's populace. A mayor might point out a promising gymnast. An aged Lox would identify an amazing chef. Some aunt in the island's largest house would grudgingly mention a new mother who had given birth to healthy and beautiful triplets. A renowned limner would mention a mathematical prodigy. And so on. The council members would then come together and validate the claims, eliminating any individual who lacked endorsements in at least three areas. Next, via a series of ever more probing interviews, they separated out the merely special from the truly exceptional.

The council could manage two islands in a tenday. They were

picky. They were fastidious. They were jaded. The most recent
pair of recipients notwithstanding, decades usually passed without a council identifying a new Bearer. But as with each of those
fifty-seven that followed Margda, when the council agreed on a
candidate they marked them with the aleph. The proud moment
took place in the largest community space that Civilized Wood
possessed. Local poets would write songs of the event. Word-
smiths would compose novels and plays, penning ever more absurd fictions about the new Bearer's history. Historians would
craft detailed monographs describing every facet of the marking
ceremony. And even though all in attendance could tell you every
step of what was about to occur, they all nonetheless held their
breaths as it happened in the flesh before their eyes. The candidate would step forward, dressed in their finest garb, approach a
raised dais upon which stood the island's leaders and a single
member of the council. The candidate knelt and the council member would write the mark of passage onto the forehead, a permanent tattoo inscribed using a proprietary, glowing ink of Margda's
own invention.

Pizlo wanted that ink.

He didn't want an aleph. The council wasn't ever going to give
him one, no matter what astonishing things he'd already accomplished, like being an abomination and still alive after fourteen
years, or making his way alone up to the planet's space station, or
swiping the ring of office from a senior senator only one other person in the entire galaxy could remember, or hearing the voices of
clouds and trees and waves. Pizlo lacked sufficient advocates who
might offer up his name, and it was a certainty that the council
themselves were never going to interview him. No, he'd never get
an aleph, but that was fine. He possessed moons.

He'd been drawing them on his chest ever since his trip up the beanstalk to the edge of space, a series of seven circles, one for each of the planet's moons. And one by one he had filled in each circle after gazing upon and communing with each particular moon. Given Barsk's near constant rain and clouds, and because most Fant spent their time deep in the tree cover of their island's Civilized Wood, a Fant could go his entire life without seeing any moons at all. Experiencing even one was rare, and carried bragging rights at most drinking establishments.

Pizlo had spoken with all seven. And as he had learned from the Archetype of Man, if he was the hero of his own life it followed that he needed a quest, something fresh and important that was his alone to accomplish. That morning he'd retrieved the recording amulet Druz had given him and fastened it about his neck. He stood now, on a small platform high up in the canopy, the same research station where years before Arlo had set himself aflame and jumped to his death. Pizlo gazed down into the shaft that defined the last journey his father had taken. He activated the amulet and spoke into the darkness.

"I have decided. It is time, no, it's past time, that I stopped inking the moons on my chest. I suppose I could tattoo them myself with traditional dyes, but then there'd be no quest. So, instead, I vow to seek out the council that awards the Aleph and whether by persuasion, trickery, or theft—all celebrated practices of heroes throughout the ages—to obtain the very same ink they use to mark someone as an Aleph-Bearer. This recording is the proof of my decision. Let those who eventually tell my story take note. This was the day I began my quest."

Being resolved to a course of action both thrilled and frightened him. His quest would produce an imram, sailing from island to island, like no other abomination on Barsk had ever done in pursuit of the council. That was the trick. Though they visited every island in both archipelagos, they did so without concern for convenience or pragmatism. Within any pair of seasons they usually stayed within either the western or eastern island chains, but they might visit adjacent islands in rapid succession or just as likely pass by ten before opting to go to shore at the eleventh. Currently they were still near, in the western chain. It was common knowledge that they'd been to both Telba and Kelpry this season, going to one and then the other, though a third of the archipelago lay between them.

He knew where they were now. The sky had told him the council was nearing the end of their visit on the island of Senjo, far to the south. But they'd move on to another island before he could reach Senjo and that destination was hidden from him. If the council hadn't yet decided themselves, the future was not fixed. They hadn't made a choice. That fit Pizlo's new understanding of the ongoing battle between determinism and agency. Though it put an added burden on him, he found comfort in it as well.

He planned to start by sailing south, until such time as the world revealed where the council had landed. Then he'd adjust his course for that new island. If they left before he arrived, he'd repeat the process however many times was required. Eventually he would catch them, walk ashore where no one but that island's residents knew them to be, and acquire their ink to create his moons. It was a quest that only he had the ability to pursue, and one that would only benefit him. The quest for moons.

~~~~~~

YEARS before, Pizlo had walked into a shop and "acquired" an inflatable boat which he'd rowed all the way to Zlorka. That had been his first time off Keslo and while his gifts kept him on course and helped him to learn how to handle the boat, in hindsight he'd come close to permanently ruining his hands. This time he needed to travel smarter, and Jorl's boat waited in the harbor. One could, in theory, consider that an invitation of sorts. And it wasn't as though Jorl would mind, he hardly ever used the boat, mostly just to sail out to meet with Druz when she visited. He'd make a point of asking the boat, but couldn't imagine it wouldn't want to set off on a trip. That's what boats were for, right?

Avoiding the attention of dock workers and harbor staff was a familiar game, and it took only a short while for Pizlo to secret himself aboard Jorl's boat. Freeing its mooring lines without anyone seeing him do so required a bit longer. Then he fired up the engine, eased the boat from its slip, and set a course for Senjo. Fewer vessels moved through the harbor during flood, and fewer still sailed to and from nearby islands, but that presented no problems. The limited visibility imposed by the constant rain and the shadows cast within the wheelhouse ensured that all anyone saw of him was the outline of a Fant and not the pale skin of Keslo's resident abomination.

As a sailor, Jorl was a fine historian, and so his boat came equipped with every technological convenience available on other, more tech-friendly worlds. Pizlo kept one eye on the boat's modern display screen and the other on a point on the horizon where his gut told him Senjo lay two days' journey to the south. This was the start of his imram, and though he didn't expect to encounter giant cephalopods or other monsters of the deep, he couldn't rule them out, either literally or metaphorically. He was on a hero's journey. As the harbor fell behind, he squeezed the pendant at his throat.

"This is day one of my quest," he said. "I am at sea again, for the first time since I set off up the beanstalk to help Jorl on the station. It's a very different trip though, and not just because I'm heading in the opposition direction. And that's okay, because I'm different too . . ."

He sailed without incident the rest of the day and into the night, passing several other islands and ignoring the calls of greeting and inquiry from other vessels. He snacked from the stores Jorl had provided and when he eventually tired and found himself dozing at the wheel, Pizlo dropped anchor and bid the sea and sky all around him a good night, went below deck to the cabin, and slept. The second day and night were more of the same.

He passed Gerd, feeling a frisson of satisfaction at sailing beyond the archipelago's focal point. He continued south and west. On the third morning, he awoke to the certain knowledge that the council he sought had completed their interviews on Senjo and moved on. Returning to the wheelhouse he called up maps on the boat's display and considered where the council might have moved to. Senjo was about as far south as one could go. But east to north to west of it were plenty of potential destinations. He could set off in one direction or another, but when awareness of where they'd arrived finally hit him, he was just as likely to have guessed correctly and so be close on their heels as to be wrong and even further from his goal. He sat and waited, considered visiting with the Archetype but stayed his hand and conserved his supply of koph. The council had a much bigger boat but his was swifter. He remained anchored and waited for them to reach a destination. Another day passed and boredom clubbed him. He waved off a handful of passing vessels that drew near with concern over his floating in place. He swam in ever increasing circles around the boat until his arms and legs began to fail him and he had to drag himself back aboard to collapse onto the desk and let the falling rain wash the fatigue from him. He fished, seeing how many different varieties he could catch and release before reeling in one he'd seen before and deciding that was justification to consume it. But mostly Pizlo mourned the missed evenings telling Rina stories.

After six days out from Keslo, the morning rain whispered that the council had made landfall on Fintz, a somewhat more isolated island a couple days further east and a bit north of his position. He could be there in three days, two if he let the boat sail on while he slept. The council would still be there, still meeting with civic leaders or, in the worst case, interviewing potential claimants. He could catch up to them, perhaps even catch them unawares, simply take some of their ink and avoid a direct encounter. He set the new course, weighed anchor, and started up the boat's engine. Only then did he allow himself breakfast.

~~~~~~

A faint but persistent tone woke Pizlo from a dreamless sleep. Morning light, such as it would be, was still a long way away. Despite the dark and the rain, devices on the boat insisted he'd arrived and demanded his attention. He climbed to the wheelhouse, shut off the alarm, and took stock. Fintz boasted three main harbors, two of them larger than the one Pizlo had departed from at Keslo. One lay directly ahead of him, but after only a few minutes at the controls he had the boat skirting past, choosing instead to follow the call of the second harbor and execute a northern curve that took him around a quarter of the island.

He hadn't intended to arrive at night. A mass of gleaming lights shone through the rain as he approached the harbor, making the council's boat impossible to miss or mistake. Pizlo guided his boat past row after row of local vessels until he reached the visitors' dock. The council's boat was one of only four craft moored. Pizlo maneuvered into an open adjacent slip, powered down, and took his time securing the lines.

He disembarked and crossed the pier until he reached a gang-plank that connected it to the council's ship. Glowing lanterns hung from it, hundreds of them, from spots barely above the wa-terline all the way up to its wheelhouse. The entire ship was lit up like a floating celebration. By now the councilors themselves would all be abed in assorted guest quarters high in Fintz's Civilized Wood, but as he climbed aboard and his hand moved across the gunwale the ship whispered that a crew of five remained as well as where each lay sleeping. More importantly, it told him where he would find the object of his quest.

It was a very large vessel, many times bigger than Jorl's boat, though less than a quarter the size of his senatorial space yacht. Slip-ping belowdecks, he left the glare of the ship's lanterns behind. He moved as silently through the narrow corridors as he might have traveled through the Shadow Dwell back home, and soon reached a minor supply hold. Amidst a great many bottles of dis-tilled spirits—gifts from other islands the ship had visited—he found several vials of the special tattoo ink. He took one lightly in his trunk and grinned. "In the Archetype's stories, finishing a quest always seems harder than this," he told the vial, then slipped it into a pocket of his bandolier. He reversed his path and retreated back through the ship, up onto the deck, and then over the side to the pier without incident. In fact, he felt a bit of disappointment that there hadn't been any complications to overcome.

"There are supposed to be trials," he said, tapping the disc around his neck and recording his thoughts as he stood in the rain. "It's not a very good story without them. I mean, I want to suc-ceed and all, but what kind of quest ends so easily?" Something was missing. No one had witnessed his actions, which meant there was no one to tell the tale. He turned back toward the councilors' ship with half a notion of waking up one or more of the crew so they could see he'd taken the vial of ink, but a better idea came to him. He set off along the pier, aiming for the harbor buildings and routes up into the forest and the city that waited within. There was a better place that he needed to reach.

In the unlikely event that the council found someone on Fintz that they deemed worthy of an aleph, the inscribing ceremony would take place in the city's largest public space. As he left the harbor, Pizlo consulted a visitor's map of the island's Civilized Wood, located an amphitheater labeled "Spoonbender's Place," and charted several landmarks along the way. He expected his timing would be near perfect—there were always people about in such a place at first light, groups doing morning exercises and stretching, oldsters who slept little enough by night and gathered with the dawn to greet one another and rehash old arguments, merchants crossing through the open area on their way to their shops and markets. What better spot to tattoo his moons than the center of this city as the first lights of a new day trickled through by vents and lenses and mirrors?

And so he climbed. The meta-trees here were the same as back on Keslo, as were most of the lesser trees and other plants that grew from its Shadow Dwell up through the Civilized Wood. The only real difference was the placement and quantity, and every few moments he caught himself in a blur of confusion at a feeling that something was not as it should be. A lifetime of moving through every bit of green space on Keslo, of hearing the voices of each leaf and vine proclaiming its spot in the mosaic of life there, assailed him with surprise and delight that they could exist here in new arrays and concentration and still be themselves, familiar but unique.

Pizlo emerged onto the upper edge of the amphitheater as first light began to warm the upper levels. He squinted into the fading darkness expecting to detect movement and infer people. But no one was there. Not a soul. Perhaps they were running late or sleeping in. Annoying, but not critical. They'd flee once they saw and recognized him for what he was. It was only the symbolism of marking himself here that mattered. Holding the vial of ink aloft in his trunk, he skipped and danced along the rows of wooden benches, descending toward the center of Fintz's public space that still lay entirely in shadow.

He reached the bottom—the main stage that had seen untold performances of professional orators and school children and dance troupes and choirs—just as the first bits of light gleamed across the polished floor. He wasn't alone after all. A tiny bundle, smaller than a child's ear, barely bigger than both his hands together, mewled once and coughed.

He rushed to it, mind racing as he looked in all directions, trying to find the parent who could possibly leave a tiny infant unattended. It made no sense. Helpless and defenseless, he knelt alongside the bundle and scooped it up, cradling the sleeping child in the crook of one arm. He shoved the ink vial into his bandolier so he could use both hands and his nubs to tuck the blankets more securely around the infant. It was horrific and irresponsible and clueless. What had they been thinking?

And then he knew.

This wasn't a normal baby and its parents hadn't forgotten him. The newborn child in his arms was exactly where its parents—or more likely its maternal grandparents—had left it. Where they had deliberately abandoned it here in the heart of Fintz. It was the way things happened for a child born out of a couple's proper time. It was what society required when giving birth to an abomination.

"No no no no no."

He rocked in place, clutching the infant to his chest, still searching the empty amphitheater for someone, anyone.

The child was broken, hideous. Albinism was the least visible defect. Its trunk ended in a featureless knob at half its proper length. Its arms bore fingerless flippers below the elbow. And a thin, translucent membrane in the center of its chest showed the movement of its tiny heart several times too large for its new body and beating much faster than it ought, racing as if in fear for its life.

"Shh. It's okay. You're going to be all right. I'm here. Pizlo's here. See? You can grow up and be strong and free. This doesn't have to end the way they want it."

He whispered to the baby, helplessly cataloging its injuries and deformities. Most horrific of all, its body was cold as the worst storms of the season. He held it closer, feeling it warm from contact with his own heat. Its tiny eyelids fluttered open showing the barest of slits, revealing eyes of brilliant blue. Pizlo looked to the back of the amphitheater and the boardways leading to all parts of Fintz's Civilized Wood. The population of an entire city lay near at hand. All the assistance he could wish for.

"Help. Please someone, help."

Pizlo struggled to stand. Not because of the burden of the infant in his arms but rather his legs didn't seem to work right at first. He staggered upward, and then firmed up his gait and began running up the stairs, crying out.

"I need a doctor. Please! Someone. Anyone. This is a medical emergency. Help!"

He crossed onto a major boardway, a mixture of prosperous homes and high-end shops. Few people were abroad yet, but those few who saw him, saw the bundle he carried, rushed to the nearest doorway and literally flung themselves within. Pizlo ran to the first of these, kicking at the door but it didn't open. Faces peered at him from adjacent windows, and from cracked doors further along the street; doors slammed shut at his first hint of movement in their direction.

He kept on, running down another boardway for a greater distance than he'd ever gone in his life, out in the open the way normal people traveled, driven by the frantic and fragile heart he could feel beating so close to his own.

"No no no." He muttered, half to himself and half to the infant. He felt sick. His eyes were watering and his throat had seized up like something was choking him. Words tumbled from his lips. "You're someone's child. You've done nothing wrong. You don't deserve this. If Druz was here, if we were on Jorl's yacht, there'd be all sorts of things that could be done to help you, heal you. Maybe you wouldn't be normal, but I'm not normal. Normal people did this to you. They're doing it to you. Innocent baby, you don't deserve this."

He arrived at a municipal building. A sign out front indicated the mayor of Fintz had offices inside but held an open meeting for any interested citizens each morning beneath the statue of the island's founder. Several had gathered there, speaking to a well-dressed Eleph who stood with his back to Pizlo.

"Help me, please. I need medical assistance!"

The citizens of Fintz scattered, all but the one that had been facing away. That one, the mayor, turned and cried out as Pizlo closed with him.

"Please. You can't condemn an innocent infant like this. Get us to a doctor. Now."

The Eleph opened his mouth, whispered "two of you," and passed out, collapsing at Pizlo's feet.

Still it was an answer. The highest elected official in Fintz would rather flee consciousness than aid him. Bells began ringing throughout the city, the kind of public alarm that told people to stay in their homes. Bells that normally rang only in the bedtime stories parents told about the terrifying abominations that came to torment naughty children.

He marched on, setting a course back down to the harbor and his borrowed boat. He'd take the infant back to Keslo. His mother would help him. She'd find a doctor, get the newborn whatever it needed to survive. She'd done it for Pizlo, and with his help she would do it for this baby, too.

At the edge of the Civilized Wood he boarded one of a series of elevators that ran down to the Shadow Dwell and opened onto the beach of Fintz's second harbor where he'd left the boat. No one challenged him. The bells had seen to that.

He reached the harbor and had crossed to the guest pier and nearly arrived at his boat before realizing that somewhere on the way he'd stopped feeling the pounding of the infant's heart. Pizlo fell to his knees, midway between the traveling counsel's vessel and his own, frantically peeling back the thin blankets that wrapped the baby. It was warmer than when he'd first picked it up, but that was all his own body heat. Its eyes had closed. Its frail body gone stiff. That breath of life that had inhabited it had fled. The infant that any right-thinking Fant would recognize as one that should never have been born, had died in his arms. He had been unable to save it.

Kneeling on the pier, Pizlo wailed. In all his fourteen years he'd never experienced pain. He'd born countless scrapes and cuts, shredded his hands, dislocated limbs, once even caught his trunk in a door—none of it had hurt. He understood what pain was, had seen those he loved afflicted with it, but his inability to personally experience physical suffering was part of his abnormality, like his weak eyes and his lack of pigmentation.

How then did he hurt so much now? He felt it in his gut, a twisting and strangling. His head pounded. His body wanted to vomit until it turned him inside out and then begin again. Tears streamed down his face, and his throat ached with a rawness.

And more, he knew, knew with useless hindsight, that his hero's quest had never been about acquiring a vial of ink. He was supposed to have saved an innocent, a fellow abomination, because in all the world who else could be expected to do so. And he failed. Failed his quest but gained something he'd never understood before.

At fourteen, after a life apart from Fant society, Pizlo now knew what anguish was.

FOURTEEN
CONSEQUENTIAL TRAFFIC

~~~~~~

K LARCE studied the reports on her desk a third time and for a third time the words swam before her eyes. Temmel had long since left for the day. A glance at the time stamp on her display screen hinted that his morning shift neared and he could be walking in fairly soon. *Oh surely not*, she thought. *I haven't worked the night away. Again.* She reached for her cup of tea, a vigorous blend imported from Telba during the season of mist on those years when circumstances allowed a field agent making the trip to bring back some of the leaves. Reached for but failed to grasp as her hand and arm spasmed and she knocked the cup off the desk even as she wrenched the offending limb back. Too late. It shattered as four of its mates had done over the past few seasons. She'd lost track of the hour often enough, the workload never ending, and had failed, again, to take her tablets. Even the buffer she usually enjoyed had been worn through, a gift of the added stress brought about by the need to end the Speaker on Keslo. It was hubris to think the delicate balance of medication that kept her whole wouldn't react to a murder decree. And so she had lost another cup, a worthy vessel filled with a stimulating brew that could have allowed her to keep working at least until her assistant turned up to insist she take a break. So, too, Jorl ben Tral would lose his life, and whatever promise of future deeds and contributions he might make to the world. Such a waste. Klarce snorted at the maudlin symbolism burbling up through the fatigue of her own thoughts.

She pushed back from her desk, a modern and fully automated information station, advertised on Dawn as the premiere data processing for executives with an obsessive need to manipulate the minutia under their direction. Well, the manufacturer hadn't phrased it quite that way. Two such units had been "acquired" through channels, delivered years ago to a mixed world's obscure tourist trap during the off-season and then surreptitiously delivered to the Caudex, one for her office here and the other occupying her office on Ulmazh high overhead. The thing was as close to a true artificial intelligence as anyone had managed, and not for the first time she wondered how her predecessor had gotten along without it.

"Your pardon, ma'am." Regina stood barely a trunk's length away. For how long? Judging by the concern on her face and the droop of her ears it had been too long. Had she dozed off? What had she been doing? She glanced about, saw the spill and shards. Another cup. Damn.

"What is it, Regina? Why are you here?"

Her second assistant pointed at the band Klarce wore on her wrist. She followed the younger woman's gaze, saw the blinking light and muttered a curse.

"Damn. Low enough to trigger the monitor, eh?"

"Yes, ma'am." Regina offered her a pair of tablets and a cup of water.

She took her meds, waving off the water and swallowing them dry, noting the larger than normal dose. It would help her return to baseline in the short run but cause her to sleep more than she'd like later on. Perhaps that was just as well. She let her eyes close and waited for the first trickle of the drug into her system, counting off the seconds. She hadn't yet reached a hundred when some of the fog cleared from her mind. Good. There was work to do. She opened her eyes to find her assistant still standing there.

"What?"

"There's a call for you from above."

"Regarding?"

"A ship. 'Nestwhistle' summoned the duty officer on Ulmazh with the news. A ship is headed to the portal. She estimates it's still five days out."

Klarce frowned. Nestwhistle was the code name of one of the agents currently floating adrift in little more than a cargo container retrofitted with pressure and atmosphere, limited hydroponics and waste recycling. Ethernauts called them luxury pods, and this one hung on the other side of the Alliance's portal in Barsk's star system. Nestwhistle's monitoring assignment gave them advance notice of anything coming their way.

"What of it? The Alliance sends its ships through to rendezvous with the station every season. Has it deviated from routine procedures for passage into the system?"

"No, ma'am, but it's not a materials transport ship, which is what prompted the agent to contact Ulmazh, and why they in turn sent word down to you. She says the ship's call signal identifies it as the same senatorial craft as has visited regularly for seven years. Passive imaging from Nestwhistle's sensory arrays scattered throughout that system confirms this."

Yes, and that was another problem that would be resolved with the passing of the senator Jorl. No senator, no need for a private yacht dropping in twice a year, piloted by who knew what race. She'd seen the images. The luxury vessel never landed, oh no. Instead it flouted the spirit of the Compact while observing the letter of the treaty. Its occupants never stepped off onto Barsk soil, preferring to float like a boat just offshore.

Klarce felt in possession of most of her faculties once more. She waved Regina away with her trunk. "There's nothing unusual about that. It visits twice a year, late every dark and early in wind. Dependable as the seasons themselves."

"Yes, ma'am. Only . . . we've just started flood."

And so it was. Damn. She brought the nubs of her trunk up and pinched at the spot between her eyes. Meds or not, she needed to think.

"Is it following its usual heading and speed?"

Regina nodded.

"So, not in a hurry, not drawing any extra attention to itself other than coming in off schedule. Not that there's any reason it should suspect its being tracked. Assuming nothing changes, once it's through the portal how long until it's due to break atmosphere here?"

Her assistant consulted a handscreen. "An additional four days. A total of nine days from now."

"All right. Well, don't just stand there, get me some koph, girl."

"Koph? Ma'am, you shouldn't ingest that so soon after your other meds. It's contraindicated—"

"So is killing an Alliance senator when his ship is paying a surprise visit, but there's nothing else for it. I have to Speak to our field agent on Keslo and rescind my previous instructions. What was her name?"

Regina consulted her device again, tapping at it with her nubs. "Dabni. Her cover has her as a clerk in a bookshop."

Klarce waved the specifics away with her trunk. "I don't care what her damn job is. I just need her name so I can pull a signature from the index."

"Yes, ma'am. I just thought . . . well, some details would facilitate the summoning—"

"I spoke with her earlier today. There are enough of her nefshons still lingering near me to pull her in quickly, if you would stop dawdling and fetch me the koph!"

"But, ma'am, the meds. Surely another member of the Quick Council can contact her if the need is so pressing."

"I told you, damn the meds! She won't accept the change in orders from anyone else, and I can't allow myself the luxury of waiting for my body to metabolize my medication. But . . . fetch me a snack from the kitchen. Some food in my system will help a bit, albeit after the fact. But the koph first. And hurry, girl. It may be too late as it is."

~~~~~

BY the time Temmel arrived for his morning shift the deed was done. Klarce didn't believe in luck, but she nonetheless felt grateful for whatever random factor had stayed the agent's hand from delivering the meme that would trigger a physicality cascade in this senator Jorl. Doubtless an explanation for the delay would be included in Dabni's report but that didn't matter now. Not for the first time, Klarce wondered if his involvement with the Alliance government was why Margda had chosen him so long ago, but nothing he'd done while in office was especially unusual, not for a senator nor an academician. There had to be something else.

Meanwhile, Regina had placed a bowl of her favorite mixed fruit near to hand, cleaned up the broken crockery, brewed a new pot of tea, and placed the sole surviving mate out of the set of six cups on the desk within easy reach. Head pounding as the koph warred with the meds that kept her alive, Klarce had rested her head on the desk, closed her eyes, and sampled tea and fruit with her trunk. At some point in the process she passed into sleep.

"Ma'am?" Temmel's voice had acquired the timidity that defined Regina. Not a good sign. She opened one eye and found her primary assistant standing over her.

"What?"

"Sind has convened the Full Council. Your presence is required."

"Damn. Do I have time to bathe first?"

"No, ma'am. Regina and I conferred and determined it was better to let you use that time sleeping. Your pardon if we erred in our concern."

"No, it's fine. The dead won't be aware of how I smell and won't care, and if Sind doesn't like it he has only himself to blame." She lifted her head from the desk. The room swam only a bit. "I don't suppose this is a session I can attend remotely?"

Temmel's ears dropped back aghast. "Ma'am! This is the Full Council."

She pushed away from the desk and rose to her feet. "Oh please, it's not like I'd be the only one there who wasn't corporeal. But never mind. Just wishful thinking. Very well, let's go see what Sind thinks is so important."

For the second time in less than two days she made her way to the council chamber. Temmel hurried after her, juggling an assortment of data records, recording equipment, and packets of koph. This time, Sind wasn't waiting for her outside the door. She entered to find him oblivious to her arrival, his head down on the table much as hers had recently rested on her desk. Melko, the Lox who was the third of the four members of the Quick Council occupied a chair on the other end of the room from Sind and was similarly at rest. She stepped to him first and placed a hand on his shoulder. With no transition he opened his eyes and gave her a smile that spoke of relief mixed with fear. She gave his shoulder a squeeze, offering reassurance for a concern she hadn't learned of yet. But Melko was a kindly soul. He had the talent and the intellect for the position, but his passion was research not governance; making policy invariably left him aquiver.

Klarce moved around the room, passing a quartet of Speakers arrayed in hammocks strung along the back wall. She knew them all. Each possessed the high clearance levels necessary to do the work of the Full Council. Each lay in a state like deep sleep. Her ears twitched. This was *not* the way things were done. She continued her circuit, passing an empty chair that should have held Kissel, the final member of the Quick Council. Klarce nodded to Temmel who had begun setting up further down the table from Sind. When she reached the senior member of the Quick Council she employed a kick to his shin rather than a gentle touch to gain his attention. His eyes jerked open more violently than Melko's. Perhaps she'd kicked the old man too hard.

"You started without me?" She frowned at Sind. Hadn't she taken a problem off his hands less than a day ago? Why was he pulling this nonsense now.

"The dead needed to be briefed."

"Then why isn't Kissel here? It's not a 'Full' Council without him."

"He's in surgery. He'll join us when he can."

"And you couldn't wait? I would have happily slept a while longer."

"This isn't the time to be petulant, Klarce. This may be a critical juncture."

"This is about the ship?"

"It is."

"Then why the rush? It's days out by all accounts."

"I'll explain in council. Sit. Your assistant has your koph ready."

"Damn it, Sind. I don't need more koph in me just now. My body's still unhappy with the dose from earlier this morning. You knew that. This could have waited."

"I felt otherwise. Please, you'll understand soon."

Scowling, Klarce seated herself where Temmel had placed the ceremonial koph used for Full Council sessions, formulated to activate perceptions of nefshons more quickly while also containing a small enough dose that wouldn't allow the user to control the particles for long. But that wasn't needed. The foursome of Speakers lining the wall were doing the summoning. She and Sind and Melko—and presumably Kissel, if and when he staggered in from his operating theater—only needed enough of the drug to let them see the results. She popped it into her mouth, folded her arms on the table, and again lowered her head and closed her eyes.

Quickly the nefshons showed themselves. She sat alert and upright in her seat in an imaginary scenario, an identical conference chamber that existed as shared illusion in a mindspace provided by someone else. Sind and Melko nodded in silent greeting as her personal construct took form. The quartet of junior Speakers existed as little more than shadows on the back wall. Their presence wasn't important. Rather, each had summoned one of the other members of the Full Council. Everyone in the room was a Speaker; the ability to manipulate nefshons was a requirement of the job.

But the other half of the council had all died long years past. Each had served on the Quick Council while alive, and these four had been among the best, invited back to share their wisdom even beyond death. The first time she'd participated in Full Council, Klarce had been intimidated to be in their presence. Now she knew them as colleagues. Brilliant, dead for centuries, but individuals like herself who served the Caudex and had the best interest of Barsk guiding them.

"Bring me up to speed," she said. "What have I missed?"

"The Alliance ship associated with Margda's chosen has arrived out of schedule." This from Genz, speaking first as seniormost of the Full Council.

The nefshon construct of Soosh, dead three hundred years, took up the narrative. "We have been informed that yesterday this Jorl ben Tral made contact with one of the island's dead Speakers. Standard protocols were followed but proved ineffective."

"Which is why, after consultation with Sind, I instructed our agent on the scene to distribute a meme to initiate a physicality cascade. The timing of his ship's appearance is disturbing but cannot be related to his discovery of a member of the Caudex. Nonetheless, prior to coming to this session I again contacted our agent and rescinded the order. No harm has been done."

"That's not why we're concerned," said Nirl, the youngest but also the most brilliant of the other side of the council. "Sind has intercepted a transmission from the vessel, relayed through the portal and on to the Aleph."

"What kind of transmission?"

"The Brady who serves this Jorl is not alone. Her cargo includes a Procy from Caluma. And that individual has a petition she intends to set before the senator. She wishes to present her case face to face."

Klarce shook her trunk from side to side. "What does that matter to us? Jorl is an academic and the least powerful member of the Committee of Information. What possible interest could a petition to him have for us?"

Genz regarded her with tired eyes. "Indeed, a reasonable enough interpretation. However the society in question is our own. The Procy intends to petition the senator from Keslo to allow non-Fant to settle on Barsk."

"What? That makes no sense. Toward what end?"

"That," said Sind, "is the question we must address. It's one thing to hide our operations from other Fant. We've had centuries to build the societal memes that allow us to proceed without detection and thus serve the best interests of our people. But the Caudex is still centuries from completing its work; we cannot yet commit to a final exodus."

"Outsiders will bring fresh eyes, newer and plentiful sensory technology, making it harder for us to hide. And hiding things in both plain sight and through illusion has been our way," said Nirl.

"And questions," added Marsh, the last of the dead council members, an Eleph who in his day had been a persuasive politician second only to Margda. "They will gaze upon the commonplace and ask questions that no Fant would think to ask, because they have not had the discontinuities that spark such thoughts shunted aside by cultural memes. Questions that we are not yet ready to entertain, and never want to respond to if the Alliance might hear the answers."

"So what are you suggesting? That my decision to rescind the order to take the senator's life was an error?"

"Less drama, please," said Marsh. "Killing is a last and extreme resort. We understand the urgency that drove the original decision, but if we can find another way, then the rest of the council would prefer not to take the life of another Fant."

Klarce nodded. "On that we are agreed. Then . . . what?"

"We must know more," said Sind. "Why did the Brady agree to bring this petitioner to Barsk? What are the particulars of her proposal? Is it even remotely possible for this historian-turned-senator to accomplish the thing, if he had the will?"

"So you're saying your intention is to 'wait and see.' How did this require an emergency session of the council?" Klarce didn't pretend to hide her irritation, even as she considered the toll this second round of koph would take on her body given the other meds in her system.

"No, there is another factor." Soosh looked like she wanted to spit. "The boy."

Klarce turned to stare at the dead Lox. "What boy?"

"I will not name him."

"The abomination?"

Nirl flinched. "I will not discuss such a one."

"That is precisely why we must. He comes and goes in this senator's home. They have been seen walking and talking together in public, numerous times."

"No one has seen any of this." Nirl's insistence bordered on strident.

"No one admits to seeing. But they see. Would you have this council turn a blind eye as well?" Soosh appeared to be arguing directly with Nirl at this point, and Klarce wondered how long they'd been going round and round on the issue, just prior to her arrival today, or was this an old feud?

"Would *you* have us turn away from tradition? From culture? This creature—do not call him a boy, it is no more a boy than this table is—does not intersect any aspect of Fant behavior. We do not apply the term abomination lightly, but we must respect it."

"I do respect it," said Soosh, and she turned back to Klarce. "Which is why the need for this session." She held up a hand and began ticking off her fingers. "A historian who has traveled beyond Barsk and lived among other races. An Aleph-Bearer who was foretold, some would say 'chosen,' by Margda herself, for purposes we cannot fathom. A senator with a seat on a critical committee, despite no formal election or history of any Eleph or Lox serving in the Alliance government. And finally, a Fant who sets aside our beliefs and traditions to not only consort with an abomination, but to educate it as well. There is too much here we cannot explain or account for. And the arrival of the Procy and her petition is one more anomaly too far."

"Which is why," said Genz, "That 'wait and see' will no longer suffice. We must prepare. Imagine all possible contingencies and have a plan in place for each."

FIFTEEN

FUTILITY ALL AROUND

DESPITE the season, despite this being only one of the island's ports, Fintz maintained a very active trade with dozens of surrounding islands, and as the morning brightened through the heavy rains, the pier where Pizlo knelt filled with people. No one spoke to him or sought to offer any assistance. Astonishing and unprecedented as the facts appeared, word that an abomination from another island had come to Fintz had spread far and wide. Eyes averted, they walked past him and went about their errands, each person wondering at the ill omen of two such creatures upon their shore.

Pizlo rose, the dead infant cradled in his arms, letting the rain wash away his tears. He stood, surrounded by denial, and rushed back up the pier to the main boardwalk of the harbor. He strode into the mass of people, scattering them with his presence and shouted.

"This is what you are. This is what you've done. I don't care that you won't answer me." He said the words over and over, his voice soft and hoarse from crying. It didn't matter that they refused to hear him. He accompanied the spoken message, pounding out an infrasonic beat that demanded attention like a lost child. They turned at that, driven by instinct hardwired into their cells, and then recoiled as conscious thought informed unconscious behavior. Abomination. Using their own humanity against them. If anything, they turned away from him even faster.

"You can pretend not to see or hear, but you do." Pizlo sobbed. "You know. *This* is part of your story, each and every one of you. You think yourselves the heroes of your tales, but explain that, tell me how that can be? What heroes embrace infanticide? What heroes laud neglect and suffering of a helpless newborn? Every last one of you is a baby killer by your inaction, your silent acquiescence." His words reached more than a hundred Fant, but they were all too busy turning away and denying his existence to react to what they heard.

Pizlo wandered back down the pier toward Jorl's boat. There was nowhere to go but home now. He had been so confident, armed with knowledge of the meta-story, the awareness that he was the hero of his life. He had identified the call to action, wavered, and then heeded it. He had embraced advice from his mentors. Leaving Keslo, the only home he had ever known surely counted as crossing the threshold into a new world. And he had been tested, pursuing the council, stealing their ink, achieving his goal. But that hadn't been his quest at all. Or if it was, it didn't matter. What satisfaction it might have brought him turned to ash when he'd found the abandoned infant.

He had always been different, always been the Abomination of Keslo. He knew the reasons for this; Tolta had never hidden it from him, and when he'd been old enough Jorl had explained the biology and the cruelty of that part of Fant culture. But even knowing the rhyme of it, he had never stopped to think that other islands might hold other abominations. "One in a million" Jorl had called him, but Barsk's archipelagos were home to five and a half million Eleph and Lox. Surely that meant that other biological mistakes happened around him. Yes, he was a rarity. Jorl said that in all the history of Barsk, only a handful had lived even a few years. But here he was, Pizlo, a fourteen-year-old, older than any of his kind had any right to be. A fluke among flukes.

Tracking and finding the council, acquiring the ink to render his moons had been a false quest. What if all along his destiny had been to seek out others like himself? What if his purpose was to arrive at the moment some city abandoned a living abomination to the elements instead of placing the baby in its mother's arms? Had he reached Fintz two days earlier might he have provided assistance? Was there some medical aid he might have brought to change the outcome? Or even the simple favor of his regard, the warmth of his own body cradling the infant, could that have saved it from its own genetic anomalies?

The realization that others like him lived and died exploded everything he thought he knew. It meant he didn't need to be alone. All of the Archetype of Man's stories of heroes and isolation came to him, and many heroes had found in the course of their own journeys the friend or companion that completed them and gave meaning and purpose. Had he, then, arrived too late? Surely if he had been Sundance then the broken newborn he carried could not be Butch. If he was Gilgamesh, how could Enkidu be dead before they even met?

But no, Pizlo knew, really understood, that it was futile to wonder such things. His own history notwithstanding, abominations did not survive. The timing of his arrival wouldn't have made a difference. He was alone, and no quest could change that.

While a handful of nearby dockworkers studiously *didn't* watch him he boarded Jorl's boat and at last set his burden down. If the people of Fintz didn't want their child while it lived, they didn't deserve the corpse. Pizlo ascended to the wheelhouse, accessed the controls, and set a course for Keslo. He wasn't a hero, and he just wanted to go home.

~~~~~

BARSK had a marine force. Boat theft was uncommon and piracy nonexistent. But plenty of drunken bachelors managed to strand themselves between islands, either running out of fuel if their craft had an engine or more commonly losing their oars or even falling overboard because of foolishness. And accidents happened, particularly given the extremes of the weather. Vessels capsized, or sometimes rammed one another when visibility dwindled and the ocean took matters into its own hands. The marines patrolled and responded quickly and efficiently. Many a Fant had a tale of being fished out of the water and owed their lives to those men and women.

Charting a direct course to Keslo and traveling at full speed, Pizlo drew the attention of his archipelago's marines. Repeatedly they flagged him to slow down. He ignored them. They hailed him to stop. He didn't and simply raced onward. Twice, marines in a smaller, swifter craft pulled alongside him, threatening to grapple their own boats to his with the intention to impound his vessel and arrest him pending trial, but each time he simply glared at them from the wheelhouse and within moments they fell away. Once the marines recognized him for an abomination they couldn't demand he stop, couldn't arrest him. Impressively, they followed him, perhaps telling themselves they didn't so much pursue an abomination but rather a vessel in distress.

In two days he reached Keslo. As he docked the boat back in

Jorl's slip the marine escort put in at adjacent piers. There would be questions asked, obliquely at best. Pizlo gave no thought to how the harbormaster would explain any of it without talking about the unmentionable. He had other concerns. As he stepped onto the pier, the infant body once more in his arms, he couldn't bring himself to feel any guilt over the inconvenience his travels might have caused anyone. In the scope of things, it just didn't rate.

He ignored the routes that would take him up into the Civilized Wood and instead made his own path ever deeper into the Shadow Dwell. The boles of every meta-tree acknowledged his presence in hushed voices within his mind. Every rock and stream greeted him somberly. The small creatures that lived there in the island's darkest places scurried and raced around him but never paused and he continued on with determination. He knew every step one could take in the Shadow Dwell, had rambled through the mud and dark of each bit of it from his earliest days. All of it spoke to him, guiding him to his destination. And in time he came to the spot where Jorl had buried Arlo, where he had watched from hiding as his father's remains had been laid to rest. A cairn lay at the base of one of the city's meta-trees, Arlo's name carved into the wood. Pizlo set the tiny unnamed, unloved body down alongside Arlo's spot. He roamed a while, gathering stones from brooks and riverlets, and when he had enough he covered over the child. Then he raised his head, gazed up as if through the forest and clouds to where Telko would hang in the sky.

"This could have been me here," he said. "If I had died instead of lived, perhaps Arlo and Tolta would have given me a grave. It would have shocked everyone in Keslo, but surely no more than they did by acknowledging me as theirs. I don't know if that's ever happened before. I never thought to ask. Jorl might know. Fintz doesn't deserve this child. Keslo neither. Probably no island does.

But . . . Arlo does. And so it's here now. And . . . and that's all I have to say. People are all so stupid. Why are we so stupid?"

Safely hidden, Telko did not reply. And honestly, Pizlo didn't want an answer anyway.

SIXTEEN

A COMMITTEE OF ONE

~~~~~~

JORL'S workspace contained an old desk that he had acquired when a physiologist he'd once met at a faculty mixer had decided to sell off all his belongings and use the resulting cash to travel somewhere far away and start over. He'd told Jorl the desk had been his grandfather's, an artist of insatiable appetites that ranged from the sweet and savory to the carnal and unsavory. Allegedly, the desk had been an altar of sorts, the physiologist's grandfather supposedly performing acrobatic acts with both men and women upon its broad surface. Upon taking possession of the desk, Jorl had it disinfected, sanded, and refinished with multiple layers of resin before moving it into his home.

As he had no intention of using its surface as a sex platform, he commissioned the construction of a matching hutch, a structure of shelves and cubbies and compartments where he could sort and file various projects, keep reams of paper and cups of fresh ink bamboo, hide snacks away for later consumption (the hiding becoming a critical feature with Pizlo in his life), and once upon a time store a supply of koph. He no longer needed koph in order to see nefshons. The drug Arlo had died to protect remained in his system, constantly reactivating the ability far better than an application of koph ever could. Instead of koph that cabinet now contained the latest in Alliance communications technology, a device that connected to a relay in the space station in orbit above Zlorka and from there to every inhabited planet in the galaxy. As the juniormost member of the Committee of Information, he had access to every published book and article, magazine and flim, recording and vid that existed in the Alliance, assuming he could figure out how to find it in the arcane and necessarily complex filing system that had grown up piecemeal as different administrations attempted upgrades and streamlining of the library.

It also served as a more mundane method than Speaking for conversing with his fellow senators, would-be petitioners, and Druz. Jorl had been sitting in his hammock, jotting down some thoughts on his aborted attempt to Speak with Fisco, the Speaker from Belp who had sailed off more than two centuries ago. Being summoned hadn't surprised her, as it had every other Speaker of the past that he'd contacted for his project. Indeed, the old woman had reacted as if she were already in the middle of someone else's summoning when he'd reached her, giving a lecture of some kind. That made no sense. Nor did the name she'd mentioned and bid him forget. Caudex. Had he misheard or was the elderly Lox attempting to cover a slip? The only other interpretation he could imagine involved Fisco having slipped into senility at the end of her long life and somehow believed herself to be part of the roots and stem of a plant. It made no sense. Jorl'd set the question aside for a time, allowing it to turn over in the back of his mind while he focused his attention on other concerns, but nothing satisfactory had emerged and he was on the verge of summoning her again when the transceiver hidden in his desk called for his attention.

Druz was signaling him, and from the pattern of the call's tone she was in the star system. Except . . . she wasn't supposed to be, not for another season.

"Attend," he said to the air in front of him, shoving aside the pages of his notes and resting his elbows on his desk and his head in his hands. "Open the incoming circuit and record." The device behind the cabinet door gave a faint ping in response and implemented his directives.

"Druz, is everything all right? I didn't expect you until wind. You're supposed to be making a circuit of Alliance worlds and scheduling appointments for me."

An image of his assistant took shape above his desk. It wasn't as clear and realistic as he'd expect from even the most inexperienced of Speakers to create from their imaginations and render in nefshon space. Rather it was made of light and sound generated by the Sloth and transmitted from her ship. Silence answered him, but that was to be expected with Druz. He'd long since learned that the Sloth's carefully prepared speeches needed pauses before and after. Regular conversation, when he could convince her to speak to him as just an ordinary individual and not as the senator she served, ran more casually, but whatever had brought her through the system's portal wouldn't be ordinary and he'd just have to endure the delays that were part of her nature.

Eventually, she spoke. "Greetings, Senator. I apologize for the unscheduled call. Has my intrusion occurred during an acceptable time? I am still several days out from Barsk and can call back at a more convenient moment if you'd prefer."

"This is fine. I'm fine. Well, no, actually, I'm curious what you're doing here."

"Yes, sir. Understandably so. As you already surmised, prior to diverting to Barsk ahead of schedule I was following your last directive, traveling among the worlds of the Alliance and screening potential petitioners. As established, I redirected those who could find better support and assistance through other, lesser, governmental channels and assigning priority ratings to the few who remained and scheduling them for you to meet using your, ah, gifts. I trust you've been receiving my field notes and reports?"

"I have. And I've been meeting from here with those you've scheduled in my offices throughout the Alliance worlds. What's come up to change that? I've had no new report."

Another pause and then, "No, sir. The circumstances have been peculiar, and I'm still writing it up. I'll have it for you before we reach Barsk."

"We?" Jorl's ears fanned with a trace of concern.

"Yes, sir. One of the petitioners I met with presented a peculiar observation along with her request to meet with you."

"Peculiar in what way, Druz. I'm not following."

"Yes, well, your special techniques notwithstanding, sir, this individual—a Procy by the name of Abenaki—had deduced that you would not actually be present at your scheduled meeting with her. I reviewed the facts of her arguments and they were quite convincing, though I'm sure you'll want to hear it from her yourself. In any case, as her petition did meet the criteria for your hearing, and as it didn't seem prudent to turn her loose with the results of her deductions, and as she'd actually brought up the matter of your lack of genuine presence as an argument for allowing her to meet with you directly . . . well, it seemed best to depart from my schedule and transport her to you at once."

Jorl's ears dropped flat against the sides of his head in disbelief. "You're bringing a petitioner to Barsk? Are you mad?"

The silence that followed went on long enough that he wasn't sure if it was one of his Sloth's legendary pauses or if he'd offended her to the point of breaking off the call, but then he thought he could hear her clearing her throat as if to start again. When she spoke, her tone was different, anxious. And she'd replaced her usual diffidence with excitement. "Senator . . . *Jorl* . . . I'm quite sane and this Raccoon's petition is truly something you'll want to hear face to face. If I have acted in error, well, then I can depart without awakening her and the meeting need not take place. You'll decide the proper course once you've had the opportunity to review my report. In the meantime, I'm transmitting all the backup documents to your location now."

"Wait, what do you mean *awaken*?"

"It did not seem prudent to allow her free access to your ship in the event I'd misjudged things and she intended some mischief or sabotage. I placed her in the medical suspension chamber in the ship's infirmary for the duration of the trip. From her perspective it will be as if she'd only gone to sleep the night before."

"Druz, that gear is for medical emergencies, not for transporting inconvenient passengers as if they were cargo."

"Yes, sir. But it seemed the best course, as I hope you'll agree once you've reviewed all the facts. In three days' time, it's my intention to set down in the waters a short distance from Keslo as I have in the past."

She stopped and Jorl waited, counting to himself, moving his trunk like a metronome to distract himself and give his assistant the time she needed. Something extraordinary was happening and, right or wrong, he'd have to deal with it in three days.

"Please review the documentation, sir. I'll leave a channel open in case you have any questions you wish me to address prior to touchdown. I should tell you, though, the Procy has said she won't answer any queries until she stands in front of you. I apologize for her rudeness. We'll be there soon, sir."

Which left him with no real answers and questions that wouldn't or couldn't be satisfied now.

"In three days then. Jorl out."

The image of Druz winked from existence. Jorl pulled a fresh sheet from a bin in the hutch and spoke aloud. "Attend," he said again, getting the device's attention. "Begin display of incoming reports. Normal scroll." Immediately the air above his desk filled with the first page of the information his assistant had started sending. He snatched up a piece of ink bamboo in his trunk and began taking notes as he read.

THE senators of the Alliance maintained a rotating constituency. It tended to limit political decision-making and legislation that favored particular planets over others. This was even more true for the Committee of Information. Its twenty-five members had to represent all the worlds of the Alliance. Of necessity, these senators constantly moved from planet to planet, local offices where they could meet with constituents, hear petitioners, receive lobbyists. Vessels and assistants like Jorl had inherited came with the job and his colleagues spent a significant portion of their lives simply traveling from one senatorial suite to another.

Jorl's ability allowed him to do the job without leaving his home and in a fraction of the time. Unlike any other Speaker, he could perform multiple summonings at once, dividing his consciousness into as many separate pieces as needed.

In a typical day at the office, he might maintain multiple independent aspects of his awareness—just yesterday his agenda had required him to create eight of himself. And, much as he'd met with Welv in a mindspace replica of the Cynomy's office, so too had he spun images of the offices he kept for interviews on differ-

ent worlds. In eight separate rooms, behind eight desks, he by
turns listened, discussed, and even argued with a succession of
petitioners—who to their credit had overcome both their personal
philosophies and the labyrinthine requirements necessary to land
a meeting with him. None of them were Fant, none had previously
met a Fant, nor likely ever imagined doing so. Ambition trumped
racial prejudice and he was the newest, most recent member of the
senate's Committee of Information.

Not traveling from world to world and conducting several meetings at the same time had allowed Jorl to complete most of his
senatorial obligations at one go every tenday. Druz handled the
particulars of his schedule, screening petitioners and providing
background details sufficient for him to summon them into his
mindscape. After each of these marathon sessions Jorl typically
slept most of the following day. He didn't find the manipulation
of all the nefshons or the juxtaposition of multiple versions of himself tiring. Rather, it was the concentrated punch of so many
pleading, cajoling, desperate individuals who saw him as their immediate salvation that drained him.

And now, for reasons that were annoyingly absent from her reports, Druz was bringing one of them directly to him.

⁓

OVER the next couple of days Jorl made several trips to various
merchants, placing orders for foodstuffs, fuel, and bits of gear.
He arranged for all of it to be delivered down through the Civilized Wood to the harbor where he kept the boat that Phloda, the
provost at the university on Zlorka, had allowed him to retain
some years back. He wasn't much of a sailor and mostly only
used it twice a year to meet Druz. By design, none of the edibles
he'd arranged for were perishable. He'd pick up something fresh

from Hearne, a vendor at the dock, before he took the boat out; rather, acquiring the supplies was an exercise in restocking what Pizlo had invariably acquired during his frequent raids.

Over these days, Druz sent regular updates, not just the final particulars of her report but also specifics of her progress traveling insystem. The final message had reached him late last night and specified the precise time of her arrival. In the morning, Jorl traveled by funicular from Keslo's transit center down to the Shadow Dwell and the harbor beyond. He had the car to himself and used the slow trip from forest into rain to review what he knew about Raccoons. Based on the most recent census information he had downloaded from his senatorial archives, one variety or another of Procy could be found on fully half of the Alliance's four thousand worlds. As a race, they tended to get along well with everyone, generally excelled at technological innovation and sculpture, and adapted their own diets to the regional or preferred cuisine of the dominant people wherever they lived. That last point came in handy as he exited the funicular at its base, stopping at a food stand. He'd long since established a traditional meal for these visits, finding a common assortment of shoots, buds, and leaves that both he and Druz favored. He added an assortment of nuts and berries—mostly for his uninvited Raccoon guest—before leaving the protection of overhangs and awnings and continuing on to the docks through the unrelenting deluge that defined the season of flood.

The harbormaster's young son, a likable boy barely a year out of his mother's house, had supervised the delivery of his ordered goods to the berth where his boat was moored, and as Jorl approached he observed the youth jumping nimbly back and forth from the surface of the pier to the boat's deck, each time carrying a different mesh bag of supplies, heedless of the downpour.

Frowning, Jorl arrived in time to pick up one of the remaining bags. "Chisulo, you don't have to do that. I'd have taken care of it."

"No disrespect, sir, but that's not so. You ordered all this, right? And paid for delivery?"

"Yes, but just to the dock. Getting them on my boat is my problem."

Chisulo shook his head, ears flapping wildly with his denial. "I looked at the bills of lading. They all specify your boat as the address, not the dock's main address."

Jorl sighed. "That may be, but they're not allowed to set foot on any of the boats. That's your mother's rules."

"Too true, sir. Only owners and guests of owners can come and go, excepting of course my ma, or whoever she leaves in charge. And seeing as how that's me just now, it falls to me to finish the delivery."

"But . . ." Jorl let his words trail off. Chisulo had followed his own line of logic that didn't have room for the alternate possibility of just leaving the stack of bags for a boat's owner to handle once they arrived. The boy had likely spent more time on or around boats than in the meta-trees of the Civilized Wood, and knew the value of leaving nothing unsecured. Jorl settled instead for a gesture of his trunk and a muttered "Thanks" and boarded the boat himself.

"You want, I can stow everything below decks, sir. Get it all tied down for you."

"That'd be a great help, thank you. The packaged food can go anywhere you find space for it in the galley. The other supplies can all go in the utility chest in one of the benches. I'll keep the fresh food with me."

"I'm on it." Chisulo wrapped a hand around a third of the bags' straps, did the same with his second hand, and grabbed the rest in his trunk. He nodded once and vanished below, leaving Jorl to step into the wheelhouse and upload Druz's coordinates to the boat's navigation system. As he finished, Chisulo popped up behind him.

"You taking her out far, sir? It's a good craft, I know, and with lots more gadgets than most, but you don't normally sail in flood."

"Not far, Chisulo. Not even as far as another island. Just out into open water for a span. No need to worry, I'll be back before nightfall."

"Yes, sir. I'll keep an eye out for you then. Safe travels."

~~~~~

SEASONED sailors never traveled between archipelagos during flood. Fisherfolk cast their nets closer to their native islands. Even the traffic between adjacent islands dwindled in this kind of weather. Jorl knew better than to travel in this season and he intended to make sure Druz understood this, too. He had zero visibility, and if not for the navigational computer and Druz's satellite coordinates he'd never have found the yacht until he'd rammed it.

The protocol they followed required Druz to set the yacht down in the water far enough away from Keslo that it would have been unseen by anyone on the shore in even the clearest weather. The pounding of rain on the wheelhouse and the gentle thrum of the engines provided the only sound, the roll of the open water the only sense of motion. A counter on the navigation display assured him he moved ever closer to his destination at good speed. A proximity alert gave him time to cut the boat's engines and continue forward by momentum until the yacht loomed over him and he floated through the gate of its flooded cargo hold. He dropped anchor and moved to the deck, pausing to pick up the parcels containing their meal.

"Welcome, Senator!" Druz's familiar voice called out to him. He fanned his ears, orienting on the sound, stepped to the bow and cast her a line. "Got it." Moments later his boat rocked gently forward and came to rest at an internal mooring. Druz stood upon a gantry level with his deck and greeted him.

"Good to see you again, Senator." She stood waiting with a bath sheet.

Jorl crossed from boat to ship, took the towel, and handed over their lunch. With a nod for her to lead the way, he followed his assistant out of the hold. "And you, of course. Now, what could possibly be so important to bring you here a season early?"

"I really think you should hear that from the Procy herself."

"I gathered as much from the lack in your reports. What's her status?"

"She awakened from suspension without incident. A touch groggy at first, but that passed after she'd hydrated."

"And she's where now?"

"Awaiting your pleasure in the guest parlor, sir."

Seven years ago Jorl would have rolled his eyes and trumpeted at the absurdity of a spacecraft having a parlor, let alone the pair of them this ship enjoyed. His first experience with extra-planetary vessels had been the Patrol craft commanded by the first Sloth he'd ever met, and he seriously doubted if Brady-Captain Hrum had much more luxurious space for space's own sake to her cabin than the spartan quarters he'd been required to squeeze into and share with a trio of ensigns. But that ship had claimed a crew of thirty and was less than half the size of the yacht he'd inherited from his predecessor.

Manners drilled into him since he was ear-high surfaced as they strode through the ship. "I hope you've made her comfortable, Druz. Unwelcome as I expect I'll find her to be, she's still a guest."

"Yes, sir. I left her just a few moments ago. She's preparing tea for the two of you."

"Why is a guest preparing tea?"

"She insisted. I believe that now that she's about to meet with you, the bluster that carried her this far has deserted her and she finds the rituals of preparation soothing."

Tea wasn't his favorite beverage, but the warmth of it would be welcome after the unseasonal trip, even so brief as it was. At the entrance to the guest parlor he handed the towel back to Druz. "This is beyond irregular, Druz. Is there anything useful you care to tell me before I meet this Raccoon, or are you determined to keep the entire thing a mystery."

"Her name is Abenaki. As for the rest, it's hers to tell."

Jorl snorted, shook his ears back, and stepped into the room leaving his unassisting assistant in the corridor.

The guest parlor was a simple room, even by the opulent standards of the yacht. A semi-circular couch faced the entrance, its broad seat and low back able to offer a comfortable place to any of the Alliance's races. A low table hovered in front of the couch, suspended from the ceiling so as to accommodate long or short legs of the couch's occupants. As expected, a tea service lay upon the table and a Procy sat upon the couch. The latter jumped to her feet before he'd finished closing the door behind him.

"Senator Jorl! An honor to meet you. Truly, a singular event in my life." She rushed forward and caught herself barely a trunk's length from him, clutching her right hand in her left, fingers dancing.

"My assistant tells me you're called Abenaki. Is that right?"

"Perfectly correct."

"Good. Good. Names are important things. Don't you agree?"

"I do, yes. Critical things."

"Yes, indeed. As are . . . policies and procedures. Mine include meeting petitioners in one of my planetary offices. And yet, here you are, an unexpected guest on my ship, having endured a most irregular passage, and arriving at an unexpected time. Tell me, Abenaki, why are you here instead of meeting with me in the proper way and the proper place?"

The Procy's manual fidgeting increased. Among the materials Druz had forwarded him over the past days was a vidlog of several casual conversations she'd had with this guest prior to storing her in medical suspension. The logs allowed Jorl to become acquainted with Abenaki's appearance, the timbre of her voice, the rhythm of her movements small and large. Those movements, from her general nervousness to a slump in her posture, were different in the moment. More obviously though was that sometime today since her awakening and before his arrival she had inexplicably powdered portions of her facial fur, blending the black mask pattern common to all Raccoons into a uniform silver grey. If it had significance, cultural or otherwise, Jorl didn't understand it.

"May I speak frankly, Senator?"

"I wish you would. But please, let's sit first. Some tea would be welcome."

They stepped to the couch and sat, leaving plenty of space between them so each could partially turn and look at the other. Without waiting, Jorl took up the tea pot and poured for them both. They drank in silence, Jorl holding himself from saying anything further, certain that the Procy would not speak first even as whatever mainspring had driven her wound ever tighter and tighter. He finished his cup, felt the warmth lighten his mood, and refilled it as he settled in for the mystery that had so entranced Druz.

"Now then, tell me why this meeting isn't taking place in one of my offices closer to your home."

"Because you wouldn't be there, Senator."

"Excuse me?"

"I've done my research. I know you routinely meet with petitioners in offices throughout the Alliance, and I actually had put in for an appointment. But when I understood that the meetings wouldn't really be face to face, I canceled the request."

"How do you mean, not 'face to face'?"

"Senator, were I to have met with you in your office on my homeworld of Caluma, it's clear you wouldn't have really been there. Not in that room, certainly not in the city, and arguably nowhere on Caluma at all."

Jorl smiled, recalled that most non-Fant wouldn't recognize the crinkling around the eyes and wouldn't be watching the edges of his mouth as they avoided looking at his trunk. He set his teacup down and lifted his hands above the level of the table, palms upward, gesturing innocently. "Where do you imagine I would be then?"

The Procy lifted her own hands and delicately rubbed at her nose with tiny fingers. "The travel itineraries of senators is not public knowledge."

"That's a security protocol," acknowledged Jorl. "It's been that way for far longer than I've been in the senate."

"Indeed. And having your own vessel suitable for interplanetary travel—" She paused, glanced around with approval at their surroundings before continuing. "—is likewise part of that protocol. As is the mandated service and inspection schedule for that vessel."

"Service and inspection?"

The Raccoon waggled her fingers and cut him off. "That information, while not precisely public, can be inferred by tracking other data at licensed facilities and tracing ships that don't enjoy senatorial security blackouts. Based on my analyses, your ship put in for a full diagnostic at a facility at Dawn some twenty-seven days before I boarded. Even assuming the most routine and brief of maintenance operations, this ship could not have delivered you from Dawn to Caluma prior to the day after tomorrow."

"And how is that significant?"

"In two ways. First, that's when my appointment was scheduled for, before I canceled it."

Jorl made a mental note to alert the fellow members of his committee to the roundabout breach of the security protocols. His personal craft *had* been in an engineering bay on Dawn at the time the Procy referenced. He recalled speaking with Druz on that occasion, using the same technique that allowed him to take meetings on other worlds.

"And what makes you think that I couldn't have arrived on Caluma *before* my ship went in for maintenance?"

"That's the second reason. Twenty days ago you met with a colleague of mine in your office on Marbalarma. And even assuming you departed the moment that meeting ended and went straight through to Caluma, you'd still have needed a day more than the physics allows for."

"I see. And so you conclude that I wouldn't have been there for the scheduled meeting?"

She shrugged, hands fidgeting again and then stopping when she noticed them. "That's my best guess, though I suppose it could be that you were never on Marbalarma, and thus *could* have arrived to Caluma prior to your ship's trip to Dawn. Though, if that's the case, parsimony would suggest that you weren't there for that meeting, either. And of course, the fact that you're here on Barsk, which is the opposite direction from both Marbalarma and Caluma, well that just provides further proof, however circumstantial."

"I must say, this is the most interesting proposition anyone has brought before me in some time. But without regard to the veracity of it, is there a point? Surely you didn't endure the rigors needed to get a meeting with me just to cancel it and travel to Barsk to tell me I wasn't actually going to meet with you."

"No, sir. All of this was just to get your attention. I've no doubt that you hear endless proposals, many of merit, but I wanted my pitch to stand out and capture your imagination."

Jorl frowned. "I see. Well, you've achieved your goal. You're here now, whether I like it or not. You have my undivided attention. What exactly is it you want from me?"

Abenaki nodded. Her hands danced, fingers flying almost faster than the eye could track. She took a deep breath and her entire body froze with a preternatural stillness. She let out her breath and just sat a moment, gazing at her cup. When she set it down, her movements were slow and deliberate, much as she'd shown on Druz's vids. No trace remained of the nervous energy that had defined her since he'd stepped into the room.

"Senator Jorl, with respect, sir, I represent a consortium of Raccoons who want to emigrate to another planet, one where no Raccoon has ever been."

Jorl's ears fanned in surprise. With rare exception, and excluding the inhabitants of Barsk, Alliance citizens, whether individually or in groups, were free to relocate to whatever world they wished. "Emigration is hardly within the purview of the Committee of Information. I don't see how I'm apt to be of much help."

"On the contrary, you're the only one who could help. You're the only Fant with any governmental involvement."

"And what does my race have to do with your desire to move to a new world?"

"Everything, Senator. The world we want to move to is Barsk."

After seven years of listening to lobbyists and representatives of every special interest group in the Alliance, Jorl had come to believe that nothing he heard in any of his offices could surprise him. The Procy had just proven him wrong. If this is what she'd told Druz, no wonder the Brady had brought her to him. But . . . revolutionary though the idea was, it was also pointless. He stared at her in silence for a moment as he recovered his wits and said, "Barsk is a closed world."

"That's exactly why we want to relocate there."

Jorl waggled the tip of his trunk from side to side. "I don't follow."

"Senator, are you familiar with the Quality of Life Commission?"

The Fant nodded. The QLC had existed for hundreds of years, gathering long-range survey data across the thousands of planets of the Alliance. His predecessors on the Committee of Information had routinely authorized the minimal request for funding it submitted annually. "Is your consortium connected with that commission?"

"Not directly, no. Their work is purely descriptive, whereas my people have taken their data and performed extensive meta-analyses with respect to global satisfaction and social hypothesis testing."

Jorl blinked. He understood all of the Raccoon's words individually and in small groupings, but the entire phrase rang like something a graduate student might try to pass off as insight in the absence of substance during a dissertation defense. "Meaning?"

"Let me back up," said the Procy. "Throughout the Alliance, approximately eighty percent of planets are what we call "mixed worlds," containing cities in which ten or more different sapient races coexist. Of the remaining twenty percent, more than half are moving in that direction and have one or more cities with at least five merged populations. That leaves less than thirty planets with four or fewer distinct sapient races upon them, all of them worlds that have been settled sometime in the past millennium. Only five of these consist of a single people, and of these only Barsk has been inhabited for more than three hundred years."

"The Fant are not a single people, Abenaki. The Eleph and Lox that reside on Barsk are two separate races."

"I'm aware of this, Senator, but it's a distinction that is not appreciated anywhere else in the Alliance. But you make my point by referring to both by the common term *Fant*. Pragmatically, both races are so unlike any others and so like one another as to make no difference."

"And what precisely is your point?"

"I'm getting there, please, bear with me. Among its measures, the QLC assesses individuals' sense of self-worth, overall happiness, psychological well-being, and social and environmental relationships. One version or another has been used on every world in the Alliance, repeatedly, in some instances going back more than six hundred years to the commission's founding. And one of its most consistent findings has been that sapient beings show higher scores across all levels on worlds with a greater mix of races. Moreover, in places where we've had data from worlds moving to more diverse populations, these levels increase across the board."

"Are you suggesting that the people of Barsk are somehow lacking in their happiness or psychological well-being?"

"No, Senator, I'm saying that the quality of their lives would be enhanced by the presence of greater variation among the world's inhabitants, and that they in turn would enhance the experience of those who shared their planet."

"You're saying that the presence of Procy on Barsk will improve the existence of the Lox and Eleph already there?"

The Raccoon's fingers danced with excitement. "And vice versa. Ideally, I would suggest more than just Procy be allowed to establish themselves on Barsk, but since their isolation eight centuries ago the negative stereotyping of Fant has only grown; building a coalition with a strong racial identity who are willing to live among you hasn't been easy. But I've assembled one thousand people who are willing to pack up and move now, today. I believe that in as little as twenty years the resulting changes they effect, on both sides, will inspire other groups from other races to follow suit. If only Barsk will give us the chance. It's a win-win, Senator. Can you help make this happen?"

Jorl rose from the couch and began pacing the room's circumference as he flapped his ears in contemplation. The timing of the Raccoon's proposal, coming so soon after his conversation with Senator Welv pushed the bounds of coincidence and smacked of destiny. But even if Abenaki's idea accomplished some of the same ends as his own goals—blending the Fant with other races of the Alliance—he'd had his fill of destiny seven years earlier, and the taste of it soured in his mouth.

"You make a compelling argument," he said, drawing the words out as he argued pros and cons in his mind, "appealing to the best interests of both Barsk's people and the greater good of the Alliance."

"Thank you, Senator."

"Yes, but you've left off the rather significant stumbling block of our Compact."

"Surely your people could call a referendum and amend the provision that prohibits—"

Jorl cut her off with a wave of his trunk. "It's not so simple. The Compact is not a constitution, it's a treaty. It's not enough to convince the Fant; you'd need approval of the full senate, and likely a majority vote of all the worlds of the Alliance. There's probably procedure for such a thing, maybe even precedent, but I seriously doubt it could happen in this circumstance."

Abenaki slumped back against the couch, one hand rising to brush back tears and smudge the makeup blurring her natural mask. "But you see the value of it, don't you, Senator?"

"I do. And I promise I'll review all of your documentation personally. Bringing the Fant back into contact with the rest of the Alliance is a goal of mine as well. Perhaps I'll find a loophole that can deliver what we both desire."

The Raccoon's eyes welled up. "You mean that? Truly?"

"I do," said Jorl. "I'd like to review your data, as well as the details of the formal proposal you've put together. If you'll give those to Druz I'll begin going through them at once. And, when I've had a chance to digest the materials, I'd like to come and discuss them with you here at length. Assuming you don't mind being my guest a while longer. Awake this time."

The Procy swallowed back emotion. "Senator, there is nowhere else in all of space that I would rather be."

SEVENTEEN

COLLECTING THE DEAD

~~~~~~

RYNE stepped from the elevator into the Shadow Dwell. Turning and looking up, he saw what he hadn't noticed on the day of his arrival: an artificial enclosure grafted to the side of a meta-tree, providing a shaft for the spacious car that had just delivered him from this final Civilized Wood. Bernath waited for him a few steps away.

"I've been reading your reports with great interest," she said, stepping forward and linking her arm in his, much as she'd done that first time on the beach. "In hindsight, the applications are obvious, but impossible to generate without the precepts you've discovered."

He shrugged off her praise with a flap of his ears. "There's no such thing as discovery. That word makes it sound like the thing didn't exist before someone wrapped it in language and math. That's not how science works. We're talking about fundamental laws of energy and properties of matter. Gravity existed before someone spilled a sack of berries and saw them fall and bounce.

Nefshons existed before the Matriarch first ingested a drug that let her perceive them."

Bernath laughed. "Fine, I take your point. But until people— philosophers and physicists—generated models to describe these things, we didn't have the language, or the math, to talk about them."

"That's fair," said Ryne.

"Well then, the models you've crafted have sparked others to think about nefshons in fresh ways. That's all the more remarkable because the Caudex began that way, eschewing the limitations Margda imposed on Speakers and pushing beyond them. They've been at it for centuries and here you come along and show them something new."

Arm in arm they walked a slow path through the gloom of the Shadow Dwell. The quiet burble of streams and the rich smell of mud and muck gradually gave way to the murmur of waves and the scent of the ocean.

"Everyone keeps saying things like that to me, and I keep telling them that I don't know anything about Speakers or how they use nefshons. My work is on the properties they display, how that can be manipulated with respect to space-time."

"Which is precisely why I asked you to join me here today. I appreciate you breaking with your normal schedule to do so."

He shrugged. "I don't mind." And he didn't. This was the time of day when he might otherwise have walked the boardways of the Civilized Wood, wandering aimlessly as he mulled over his thoughts. He could do so well enough accompanying Bernath to the beach. So far, her conversation was only a minor distraction to the math that ran through his mind.

"You've never asked about my work," said Bernath. "Which neither surprises nor offends me. I'm one of three people who are generally responsible for meeting Dying scientists when they arrive, and in my experience fully half of you are so focused on your ideas that it doesn't occur to you to wonder about other people."

Ryne stumbled, the remark like a stone he'd tripped over. "I—huh. You're right. I hadn't looked at it that way. Uh . . . sorry?"

"Don't be. We need you for who you are, and as I said the behavior doesn't offend me. But I wanted to share the observation with you because I think we are engaged in similar tasks."

This time he came to a complete stop. Bernath continued a few steps ahead, her arm leaving his. She turned to face him, smiling and laughing softly. Was she laughing in general or laughing at him?

"Explain that to me, if you would."

"Happy to, but first, tell me how you would describe your work."

He frowned, ears flapping forward. "As I said, I'm studying the relationships between nefshon particles and how they manipulate—and can be manipulated by—space-time. It's a poly-dimensional model that holds up well through six dimensions and makes predictions through eight. Most of the work with nefshons never gets beyond three or four."

"You realize there are only twenty-seven people in the entire world who could even begin to follow the math that has led you to that description, and we have five of them here, and that's counting you and me."

She wasn't laughing at him then. Good. "You understand the math?"

"Not exactly. I said I can follow it. I can see when you point something out, some piece where you've already been. I can't run with it. But I understand enough to direct some of the engineers to create applications. And that's because I'd describe what you're doing very differently than you do."

Maybe it was the drug that Lolte had been giving him, maybe just the pleasure that this woman had been making the effort to read his work. He wanted to see what she thought of it, understand it through her eyes. "And what is that, exactly?"

"You're collecting the dead."

Ryne frowned. That wasn't anything like he expected. And surely wasn't true. He shook his head. "I don't follow."

"Speakers use nefshons to re-create enough of a person to in effect summon the dead. To . . . well, to speak to them. And when they're done, or when the drug that allows them to interact with nefshons is exhausted, that recovered decedent discorporates again and is lost."

He nodded. "That's a good choice of words," he said. "Like other forms of matter, albeit at a much more fundamental level, in the absence of an organizational focus nefshons will disperse."

"Well, to use your words, the Speakers are what supply that organizational focus. As far as anyone's been able to determine, they're the only thing that can."

"That's a fair description."

"It was, prior to your work. Your theories describe the underlying mechanism. But what Speakers do by imposing their will, working at cross purposes to the natural tendency of dispersion, from your work we now have a model that allows that organization to continue more or less indefinitely."

"I wouldn't go that far," Ryne protested. "Even at the subatomic level, you don't get perpetual motion."

"True, but from the time scale we're talking, little enough energy needs to be put into the system to keep it running. And so instead of a Speaker summoning the dead and then having to let them go in short order, we'll soon be able to capture and maintain that nefshon construct."

He was nodding now. "That's what you meant by 'collecting the dead' then? That's metaphorically true, but it doesn't begin to describe the math."

"No, but as most people aren't equipped to understand the math but can embrace the metaphor, it has more utility. Which brings us back to how we're similar."

They'd reached the edge of the Shadow Dwell. Bernath led him out from between the trees, but stopped short of taking him down onto the beach and into the rain. Through the downpour he could just make out a boat approaching the shore. It clicked.

"I collect the dead, and you collect the Dying?"

"And like with your models, it's not a permanent collection."

"Nothing's permanent," he said, and knew he was saying much more than words alone could convey.

"Indeed not. But for a time we put off the natural flow of things. Your constructs will be able to linger beyond the usual duration of a Speaker's session, and the men and women I bring in from this shore will enjoy more time and in some cases renewed life."

Ryne rolled the metaphor around. He could almost taste it, touch it. He'd often thought of the math that way, as something to be grappled with using all the senses and not just as thought experiments. He found himself looking at Bernath with renewed appreciation and made a mental note to seek her out for subsequent walks and conversations, assuming her own schedule allowed.

"You may not have the Speakers' gift, Ryne, but between us we make possible so much more than the world ever dared imagine. Our contributions are helping the Caudex to define the future."

EIGHTEEN
MOON THREADS

~~~~~~~~

EVERYTHING had changed, but no one on Keslo knew it, *yet*, and Pizlo himself still needed time to sort it out. He stopped at Jorl's home and accessed his link to the Alliance archive, hoping to find something to lift his mood. He managed a search for the top ten humorous plays as related by a previous generation of Jorl's committee. He found and memorized a story that involved a Marmo and a Myrm who'd had a huge misunderstanding and cost each other their respective hearts' desires because the Myrm couldn't see the simple truth of its own snout and the Marmo refused to learn to whistle. It had been a popular story many years ago on Sleipnir, a world that had almost no population of either Groundhogs or Anteaters, which may be why the people there found it so funny. Later, he'd told it to Rina and she had smiled throughout and laughed in all the right places. In the telling though, something inside Pizlo shifted to quiet and serious. Dark truths that he hadn't known lurked inside his skull had burbled their way to the surface of his awareness.

He tucked Rina into bed and left Tolta's house, passing like a ghost in one of the Archetype's stories. Pizlo wanted to curse, to swear, the urge coming upon him suddenly, and gave a mournful cry when he realized he didn't possess the vocabulary.

It wasn't because of what had happened on Fintz—well, not *just* that. It was hard to imagine anything that he might think of for a ten of tendays that wouldn't be affected by that—it was everything.

Everything was connected to everything else. Everywhere. Always. Forever.

The insight stopped him cold. Far from being revelatory, the simple truth of it felt both damning and a relief.

Did Jorl know this? Did he see how the galaxy and all the people in it touched one another in a complex network that was more basic than even his precious nefshons? Did Tolta understand? Was this why she had stopped mourning Arlo? Had Arlo seen it, and was that the reason he had taken his own life?

Because not only was everything connected and therefore a part of everything else, it was all both true and false at the same time. Meaning wasn't meaning anymore. He dug some koph out of a pocket and munched it as he climbed higher, not sure where he was going but at the same time grudgingly admitting that if everything touched everything then there was no random chance or accidents anywhere and at some level he had to know where he was going even if at another level he lied to himself about it.

He reached the top of the canopy and paused at an observation station there. He'd begun seeing nefshons and considered reaching out to Jorl to demand explanations about the interrelatedness that battered his brain, but didn't trust himself not to petulantly demand an explanation why his ex-mentor hadn't told him before. Instead, he summoned the Archetype of Man, whom he'd not spoke to since leaving Keslo.

"Hello, Pizlo. How goes your quest?"

"Brutally," he said, standing as usual upon the machine's flat surface, imaginary rain pounding down upon him. "And you knew it would be, didn't you?"

"I'm sorry, I need more context to understand and respond to your question."

"You *knew* that everything is everything, didn't you? From the smallest or nearest part to any other. You knew. It's all connected."

"I don't know any such thing. But again, it may be that I lack proper context. Can you elaborate?"

"All your stories! They're all the same."

"That's false, Pizlo. They involve different heroes performing different actions in different settings for different purposes—"

"At a meta-level, they're all the same!"

"Oh, yes, that is true. As we discussed, there are patterns that repeat throughout all of human history and storytelling, that resonate for all people, but even so differences—"

"And at a meta-meta-level?"

"I'm sorry, I don't understand the question."

"Every story, they're all about what you would call the 'human condition,' aren't they?"

"How could they not? They are human stories."

"Yeah. Not the long dead race of humans. They're everyone's stories. Humans and Fant and Marmo and Brady and . . . and . . . everyone. It's all one story. It's the story of us and what it means to be that."

"Yes, Pizlo. Every story is a way of glimpsing a different facet of who we are."

"But that's not just true of your stories, is it?"

"Again, I apologize. I am not following your questions."

In the mindscape of his summoning, Pizlo stopped the rain. He caused the sun to rise prematurely and hang hidden on the horizon, dawn brightening the cloud-covered sky. Then by an act of will he made the clouds wither and vanish until nothing rose above him but the cerulean sky in its totality that could never be seen on Barsk. One by one he spun all of the world's moons above him, running them through their respective orbits—which he knew as well as he knew every possible route between the Civilized Wood and the Shadow Dwell—until reaching a configuration that allowed them all to be visible overhead at once. He turned his attention to a point to the north where the planet's artificial satellite hung above the equator and added the existence of it though it was too small to actually perceive from that distance.

"Stories aren't just fiction," he said.

"No, you're mistaken. Stories, by definition, are constructed. They may be based upon actual events, or inspired in some way, but through the vehicle of metaphor they—"

Pizlo waved him to silence with his trunk. "No, I'm not. Don't start in again with metaphor. You're wrong. Everything we do is a story, whether anyone tells it or not. And because all the stories are the same story, so is everything we do. Everyone that's ever lived, everyone that's drawing breath right now, and even all who will be born sometime in the future, we're all living a story. The same story."

"Ah. I understand you now. Yes. And, it should not surprise you that I have stories about this too."

"About pointlessness? About futility? About asking what the value of anything is?"

"Many such stories," said the Archetype of Man. "The concepts of nothingness, of oblivion and uselessness are a popular subset of stories."

"But if it's all the same story, then the story about predestination is also the story of free will. Living and death. Joy and love and hatred and fear and indifference. Each of those stories is the same story like every story. Nothing matters because everything is everything."

"Yes. Except . . ."

Pizlo froze. "Tell me," he whispered.

"You have invoked story, and meta-story, and meta-meta-story."

"Yes."

"What lies beyond that?"

"Nothing!" Pizlo shouted and crashed the sun, tore the moons away, flooded the sky with clouds, and subjected himself to torrential rains. "Nothing exists beyond because everything is everything else."

"What if you're wrong?"

"Wha—what?"

"Even if everything is story, the fact that you can conceive such a state demands that you have rejected that there can be anything that isn't. But, to make such an observation, you first must have the concept of something that isn't. Which means you're wrong. Which means *that* story isn't like all the rest. But it has to be. But it can't be. Paradox."

"Paradox?"

"A self-contradictory statement."

Pizlo stopped the rain again, brought up winds that swept the water from the surface of the Archetype's cube. He placed both hands flat on the cloudy glass he'd been standing on, staring into the indistinct shapes that danced and swirled in ever-changing colors deep inside. He raised his palms and the glass flowed, rising up and taking the shape he desired like he might sculpt river clay in the real world. More and more of it came at his command. He stood and drew more of the glass, building a mass of it to his own height. He split its base in two, creating legs. He pulled a pair of limbs from the upper portion giving rise to arms, added a glob of still more swirling glass to the top as a head.

"What are you doing, Pizlo? This is not my shape. This is not me."

He ignored the Archetype's words, chose not to evaluate if they were plaintive or anxious or fearful. The legs grew feet and toes, the arms hands and fingers. The head sprouted the ears and trunk of a Lox, and the relative shape of the parts made it clear that he was crafting an adolescent, a figure his own age.

"You're saying that yes, because everything is everything else, then everything is pointless. Except if that's so, then saying so requires the existence of something that isn't, or how could we know? Except then the first thing isn't possible. Paradox."

"Yes, but that doesn't explain what you're—"

"I'm giving you a new story," said Pizlo, stepping back from his creation, pulling the Archetype's nefshons from the cube beneath him and imbuing them into the gleaming double of himself. "My story." He drew forth the meme he'd created, his echo now updated to reflect his aborted imram, the events on Fintz, even his conclusions of futility and this new notion of paradox. "This is me," he said and pressed the meme into the figure of the Archetype as Fant, as he'd reimagined it.

The Archetype remained silent. Time stopped. It held out arms it had never before possessed, curled its trunk, flapped its new ears, opened eyes to experience sight, and trumpeted the same sound every newborn Fant issued as it entered the world and declared its existence.

"Oh," was all it said.

"Yeah."

"Thank you. And I'm sorry. I . . . I don't think I have anything left to teach you, Pizlo. Many more stories, surely, but nothing that will inform the person you are."

"Yeah. But . . . thank you. Truly."

"What will you do?"

"That's the question, isn't it? Because it doesn't matter, but it's also the only thing that ever could. Paradox."

The ancient machine that faced him as his glassy twin nodded. "You understand the concept perfectly."

"And that's the answer. That's what I must be. Which is funny, because it's what I've always been."

"And what is that?"

"A contradiction, in every way. Every day of my life."

He dissolved the mindscape and let his perception of nefshons fall away.

~~~~~

THE next morning, Pizlo lay upon his back on the mix of gravel and sand that defined the tiny strip of beach where he had found the carving he'd given to the chemist. The forest loomed around him on three sides, its branches and leaves murmuring just below the level of his understanding. Waves lapped at his feet and whispered their approval of his decision. He tapped the medallion nestled against his collarbone.

"When I set out on my quest, I thought I would have enough adventures to justify an imram. That would have been something, the heroic narrative of an abomination's journey from island to island. And yeah, I guess you could say I had some adventures, but I got the quest part wrong so I don't think it counts. Or maybe it does. I'm not sure, just saying my best guess. Jorl will probably know clearly, one way or the other. I'll upload all of this to his system and maybe he'll get it published. Not here on Barsk though. No Fant is going to want to read my story. Just the idea that an abomination could create something is too new. Unthinkable. I mean, sure, *I'd* read it. But that's just more of me being a contradiction."

He checked a pouch on his bandolier and pulled out a packet of koph. He'd have to pay another visit to that chemist soon. Right now he just needed to talk to someone and his options were limited. Tolta loved him, but she'd never understood him, and anything he might say would only confuse her and spur her to further attempts to smother him with maternal comfort. Dabni didn't much like him, and every conversation he'd ever had with her had involved half of her attention trying to find a way to end it. Rina would be a sympathetic ear, but would comprehend what he was going through even less than Tolta, and though he treasured her unconditional support he needed an adult. Druz, however much she might try, anchored all her interactions with him to their first meeting when she'd named him "Little Prince." And besides, she was off on the ship somewhere, and he had promised Jorl he wouldn't Speak to the living, excepting him.

Which is why he'd taken the koph. While he and Jorl had been spending less time together over the last many seasons—and Pizlo acknowledged it was as much due to his desire to grow beyond a definition of being student to a mentor as it was Jorl being ever more busy—the historian was still his best friend. Likely much as he had been Arlo's best friend. And though busy, he'd make time, interrupt what he was doing, if Pizlo reached out to him via nefshons. Jorl would see his pain and help talk him through the worst of the confusion and emptiness that gnawed at him.

The glowing gold appearance of his own nefshon sheathe let him know the drug had worked and he filtered it out at once. But before he could close his eyes and begin summoning enough of Jorl's particles to create a strand leading back to him, something in the real world caught his eye. Something completely impossible. Here and there, widely spaced and visible only because he lay outside the forest gazing upward, he saw nine gleaming strands falling from the clouds above like shafts of purest sunlight racing down into the forest. But they weren't beams of sunlight; he hadn't been able to see them before he took the koph. Which meant they were nefshons. And because they weren't simply random particles but rather coherent strands, meant they were lines tethering a living person on either end, much like he'd intended to create to Speak with Jorl. Or like the strands he'd seen Dabni create that day in the park. One end of each of these nine nefshon strands connected to a living person somewhere in Keslo's Civilized Wood, and maybe those Fant were unaware of the event. But who was on the other end, and where were they?

There were of course endless nefshons all around him, but those had been filtered out when he'd banished his own swirling cocoon. These strands remained because they were contrived, the imposition of a will on the raw stuff of the particles. As questions flitted through his mind, first one and then a second of the nine strands lost coherence, dissolving as their individual nefshons began drifting apart, much like when Pizlo finished a summoning of the Archetype of Man and let his constructs fall away. Which meant that two of the nine people doing this thing—whatever it was, and from whichever end—had stopped. He couldn't know how long it had been happening; before his dose of koph allowed him to see the strands had they been hanging here in the sky? A third flickered and was gone.

He focused his attention on the nearest of the remaining strands, impossibly far above him but reachable because they presented themselves as coherent and thus more readily summonable. In that instant, his own nefshon construct hung in the air and gripped the glowing line with hands and trunk midway between the clouds and the top of the forest. It felt a lot like the mindscape he'd create to Speak with the Archetype or Jorl, but with fewer pieces and no walls. Realizing that, his volition was everything and he sent himself hurtling downward. The journey was instantaneous. One moment he was hanging in the sky and in the next he had followed the strand into Keslo's canopy, passing through leaves and limbs and vines until he came to the uppermost level of the Civilized Wood. He'd plunged further, through buildings and boardways and three different people—none of whom noticed his nefshon construct sliding dizzily down the strand—until he slipped into a house, into a bedroom, onto the head of a slumbering old Eleph. He recognized her as one of Rina's gymnasium teachers.

"This is so weird," he said, but his construct had no physicality and produced no sound. He lingered a moment, studying the face of the woman, so calm in sleep with none of the passion she projected when teaching rhetoric. A pattern of thought flowed down the strand from above, passed through him, and slid into the sleeping woman. Pizlo gasped. Knowledge flowed into his mind. His own thoughts raced after it, but like water slipping through cracks in the mud and rock of the Shadow Dwell the new ideas fled into the under thoughts that Jorl had described as his unconscious, a place that was his mind but not any part he could deliberately reach. It was like when he had stood upon the space station and Telko had filled him with knowledge, more than he could comprehend in the moment. Information had come down this nefshon strand, a story that he couldn't quite hold on to; something about a time for this woman—he now knew her name, Shelby—and an awareness her death was near and where she needed to be and soon. Pizlo knew the story, but this felt less like a tale the Archetype might have shared and more like something he had lived. Only he hadn't. Someone had poured actual experience and not simply narrative into him and into the sleeping Eleph rhetoric teacher.

He hadn't known such a thing was possible! This wasn't like his echo, not simply content but directive! He reeled, at the implications of encoding instructions into nefshon patterns and sharing them directly. Someone, somewhere on the other end of this strand had done that. He had to know who and how and where. The need generated the action and he willed himself back up the strand, seeking its other end.

That journey, though it also took no time, led to something even stranger. He retraced the path back, intangibly racing through all obstacles. He reached the open sky and continued to climb. His awareness rose to the clouds and through them, higher and higher until he soared above them and still he climbed. Had he been able, had traveling along the strand required time and not just distance, Pizlo knew his will would have failed. But there was no time to contemplate that this was real and not merely a construct in some mental space. With impossible speed he left atmosphere behind and crossed into airless space, up the golden strand of nefshons that he knew had been formed from the Eleph sleeping far below.

And still he rose, higher and higher in that single instant, through darkness and cold, until a dim circle appeared far above. It grew larger, and resolved itself into one of Barsk's seven moons. He was hurtling up to Ulmazh. Closer and closer, until up became down and he could see the strand he followed originated in a crater. That made no sense. There had to be a Speaker on the other end of these nefshons, but what would a Fant be doing on the moon? How would they have gotten there? How had they managed to stay alive? And most importantly, why connect a trail of nefshons to a rhetorician on Keslo far below?

All of it happened in the same instant. The moment when he'd willed himself back up the strand from inside that bedroom was the same moment he'd been in the clouds. It proved to be the same moment that he struck the crater and passed on through layers of rock and metal and into atmosphere again. The strange thread stretched through walls and rooms that were like those found in a Civilized Wood but different, too, fashioned in part with ceramic instead of wood. Pizlo snatched glimpses of other Fant, all of them oddly dressed as he passed through levels deeper and deeper as if he were bound for the center of the moon itself. But the thread stopped long before that point, stopped in a simple room with a desk and a couch and cupboards and art on the walls and a rug on the floor. And a Fant. Like Rina's teacher this was another Eleph woman. But this one lay on the room's couch, eyes closed, face lax, while her nefshon construct stood alongside her real body, holding the other end of the rhetorician's golden strand in one hand and gazing upward as if all the way to her bedroom.

Pizlo barreled into her, one nefshon construct colliding with another, both surprised beyond their experience. His hand still touched the strand as he pulled himself upright and stared at a Fant here in the moon. Time resumed. She stared back, eyes widening, and she screamed.

"Abomination!"

Before Pizlo could think or react or do anything, the Speaker was unraveling the nefshon strand that had brought him there. In that instant, he was thrown back, out, down, and found himself breathless and returned to his body in the little cove on the edge of Keslo.

NINETEEN

A CHILD'S VIEW OF SPACE

~~~~~~~~

WHAT did you do in the Patrol, Papa?"

Rina walked hand in hand with Jorl as they made their way from one of Keslo's public performance spaces where they had just enjoyed a retelling of the story of Pholo performed by a traveling troupe of Eleph shadow puppeteers. Jorl regarded his daughter, trying to fathom what had prompted the question.

"What makes you ask, little twig?"

"Cuz didn't you fly? When you were in the Patrol? Like Pholo did."

"Pholo flew because . . . well, no one really knows how Pholo flew. But I flew in a ship."

"Right, I know. But what did you *do*? Why were you flying?"

"Oh, got it. Well, we did a lot of things in the Patrol. Sometimes we helped out with emergencies at one or another of the outer colonies where things were spread a little too thin. Once our navigator caught a glimpse of a smuggler hiding quiet and hoping to slip away just as we came into a system, and that got . . . messy. But

mostly we were following up on cartographic data from earlier unmanned craft."

Rina whuffed a put upon bleat from her trunk and gave her
father *that* look, the one she saved for when he forgot that smart as
she was she was still just a kid and couldn't always follow everything
he said, particularly if she found it boring. He acknowledged his
error with a little squeeze of her hand and tried again.

"Most of the time we were looking for new planets. The Alliance is always expanding, and to do that it needs to find new
worlds where people can set up colonies. For that to happen, the
Patrol has to constantly push portals further and further out there.
The galaxy's very big, and without the portals it would take far
too long time to go from one place to another."

Their walking had taken them to the door of Dabni's bookshop
and they stepped within. Rina's mother was helping a customer
but she paused long enough to wave her trunk at the pair of them.
Rina lifted hers in response and then led her father deeper into
the store to a small table surrounded by several chairs. Kokab
waited patiently, propped up on one of the seats, a miniature teacup set in front of it. Rina sat at the table and waved Jorl to sit at
the sole adult-sized seat. As he got comfortable, she went through
the motions of filling a dainty cup full of fantastical tea, a blend
composed of made-up words she'd overheard from different visitors to the shop. Today they were drinking ontologically thespia-
nation with just a hint of cribble. She waited for him to delicately
lift the cup with one hand and only then picked up the conversation again. "But why?"

"Why?"

"Why push portals?"

Jorl frowned for a silent moment and then set his cup down as he pulled a pair of books off a nearby shelf. "These are two books in a set, volumes one and two, do you see?"

"Yes, but—"

He lifted his trunk interrupting her. "You could read them from the beginning of the first page in volume one all the way to the last page in volume two. Right?"

She nodded, clearly still *not* seeing but understanding that she had to wait for him to finish.

"That's a long distance, from beginning to end. But when I put them back on the shelf, I put volume one to the left of volume two. Now the actual distance from the beginning to the end is shorter, do you see? It's just the thickness of the front and back covers and not all the pages in between. Portals do that for the space between stars."

"How?"

Jorl smiled. "That I don't know, little twig. That's physics, and I studied history. I don't know how it all works, but I can tell you that portals always come in pairs. A lot of what we did when I was in the Patrol was to push one piece of a portal further and further through space away from its matching piece. Even though our ship went very fast, the distance between stars is vast. It takes a long time to push a portal from one star system to another, much longer than anyone wants to do it."

"Then how does it get there?" Rina picked up the teapot from the table and filled her own cup to the brim with imaginary tea.

"We took turns, like the runners in a relay race. Part of the time I was in the Patrol, my ship went through what we called an "ongoing portal"—because usually both parts of a portal are fixed in space and people travel from one place to the other. But we flew through a kind with only the first part fixed, because the other end wasn't at its final destination yet. When we came out the other end, there was another Patrol ship waiting. They'd been pushing that side of the portal for a long time. We took over for them and they went back through so they could have a break and do something else. We pushed it for a while until, seasons later, a different ship replaced us."

Rina pondered and then pointed to the books Jorl had returned to the shelf. "So . . . when you were done, it was like you'd added more pages to the books but the distance from the front cover of the one to the back cover of the other hadn't changed?"

"That's it exactly."

"That's neat. When I grow up, I want to push portals, too!"

Jorl smiled and carefully dipped his trunk into his teacup, miming pulling deeply and then placing the end into his mouth as if to drink. "Trust me on this, Rina, you really don't. It's boring work. It's important, the Alliance can't colonize new worlds without the work of the Patrol, but I think you'll find much better things to do right here on Barsk when you grow up."

She busied herself preparing Kokab's cup before asking, "The others in the Patrol, people you were pushing the portals with . . . they weren't Lox like us?"

"They were not. Nor Eleph."

"That's not fair. I want to meet other people. Other races. I've read about them here in Mama's shop. And you talk with them all the time. You said the other senators are all different. Brady and Cynomy and Marmo and lots of others."

"That's true."

"And Pizlo has told me stories about how he got to meet some when he wasn't much older than me."

"Well, to be fair, Pizlo is always a special case. I didn't meet anyone who wasn't a Fant until I left Barsk, and that didn't happen until I was older than you and Pizlo combined."

"But Papa—"

Jorl raised a hand and she stopped. "There may be an opportunity at hand. Let me talk to your mother about it and we'll see."

"Talk to me about what?" Dabni had come around the corner of the bookshelf, knelt alongside one of the child-sized seats and helped herself to a teacup. Rina's head turned to regard first one parent and then the other. Her mother's eyes held a twinkle that she now also saw in her father's.

"Rina was just bemoaning the fact that she's never met anyone who wasn't a Fant," said Jorl.

Dabni laughed. "You mean, like nearly everyone else on Barsk except you?"

"And Pizlo," added Rina.

"Well, yes," admitted Dabni. "And Pizlo."

"I've not had a chance to mention it to you yet, but Druz is here."

"Here? Here where?"

"Here onworld," said Jorl. "Something . . . came up and she's arrived a season ahead of schedule. And she brought a Procy with her."

"You're telling me that in addition to your personal Sloth, there's also a Raccoon on Barsk?"

"Really?" squealed Rina.

"Not *on* Barsk," said Jorl. "That would be unlawful."

"And what does this have to do with Rina?"

"I thought . . . well, Druz has my complete trust, and it's long past time for Rina to meet her. And since Abenaki is here and desperate to make a good impression—"

"Who is Abenaki?"

"Sorry, that's the Raccoon. She's from Caluma."

"Caluma? What does that have to do with—"

"Absolutely nothing. Just another datum. But my point is—"

"You want to take Rina to your yacht so she can meet your visiting Brady and Procy."

"Well, they're not *mine*, but yes, it's an opportunity—"

"Of course they're yours, Jorl. You're the senator. That's the only reason either of them are here. And that's fine. I do think that Rina should expand her horizons, though I'm not so sure this is the best way to do it. She's not going to have the kind of wanderlust that boys get, and she's certainly not leaving the planet like you did."

"Mama?" Rina bit her lip, having tried and failed to keep the hint of a whine from her voice.

Dabni regarded her daughter. "Yes, dear?"

"Are you saying I can or can't go meet the people on Papa's ship?"

"Yes, Dabni, what are you saying?"

The sound of amusement in her father's question wiped away her own worries. Her mother rolled her eyes, a gesture that sometimes meant that patience had been exhausted and she was in trouble and sometimes that her mother was about to give in to one of her father's more silly suggestions. It was never easy to tell which until it was past the point of doing anything about it. Then Dabni ran her trunk behind Rina's ear in a gentle caress and the girl knew the answer, if not the particulars.

"I'm saying a great many things, Jorl ben Tral, all of which you know and none of which you want to hear. That women are more stable. That men are more prone to foolishness. That young girls adore their fathers despite the good sense of their gender. And that this is an unsought-for situation and I won't let my own bias withhold the opportunity from our daughter, so yes, take her to meet with your visitors. I'll speak to her teachers and maybe she can write up the experience for some extra credit."

"I think that's a fine idea," said Jorl and ran his own trunk lovingly around Dabni's ear.

Rina's squeals of delight broke off suddenly and she leaned in, folding one ear to envelope her doll. "Papa? Can Kokab come, too? He says he's hardly met anyone."

Jorl smiled, cast a glance to Dabni, and then nodded. "I think we can manage to find room for Kokab, too."

"We're gonna meet a Sloth *and* a Raccoon! I can't wait to tell Pizlo!"

TWENTY

LIFE AND LIES BEYOND DEATH

~~~~~~~~~

ORL'S time in the Patrol had taught him the basic skills to navigate and pilot most spacecraft. Druz freed him from such responsibility, and really there was nowhere he wanted to go. He'd vowed never to leave Barsk again, regardless of the ability and resources to do so.

Still, his yacht was here ahead of schedule and he had a mystery to solve. It was as much pragmatism as serendipity to arrange for a quick, suborbital flight. The ship contained equipment available nowhere else on the planet. If his hunch proved wrong, Rina would still get a chance to see her home from above its ubiquitous cloud cover, as well as meet members of two races that had never set foot on Barsk. But if he was right . . . well, Dabni might give him some grief on bringing their daughter along, but the defensive capabilities of the yacht exceeded by several orders of magnitude anything his world could throw at it.

~~~~~~~~~

HE'D awoken early this day—Kentl having recently hired a local gardener to cut back the sartha beneath his window. A stack of minor things required his attention before taking Rina on her adventure. He threw himself into the sea of minutia, absently consuming breakfast as he waded through the stack. Midmorning brought a knock at his door before he had completed his labors. He welcomed the interruption but threw his ears back in surprise as he opened the door.

"Chisulo? What are you doing here? Are you all right? Is your mother okay?"

"Yes, sir, she's fine. We're both fine. Only . . . she meant to say something the other day when you were at the dock but you came and went so fast. So she sent me today, said it couldn't wait for you to come by again, particularly it being flood and all and you don't normally use your boat this season, which is part of why we missed the whole thing in the first place, and anyway she thought I should come tell you personally."

He waved the youth into his home. "Missed what whole thing?"

"Theft," said Chisulo. "Sorry, I should have said that right off. Your boat. Someone made off with it some days ago."

"I don't understand. I just took it out. You saw me, helped me load some provisions."

"Yes, sir. That was after it was stolen."

"If it was stolen before that, how could it have been there when I used it?"

"Oh, as to that, the thief returned it."

"The thief? So you know who took my boat?"

"Well . . . we didn't see no *person* at the helm, not coming or going. And my ma, she says, and meaning no disrespect but she says, we can't have that happening at the harbor. There's paperwork and it's not the kind you can fill out easily all things being what they are and it makes people think we don't know our job and that's not fair to us if you see what I mean, sir. Ma says."

Jorl stood there a moment, just blinking. Thievery was uncommon on Barsk, much more so than any of the other Alliance worlds he'd visited while in the Patrol. And theft on this order was a greater rarity. Moreover, unlike most of the vessels in the harbor, the navigation gear on his required specialized training. Almost any other boat would have served even joy-riding adolescents better than his. Unless . . .

"Will you excuse me a moment? The pantry's just in there. Please, make yourself at home and help yourself to a snack. I won't be long."

Without waiting for an answer Jorl stepped into his office and sat in front of his desk. He didn't need koph, but he did need to calm himself because the only thing that made any sense was that Pizlo had taken it upon himself to take his boat without so much as a by-your-leave, and the boy's timing was inconvenient and maddening. He reached out for his protégé's nefshons and made contact, lightly at first, because unlike other people he might Speak to in this way, Pizlo often as not could be careening through the space between the Civilized Wood and the Shadow Dwell, and he didn't want to risk causing the boy harm by disrupting his concentration.

The connection firmed as another mind quested back along the lines of his nefshons. "Jorl?"

An instant later they were in a simulacrum of Jorl's office.

"Where are you, Pizlo?"

"Lost in thought."

"Are you being evasive?"

"Sorry? No, just . . . trying to make sense of things I've seen lately."

Jorl rolled his eyes and made sure Pizlo saw him do it. "I don't have time for this, so I'll be direct. Did you take my boat without asking?"

"It's flood, Jorl. You never take the boat out this time of year."

"In fact, I did just recently. Druz is here early and I had to go meet her. And I'm going out again today."

"Oh. Huh. I didn't know. I didn't inconvenience you, did I? You didn't need it while I was away?"

"No, but that's not the point."

"Then what is? You weren't using it. Mostly nobody's traveling around during flood. I needed it. I returned it when I was done."

"The point is the harbormaster is reporting the boat as stolen."

"That's stupid. I put it right back in its slip."

"They know that."

"Then what's the problem?"

"Pizlo, you know they can't say you returned the boat."

"They can't . . . Oh. Right. I didn't think of that. I was all focused on my quest when I was leaving and . . . and distracted with other things when I came back."

"Quest? What are you talking about?"

"It's not important. I was wrong. It was important that I went, but not for the reasons I thought it was. I . . . I'm sorry if I caused you or the harbormaster any trouble. It won't happen again. And I'll try to think of some way to make up for it."

"You sound like you're upset. Where did you go? Why didn't you tell me before now?"

"It's complicated. Maybe I can come by and we can talk about it? I'd really like your input on things."

"I can't today. I'm taking Rina out to meet Druz, and maybe going on a bit of quest of my own, back to the final island we visited once before. But yes, as soon as I get back, let's talk. Over breakfast. Or lunch." He paused and smiled at the image of the boy, not really a boy any longer. "Maybe both," he added.

"Thanks. I'd like that. Say 'hi' to Druz for me."

Jorl broke the connection, shaking his head at the historic significance of it all. The Abomination of Keslo had taken to the high seas. Nothing like that had ever happened before, and ultimately he'd enabled it. For a moment he tried to wrap his head around how that would work. Paperwork for the harbormaster here on Keslo was the least of it. It was one thing for ordinary folk who encountered Pizlo on a boardway to turn their gaze away and keep walking. How would other ships manage to ignore him? Or the harbor patrol if he tried to make landfall at some other island as he almost surely had. Officially, once they recognized Pizlo for what he was—and one glance at the abnormality of his skin would lead any observer to an instant conclusion—they'd ignore him and the boat he arrived on, but they'd also check the boat's registry, which would lead back to Zlorka. Likely it was only a matter of days before he received a very obliquely worded reprimand from Provost Phloda on university letterhead and a private note harping on him for tasking their friendship so.

He returned to the parlor to find Chisulo contentedly working his way through a bowl of fresh leaves.

"Tell your mother she can stand down."

"Sir?"

"My boat wasn't stolen. It was taken by a friend who . . . forgot to tell me. It's all fine. Tell her I'll send a letter explaining the matter and taking full responsibility. And that I'm sorry and my friend won't be doing that again."

"Oh. Okay. She'll be glad to hear that. She's never had a boat go missing on her watch."

"Yes, well, as it happens, I'll be taking it out again for a short trip later today."

Chisulo's ears fell back. "Again. That's three trips in flood. You sure you don't want to wait for the weather to improve?"

"I appreciate the concern. We both know I'm not much of a sailor. I'll be relying on the engine and navigation equipment. And I'm not going far. As you say, it's flood."

Chisulo nodded, shoved another trunkful of leaves into his mouth, and headed for the door. "I'll make sure she's ready for you then, sir. Fuel topped off and such. Don't you worry. You want me to see it gets stocked with anything?"

"That'd be very helpful, thank you. You know Hearne's?"

"Sure."

"Tell him it's for me. Same order as last time but double it."

"Yessir. I'll take care of it." He opened the door to let himself out but paused to turn back for a moment and add, "Thanks for not having your boat stolen."

Jorl watched him hurry away and then returned to his study to inform Druz of his impending arrival and task her with locking in their ultimate destination.

⌇

RINA waited for him at her mother's bookshop, standing by a table of sale books, restlessly swinging her arms. She held a small travel case in one hand and her rag doll hung from the other. When Jorl came through her head jerked up. She fanned her ears wide and her eyes shone with delight.

"Papa! Are we really going? Is it time?"

"It is, little twig. I'm sorry I'm running a little late. I had to talk to someone about the boat."

"What happened to your boat, Papa?"

He considered brushing off the question, but it was an honest enough inquiry and deserved a like reply. "Pizlo," he said.

His daughter nodded solemnly, turned to call back into the store where, one supposed Dabni was busy with a customer or working the stock. "Mama! Going now! Bye!" She preceded him out the door onto the boardway where she stopped, and looked back at him impatiently.

Jorl followed. He took her case from her so she wouldn't tire, and held her hand as they walked to the transit center and took the funicular to the harbor. Chisulo waited for them with receipts from Hearne's that had been billed against his harbor account. Around them the rain came down in torrents.

"Are you sure you want to be going out in this, sir?"

"I'm not going far," said Jorl. "Not even half the distance to the next island."

"Well, I don't know as that would reassure anyone much, having you anchor in the open water overnight."

Jorl had no such intention. As before, he'd be mooring the boat inside the yacht's hold. He'd already warned Druz of the need to secure it as the larger vessel would be traveling. But explaining all of that to Chisulo would take too long. Still, the boy had a point. Jorl glanced at Rina.

"I don't know if my daughter has her sea legs," he said. "And while my boat handles well, you're right, in this weather we'll feel the waves more. I'd like to keep her lunch inside her."

Rina trumpeted with embarrassment and whispered, "Papa!"

Chisulo affected not to have heard. "I can't speak to that, but best to make all possible speed to wherever you're going."

"Good advice. Thank you, Chisulo." He gave Rina's hand a squeeze and together they strolled down the pier toward his boat, leaving the harbormaster's son behind.

"It's an adventure," said Rina, giggling and smiling up at him as rain pelted them both.

"Every day."

They left the harbor without incident and in due course found the yacht where it had been. Similarly, docking the boat went as smoothly as a few days earlier, with Druz on hand to pull them into position. Even quick as it had been, the trip through the choppy water left Rina a bit green. She didn't vomit, but she'd remained silent as if the only way to ensure the contents of her stomach stayed where they belonged was to refuse to admit that her mouth could open. Her nausea faded once they'd entered the calm of the hold, the yacht sparing them the onslaught of rain and waves. Her ears fell back and her eyes widened as she beheld the first person she'd ever seen who was neither Eleph nor Lox. Any shyness she felt fled at once. She practically bounced over the railing to land in front of the Sloth.

"Hi hi! I'm Rina. I'm a friend of Pizlo's."

Druz reached out a hand with quicker than normal speed and steadied the girl. She bowed solemnly. "It is a privilege and delight to meet anyone who calls the little prince friend. Be welcome here, senator's child."

Rina giggled. "Pizlo's not a prince. That's a title from storybooks."

"You know, he has said the same thing to me many times. And who is this?" The Brady gestured to Rina's doll with the same seriousness she might use for a diplomat.

"That's Kokab. He wanted to come along. He's very smart."

The Sloth nodded. "A trusted advisor then. Welcome to you also, Kokab."

"And what about me?" asked Jorl, as he came up behind his daughter carrying her travel case and the assortment of meals from Hearne's which Chisulo had stowed aboard his boat.

"It's all as you requested, sir. I've determined the coordinates, but much as we experienced when I flew you there seven years ago, the ship's instruments as well as satellite imagery insists there's nothing there."

"Well, at a minimum, we know there's an island there," said Jorl. "It's an anomaly, all right. And since I've found another one, I'm thinking why not keep both of them in one place. But first, let's try to explain away some of the mystery. After that, well, worst case, we park close enough for me to wade out and go ashore and I waste a day and get a good hike."

"If that's the worst case, what is the best one? What do you hope to find?"

Jorl smiled. "Same thing Rina came to the ship to find. People."

~~~~~

DRUZ took them up into the planet's mesosphere and then due east until reaching a spot nearly equidistant between the nearest islands of the western and eastern archipelagos far below. Nothing was visible except the tops of distant clouds beneath them.

"I don't understand," said Abenaki. "Druz tells me we're traveling to an island that doesn't exist? Why, when you have hundreds of perfectly good islands to visit."

"It exists. I've stood upon its shore. Druz, were you able to confirm my suspicions?"

"Yes. From our current position I have identified a vast array of atmospheric drones near the top of the troposphere, spread out above an area of ocean with the island at its center. They appear to be scattering the spectrum above. There's some data loss, but it's well within the tolerance that weather would cause anyway."

Jorl nodded. "Rendering the island invisible to the initial survey mapping from early in the first century."

"Yes, sir. And from any subsequent scans from the station above Zlorka."

After being introduced to the Procyon, Rina had sat quietly on a low couch, her gaze flitting back and forth from Druz to Abenaki, now and then whispering to her doll but otherwise seemingly engrossed. Jorl kept looking her way, unsure of how much of the conversation she was following.

"I'm assuming those drones aren't something that could just be put up once and function indefinitely?"

"They're lightweight and durable, but no, even drawing energy from the weather they'd still need regular, albeit infrequent, maintenance. In fact, their manufacture suggests materials not otherwise available on Barsk."

Jorl chuckled. "Care to wager that someone on that island is producing such materials?"

"No, sir. The fact that they exist to hide the island suggests there may be other things occurring there worth hiding."

"I agree. So, for as much as seven hundred years there's been an ongoing and deliberate effort to keep the existence of this island from public record and awareness. And yet, almost every Fant on the planet sails here as the last thing they do before they die."

"Papa? You're not going there are you?" Rina's question rang like a cry for help. In fact, intentionally or not, she was sending out an infrasonic pulse of profound distress that neither the Sloth nor the Raccoon detected. Jorl rushed to her couch and knelt alongside her.

"What's wrong, Rina?"

"That's where people go to die. Please don't go there, Papa. Don't die."

"Hush, little twig. I'm not going to die. I didn't wake up this morning or any morning suddenly knowing where it was. And besides, I've been here already, back before you were born. I'm going back and so this isn't like when other people travel here."

Rina clutched her doll to her chest, some of her fear fading and the thrumming of her emotions falling away. "How did you know where to go the first time?"

"Pizlo told me," he said. "He actually came with me."

If there was any real magic in the world it was saying that name to his daughter. She smiled like the sun peeking from behind relentless clouds.

"Okay, then," she said. And then added, "Maybe we should have asked him to come with?"

"I thought about it, little twig, but he's been busy with other things lately. He and I will be having breakfast and probably lunch together after we all get back. I'll ask your mom about having you join us for that lunch. Okay?"

She nodded solemnly, still smiling brightly.

"All right, Druz. Take us down as we discussed. Come in from the north so we don't disturb or distract any Dying who are sailing there. Find us a nice piece of beach where you can put down, and hopefully I won't have to wade through too much water to get ashore to see who's there."

Abenaki drummed her fingers in what Jorl had come to see as a nervous tell. "Even if there are people on your invisible island, Senator, do you really think they'll be waiting for you when you arrive?"

"Stands to reason," he said. "If it was me going to all this effort to hide, I'd make sure to keep an eye open in case someone found me anyway. And given they have no compunction against technology, I wouldn't be surprised if they knew we were on our way almost as soon as we did."

TWENTY-ONE

REVISIONIST HISTORY

~~~~~~~~~

EVERY season, a member of the Quick Council left their
home in the Civilized Wood of the nameless island and
boarded a hidden shuttle housed beneath a shallow bay. Despite
being possessed of better stealth technology than the Patrol, the
protocols of the Caudex insisted this shuttle could only be used
when no other ships were within a day's travel of the planet, when
its destination—the moon the Fant had named Ulmazh—lay on
the far side of the globe from the island of Zlorka and the space
station in geosynchronous orbit above it. Despite centuries of successful missions to star systems beyond their own, the core of the
Caudex's program remained at the base its earliest visionaries
had established within this moon. Theory and practice of the best
developments of Alliance technology were explored, adapted, and
enhanced there before being sent out to be implemented in still
more ambitious projects. Ulmazh was the seat of Caudex manufacturing. The smaller portals that their ships had pushed for
centuries were constructed there. Teams of ethernauts trained
and drilled there, building up reflexes for contingencies that had

never occurred but that some day might—for the Caudex, preparation for even the unlikely was mandatory. The moon also housed a modest shipyard, depending on the lesser gravity there to turn out new craft every decade. Small wonder then that a councilor spent a portion of each season on Ulmazh.

If Klarce enjoyed her rotation up to the moon more than her peers, well that was fine, too. If one of them wanted to let her take their turns, she'd be beyond delight. As it was, she'd been looking forward to the day's trip all season.

Temmel arrived at Klarce's office as she finished off several smaller tasks that would not wait for her return. Regina swapped out memos in front of her as quickly as she could skim, verify, and sign them, whisking the completed documents away to eventually distribute as necessary. When she was down to the last stack she didn't bother to look up but acknowledged her first assistant's presence with a simple question.

"Are we loaded and ready to go?" She knew the answer. Temmel was the very definition of efficiency. Klarce had traveled from world to moon and back with him many times and he wouldn't be waiting on her now if there were anything left undone. In fact, he'd doubtless been yearning for the trip even more, eager for the chance to gain more flight time. Years before she'd joined the council, she'd been one of her predecessor's assistants. Among the skills required for the job was piloting, a rarity on Barsk. Outside of the Caudex, she suspected that only Jorl could fly a shuttle. She'd enjoyed the rare opportunities to command a spacecraft, even within the restrictions of a covert dash from planet to moon and back again, and Temmel felt the same. For him, her turn to visit Ulmazh brought the satisfaction of sitting in a pilot's seat, fingers and trunk hovering over the command board. As for her own hunger to pilot, Caudex protocols required someone else command the craft on such trips. Even so, Klarce had set aside time in her schedule over the next few days to drill with some ethernaut cadets and renew her certification. Should the need arrive, she liked knowing she could take the helm herself.

Time passed, and when Temmel still hadn't responded she glanced up from her paperwork and saw a different answer in his eyes. "Tell me," she said.

"Yes, the shuttle is ready, but . . . the launch has been countermanded."

Klarce had feared as much but hoped she'd be wrong this once. Her travel plans had been overturned by the rest of the council. The Caudex would not allow a shuttle to lift today, not with a senatorial yacht afloat off the coast of Keslo. Which, she supposed, was why contingencies existed.

"We adapt," she said. "Regina, send word to everyone I was scheduled to meet with over the next few days and express my apologies. Reschedule, loosely. With luck, whatever brought our senator's private pleasure boat here ahead of schedule will send it back on its way promptly and we'll have only minor delay. Temmel, is there anything that can't wait?"

"We have three candidates for flight school who were going up with us to replace the team that's graduating and preparing to start pushing a portal from the Thrax system, but I'm sure they have plenty to occupy themselves until we're ready to leave. And actually, this may be a good thing for us in another area."

"What are your referring to?"

"Ryne's work."

"The physicist? What of him?"

"Bernath informs me that the engineering team is preparing to test the prototype he designed. She says it's really quite elegant and if successful production can begin immediately."

"What's that mean in terms of having working units?"

Temmel smiled. "Days. We can probably have the first batch to carry up with us when your flight is cleared."

Klarce shifted in her chair, ears fanned wide with pleasure. "Now that is a piece of good news. Pending confirmation of the test from Bernath, I want you to review the schedule of outbound ships. Not much we can do for any ongoing portal-pushers already in transit, but I want one of the new units onboard any relay vessels. And when those are covered, create a timetable for delivering a unit to every watch station on both sides of our existing portals."

"Providing the devices to the watch stations is to be our first priority?"

"Eventually we'll distribute them to our more ambitious projects, but our first concern has to be preparing for emergencies both near and far. The greatest danger to our longer range plans remains the possibility of something coming through a portal that we hadn't planned on."

"But, ma'am, they're *our* portals. It shouldn't be possible for someone we don't want coming through to use them at all."

She reached out with her trunk and circled his wrist, like a parent focusing a child's attention. "That's exactly the kind of thinking that almost guarantees we've overlooked something and ensures it will catch us unprepared. Heed me, Temmel, if you want my job one day; factor the impossible into your plans. Now, since Regina has gotten me caught up and we're not actually leaving, I'm taking the rest of the day off. Follow up on the last bits I've given you and then feel free to do the same."

"Yes, ma'am."

"But . . . keep an eye on the senator's ship. If there's any change, anything at all, inform me at once. There's no good reason for it to be here out of season, which only leaves bad reasons. Understood?"

Temmel turned and fled. Klarce nodded to herself. She had no complaints regarding her first assistant's competency, but it would do him good to reflect on his own confidence. The galaxy had a nasty habit of rewarding hubris with ruination. That was another lesson Margda had taught them long ago.

~~~~~

WITH the intention of making mash out of fallen fruit, Klarce left her office with no greater purpose than to walk the boardways of the unnamed island's Civilized Wood. She smiled and responded to greetings and well wishes from passersby, paused at a park to talk to a group of children playing some game with a long set of half-imagined rules, lingered at a fruit stand to select a few melons that would make a nice dessert that night when she surprised Adolo by actually having the time to cook dinner for them both.

The world-weariness that defined her responsibilities as second-in-line of the Quick Council fell away. The constant ache from her disease—however well managed—faded into the background. She felt happy, as much because she stood at the edge of an event that future generations would look back on as a benchmark of Fant history as because she had a free afternoon for the first time in more seasons than she could count.

That ended with such abruptness that she nearly stumbled and spilled her melons. Temmel had plucked a thread of her nefshons like a harp string, summoning her without warning, and even as she registered that he appeared to be back in her office she understood that to reach for her meant something critical or dire. Before he could apologize she interrupted him. "What's happened?"

"The senator's ship. It's moving."

"Leaving? Quicker than we thought. Does the rest of the council know? Are we back on for launch?"

"Ma'am, not leaving, moving. It's still in Barsk airspace. And . . . hold a moment." He looked to one side, as if someone stood next to him. Presumably, in her actual office, someone did. "Regina just shared an update. In the time I needed to take koph to find and tell you this news, we've confirmed the ship's vector. It's heading for us. We estimate it'll reach the unnamed island before day's end."

"One of the western landing spots?"

"Unlikely, ma'am. They look to be aiming slightly north. Almost as if they want to avoid seeing or perhaps being seen by anyone who's sailed away and is making landing here."

She snorted. "As if anyone arriving after days of traveling to us during flood is apt to notice anything beyond their own trunk in the deluge."

"It was just a guess, ma'am."

"No, no, you're probably right. A point to the senator for attempting discretion."

Temmel nodded, then frowned. "But ma'am, why is he coming? He knows there's something called the Caudex, but why would he think we're here of all places?"

She considered this a moment and nodded. "Because he's a scholar."

"I don't understand."

"It's a matter of *parsimony*. Where else on Barsk could we be? And we know he knows how to find the island. But he's never done more than land on the beach. Never had cause to. If he's looking for the Caudex though, he'll be looking for a city. Have you informed the rest of the Quick Council of this development?"

"Regina is doing so now."

"Fine. Doubtless they'll convene, but I can guess what they'll decide. I'll be asked to meet with him, learn what he knows, and determine what he wants."

"What does he want?"

"This is just a guess, but if he's being true to what we know of him, he's coming to confirm a hypothesis, vetting his source. Send word to Sind that I'm on my way to the council chamber now. But also, let Adolo know that I need her to oust her family from their guest parlor and that she'll be hosting an intimate reception for our guest."

"Will the council sign off on such an informal venue? Wouldn't something more official make a better choice?"

"First impressions are critical. He's not showing up as an Alliance senator with a formal presentation to the council. He's using his senatorial perks to hitch a ride here and showing up as an individual, relying on his aleph to open any doors. I intend to reinforce that by treating him as such, and guide him toward the doors I want to open by inviting him into a home."

"But not your home."

Klarce snorted. "My home is my office, more often as not. Adolo won't mind being pressed into service as hostess. And if the rest of her household doesn't like it, well, they can file a complaint. It wouldn't be the first time. In any case, they can certainly spare the guest parlor, and it has its own, discreet entrance."

"Yes, ma'am. I'm on it. Anything else?"

Klarce considered. She pulled back from the connection with Temmel to get her bearings in the real world. She hadn't made it all that far from the fruit stand and had come to a halt in the middle of the marketplace's minor boardway, a confectioner on her left and a spice shop to the right. Sweet and savory, she wondered which would ultimately describe her face-to-face meeting with Margda's chosen.

"One thing more," she said, returning her focus to her assistant. "Send someone over to the council to pick up a parcel and take it to Adolo. I no longer have time this afternoon to deliver these melons myself."

THIS Full Council meeting was much like the last, tedious and pointless. Arguments ranged back and forth between cautious and proactive. Marsh even went so far as to suggest pretending the island was uninhabited, and if necessary using the same lightning manipulation they used to clear debris from the beaches on Jorl if he appeared determined to cross the sand.

"Once he enters the forest, he'll realize it's truly a Shadow Dwell, and find signs of and access to the Civilized Wood above. He has to be stopped before that."

Soosh disagreed. "Would you have us throw away centuries of tradition?"

"What are you talking about?"

"He has an aleph. By tradition, none may bar the path of a Bearer. He is free to go where he will."

"The aleph was created by Margda," said Sind. "The only reason he has one is because she foretold he would. Perhaps this is why she chose him, perhaps she foresaw his arrival here and she wanted to tie our hands in the matter."

Genz trumpeted with disgust. "Impossible! If such a future were fixed, there'd be no point to this council even existing."

"There have been few precognitivists since Margda," said Klarce. "It's far too late to lament we haven't made a proper study of the phenomenon, and it's moot besides. We don't know for certain if he's coming to us as a scholar or a senator. We don't know what he knows or what he intends. Moreover, he—" She broke off

mid-sentence as someone tugged on her sleeve back in the physical world. She shifted her attention and there was Temmel handing her a note. She read, nodded, and shifted her attention back
to the council's shared mindspace.

"Further argument is going to have to wait. I've been informed
that the senator's yacht has landed just off a strip of beach on the
north side of the island. He's on foot, wading to shore even now
and he's alone."

"Alone?" asked Kissel, uttering his first words of this session
and drawing all eyes to him.

"Yes. Just him. No Sloth. No Raccoon."

"But we haven't reached a decision." Marsh's trunk slashed
from side to side. "We don't have consensus."

"No, said Klarce, pushing back from the circular table of the
mindspace. "But what we do have is a visitor to our shores, one who
strongly suspects there's more to this island than the rest of the
world believes. He's coming. You can keep arguing what you'll do
but he'll be walking down our boardways before you've reached
agreement. As for me, I'm going to go meet him."

"You can't do that," said Marsh.

Klarce silently looked around the table, pausing to lock eyes
with each of her fellow councilors. "I don't imagine any of you are
going to actually attempt to stop me. Chastise, perhaps even sanc-
tion me after the fact, but not stop me. I'm fine with that. But one
way or another, we need closure on him, and I'm going to get it."

~~~~~~

KLARCE opened her eyes to the real world, dipped her trunk into
the water pitcher on the table, and rinsed the taste of koph from
her mouth. She'd have liked to take a moment, splash some water

on her face and ears, but there wasn't time. She left the council room to find both Temmel and Regina waiting for her outside.

"How quickly can you get me down to the northern edge of the Shadow Dwell?"

Regina shook her head. "Not quickly enough. Even if he takes his time, the senator will easily have climbed the beach and reached the forest before we can stop him."

"I don't want to 'stop' him. I want to greet him. Likely he has only wild conjectures as to what he'll find here. The last thing we want is to put him on the defensive. He mustn't begin his visit here in a foreboding manner. We need to welcome him."

"There's no way to get there in time," said Temmel. Regina nodded beside him.

"Go," said Klarce.

"Ma'am?"

"Get to him, the both of you. Clear a path back, use my name, invoke the council if you have to. You're his honored escort, the personal assistants of a member of the council."

"How will we find him? By the time we reach the Shadow Dwell he could be anywhere."

"No, he won't. He'll be waiting just inside the forest for you to come and guide him to the Civilized Wood."

"How can you be so sure?"

Klarce smiled. "Because he'll be busy chatting with me."

~~~~~

SHE rushed down the hall to her office, fumbling with yet more koph as soon as she was through the door. Another dose, so soon after the last, and not the abbreviated mixture used in council. She'd pay for this later, possibly when she most lacked the resources but there was no other way. She dropped to a couch, calling up the index as soon as she had perception of nefshons, and swiftly singled out Jorl's thread. She let the rest of the index fade and yanked on that single strand.

"Jorl ben Tral!" She hailed him, spinning the scene to match the one he actually stood in, there on a rainswept beach, the bulk of his vessel in the water a short distance behind him, himself but a moment's walk from the forest's edge. "I bid you welcome. I am Klarce, my mother's name was Kolleen."

He stopped, the construct she'd spun of him reflecting his self-image, moving as he imagined he should move. And then he smiled, an expression that spoke volumes, revealing that he understood what had just happened and that he had experienced nefshon-based conversations with other living beings before. The realization rocked her more than she dared reveal; Margda's chosen one had violated more than just one piece of her precious edict.

"A pleasure to meet you. Klarce? Perhaps our mothers knew one another."

And that simply she set aside half her fears. However tainted this fool might be, whether from Margda's influence or some Alliance contagion, he was civilized. He was Fant. And so he must surely understand that the Caudex's work was as much for him as for anyone on Barsk. It was a place to start.

She returned his smile. "I suspect we both have seen far stranger things than that possibility. I hope we can compare notes."

He nodded. "I'd like that. But, and pardon this next question, I intend no disrespect, but I don't want to proceed from false assumption. Klarce, I know where we are in this moment, but before you spoke to me I stood on the last island. I am not of the Dying though. Are you? Are you here as well?"

"Yes, to the second, and no, to the first. The Dying do indeed come to these shores, though perhaps not to the particular beach you've selected. But those that proceed further are no longer Dying. They join us, high above your head in the Civilized Wood as full citizens and participants in our endeavors."

His ears rose and spread with obvious delight. "An entire Civilized Wood? Here? How large?"

"Not so small as you'd find on the smallest island of your archipelago, but near enough. I'm sure I can arrange a tour."

"Like this?"

"Oh no, that would never do. You need to appreciate it with your own senses. This, this was just so I could be here personally to welcome you. Your arrival took us by surprise."

"Not completely though."

"No. But we'll talk more of that soon. I've arranged a simple, home-cooked meal for you, if you're agreeable to dining with my partner and me."

"That sounds very agreeable. How am I to find my way there?"

"I've sent my assistants down to escort you. They should reach you shortly. Pardon their appearance if they are out of breath or otherwise disheveled. I emphasized speed in reaching you. I assure you they will take a more leisurely return."

He looked at her strangely. What did he see? Could he read her fatigue?

"Very well. Then I will abide here until they arrive. I look forward to seeing you and your spouse soon."

"Soon," she said, and broke the connection.

~~~~~

KLARCE'S assistants delivered Jorl to her on the front porch of Adolo's family home and then departed. Adolo had met them at the side door to the small parlor. Traditionally, it was a place for would-be suitors to some daughter of the house to meet without the pressure and attention of unwanted siblings and cousins—to say nothing of meddling aunts and grandmothers—and it served the need for a private welcoming of an unexpected visitor. From the look on his face and the posture of his ears, Jorl had not expected such a homey reception, and was embarrassed to have arrived without a visitor's gift. Adolo had waved away his discomfort by placing a hefty mug of day beer in his hands and ushering him over to the very chair that Klarce had occupied over the span of many visits while wooing her.

Klarce had expected Adolo to be put out at the prospect of hosting Jorl in her own home, but in fact she had embraced the idea with delight, perhaps seeing it as an opportunity to bring their personal lives closer to her work in the council. And certainly the Full Council had demonstrated a pronounced inability to come up with anything better. But now, having this Aleph sitting in her parlor, occupying her favorite chair, nibbling dried vlarjna berries from a dish Adolo had made for her during an ill-conceived couples' pottery class, it was all too much. She wasn't entertaining some visiting leader or scientist recovered from among the Dying, this was an Alliance senator in Fant guise, and always and above all the chosen of the Matriarch. More, he had somehow resisted the efforts of two teams to disrupt his memory. What secrets did he hold and what game was he playing?

They'd settled in and Jorl blandly held forth with a string of seemingly sincere compliments of the parlor, the courtesy afforded by Temmel and Regina, the appearance of what portion of the Civilized Wood he'd seen on his way here. It was all polite and empty and demonstrated he had no intention of volunteering anything. Before she could organize the myriad thoughts in her head and begin to properly but surreptitiously interrogate their guest, Adolo broke the conversational ice.

"I am led to understand that you are a scholar with an unparalleled knowledge of the Matriarch's prophecies," Adolo said, even as she stepped up to refill Jorl's cup with another serving of beer. If she caught Klarce's glare she gave no sign but continued making small talk, ever the perfect hostess. "That must be fascinating."

"Margda was a manipulative bitch," snapped Klarce, diplomacy giving way to the effects of too much koph on her illness. Schooling herself, she elaborated, attempting to soften her outburst. "Her many accomplishments not withstanding, nor the tragedy of the illness that caused her such discomfort in the latter half of her life, but she was the most disagreeable, single-minded Fant that ever lived."

Adolo had blanched at her lover's vehemence, but Jorl showed no offense. He sipped from his cup, scooped up another helping of berries with his trunk, and nodded thoughtfully as he chewed and swallowed. "That doesn't come through if you're just reading her texts or the other papers she left behind, but that was my assessment of her as well." He paused, turned his attention to Adolo, and smiled. "Thank you, these refreshments were exactly what I needed after the voyage here."

Klarce bit back a scowl. Let her love be taken in by his charm for the moment, she knew better and would sort her later. "Assessment, scholar? That sounds more like a personal opinion than a conclusion reached by many hours of research. Surely you never conversed with her yourself?"

The historian had been raising the cup to his mouth again and halted, likely realizing he had slipped up. His eyes revealed him in the midst of a calculation, whether he ought to dissemble or bluff his way through, or minimize the truth by treating it as a triviality.

He nodded. "Actually, I did. Only a few times over a couple of days. After so many years immersed in her work, it was a singularly . . . disappointing experience. I tend to let it fade from memory."

"How, disappointing? As a student of her life, someone actually foretold by one of her prophecies, you were marked with the aleph and forever changed on her word alone, and you found conversing with her disappointing?"

Jorl shrugged and fanned his ears, pretending a nonchalance that she knew was all fiction. "Say rather the conversation itself was disappointing. My apologies, I'm not at liberty to discuss the particulars of it."

"As may be," said Klarce. "And yet, if you had words with Margda, dead now the better part of eight centuries, you must perforce have been in violation of the first law of the Speaker's Edict. Was that what made the conversation less than the pinnacle event one might expect of a scholar meeting the source of his life's work? The utter betrayal of one of her most fundamental precepts, by her chosen one no less!"

From the corner of her eye Klarce could see Adolo flinch at still another display of bad manners, but her intention here wasn't simply to be rude to a guest. Rather, she had selected her words deliberately. She needed Jorl unbalanced, needed to gain the upper hand with him, no matter how convivial a visit Adolo had created. And yet, she had somehow failed. Far from appearing mortified, Jorl looked to be striving to fight back a smirk. He hid his mirth behind another swig, draining the cup and waving off Adolo's move to refill it again.

"I can see why you might think so," he said, "but in fact, I didn't summon her."

Now Klarce snorted, ignoring the horrified stare she drew from Adolo. "You say you spoke with her?"

He nodded. "I did."

"But didn't summon her? The Matriarch of Barsk, dead for all those years. Pray, tell me how you two managed to converse if you didn't discard the first law and summon her?"

His ears fell back and went still. He'd managed to school the amusement from his mouth but his eyes twinkled. "She summoned me."

"What?"

"Margda summoned me. She broke both the first and second law of the Speaker's Edict in doing so, but I suppose since she created the rules in the first place they were hers to break."

"Impossible! How could a dead Speaker summon a living one?"

The smile came back and as it spread across his face Klarce knew she'd lost this round. The smug bastard had stopped any pretense at hiding his amusement. But more, the gleam in his eye had transformed into something shrewder.

"I think you of all people would know the answer to that better than me. That's why I'm here, after all. Ignoring the Speaker's Edict is the least of the surprising things that take place in this city that is found on no map. How many people not on this island even know of its existence?"

Klarce bit back a laugh and resisted the temptation to quote the number, or lay claim to the handful or more for every island on Barsk, or mention the residents of Ulmazh above, let alone those beyond this star system. Any one of those responses would give too much away. He'd scored a hit, and knew it, but not to what extent. So, she could return his game and minimize, downplay what he thought he knew.

"This community was founded by Margda's contemporaries. They respected her work, but didn't agree with all of her ideas or how they should be used. But she had the support of the sitting government and she did not tolerate differing opinions, let alone differing schools of thought. That was in the time of the planet's first native-born generation. Less than half of the islands of the eastern archipelago had been colonized yet; the western islands had been charted from orbit but had yet to be visited. Those first Speakers who disagreed with her banded together and vanished from the world, creating a city on an unused spot beyond the western border of any settled land."

"So this island wasn't hidden back then?"

"Far from it. Back then you could even find it on maps—not that any of those maps exist today. And, of course, the cultural prohibition against technology was in its infancy so settling this place was easier because those who came here chose to embrace modernity rather than turn from it. That was the crux of the difference. Margda was a politician turned scientist. Our founders were scientists turned revolutionaries. While she was laying down her edict and defining the 'one true way' of Speaking, they were exploring the possibilities of nefshons in manners and directions that never occurred to her, generating hypotheses and testing their limits. I don't know why she failed to examine any of those possibilities. She wasn't stupid. Even those who hated her for her controlling personality acknowledged her brilliance. But she never pursued any of those other avenues of nefshon research."

"I suspect she couldn't," said Jorl. "The visions she had of the future and her goal of keeping Barsk strong in the face of an antagonistic Alliance shaped her work."

Klarce nodded. It stung to agree with the scholar, but he made sense. And it fit with things she and a handful of other living Speakers knew from direct experience. "Yes, always the visions. Lacking a scientist's curiosity, perhaps she had to rely on direction from her own damaged brain."

Jorl scooped up more berries, used chewing as an excuse for a moment of silence rather than reply. When he did speak, it was to direct the conversation back to an earlier topic.

"You said my assessment reflected conversation, but I was simply affirming what you'd already said. Which I take to mean that you have spoken to her yourself. Even unhindered by the edict, I have to wonder how that came about."

She laughed. "Oh, not just me. Speakers in this city have been summoning Margda since word of her death reached our shore within days of her passing. She's doubtless the most frequently summoned person in all of history. Doing so is a rite of passage among our leaders and most talented citizens. I myself have experienced her cutting intelligence, her contempt and disdain, seven separate times."

That had struck a nerve. His eyes had widened with each word. By the end, his trunk dropped into his lap, limp and weak. But what had he expected?

"I . . . I find that difficult to credit," he said. "Such a thing changes the deceased. I've seen it myself, before I learned better, from summoning a loved one again and again. I would have seen it in her when she summoned me. Heard it in her voice."

"No, scholar, you wouldn't. None of those thousands—yes, that many and more—thousands of summonings left any mark on her nefshons."

Emotion became animation and he swung his head and trunk from side to side in violent denial. "No. That's impossible."

Klarce relished her turn to be smug. "For you, perhaps. For those trained only in the knowledge that the Matriarch passed along. But here we studied not just those teachings but many different things as well. We learned to control and influence and disrupt the formation of memories. Every Speaker in this city who ever summoned Margda stripped her of the experience as the final part of the event. She recalled no summoning, nor any word shared with her, and thus each time one of our Speakers drew her here it was the first time all over again for her."

He took a moment, absorbing what she'd shared. "You left her only quiet," said Jorl.

"A colorful description, but apt."

"She had to have known though. Given how much of the future she saw in her visions, how could she not have seen that others would summon her?"

"You're probably right at that, scholar. Careful notes were taken every time we spoke with her. Invariably, once the Speaker had established her construct, her expression would begin with something I thought bordered on amusement and then change at once to disappointment and disregard. As if she knew she'd be summoned, but that none of us were the one she expected."

"That . . . that makes sense to me," he said, but didn't expand on how or why he thought so.

"Does it? A pity then that we cannot ask her to elaborate. But that doesn't surprise you, does it, Jorl?"

"I don't understand what you mean."

"No? Because as I've noted, the Speakers of this island have been conversing with Margda regularly since the time of her death. That tradition ended unexpectedly just a few years ago. Specifically, seven years. Does anything stand out for you from that time? Because we've had reason to examine it carefully, trying to tease out possible explanations. A time that is marked by you, her designated aleph, causing some kind of ruckus in the station that is the Alliance's sole link to our world. A time that also corresponds with an unexplainable appointment of a Fant to the Alliance senate. Never mind that no Fant has ever enjoyed such an office, yours included permanent standing among that body's most important committee."

She stopped speaking and glanced up at Adolo, sweet Adolo, who had never had an interest in politics or science but was ever content to teach children their numbers and letters and ensure that life had some semblance of normalcy for those growing up in this strange place. Adolo stared back at her, the back of one hand raised to her mouth, her eyes wide but not really seeing. She turned and hurried from the parlor. It was just as well.

Klarce returned her attention to her "guest." "Tell me, Jorl, you're the historian here. Surely you don't believe in coincidence. Not one of such magnitude. Surely you have some inkling of why, despite the efforts of the most powerful Speakers on this island, none of us have succeeded in summoning Margda since that day."

He nodded. "I do."

"You caused this, didn't you."

Again the nod. "I did."

"What did you do? What could you possibly do to prevent so many talented people from doing what we have done for centuries?"

"I . . . I removed her from the range of your talent."

"Excuse me?"

"It doesn't matter. It's clear you have studied the science of summoning in ways unknown to Margda's students and their successors, just as it's apparent that you've also schooled yourself in the things she taught. But it hasn't occurred to you that someone might be able to do something you can't. Even if I told you how it happened, you wouldn't believe me."

Klarce spread her hands in front of her and gestured an invitation with her trunk. "We're nearly all scholars and scientists on this island. Try me."

He sat silent a moment, glancing into his empty cup before setting it aside again. His gaze traveled to the dish that had held the berries and found it empty as well. His head came up and he locked his eyes with hers. "Fine. Her nefshons. I dispersed them. That simply."

"That doesn't make sense."

"No, what doesn't make sense to you is that it could be something so simple. You know the process. At the end of any summoning, the Speaker releases the control that has brought the conversant's nefshons together and gives them a push, sending them back on their way, spreading out through space as everything does."

"Yes, yes, but then the next Speaker pulls them together again, or gathers other particles from that conversant until enough are present to allow a summoning. What did you do differently? Something else is in play here. I've attempted it myself. Her nefshons no longer come when called."

"Oh, that's not true. I'm sure they still come. But as I said, they're beyond your range. Summoning someone is all about pulling particles to you. But I didn't want to Speak with her, not ever again. So I pushed them instead. When I sent Margda's nefshons away, I spread them far. Unimaginably so. A single Speaker doesn't have sufficient time, not on the duration of a single use of koph, not in the span of a lifetime of such attempts, to bring them back far enough. It won't happen."

Klarce frowned. "Manipulation of nefshons, whether pulling them towards the Speaker or as you suggest pushing them away, works at the same rate. To move them too far to be retrieved would require a comparable amount of time. But physics aside, even if such a thing were possible, what would be the point?"

"For the reasons you said at the beginning of this conversation. Calling Margda single-minded and disagreeable doesn't begin to describe her. She played with the lives of generations of Fant in pursuit of her own agenda. I wasn't going to risk her ever being able to do that again."

"So you dispersed her? Beyond all recall? No, I don't believe that could be done."

He just shrugged. "And yet, you haven't been able to summon her since. If you have a better explanation, I'd welcome the telling of it." He sighed, as if he'd relived something that had cost him dear, something Klarce wished she understood if only to use it against him. Again he picked up his empty mug. His trunk quested across the dish Adolo had made for her.

"Could I get something more to drink? And do you have any more of those berries?"

She ignored him, his outlandish claims somehow relieving her of the responsibility of hospitality.

"Your ship is here out of season."

He held the mug up, a prop to hide behind. "That's not the sort of thing I would think you'd know. That it's here, certainly, you'd have detected it at your shore. But that it has a regular schedule. . . ."

"The Caudex pays attention to a great many things, Senator."

"Ah, that's the name I was waiting to hear. The one Fisco mentioned. That's what you call yourselves? All of this?" He waved his trunk in a circle as if encompassing the island.

"And more," Klarce said. She frowned. How was it he kept gaining more from all this than her?

"Hmm. Well, as to my ship, yes, it came early. A . . . special circumstance. Senatorial business, I can't elaborate."

"Bringing a Procy to Barsk seems beyond the purview of your office, and a violation of the spirit—if not quite the letter—of the Compact."

Ah, she'd scored another point. She saw it in his eyes, a widening of surprise followed by a narrowing as his mind raced to fabricate something vaguely convincing and wholly false. It was time to switch tactics and keep him off balance.

"Would it amaze you to learn that I know a great deal more about your situation than just the comings and goings of your yacht? I have personally read every book you've written, reviewed every journal article you've published. I know you've maintained the same abode longer than any other male on Keslo. I'm aware that, perhaps out of a misguided sense of loyalty to a dead friend, you have acknowledged the existence of an abomination—"

"His name is Pizlo."

She lashed from right to left with her trunk, symbolically and mentally waving away the name.

"I know your daily routine, Jorl. I can access your tenday grocery list, the people you correspond with on other islands, the names and details of the last play you attended. Shall I tell you the title of every book you've ordered from your wife's bookshop?"

Through most of her recitation he had sat still, showing no emotion. At this last piece his ears flapped back and up and he leaned forward in his seat. When he spoke, his voice had dropped an octave.

"I came here seeking an understanding to a puzzle, and you tell me that you've been treating me as such for some time. That's fine, and if you have specific questions I'll do my best to provide you with answers. But your curiosity stops at me. I will *not* have you scrutinize my family. That ends now. My wife and daughter are no part of anything that should interest you."

Klarce kept the reaction from her face. Daughter? How had she missed something as significant as the historian having a daughter? What else had Dabni left out of her reports? She raised her trunk in a halting gesture and extended an open hand as if revealing a peace offering.

"Be at ease, please. Your daughter has never been of interest. Believe me when I tell you she isn't mentioned in any of the reports I receive on you. Your wife, however, is another matter."

"She shouldn't be of interest to you either."

"You give her far too little credit, Jorl. After all, who do you think has been filing all those reports?"

And just that easily she saw she'd defeated him. The self-assured smirk, the smug confidence, fell away. He slumped back in his chair, arms limp at his side, trunk flat across his chest. His ears hung back. He seemed to age a decade in that instant and Klarce could almost believe the faint glow of the aleph on his forehead dimmed just a fraction.

"Dabni . . ."

"She's a Caudex field agent. One of thousands. We sent her to Keslo specifically to keep watch on you. You said you came here to unravel a puzzle; I share this with you so you can ponder a new one of which you were unaware. Doubtless you and your spouse will have much to discuss when you return. But frankly, I don't care. Your personal life doesn't concern me. It's your professional life as a member of the Alliance senate that worries me."

He shook his head, following the direction of the conversation like a man dragging himself through the mud of the Shadow Dwell. "There's nothing to worry over. I'm not here to play power games with you and your Caudex, regardless of what you believe of my situation with the Alliance senate."

She'd broken him. It was only a matter of changing tacks again and she would own him.

"We've been quite frank with one another thus far, and whether you believe me or not, I am with all sincerity the closest thing you have to a friend on this island. You say there's no cause for worry, and yet my people are concerned. Tell me why a Raccoon has come to see you, tell me so I can alleviate panic before it runs away and cannot be stopped."

"She . . . she has a proposal."

"For?"

"For immigration."

"She's seeking Eleph or Lox to immigrate elsewhere in the Alliance? That hardly seems likely given the lengths they went to to put us all here."

"No, not Fant. She wants to have other races emigrate to Barsk. To share this world with us."

In a million years Klarce would never have imagined someone would sit in her parlor and speak those words. Adolo might as well have come back into the room and slapped her full in the face with a sack of barley.

"That's . . . impossible!"

Jorl nodded. "At the moment it's merely a thought experiment."

"A dangerous one. And what is your position?"

"Although I feel the only way our people are to survive in the galaxy is for us to once again live among other races, whether here on Barsk or out there on other worlds, I've yet to come up with a scenario that gets past the pragmatic without ending in disaster."

Klarce composed herself. "The Full Council will be relieved to learn that."

"Full Council?"

She inclined her head. "The governing body of the Caudex. I wonder, would you be inclined to meet with them?"

"That depends," he said, drawing out his response, regaining some of his composure before her eyes. "Will they answer my questions, or just ask more of their own?"

Her ears flapped at his wryness. It would be easy to like this scholar, his sharp wit, his insight. But no, even if as he claimed he had banished the Matriarch from all reach, she had nonetheless chosen him. Whether he understood it or not, he would be forever at odds with the Caudex.

"I think an accommodation can be made. Tomorrow, at midday?"

"Thank you, I'd like that." He stood and, damn him, despite the knowledge of his wife's betrayal the fool was smiling. "Then, if it's not too much trouble, I should get back to my ship."

"I'll have one of my assistants escort you down to the beach."

He nodded, paused, and to Klarce's surprise extended his hand to her. "I wasn't sure what I was going to find here, but this . . ." his trunk swung round again, though something in the gesture this time limited the inclusion to just the room. "Not what I expected. Thank you. And if you would, pass along my appreciation to Adolo as well."

She escorted him to the door. Regina and Temmel waited outside, alert as it opened.

"Regina, would you kindly escort the senator to the spot of beach where he came ashore?"

"Yes, ma'am. Senator, if you'll follow me please?"

"Of course." He paused and turned back to Klarce. "I'll be back on that spot a bit before noon."

"And Regina will be waiting to escort you to our Full Council, Senator. Until then."

He nodded and followed Regina down the boardway and a moment later was gone to her view. She took a deep breath, made a mental note to take her meds early tonight, and focused her attention on Temmel.

"Send word to Sind. Regina will escort the senator to the council room tomorrow for a midday session of the Full Council."

"Regina? Not you?"

"No, you and I will be elsewhere, though naturally I'll still attend the council."

"Where will we—"

She cut him off. "Contact Bernath. Get an update on the physicist's devices. If they're ready, have them put aboard the shuttle. If not, bring what you have and him as well. Likewise the three flight school candidates. We'll be leaving at dawn."

"Ma'am? The council countermanded the shuttle's departure—"

"Because of the presence of the senator's ship. But we know where that ship is, and we know where it's going to be, at least until he returns to our shore. I intend to use that window to get us to Ulmazh. If the Full Council judges him to be a problem, I'll have far more resources available to me there than here. Now go, set it all in motion and then grab some sleep. Tomorrow will be here soon enough."

Not waiting for a reply, she stepped back into Adolo's family home. Somewhere in that vast collection of rooms and hallways she still had to find her lover, and apologize for her rudeness to their guest. As if that was the most important thing that had taken place there today.

TWENTY-TWO

CHOICES

~~~~~~~~~~~~~~

OLTA was away when Dabni had returned home, a small grace. One of Tolta's younger sisters had been due to deliver her first child a tenday ago and the delay had worn the mother-to-be to a frazzle. Dabni found a note pinned to a cupboard, a quick explanation that the sister had gone into labor at last and all signs pointed to a prolonged delivery. She wanted all of her siblings gathered around her when she gave birth—even the disowned one. Tolta might be gone for days.

Rina had gone off with her father on an overnight field trip to meet his Sloth assistant, which meant Dabni had the house to herself. When she awoke the next morning, it occurred to her that instead of rising and beginning yet another day, she could just sleep in. Allowing the book shop to remain closed for a day or maybe two struck her as a compelling idea. Jorl was beyond the range of her watch, and her index of the people of Keslo was up to date. She could just roll over and go back to sleep.

A sudden tug on her consciousness wrenched the fantasy from her and left her fully alert, as if she'd been plunged into an icy rain.

Her simple bedroom vanished, replaced by the imposition of Klarce's office flooding her senses.

"Your target will be on his way back to you soon," said the councilor. "You'd indicated that the senator had gone off on an outing, transported by his assistant. Is it possible you didn't know he was coming to the final island?"

She fanned her ears frantically at the news. The frown on Klarce's face reflected Dabni's ignorance back at her. She was still processing the councilor's words. Last island? How did Jorl even know the location of the last island? Centering herself and blushing as she struggled to regain control she asked, "Surely he did not allow the Sloth to land with him."

"No, though one might argue that as this island exists on no map of Barsk it cannot be considered a part of the Compact. In any case, neither of us pressed the point and the Brady remained aboard his yacht for the duration of the visit. I spoke with him at length and in a short while he'll be interviewed by the Full Council. I'm sure he'll brief you fully upon it when he returns to Keslo."

"Brief me? Why . . . why would he do such a thing?"

"He has been informed that you are an operative of the Caudex and our agent on Keslo."

Dabni lost all composure again, gasping before she could stifle the reaction. "But . . . doesn't that compromise my assignment? How am I to keep watch on him if he knows I'm doing so?"

"You compromised it long since. Or did you imagine it an unimportant detail that he had given you a child?"

Rina. Rina had been onboard the yacht. The "field trip" had been to the final island. Had Klarce met her daughter?

"Councilor . . . I can explain. You see, I—"

"Spare me. Consider yourself on probation until the Full Council can take the time to properly assess whether your action reflects a simple lie of omission or deliberate treason. Rest assured, a new agent will be assigned to your husband."

"That's hardly necessary, I'm right here. My loyalty has never swayed. Please. You have all my reports. In all the time I've been here, Jorl's done nothing to warrant suspicion. Whatever reason the Matriarch had for marking him, he's never threatened the Caudex's purpose."

Klarce's response lowered the temperature in the imagined office. "That's not for a field agent to say. You have only a tiny piece of the entire picture. Jorl ben Tral may not be a threat, but he is far from harmless. That said, the council will likely reach an agreement with him and be content, for now. But we would be foolish not to keep him under surveillance. And, as you've demonstrated a lack of objectivity, that task is beyond you and will be assigned to another."

She swallowed, holding her body still. "I understand."

"You are not completely out of favor, Dabni, but the council is *very* disappointed with you. Consider it a sign of our regard for your previous work that I have reached out to warn you that your husband is aware of your double life. Goodbye."

Like the closing of a book, the conversation ended and Dabni was back in the warmth of her bed. She let out a great breath and shuddered, as her body reacted to the information. Had they also told Rina? And if so, how much had they told her about the Caudex? The child was bright but she couldn't possibly fathom what it all meant. And somehow Jorl had learned of the final island, which meant if he hadn't already known to find the Caudex there, he knew it now. But again, what else had they told him? About Ulmazh? About their long-range plans for saving the Fant? Even now his keen mind would be reviewing the time since they met, putting together any pieces that had seemed slightly out of place over the years. And again, how much had Klarce told him? That she had been assigned to watch him was certain, but what about the order to end his life?

A sound at the foot of her bed pulled her attention from her thoughts. Pizlo stood there, red-rimmed eyes intent on her.

"Who were you talking to?" he asked.

"What? I—no one, of course, there's no one else here."

The boy frowned and she felt a tug on her awareness much as when Klarce had summoned her. A duplicate bedroom formed in her mind, one in which Pizlo now sat at the end of the bed.

"I saw you, in a park a while back. I saw you plucking people's threads and doing something that Jorl never said Speakers could do. That got me wondering what other things you might be able to do. So now when I know I'm going to see you I take some koph first. In case you're doing something special, I don't want to miss it. And just now, you were talking to someone. Jorl taught me the trick of it, because he worries about me and wants to be able to check in. I don't know if he does it with anyone else much though, because it's against the edict. But that's what you were doing, right? What I'm doing now. So it's not just Jorl breaking that rule, and that's another way you're not like other Speakers. And I bet that's probably so about whoever you were talking to."

Even after so many years, talking with Pizlo made her feel like someone had shoved her trunk in a vice. For Tolta's sake she'd tried to see him as just another child. But it was one thing to steel herself for an encounter with him and quite another to be taken by surprise. Still, here he was asking questions that she'd never anticipated from him. She took a calming breath and her training reminded her that she needed to reframe the situation and establish her control.

"It's rude to spy on people and listen in on their conversations."

"I wasn't listening in," he said. "I might have, if I'd gotten here sooner. But by the time it occurred to me to try and grab some of your threads like I'd seen you do, you were done."

"Fine, then it's rude to grab people's nefshons."

"Is it more or less rude, if the nefshons being grabbed are those of someone you know—like my grabbing yours—or strangers like the people in that park?"

"There are some things that simply aren't any of your business, Pizlo. Just because you share everything you know does not mean everyone else does or must. Adults often have secrets."

"Like that you're a Speaker? Does Jorl know?"

"He . . . no, no he does not. There's no reason he should know. I don't use the ability to Speak to the dead."

"But you do use it, just in other ways. Like at the park. Will you tell me what you did?"

Dabni glared at him and thought—not for the first time—that maybe the Caudex would be well served having an agent keeping an eye on the island's wild child abomination. Perhaps she could convince Klarce to allow her to remain by offering to take on a task no one else would bear. "Have you grown up to be an extortionist, Pizlo? Are you demanding I show you this thing or you'll tattle to my husband?"

Pizlo's ears fanned out in surprise. She'd guessed wrong.

"I'm just trying to understand what I saw. It looked like you were taking nefshons from people and building something. Will you show me how you did that?"

She shook her head. "Honestly, I cannot."

"But you had it in your hands. I saw it grow."

"You misunderstood. I don't know how to build such things. I was given the thing you saw me holding. I only know how to add to it, I can't create such a thing from scratch."

"Oh." Pizlo regarded her silently and moved closer up her bed. "If you show it to me maybe I can help you figure it out."

Dabni almost dismissed the absurdity of Pizlo's offer out of hand. She was Caudex trained. What could a wildling teach her? And yet . . . until he'd asked the question, she'd never considered the implications behind the index, had never thought or realized that though she could modify the structure, she wouldn't know where to begin if she wanted to craft such a thing herself. Perhaps his unique perspective could show her something new, which in turn she might use to stay in favor with Klarce and the council. She doubted the Caudex would have any compunction of moving her to another island and not letting Rina to come with. Or, even if they allowed her to come, Dabni hardly liked the notion of taking the girl away from ready access to her father. For her child's sake, if she could learn something valuable from Pizlo she had to try.

"We call it the *index*," she said, bringing her hands together and summoning the complex structure into being whole from memory. Its shining shape hovered above her open palms."

"We who?" asked Pizlo.

"Myself and another Speaker who gave it to me."

"Oh. That's not the same Speaker as the one you haven't told?"

"Told? Told who? Told what? What are you talking about?"

He shrugged, all of his attention still on the index. "There's a Speaker who gave you this, and there's at least one other who gave you something else. You were supposed to give that other thing to Jorl, but you never did."

"I . . . how do you know anything about that? Who told you about Klarce?"

Pizlo sighed, sounding much like her daughter did when she'd exasperated Rina by treating her like a child at a moment where she felt herself the epitome of adulthood. "Nobody tells me, not like you mean. Sometimes I just *know* things. But I don't have all the details. Like, I didn't know her name until you just said it or what the other thing was—"

"Fine. That's as it should be. It's private and none of your business."

"Well, can I at least see it? You're letting me see this one."

"What? No, absolutely not! Tolta would never forgive me!"

"What does Tolta have to do with it? She's not a Speaker, not like you and me and Jorl."

"Because it's a bad thing, Pizlo. It's a meme designed to hurt people."

He frowned. "Oh. Is that why you didn't give it to Jorl?"

"I . . . well, yes."

"But this Klarce, she wanted you to? To hurt him?"

She wanted to cry. The innocence of the boy's perspective unnerved her, cut through the rationalizations she'd told herself, the lies. With a sob, she confessed, amazing herself as she did. "They didn't just want him hurt, Pizlo. They wanted me to kill him. They didn't give me a choice. They rescinded the order or he'd be dead by now. Do you understand? They asked me to murder my husband, the father of my child."

"But . . . you didn't."

"No."

"That's what I thought."

"But I might have."

"No. Not for a long time. You just haven't realized that. Not yet." And just that quickly, he let it go. No judgment, no guilt. He'd gone back to studying the index in her hands. "How do you make it work?"

Dabni shook her head, sorting her thoughts, shunting aside the strange sense of absolution and focusing on the need to pluck something of success out her failure. "Look more closely and tell me what you see."

He settled next to her on the bed and pressed his face as near to the index as he could without actually touching it. "It's big and small at the same time. It's like . . . it's like a map!" His ears lifted up and he grinned. "Like a map of the archipelagos, but instead of islands and their locations it's made up of people."

"You're right. Mmm. I never looked at it that way. I've always thought of it more like a complicated jumble of connections."

He shook his head and moved around the bed, trying to look at the index from the side. "That can't be right," he said. "If it were then it couldn't have a shape. There'd be no starting point to hook the first things together." He reached for it.

"Don't touch it!"

But her warning came too late and though the construct of the boy's hand didn't actually touch the index, he made contact with it. He gasped as he drew his hand back, holding a copy he'd somehow made. That was further than she'd been prepared to allow, but no matter. She would snatch it back as the onrush of information dropped him and then disrupt his memory of it before he could recover.

"Wow! That's incredible." Pizlo tossed his copy of the index back and forth from hand to trunk to other hand like a ball.

Dabni gaped. "How are you doing that?"

"I kinda have to. It tickles. No, itches. Well, no that's not exactly right either. It's prickly. All those people trying to talk to me at once. They're settling down now, a little." He continued to juggle it.

"You're not feeling overwhelmed?"

He shrugged. "Not really. I mean, a little, maybe. It's a lot like when I see one of the moons through the clouds and it pours a lot of knowledge and facts into me. It's like drinking the rain; you don't have to swallow all the time, you can just let it flow into your open mouth and down your throat. You don't need to taste it all."

"That's . . . okay. I have to think about that. No one has ever described it that way." She let the index fade from her grasp. And Pizlo did the same with his. A moment later he manifested it again in his other hand.

"How did you take a copy from me? You shouldn't take things that aren't yours."

"I didn't mean to, and like you said, it's a copy, so you still have yours. As soon as I touched one thread in it the whole thing came rushing into me. First the structure and then all the people."

"You saw the underlying structure?"

He grinned, still not overwhelmed as she had been that first time, but looking a little drunk. "Oh yeah."

"Can you tell me anything else about it? How it was made?"

He nodded. "Oh sure. Kind of like rain, too. Well, like a drop."

"I don't understand."

"A raindrop. You know, it's not just water, right? The water forms around a particle of dust. This is like that. Only instead of dust, they used an idea."

"A particle of an idea?"

"Uh huh. Because nefshons are particles, too, just smaller. That's what's at the heart of your index. Somebody's nefshon of an idea."

"Can you tell what that idea is?"

"You don't know? The whole thing resonates with it. It's what's holding all the pieces together."

"Humor me. What's the idea?"

"Everyone. Every bit you add tells every other bit that together they're everyone."

"That's it?"

"Well sure. The best ideas are big but simple. Because everyone is in it, it always wants to include everyone. I think that's why it jumped into me. Your copy doesn't know me. Why is that?"

Dabni sighed and, not for the first time, wondered what the child of Tolta and Arlo might have accomplished if he had been conceived after they'd properly bonded. "You already know the answer to that, Pizlo."

His face dropped and he let the index fade from him again. "Oh. Yeah."

TWENTY-THREE
SPEAKING BEYOND SILENCE

⌒⌒⌒⌒⌒

PIZLO left the house in search of breakfast. He could have raided his mother's larder, but he wanted to get some distance from Dabni and think about what she'd shown him, what she'd said, and what she hadn't said. Adults were odd that way, breaking the world into the parts they talked about and the parts they kept secret, as if anything could really be hidden away for long. He burrowed into the green framework of the Civilized Wood and began to climb.

He liked to think that Arlo hadn't been that way, that he inherited his father's philosophy that all the world existed to be discovered. It was really the only way they were alike, although they took that view in different directions. Far from finding comfort in the physical world or the study of sciences that Tolta insisted were a legacy of his father, the knowledge that everything around him consisted of ever smaller pieces that he couldn't see or touch nagged at Pizlo. Reality, as he understood the physicality of it, had weight, took up space, possessed color. But what color was a chemical bond? How many molecules could he hold in his cupped hands? What was the weight of all the chromosomes in one of the bugs in his collection? Science, as Arlo had understood it, had obeyed very strict rules. There were constants that brooked no variation and which in turn allowed practitioners to build grand theories and design elaborate experiments, all to lock down still more rules. Like they thought the only way to understand a thing was to define it in relation to every other tangible thing that they already understood.

But that only applied to stuff. Not everything was stuff. Ideas weren't tangible. You couldn't assess their weight or volume. Ideas were never meant to be grasped in one's trunk. They lacked physicality, had no need of it, wouldn't know what to do with it in the first place. To imagine a thing was to give life to it, without the need for genetics or physics or any of those things that other boys and girls his age studied in the gymnasium. He'd hidden outside the windows of classrooms enough to be sure of it. Nor had any of the moons contradicted this understanding.

Maybe that's why Dabni was surprised that he could hold the index he accidentally copied. He'd embraced a different metaphor than she had. Years before, when he had stood upon the space station high above the grip of Barsk's atmosphere, Telko, the greatest of the planet's moons, had poured its wisdom into him. Pizlo knew that "wisdom" was an abstract thing and the "pouring" was a metaphor. It didn't have to make any sense, even if Telko had filled him beyond measure and kept on pouring insight and possibilities into him. Even if really, it had all been him anyway. You couldn't fill up because knowledge didn't have volume.

He'd been just a kid back then, not even seven years old.

Tell that to most people and they'd think it the most incredible thing they'd heard in their lives, doubly so because it had happened to an abomination. But barely a day later, Jorl had created a new kind of abomination than had ever been before and a man had ceased to exist. That Yak—a once prominent senator named Bish—lived still. Pizlo was fairly certain of it. Jorl had somehow made it so that every memory of him, every thought, every memory association, vanished. Only Jorl recalled him, because he'd made the thing happen and somehow existed outside the awfulness he'd wrought.

Pizlo had met the senator that day but couldn't recall it. But he remembered what Telko had told him, the particulars of that encounter before it happened and all the horror of what was coming. Only the two of them, he and Jorl, knew there had ever been such a senator—leader of the Committee of Information and the architect of the plot that could have killed everyone on Barsk. The man who had nearly slain Jorl! One day he had commanded powerful forces, directed the flight and purpose of space ships, dictated the policies of hundreds of worlds, possessed the ability to end or enhance the careers of thousands of politicians and industrialists and artists, and wielded the largest collection of precognitivists ever assembled. Pizlo knew that because Telko had told him so. Just as he knew that Jorl had ripped that away in a moment, leaving only silence where before there had been unchecked power.

Pizlo took another dose of koph from his pocket, pressing it up inside his left cheek to let it dissolve. The wistful scent of spiralmint filled his sinuses. He burrowed in deeper amidst the foliage that defined the back wall of this hideaway, the empty space of the chimney that bore his father's name lying far on the other side. It seemed an appropriate spot for what he planned.

As his perception of nefshons began he built a different space than he used for his summoning of the Archetype of Man, drawing from earlier memories. The details weren't as sharp as he could do now, working with nefshons had caused him to become a better observer of surroundings, the shape and texture of things. But his recollection of the past served well enough. He didn't have to make it perfect, just familiar enough that his conversant recognized it.

He started with the room, defining its size as he recalled viewing it from just within the door. Walls took shape, flowed up and down and suddenly the room had a floor and ceiling, the whole of the space dimly lit. The walls on either side sprouted boxes of white plastic that resolved into cabinets. At the back of the room he added a polished desk, all of green stone that reflected back the little light in the room. More furniture then, a table of the same stone, and around the table on three sides a massive sofa covered over in a brown fabric that he recalled had been so very soft. Beneath the table, and both behind and in front of the desk, Pizlo conjured thick rugs of sweet smelling grass. As an afterthought, he conjured two mugs of vanilla cocoa for the table, wisps of their flavor painting the air with a faint sweetness. He stepped into the room, walked behind the desk, and sat in a chair whose size threatened to swallow him, a chair that hadn't been there a moment before. He tried to lean on the desk, found himself too low, and managed it in his second attempt after creating a stack of books under him on the chair. It was as good as his memory could make it. That was the easy part.

Speakers, both on and off Barsk, had rituals when summoning someone. They'd emerged about the same time as the rules for what one should and shouldn't do with nefshons. Margda's rules. He knew of them from his studies but had never used them. He only ever summoned the Archetype of Man, and Jorl himself had assured him the establishing ritual would be meaningless to it. Which meant it wasn't a necessary part of the process, just a commonplace one. So, if the nefshons didn't care, he didn't see any reason he should. With no more thought for protocol, he reached out for the particles he desired.

Pizlo was one of the few people who knew that Jorl had broken the rules of the Speaker's Edict. And yet, he summoned people just the same. So, like the establishing ritual, the rules of the edict were just another lie of the Matriarch. With that in mind he broke one of them, reaching out for the nefshons of a man he believed still lived. Jorl had sent him far away to a frontier world that might one day become a new colony of the Alliance. But seven years earlier all of his nefshons had been pulled to the space station in orbit above Barsk. They'd dissipated in that time, but not so far that Pizlo couldn't call to them, not much harder than another Speaker might reach out to a relative that had sailed off a tenyear ago. Soon he had a portion of those nefshons gathering in front of him. They in turn connected back to the source, defying rules of time and distance, a trail of particles that allowed him to capture more recent nefshons from his living target. It was like he held a string made of connected particles, running all the way from Barsk to the other side of the galaxy. Like—and Pizlo gasped as he made the connection—like the nefshon thread he'd seen Dabni manipulating.

As the connection solidified, he had a sense of the man as he now was. Pizlo let him take form, drawing the appearance from a blend of self-image and unconscious admittance of how he appeared to others that were present in the memories sloughed off from the moment before.

The Yak took shape, aged far more than he appeared in Pizlo's seven-year-old premonition. He'd lost a lot of weight, muscle mass mostly, and his body sagged as if his horns sought to drag him to the ground at every moment. Gone were the former senator's fancy robes, replaced by a utilitarian and heavily patched jumpsuit somewhere between dirt brown and mottled green. He appeared tired beyond the power of simple sleep to repair, his eyes as dead as any Pizlo had looked upon. He looked defeated, or worse, broken.

"Do you know where you are?" he asked the Bos.

Slowly Bish lifted his head. His eyes widened as he took in the room, the desk. He tried to speak, failed, wet his lips and tried again.

"This . . . is my office."

"No, this *was* your office. It's mine now, at least for the moment. But never yours again. Do you know me? Or if not, can you infer who I am?"

"You're a Fant."

Pizlo rolled his eyes. Why had he been so afraid of this man? "Push past the obvious. I can't believe you've met very many of us."

"You're not Jorl." He scowled and spat into the grass rug. "I'll remember him to my dying day. He killed me."

"Worse, he left you alive. But no, I'm not Jorl. Nor does he know we're having this conversation. This doesn't concern him."

Bish stood a bit straighter, meeting Pizlo's gaze for the first time. "This isn't real. I'm still on Dorrance. Still picking beans like a common laborer."

"That's right, we're a long way from your colony. You're there but you're also here."

He nodded. "This is like when Jorl brought the members of the committee together from all their worlds. But . . . you're not him. I thought only he could do that."

"There's a trick to it, but it's not important. Do you recognize me? One abomination to another?" Pizlo saw on the Yak's face when the pieces fell together.

"You're the brat." He stood a little straighter as he said that last word, anger evident in his eyes. "The precognitive wonder that Druz brought to me. You've grown up some. That makes sense. The days run together here but surely you've had years to mature. And you've become another damn Speaker, too?"

"I am. I have. Though you're one of a very small number of conversants that I've summoned."

The Bos snorted. "Excuse me if I don't feel flattered by the attention. What do you want? And how is it you know who I am? No one does. No one remembers a thing."

"They all forgot you. Everyone but Jorl."

"And you."

"No, I forgot you too. I just remember what I learned by unconventional means before I forgot. Like you said, I'm a *wonder*."

His guest considered that a moment then nodded. "Druz said your rating was likely to exceed all others when you hit puberty. Huh. Score one for the Brady."

"There's no point in keeping score or worrying about anyone but us. I brought you here to talk with you. I won't keep you long."

Bish snorted again, shaking his head. The tips of his horns danced briefly closer causing Pizlo to flinch. That reaction drew a smile from the Yak.

"Why would you think I'd have anything to say to a Fant? My time in exile hasn't made your kind any less repugnant, and I blame your associate for my fall. End this. Send me back. We're done." He bowed his head and as he exhaled his body folded in, what little bluster he'd possessed used up that quickly. The anger that had flared from some banked inner fire had spent itself. Once again he just looked broken.

Pizlo considered ending it. Bad as he'd been, this man had lost everything. What right did he have to add to Bish's torment? But then he recalled the Abomination of Fintz, and wrapped himself in his resolve. "We'll be done when I say we're done. You have the rest of your life, whatever time may be left to it, to pick beans. I don't care about that. I need to know about the life you led before you were forgotten. I need to understand how you did what you accomplished, built what you created. I don't have the luxury of figuring it out on my own. I want you to teach it to me, the high points, the underlying structure and concepts, as much as you can, right here, right now."

The Yak raised his head again, staring across the desk. "What are you talking about, boy? It's all gone. You understand that? There's nothing left that I could teach you even if I wanted to."

"There is. Your life's work, the methods, the skills, they're still in you. I need that."

"What are you talking about?"

"Power," said Pizlo. "Teach me about the acquisition of power."

Bish shook his head. "You're just a boy. Why would you crave power?"

"Why does anyone? Start there. Why *crave* instead of *want* or *desire*?"

The Bos chuckled then, weak and soft, laughing at him. "That's the heart of it, boy. The difference between need and want."

"Explain. Why is that the heart?"

Nodding, the Yak turned and stepped to the sofa, lowering himself down upon it, too tired to hold up his own frame. "Look at those words. What do people need?"

Pizlo waited, thinking at first the Yak was being rhetorical. But no, he truly wanted an answer. "Do you mean what do people need to live? Like air and water? And food? Shelter?"

"What else? What must a person have?"

"Um . . . clothing? Companionship maybe?"

"And what do people want?"

"Like I said, all of that."

"No, that was need," said Bish. "What do they want?"

"Stuff. A nicer house, maybe. Or books. Trips? I don't know . . . I don't really want much, I guess."

"How nice for you. But that's the crux of it. That's where power fits in."

"Because people want power?"

"No, the people who want power aren't the ones to concern yourself with. It's the ones who need it, like air and sustenance. That's it, right there. Power sustains. It is the means to everything else. Those who understand this, who truly crave power, are the only people who can properly wield it."

"Wield it how?"

"As they choose. That's the beauty of power. At its essence, it becomes the means to shape creation, to impose one's will on reality."

Pizlo felt a little sick. "Like here, in a summoning. I created this room. I have the power here."

Bish laughed, cackled actually. "This? This isn't power. This is fantasy. I'm not a Speaker but I know this cannot last much longer. And when it ends, I'll be back to picking beans and you'll return to being a repugnant child who thought it might be amusing to waste my time with your questions."

"Maybe you're right—"

"I am!"

"Yeah, but if you are, while I've got you here, I'm going to keep asking you questions."

The Yak shrugged and looked away. "You can ask. I don't have to answer."

"Are your beans really more interesting? I'd think you'd welcome the distraction from what your life has become."

He lifted his head, the tips of his horns glinting in the dim light. "Did Jorl teach you that?"

"What?"

"To think like that? Cruel truths?"

"I . . . I'm sorry, I just need to know these things. The way you describe it, power is about controlling things. But you haven't explained how you get that power in the first place."

"How you get . . . you don't *get* power, boy. You take it! Do you ask for the air you breathe? The food you eat? Do you wait for it to fall from the sky and fill your outstretched hands?" He lurched to his feet and came at Pizlo, stopping on the other side of the desk, arms extended over it. Pizlo pulled his trunk back. "You see it, and you reach out your hands, gripping it tightly, and you take it!"

"Like nefshons," Pizlo said, and in response to the confusion spreading out on Bish's face, he reached out and pulled apart the collection he'd gathered to bring the Yak here. Vanishing him and ending the summoning. His thoughts turned back to Dabni and the index. And that other construct which she hadn't shared with Jorl because it would have hurt him. "Like nefshons."

~~~~~

"IF all stories are really the same story just told differently—like you can take a piece of paper and fold it a billion different ways— that's one thing. But then, what about the stories that aren't tales or myths or like that? What about the stories of ordinary people? Are those stories, too? Because, if everyone is the hero of their own story, and all the stories are the same story, then doesn't that mean all the heroes are the same hero?"

After his interview with Bish, Pizlo had climbed down to the Shadow Dwell. Sometimes contrast helped him sort through things and so he'd arrived at a hot sulfur spring of bubbling mud that lay adjacent to a cool stream. The mud soaked into his skin, soothing the unfelt lacerations that were a part of his daily life. He'd been speaking aloud, as much to himself as to the world all around him, trying to work through the tumult of ideas that threatened to pull him down. The warmth of the spring calmed his mind, while the fumes made his head heavy with a need for sleep. Each time he began to nod off Pizlo pulled himself out of the mud and dropped like a stone into the stream's flowing rush of water, clearing his thoughts in the process. He'd already climbed from the stream to the spring and back again several times, expressing his thoughts to a nearby collection of grubs that were on hand to feast on some plants growing near the spring. Though the grubs themselves did not reply to his question outright, a reply resonated in his mind all the same. The world insisted on answering even his rhetorical questions.

"Right. So Jorl is a hero, because he defeated the Matriarch and that bad senator. But Dabni's a hero, too, even though she planned on killing him. And Tolta's a hero as well, claiming me as her son. And I guess that means Druz is a hero, too, though she seems more like someone who is always there to help the hero, but maybe that's just setting her up for her own quest. Maybe for her, being there for Jorl like that *is* her story."

He climbed out of the stream a final time, shook off the excess water, donned his shorts and bandolier again, and set off through the muck and roots of the Shadow Dwell making a line for a small spot of beach too small and too difficult to reach to attract anyone else. As he emerged from the edge of the forest, the rain whispered a greeting. Pizlo gazed up, paying his respects to the weather, the clouds, and the moons above them. Ulmazh and Pemma were overhead, Wella just dropping below the horizon.

"The Yak thinks he's a hero, or was; he had a quest and everything, but he failed at it. But he knew things, like the difference between need and want and how that relates to power, and he had it, for a long time. And that woman who'd given Dabni the thing to hurt Jorl, she's a hero, too, right?" He paused. Despite the intervening clouds, Ulmazh was speaking to him, spurred on by his implication about Klarce. In that moment he saw a future, one where Klarce wanted more than just to hurt Jorl, she saw his death as a necessary part of the woman's own story. Unlike Dabni who'd been ordered to harm him but refused, Pizlo saw Klarce tearing Jorl apart, using his own nefshons to kill him bit by bit.

But that didn't have to be the future. He'd repudiated the world and its moons, refused to accept that the things they told him that hadn't yet happened—*must* happen—because they'd been told. Refused . . . like Dabni had refused? Was that what she'd done, broken from her own narrative, changed the nature of her quest? Not all quests were orthogonal, that was pretty obvious. Jorl and Klarce might both be heroes, but their goals were incompatible. That conflict might even be a big part of what made each of them heroes. But if only one could complete their quest, then only one could win, and his visions were telling him which way it would go.

Unless *he* changed things. The future was fixed—even if only he could see it—but also only if he did nothing to alter it. Agency could defeat predestination. And hadn't he decided to be the embodiment of contradiction? What was that if not agency personified? It was his choice to make—or not—to accept the vision of the future or work to change it.

He shouted at the sky. "That doesn't have to happen, Ulmazh, and you know it! I was wrong about it before. Maybe my quest is to intercede for Jorl, to convince Klarce that whatever has her so mad is a mistake. Is that why Jorl went back to the final island?

Because if that's where she is, I know the way. I'll go there myself and confront her. I can borrow Jorl's boat again, when he's not using it, and I can make her see that he's really on her side and . . ." He stopped as the realization that Klarce was not on that island washed over him. She wasn't anywhere on Barsk at all.

"That doesn't make sense. She has to be here somewhere. She can't . . . oh . . . that's why you're talking to me in the first place, isn't it? She's there, with you. In you. Klarce is *inside* Ulmazh. That's sneaky. Too sneaky to take a boat to see her, but . . ."

He spun around and plunged back into the forest. Pieces began falling in place in his mind, things he had to accomplish, details that had to fit into the right time and place. He could do this, he had the power if he only chose to clasp it to himself. Bish had made that clear. He didn't know how Klarce had left the planet, and it didn't matter. Very soon, Jorl would return to Keslo, and when he did Druz would be waiting just offshore in the only spacecraft on Barsk. A trip to the moon would be almost effortless for such a vessel. That's how he would reach Klarce. He only had to convince the Sloth to take him there.

TWENTY-FOUR

BETRAYAL OR REDEMPTION

~~~~~~~

JORL had returned to the yacht to find Druz, Abenaki, and Rina working a jigsaw puzzle on the floor just beyond the main boarding lock. The complexity was far beyond his daughter's age level but far from being frustrated by it the child seemed enthralled. Instead of the simpler task of finding edges—which Rina could have done with ease—in consultation with her doll she would point out scattered pieces to the Procy and Abenaki would gather them together and assemble assorted portions from the middle into ever larger connected chunks. Somehow Druz had been relegated to the work of building the frame.

"Papa!" Leaving her doll to study the puzzle pieces, Rina leapt to her feet and flung herself at him, arms and trunk wrapping around his legs. "Did you meet the strangers? Was there a mystery? Did you bring me a present?"

"Of course I did, little twig," he said, answering her most important question first. His escort, Regina, had been kind enough to lead him past a sweets shop on his way back. Bending low, he folded his ears around his daughter to block her vision and pulled a bit of waxed paper from his pocket, revealing it with a flourish. "I think you'll enjoy this. I never tasted anything quite like it anywhere else on Barsk."

She unwrapped it, revealing a lump of rock candy. Rina immediately put the whole thing into her mouth. Smiling around the lump she mumbled. "Did you bring one for Kokab?"

"I'm sorry, I only thought to ask for the one. Perhaps you can share?"

She nodded once, let go of his legs, and returned to her doll on the floor.

Druz had also abandoned the puzzle and been rising more slowly. "Senator, did you learn what you came for?"

"In part, but not in whole. I'll need to return tomorrow."

"Return to Keslo, sir?"

Jorl shook his head. "No, another trip onto the beach."

"I don't understand. I thought this island was deserted."

"No, this island doesn't officially exist. And tucked away in the rainforest of this nonexistent island is an equally unknown city, identical in many ways to any other Civilized Wood on any island, but also critically different, too."

"So you found people there? Other Fant."

"I did. And tomorrow I have a meeting with their leaders. It shouldn't take too long. I'll be back before day's end and then we can return to Keslo."

Rina tugged on his arm. "Papa, can't we stay a few more days? Abi is teaching me all about the Procy. If I go back tomorrow, she won't be able to finish."

"I think there's much more to know about her people than she can manage to share even if we were to stay here another tenday. Nor would that be fair to your mother; we don't want her to worry.

Besides, don't you have oratory the day after tomorrow? You wouldn't want to miss that."

Rina rolled her eyes at him in a manner that would have made her instructor proud, saw it did no good, and subsided.

"And your plans for me, Senator?" All this time the Raccoon had silently continued assembling pieces. Now she got to her feet.

"Much depends on this meeting. By this time tomorrow, I may have something concrete to share with you. Possibly much more than either of us might have imagined just a couple days ago."

"Does that mean we get to have dinner here, Papa? Dinner on a spaceship?"

"I suppose it does at that."

"Would you like me to prepare a dinner for the two of you in your room, Senator?"

"No, please, let's all just eat together in the galley, if that's all right. Rina can grab a bite with me any time she likes, but who knows how long it will be before she has the chance to share a meal with people who aren't Fant."

"I'll be in the galley then, if you need me." She paused and waved to Rina. "Would you like to help?"

"Can I, Papa?"

"On this ship, you can do anything Druz says you can do."

Grinning from ear to ear, Rina offered her hand to the Sloth then glanced back to the Raccoon. "Are you coming too, Abi?"

"I'll be following right behind. I remember the way from when we had snacks earlier."

"Good snacks, too," said Rina, and hand in hand with Druz skipped out of the room.

Abenaki stepped forward, and to his amazement clasped Jorl's hands in hers. "Senator. Thank you. For anything you manage. For your willingness to attempt anything. And for hearing me."

Jorl met her gaze. "I could hardly do otherwise for the most compelling proposal any constituent has ever brought my way. At the moment, I have only the glimmering of an idea. We'll see in a day if it goes anywhere. Now, let's join the others for dinner."

~~~~~

LATE the next morning, he returned to the beach and found Regina waiting for him.

"What's the plan?"

"If you would, I'm to escort you back to the Civilized Wood. The Full Council is in session discussing your . . . situation. Councilor Klarce invites you to attend."

"This is the council that runs the Caudex, and purports to have thousands of agents spread out across the planet?"

Regina's mouth tightened but otherwise managed a neutral face. "The Full Council exists to ensure the ultimate welfare of all Fant everywhere. But this is the first time, since its creation, that a Speaker from the outside has been invited to attend and give testimony."

"I'm honored, of course," said Jorl, privately chiding himself for tweaking the younger woman. "I apologize if I gave any other impression. Please, lead the way."

The walk back through the unnamed island's Shadow Dwell and up to its Civilized Wood gave him time to reflect. Klarce had been surprised, possibly even upset, at the notion of reuniting Fant with any of the Alliance's other races, which was no more than he'd expected. But she hadn't rejected the notion out of hand. Her need to convene the Caudex's Full Council had to be a good thing. Surely the worst that could happen was that they'd dig in deeper and insist on maintaining the status quo of the past eight hundred years. If so, then he'd be no worse off than before he came here.

But the possibility that he might have stumbled upon a powerful ally, one who shared his own desire to protect all Fant, gave him hope. Then again, he reminded himself, Margda had defended her own machinations with that same logic, the continued well-being of her people justifying any and all action.

Regina led him down a different boardway than he'd walked the day before. With the exception of the detour to the sweet shop, his escort had taken him by less-used routes. Today they strolled down the main thoroughfares of the city. The layout and design of the place were familiar enough, but everywhere he noted examples of technology eschewed by the rest of the planet: artificial lighting in lieu of elaborate arrays of mirrors, the occasional automaton that whizzed by scooping up litter or fallen leaves, vid displays in shop windows. Trivial things that spoke of a commonplace acceptance of goods and services that he'd had to learn to endure when he'd been in the Patrol and then let go of again upon his return.

They arrived at an unassuming building, entered into a spacious rotunda, climbed a stair, and strode through a wing of offices until arriving at their destination. Regina paused and handed him a small packet.

"You'll need this, sir."

Curious, Jorl opened the packet to find a simple tablet of koph. He smiled. "What's this for?"

"The Full Council meets in a shared mindspace. You'll understand why in a moment."

Jorl feigned putting the tablet in his mouth, all the while secreting it in his trunk. As Regina turned to knock on the door, he slipped it into a pocket and then followed his guide inside.

A large circular table occupied most of the room, with eight seats. Three Fant had spread out like three points of a compass, each with their arms folded in front of them on the table, their heads resting upon them as if asleep. Each had an empty chair to either side. Regina guided him to the remaining compass point.

"Where's Klarce?" he asked her as he settled into the chair.

"She'll join you shortly. This is her spot. She wanted you to have it."

In addition to the four of them at the table, a set of four hammock seats hung along the wall, one behind each of the empty ones at the table; in each of these slumped a young Fant, likely—given the koph that Regina had supplied—caught up in summoning someone. Jorl sat and, with a thought, switched on his perception of nefshons and found a fully realized construct of the room waiting for him. He added himself to it and Speakers occupying the hammocks along the wall vanished just as the empty seats at the table filled with elderly Fant. He was far from an expert on fashion, but the summoned quad all appeared to be dressed in garb different from one another and from the current trends and styles. Moreover, he recognized three of them from his own reading of history. As for the three Fant he'd seen slumped upon their arms when he came in, all were sitting upright now, listening intently to one of the elders—could that truly be Nirl?—who'd held the floor but broke off as Jorl's own construct manifested. She waved her trunk in his direction and the others turned toward him. A voice spoke from behind and he turned in his seat to see Klarce standing there.

"Councilors, may I present our guest, Jorl ben Tral, lately of the island of Keslo in the western archipelago. He is a history professor at large, associated with the university on Zlorka. As you can see, he bears an aleph, the fifty-seventh to wear that mark, foreseen by Margda before her death. In her words, he is the 'one who had gone out and come back, and though of the present would look into the past.' He is one of only a handful of Fant to reject the Compact's perpetual military deferment and serve in the Patrol, the first in six hundred years. And he is the first Lox to be admitted to the Alliance senate, where he serves as a junior member of the Committee of Information."

She paused and Jorl took the opportunity to raise his trunk in a salute and execute a quarter bow to the councilors around the table.

"Jorl, allow me to introduce the Caudex Council. The living members you would have seen when you first arrived are, from your left, Melko, Sind, and Kissel. With myself, they make up the 'Quick Council.' The summoned members of our group are, again starting on the left, Genz, Nirl, Marsh, and Soosh."

"So you're Margda's chosen," said Nirl. "I must say, you don't look particularly special. And that surprises me, because like you I was a student of her madness. Every other of her prophecies sparkled in some way. I see nothing dazzling about you."

Klarce glared at the dead Speaker. "Please, Jorl is here as a guest."

Marsh snapped the nubs of his trunk for attention. "No, I believe the better starting point is to describe him as a concern. It's on him to convince us whether he is to be considered an ally and not reassessed as a threat."

"Be that as it may, we can reach some conclusions without antagonism."

"It's fine," said Jorl. "Being a part of Margda's prophecies was certainly not something I wanted. And as it happens, my role in them was more about someone I knew than about me."

Nirl smiled. "See? He admits it. I've said nothing that wasn't true."

Jorl flapped his ears. Was this council already at odds, or was this a performance for his benefit? Klarce to be his innocent advocate and Nirl his aggressive interlocutor? Though just the day before Klarce had demonstrated she was anything but innocent. Fine. As a veteran of endless faculty meetings he could handle this.

"I wouldn't go that far. But then, you're *that* Nirl. Nirl of the island of Moreb? Maybe things have changed for you here in this place since you sailed away, but in life you weren't exactly known for truth."

Nirl was on her feet, ears down and back, trunk slashing in front of her. "I was the premiere scholar of my day. A polymath beyond compare."

Jorl smiled at that and shrugged. "I'm just a historian, but I don't think you give yourself enough credit. While what you say is true, you've left out that you were also a thief and a liar."

Marsh and Kissel both turned toward Nirl and then back to Jorl.

Sind pounded the table with a fist. "What are you implying?"

"Nothing that you can't confirm for yourself, if you know where to look. Two generations after Nirl's death, one of her granddaughters came forward with proof that all of her published papers, all of her celebrated ideas, were the work of others." He turned to first one of the councilors and slowly included them as his remarks flowed in an arc. "It's true, she began as a credible scholar and scientist, and truly gifted as an orator. I've been in her presence for just moments and I can already feel her charisma. No surprise then that she surrounded herself with brilliant and talented students. She nurtured them, encouraged them, and then took credit for their insights, stealing their accomplishments and applying her name to them."

Sind waved that away and motioned for Nirl to resume her seat. "The past we're concerned with is yours, Jorl. We have been informed that you claim responsibility for our inability to Speak with Margda for the past seven years."

"That's true."

"And shortly prior to that, you say she, uh, Spoke with you?" added Kissel. "How was that possible?"

"It actually all goes back to why she singled me out in one of her visions to receive the aleph."

"Fine," said Sind. "Start there."

He sighed. "As you wish. Briefly then, Margda wanted me to have the aleph as part of a plan she'd put in place to defend against an Alliance threat she had seen, one that could have meant the end of all Fant on Barsk."

He'd expected a reaction when he said that, gasps of surprise, exclamations of disbelief. Instead, all around the table the councilors, both living and dead, nodded as if he'd confirmed what they already knew.

Soosh addressed him next. "What was the nature of this threat?"

"A ranking member of the senate viewed the current state of exports from Barsk as holding the Alliance hostage, particularly with regard to koph. He began abducting the Dying on their way to your island, believing their absence wouldn't be noticed and thus allowing him time to interrogate them."

"This doesn't explain how Margda could Speak to you."

"Part of her vision included knowing that when these events came to pass, a Speaker from another world—an Otter who was also a telepath—would have cause to break the first rule of her Edict and summon her. Margda was able to appropriate her mental abilities and imprint herself in the Lutr's mind."

"That's not possible," Nirl sputtered. She turned to Melko. "Is that possible?"

"It's . . . conceivable."

"It happened," said Jorl. "Margda basically lived again in the body of the Otter. By that point, I'd set out to find your island and learn what was happening to so many Dying who had left seasons before yet somehow never died. Along the way, I was abducted as well and soon after Margda herself broke the second rule of her Edict by summoning me."

"And this was all in service to a threat she saw to all Fant."

"That's correct."

"But that was seven years ago," said Soosh. "What is the status of this threat now?"

"Oh, it's been resolved. I ended it."

"And I suppose in recognition of your service, they made you a senator?" Nirl's question served as a vehicle of her contempt.

"Indirectly," said Jorl. "There were other factors, but that's the upshot, yes."

"And you would have this council believe that you, a simple historian, saved all our people and wooed the Alliance of a senate seat?"

"Oh no, not at all."

"Ha!" Nirl was on her feet again. "You admit this is all fabrication then!"

"No, everything I've said is true. I was responding to your question, not your implication. Frankly, I don't care if you believe me or you don't. But I'm not surprised if you don't. As I noted before, you built your entire career on lies. I suppose it's only natural for you to assume other people must be fabricating their own actions."

"Councilors!" Genz had leapt up and stared at Nirl until she sat back down. "Councilors, I choose to take Jorl's remarks at face value, because their underlying pattern reveals that we share common cause."

"And what would that be?" asked Jorl.

"Saving our people. Our founders were Margda's contemporaries. While Margda practiced politics and drafted the Compact, they looked at the result and saw it as a temporary solution at best. For more than seven hundred years, we have been working in secret, studying nefshons in ways she never considered. We have drawn the best and brightest minds of Barsk to these shores to help us. While the rest of the planet has turned their backs on most technology, we've pushed its limits."

"Toward what end?"

"Our salvation. You may wonder why Klarce is not physically here in this council chamber along with her peers on the Quick Council. It is because she is no longer on Barsk."

"Excuse me? If not here, then where?"

"Would it surprise you to learn that yours was not the only spacecraft on Barsk this morning?" said Klarce.

He nodded. "The Fant stopped being a space-faring people when we were moved to Barsk. There's nowhere you could go that the Alliance wouldn't notice. Believe me, I'd know."

"You're wrong. Not long before this council session began I arrived at Ulmazh. The Alliance doesn't monitor our activity there."

"You're on one of the moons?"

"More accurately, I am inside one of the moons. Ulmazh is the proving ground for our technology. We've learned how to take a lifeless planetoid, scoop a portion of it out, and create a viable city within. There's a Civilized Wood here, Jorl, populated with ten thousand Eleph and Lox. Generations of people who have known no other home."

"That's astonishing!"

Nirl was sneering at him again. "So you can see, we didn't need you to save us. We would have survived your scenario."

Jorl spat. He'd had enough. "Forgive me if I nonetheless take some comfort in my efforts to spare the lives of five and a half million Fant."

"No," said Sind, "forgive Nirl her foolishness. She's been dead so long, she's lost track of the value of life. Our goal isn't simply to ensure Fant continue to exist at all, but to preserve all of our people, wherever they are. Which is why we oppose the petition that brought a Raccoon to you."

"I don't follow."

"It's not a question of whether or not turning Barsk into a mixed world would be beneficial," said Klarce. "Arguments can be made on both sides. But long before that question could be tested, it would doom our other efforts."

"Simply put, we cannot risk the scrutiny that greater Alliance interest in Barsk would bring." Genz glanced at each of his fellow councilors and received nods in response.

Jorl saw the problem at once. "You're worried the Alliance would discover that you've, in effect, colonized another world. You want to keep what you've done on Ulmazh a secret."

"In part," said Soosh. "But we've done a great many things on Ulmazh. You've been in the Patrol, you no doubt are familiar with the time it takes to push portals and establish new routes between distant points in space."

"Of course, it's one of the main tasks of every Patrol ship."

"Indeed. Would you be surprised to learn we've been doing this ourselves for several centuries? That we have our own, improved portal technology?"

"That's impossible," said Jorl. "You couldn't possibly have ships traversing the galaxy. Other Alliance vessels would detect them."

THE MOONS OF BARSK   301

"Not if they only traveled where the Alliance never goes," said Marsh.

Klarce stepped closer, seating herself on the edge of the table to his left. "I said that Ulmazh has been a proving ground for us. Remember, the Caudex's purpose is to ensure not just our people's survival but their continuance. The things we've learned to do here were never meant to end here. This city in the moon is a wonderment, yes, but it is also a proof of concept. One that we have re-created elsewhere in the galaxy. Not once, not twice, but more."

"I don't understand. You're saying you're building other cities inside other dead worlds?"

"No, Jorl, I'm saying we've long since done so. And that's why we cannot permit your Procy's proposal to go any further. The fate of a single, small city existing in Ulmazh is not what hangs in the balance. We've been at this for centuries. You think the sum total of our people are the five and a half million Fant you saved seven years ago. But the Caudex has spread nearly that same number across six other spheres."

"Six?"

"For now. More in time. They are our Hidden Worlds, the legacy of the Caudex. They are the posterity of the Fant. Everything we do, the reason this council exists, is to protect them."

PART 3

REDEFINING HOME

TWENTY-FIVE

PERSEVERATION

~~~~~~~~~

RYNE hadn't seen much of Bernath since arriving on the nameless island. He heard from her several times each tenday, but always in the form of notes or messages conveyed by one of his assistants. Meanwhile, Lolte continued dropping by to monitor his ongoing rejuvenation. Apparently the reversal of the aging process happened differentially. His body built more muscle mass. He'd needed a tad more sleep. And thus far he'd successfully channeled a renewing libido into his work. Unlike in his old life, he no longer had office hours or classroom requirements, so when he wasn't asleep or taking a meal he lost himself in the math. Krokel and Gari each kept to more traditional patterns and had worked out an arrangement among themselves so one of them was potentially available to him—or more likely available to try to follow along with the products of his work—at any time, day or night.

Yesterday he'd arisen before first light, and gone immediately to work. He ate breakfast while writing at one of the slate walls, now and then forgetting whether he'd been writing with a hand or his trunk and ending up with a taste of chalk along with the leaves that went into his mouth. Gari had been shadowing him at the start and passed responsibility over to Krokel at around noon. Ryne had finally called it a day in late afternoon and tumbled onto his cot, pleased with the latest revelations of the math.

He'd awakened at dawn—much later than he'd intended—in a state of arousal, fresh from an erotic dream involving Lolte, the luxurious bed he'd been given when he first arrived, and a playful assortment of edible pigments. Donning a loose robe, he sought out the emergency shower in his lab and thought of math while the water reduced any obvious signs of his hormone-addled body. He was toweling off when the object of his nocturnal fantasies stepped into the room accompanied by Bernath. Both had the good grace to turn their backs as he completed drying himself and pulled his robe back on.

"I'm sorry, did I know you were coming today? I overslept again."

Bernath looked confused at that remark but Lolte spoke before her companion could express why.

"Not to worry," said Lolte. "That's a common side effect, and it's correlated with the slight increase in body temperature and the more pronounced increase in your appetite. Your body is repairing itself, restoring to greater efficiency systems that had succumbed to the effects of old age."

Ryne said nothing to that. While the doctor might welcome news of this latest symptom, talking about it to her would invariably lead to reviewing the graphic images he'd dreamed, and all too quickly he'd move from the abstract and scientific to the embarrassingly physical. She was barely half his age, he had no business having such thoughts, even if his body had a compelling argument that it—or at least portions of it—had been restored to that age.

"No appointment," said Bernath, providing a welcome change of subject. "But I think you'll make time in your schedule. There's been a change of plans and I'm here to invite you to a demonstration of the first application of your theories."

"Really? Now?"

"Well," said Bernath, "I think we can allow you time to dress in something a bit less informal." Her laugh sang out and Ryne smiled as he had that first day he'd heard it on the beach. Bernath was much closer to his age, and as if in response to that direction of thought he stirred beneath his robe. He turned away, aiming himself out of the lab and back to the corner of the next room over where he kept his simple pallet and a dresser of clothing.

"I'll just be a moment then," he said, turning his mind to thoughts of math once more.

"While you're at it, pack a small bag. Enough for a handful of days. This demonstration requires a bit of travel."

"Days?" he called over his shoulder. "Where are we going?"

"You won't believe me until you see it for yourself," said Bernath. "But your physician here assures me you're up for it."

~~~~~

THE trio walked down several boardways and passed an assortment of other residents all going about their own business.

"What exactly am I going to see?"

"The tests on the prototype have all gone well. Oh, there were some minor glitches at the outset, but those were all engineering problems and nothing to do with your theories. The team quickly resolved them. This will be the first full field test of the design and the councilor who's backing your research wants you on-site for it."

They walked past the spot where the council met and entered another building a bit further down and on the other side of the boardway. Bernath nodded to a man sitting behind a desk and he waved them on through to a door on the wall past him. They entered a short corridor that ended in another door.

"You still haven't said where that is. If not here, what island would be better suited? And why would you need Lolte to sign off on my travel? I'm in better health than when I sailed here, surely. So, why would there be a question of travel?"

Lolte smiled. "It's not about putting you on a boat, especially not as a passenger. And no, there's been no discussion of running tests of your work on other islands."

"I don't understand."

Bernath opened the door. Instead of another hallway or a room, it opened onto an elevator car. She waited until they were all inside and she'd accessed the control panel before she spoke. They began to descend.

"Congratulations, Ryne. You've just had your security clearance increased."

"I have a security clearance?"

"To be sure. The Caudex does many things, and knowledge of the different levels is only doled out to those who need to know them."

"What do I need to know today that I didn't yesterday? I'm doing the same work as I have since I arrived."

"What's different is that today you'll be doing it somewhere else. Up to this point, you've known only that the Caudex is here on this island."

Ryne interrupted. "That's not quite true. You'd mentioned being present at one or more of my past lectures. I've inferred that some of the time you have people visiting other islands."

She laughed—ah, that laugh. "Fair enough. Today you learn that the Caudex has gone far beyond that. Beyond Barsk."

"Yes, yes, you have spacecraft and portals. I know that."

"True, but I'm not talking about a small crew of ethernauts, but rather thousands upon thousands of Fant who live and work in a city on Ulmazh."

"That's where we're going? To the moon?"

"That's where we're going," said Lolte. The elevator stopped and Bernath again accessed the panel.

"But, how are we getting there?" asked Ryne.

The door whooshed open onto an underground hanger. The wall opposite them appeared to be two halves of an enormous gate. Occupying the entirety of the space between them was a small spacecraft.

"On that," said Bernath. "Come along. We're not the last to arrive, but the others are more experienced. We need to brief you on procedures, for your safety and ours."

~~~~~

THE actual flight was anti-climatic. Bernath and Lolte had led him to a small passenger compartment where three young and visibly excited Fant were already strapped in to flight couches. They quickly unfastened themselves and began fussing with him and his companions. One by one they were escorted to a closet-sized booth and assisted in stripping down and redressing in simple flight suits—an unlikely precaution, he was assured, but better safe than sorry, or some such. When it became clear that both of the women had traveled on such shuttles before—which was a bit of a wonder to him, but not one which he had the luxury of time to ponder—the trio left the two women to their own plans and converged on him. In the course of explaining the need for him to be properly strapped down, the discomforts he would feel during initial acceleration, the need to report immediately if he experienced any abnormal changes in heart rate or respiration, he learned they'd been training for careers as ethernauts for years and were as passionate to work in space as he was for math. It had been so long since Fant had been allowed in space that the possibility—much like the science of observational astronomy—had been beaten out of physics as he knew it. He marveled at the ideas it opened up for him, and at his own urging two of the young folk agreed to share his flight couch so he could continue to question them.

Somewhere in the course of conversation the shuttle lifted without his notice. On the couch behind him, he heard Bernath laugh at one point, and Lolte had unstrapped to come over and check on him, giving him a beverage of some sort. Overall though, much like when he lost himself to the math, the time passed without awareness and he only knew the trip had ended because his young companions gathered around him. They expressed profuse appreciation for his time and wished him well. Then the three of them rushed out of the compartment. Ryne sat there, breathless and blinking, a smile plastered to his face. He looked up and found Lolte and Bernath staring down at him.

"Everything all right, Ryne? You look a bit overwhelmed."

He considered this. Sorted it and his smile expanded. "I've spent the last many years thinking about particles too small to see. Maybe it's time I begin pondering something bigger, like stars."

"Perhaps," said Bernath. "But not just yet. Come on, we'll take you to the lab we've set up for you."

~~~~~

IN many ways it was like being in any other Civilized Wood of any island of Barsk. But also not. Just like the city he'd found on the unnamed island was and wasn't like other cities, he found himself in a place that was also different, but in new ways. Up and down felt funny. His weight was . . . off. The air tasted odd. But the boardways were much the same as other boardways, the meta-trees that provided the walls and floors and ceilings all around him were the same. And people, well, they were still people, but somehow more focused and optimistic. There was an excitement in the air and he breathed it in and felt it flow through him.

"But what am I going to see?" he'd said as they led him from the shuttle and through the Civilized Wood.

"Well, that's problematic," said Bernath. "About all *you'll* see— you and Lolte here—will be a team of young Speakers who've been assigned to the project. That, and some display boards that will show you the power distribution as the experiment's contain-ment fields take form. But to those Speakers and myself, the room should grow ever more crowded."

Lolte chimed in. "I'm coming along to monitor the vitals of the other two Speakers. So, don't feel bad, I won't see anything either."

They'd arrived before he could reply and he was ushered into a building, down a hallway, and at last through yet another door to their intended destination.

Inside Ryne found a large lab with a pair of young Eleph seated at either end of a table in comfortable hammock chairs and a complex-looking device about the size of his head situated between them. Lolte stepped past him and approached first one, then the other, withdrawing diagnostic equipment from a bag worn on her hip. Ryne looked from the pair to Bernath for confirmation.

She nodded. "Yes, those are the Speakers. Have a seat. Now that we're here, they'll be starting as soon as Lolte finishes record-ing their baseline readings."

He stepped into the room and noticed eight coppery discs on

the floor between each of the Speakers and the machine, sixteen in total. Ryne recognized them from the notes Gari and Krokel had made as he explained a particular bit of the math to them days and days past, the fruit of his work given shape. Docking rings. If his theories held true, each ring could be used to generate and maintain a nefshon containment space. Random nefshons would pass through, but concentrations of organized particles—as might be expected following a summoning—would be unable to leave the field once being lured into it. Though of course, if the organization of nefshons was a conversant, it wouldn't so much be lured as enter the field at the call of a Speaker.

Lolte concluded her assessments and joined him as he settled onto a couch against one wall. Bernath had basically swapped places with her and was now talking to each of the young Speakers in turn.

"Can you explain this to me," Lolte asked as she sat next to him. "I know that Bernath will be able to see the conversants these Speakers summon, but how will you know if your invention works?"

Ryne pointed at the display monitors that sat upon a table closer to the door. A pitcher of iced tea and a tray of glasses lay to one side of them. "We still don't know how to build a device that can actually detect nefshons or measure their concentration. But we can infer their presence by their influence on the field's resonance pattern, which we have full access to. Like seeing the presence of the wind by the leaves it's blowing."

Bernath finished her instructions and crossed to the table, passed the monitors and poured two cups of tea that she then gave to the Speakers before returning and helping herself to a cup. She nodded. "That's how you'll see it." She took a long drink, smacking her lips and exhaling a burst of spiralmint. "I hope to see what our Speakers here see."

"Which is what," asked Lolte.

"A room full of conversants. One per disc."

"There's koph in that tea?" asked Ryne.

"There is. Which is why I didn't offer you any."

"Oh."

One of the Speakers called to them. "We're ready to begin when you like."

"No better time than the present to reveal the future," said Bernath.

Lolte snorted. "Even if we can't see it being revealed."

"I told you. *I'll* see it. Begin!"

From Ryne's point of view, the beginning involved the pair of Speakers lowering chins to chests and closing their eyes, presumably as they shifted their attention to whatever illusion of place they were using to summon their respective conversants.

"Are they just re-creating this room? That would eliminate a potential source of systematic variance. Who provided the specifics of this design? I should have been consulted."

Bernath patted his hand. "Relax, Ryne. Yes, the nefshon space they're using is a replica of the same physical space. I promise you the methodology being followed is solid. I produced the design and it was vetted by a board containing the island's best scientific minds, including an old instructor of yours. So be at ease."

"Old instructor?"

"Jordover ben Ohn. He said he remembered you from an early design class. Apparently you made quite an impression."

Ryne sputtered. "That was seventy some years ago. He couldn't possibly still be alive!"

"Well, as to possibility, I'd have to defer to our systems biologist, but no, you're right. He sailed away about fifty years ago."

"Then how . . . you summoned him?"

"We have. He's too valuable a resource, and he's been happy to make himself useful. Now hush, the first conversants of each Speaker are taking form. Ahh, that's it then. Very good."

"What?" Lolte peered pointlessly at first one Speaker and then another.

Two of the monitors on the table beeped. Ryne regarded the displays. "Two of the discs are showing a spike in power utilization. They're operating at nominal levels, which suggests that a concentration of organized nefshons has moved within each and been captured."

"Captured?" said Lolte as she rose from the couch and stepped toward the nearer Speaker, medical instruments at the ready.

Ryne shrugged. "Captured. Contained. If my theory is right and the discs crafted to my specifications, the only way they'll be able to disperse is to shut down power to the disc or disrupt its battery."

Bernath swayed in place, eyes closed. "What I see are a pair of middle-aged Lox, man and woman. They popped into existence and their respective Speakers bade them to cross the floor and stand over the nearest disc. Time for phase two."

"Which is?"

Without a word, the pair of Speakers both opened their eyes and rose from their hammocks. They circled the discs on the floor widdershins and a moment later settled into the other's hammock and closed their eyes again.

"Not so much as a waver in the displays," said Ryne.

"Good. And the two conversants are still in place, even though the Speakers are gone, as is the mindspace of this room. They were maintaining it, not me."

"Do you see the discs still?"

"No, Ryne. They were also just a part of the illusion to mark where the real discs were. All I see now are a pair of Lox hovering in emptiness. No, wait, the room just came back. The Speakers have re-established it."

Ryne looked at the next monitor, peering expectantly.

"Though anyone who is sensitive to koph can witness the manipulation of nefshons, Speakers can only manage one other person's particles at a time. If you want to summon more than one decedent, you need a separate Speaker for each. Until today. Each of these Speakers has just conjured up another person. Another male Lox and a female Eleph. They're obligingly moving to stand above the next set of discs and—"

"Captured!" Ryne trumpeted, as the field utilization spiked on two more discs.

"Confirmed. Shall we move to phase three?"

"How many decedents do you intend to contain? Surely not all sixteen discs worth?" Lolte asked.

"No, I arranged for twice as many discs in case there were complications. The goal today is to hold four constructs on the discs per Speaker, plus a fifth maintained in the traditional manner. That will do for today's demonstration I think."

The two Eleph Speakers opened their eyes, stood, stretched, and once again changed seats. They settled in and, barely suppressing smiles at their own place in history, each began to summon their third conversant of the session.

TWENTY-SIX

SET FREE

~~~~~~~~~~~~

THAT morning, Dabni had gone down to the docks to await her husband's return. She'd taken the funicular to the harbor and marched out onto the pier and then to the slip where Jorl would return. She didn't imagine she'd have long to wait, but even that felt like too long in the heavy rain of the season. And yet, she deserved far worse. The full weight of Klarce's revelation bore down on her. For seven years she'd successfully compartmentalized the two halves of her life. She'd grown comfortable in the invented identity of a young woman breaking from the family business to run a bookstore, all as a cover to observe and report on the activities of a historian and Aleph-Bearer. And along the way she'd taken on a new reality, lover and wife and mother. She'd fallen for her target, rationalizing at each critical step that it was just part of her deep cover.

But no, she'd dropped that lie when she'd disregarded the order from the council and withheld the meme that would have caused Jorl's death. Yes, Klarce had rescinded that order, but what if she hadn't? How long before her handlers followed up and discovered she hadn't so much delayed as disobeyed. Because that was the moment when she'd stopped serving the Caudex. That, more than anything else, was what she needed to tell Jorl. What she needed him to understand. Everything else, the deception and manipulation and lies of omission, that was all on her, and if he hated her for it she couldn't fault him. But choosing his life over the life she'd led up to that point, that was a choice she had to have him hear.

All the way to the harbor she'd run through variations of how to tell him, rejecting them one by one. Now, when she could go no further, when all she could do was wait, she found she had no words at all.

She sat scanning the sea for the first sign of a returning boat. Visibility at the harbor was poor, something she'd known intellectually but had never actually tested by sitting on a pier during flood. Looking back, she couldn't see all the way to the dock, and only the boats in the nearest of surrounding slips showed clearly. She saw movement on one of them, two slots further up the pier. The movement resolved into a pale, three-quarter sized person. Pizlo sat on the prow of a nearby boat, swinging his legs as he too stared out to sea.

She hesitated to call to him. Even though she'd grown up in the progressive Civilized Wood of the unnamed island, she'd still learned to flinch from the mere mention of an abomination. And yet somewhere in the last few years he'd changed from an abstraction lent flesh to the bizarre best friend of her daughter. Which was to say, he was just Pizlo, no more and no less.

Moreover, there was no one else around to react to the indecency of interacting with him. "Did you follow me here?"

He turned to her and even through the rain she could see he was surprised she was there. So, no, he hadn't followed. Probably, he'd even arrived first. He clambered down from the boat, tripping and tumbling along the pier like a gymnast and then up on his feet again in a brief jog that brought him alongside her.

"No. I'm waiting for Jorl. Did the moon tell you he was coming?"

She shook her head. "No, someone else."

"Was it Klarce? I'm going to go talk to her."

"What? Don't even joke about that, Pizlo. It's not funny."

He gave her a wounded look. "It's not a joke."

"Just . . . don't. Okay?"

Pizlo looked up into the pouring rain. "Are you going to tell Jorl you're a Speaker?"

"Among other things, yes."

"Oh. Good. Because I thought I'd have to, but now I don't."

"You'd *have* to . . . oh. Um, why would you do that?"

"Because you were going to hurt him."

She leaned away from him, her ears fanning out in defense. "I wouldn't. Never."

He stared at her a moment and then shrugged. "Well, no, not now. But before. Only . . . you changed that. Huh. I bet Telko missed that."

She frowned at him. "Is this something the precognitive voices in your head told you?"

"Kind of."

"Well, I guess they were wrong."

"Not wrong. They can't be wrong."

"Didn't we just agree they must be? If they told you I was going to harm Jorl and we both know I'm not?"

"No, it's a timing thing. And an agency thing."

"Timing?"

"The future. It's mostly fixed. Unless you're able to act and choose, and the timing of that choice may or may not be enough to change things. But that doesn't mean it wasn't fixed before. Just that choice trumps destiny. I only really learned that recently." He smiled.

Choice. That single word from him summed up everything she'd been agonizing over. She looked at him, trading the smile on his face for an imagined one that she might expect to find on a boy who had grown up in a vast home of siblings and cousins and plenty of food and endless games to play. At times, his sickly pallor, as well as the bruises and lacerations that announced his hidden deformities, faded from her awareness and she had to look hard at him to see the abomination that had denied him that life. How was it he'd had no choice and yet so effortlessly pointed out hers?

"You're an odd young man, Pizlo."

He nodded. "I'm a contradiction," he said.

"That, too."

~~~~~

SHE got to her feet at the first glimpse of Jorl's boat arriving through the rain. Moments later she could see the shape of him through the windowpane of the wheelhouse. And then the boat was easing into its slip and Rina was capering on the deck and shouting to her.

"Mama! Mama! I met a Sloth and she had real long sleeves. I mean really really long! And a Raccoon and she had a mask and then another mask painted on top. And we made a puzzle, only we didn't finish it and—"

And there he was, scooping their daughter up in his arms, making her giggle, crossing the deck and descending to the pier. Her target. Her husband. Rina's father.

"We need to talk," she said as he came within quiet earshot.

"We do," he replied.

Rina squirmed in his arms as she spied Pizlo and he set her down. "Pizlo, did you hear? I met a Procy. Did you ever meet a Procy?"

The abomination came forward, stood right next to her and smiled at her daughter in a way that a creature who did not belong to society had no right to. This aberration whom Jorl befriended and taught, whom she had endured and grudgingly acknowledged in order to do her assignment, loved her daughter with a friendship stronger than any she had known.

"Never," said Pizlo.

"Never ever?"

"Not even once."

"That's okay. I'll tell you all about her."

"I'd like that, but in a moment." He waved his trunk and Dabni half turned his way. "You need to tell him."

"Tell me what?"

"Pizlo wants to be sure I mention that I'm a Speaker, like you."

"Not exactly. No one's like him. And you're not even one like me. But I guess no one else is either. Ha!"

"Pizlo, leave off. I already know."

Dabni turned back to her husband. "You met Klarce?"

His ears were down and back. His hands folded together in front of his body, his trunk low and still. "I did. She explained why you came to Keslo. Why you really came here. And what you've been doing since then right up to today."

"No," she said. "It stopped days ago. I ended it."

"Oh? Klarce didn't share that."

"She doesn't know. I haven't told her. I . . . I didn't know myself, not consciously, until just a while ago."

"What happened days ago?"

"I didn't kill you."

"Mama?"

She ignored the tone in her daughter's voice, hadn't meant to say that in front of her but in the moment it felt right. Where was that moment now?

"You'd done . . . something. Learned of the existence of the Caudex. The council saw you as an immediate threat and they ordered me to slip a meme into your mind that would initiate a cascade failure of every major organ. Your body would sicken, weaken, and in a handful of days you'd be dead."

He stood there. Not . . . angry, not even judging, just taking in her words and staring at her. As though, because the things she'd said were in the past, he could regard them the way he contemplated history. Behind her, she could hear her daughter crying.

"And you didn't do this thing?"

"No."

"Do you know why?"

"I thought so. At first I tried to rationalize it. You were my assignment. My target. For all that time. All those years watching you and writing reports and telling myself I was just playing a role so I could get close to you to do my job. But . . . you're also Rina's father. And I couldn't do that to Rina. I love her too much to cause her that kind of pain. And . . . when I acknowledged that, I also realized I loved you too much, too. And then the choice was easy."

Small fists beat against the backs of her legs.

"But you were going to!" Rina screamed, tears streaming down her face only to be washed away by the rain. "You thought about it. Someone told you to kill papa and you thought about doing it."

"Rina, sweetheart, it wasn't quite like that."

For a moment the only sounds were the rain and the reluctant movement of the boats. Then, softly, Pizlo spoke. "Yes, it was."

"See? Even Pizlo thinks so. I hate you. Hate you!"

Rina spun and ran away up the pier, arms and trunk flailing as she wailed. Her world turned wrong side over, Dabni started to go after her but Jorl's hand gripped her arm and held her back.

"Pizlo?" Jorl turned the name into a question beyond the capacity of language.

"She'll be fine. Worn out and hungry. But fine. Give her soup."

"And what about you?"

He ignored Jorl and faced her instead. "I knew you were going to hurt him. Not you as you are now, but as another person. Only, I thought that was something new, and this you, this was who you've been all along. No one ever told me that all this time you weren't like now. I should have been told."

"I . . ."

"Maybe not everything. That's too much. But, this. I should have been told this." He still hadn't looked at Jorl. Instead, he started away, back toward the harbor proper and the forest.

"Where are you going, Pizlo?"

"To think. You should too, Jorl. Different things, though. You're better at it than I am, but I need to try." He never so much as broke his stride. Soon the rain swallowed him and he was gone.

And there was just the two of them. Fitting to end as it had begun.

"Do you hate me?" There. She'd said it. Wanted to give herself credit for saying it, and then let that go. No credit for her, not after everything.

"No," he said. And that was all. She waited, in case he wanted to elaborate or qualify, but no. That was all he had to say on the matter.

"You should," she said, tears filling her own eyes. She hoped the rain hid them. She turned from him, emptier than she had imagined ever feeling, and left him on the pier, wishing she'd never come to this island or met this man, or only come to realize how much she loved him in time to lose him.

TWENTY-SEVEN

STALEMATE

~~~~~~~~~

JORL watched nearly everyone he cared for run away from him, vanishing into the rain. He'd known more drama in the last handful of days than he'd seen since he'd first set out to find the unnamed island years before. In hindsight, he might have realized that seeking that place before his time couldn't possibly lead to anything good, and yet he'd experienced wonders since. In that time, Pizlo had continued to grow and learn and defy every expectation of society. And Dabni had changed his life in so many fundamental ways which, regardless of her motivation, had resulted in him being a better man. And Rina, how could he ever doubt the perfection of having a daughter. All of that had come after his first trip to that unnamed island, and he had to believe that this second visit would eventually yield similar treasure. Not in the current moment, but eventually.

For now, everyone was still reeling from the confrontation and revelations on the dock. Pizlo had fled to seek his own counsel, Dabni had likely retreated in confusion and shame to her bookstore, and Rina had run away home. He understood that everyone needed time and space to process, and that was fair, though he worried about his daughter getting back safely. She was mature for her age, but she was also upset. She would never have allowed him to accompany her, but perhaps. . . .

He saw the harbormaster's son hesitantly drawing closer, bringing him a solution. He beckoned Chisulo to his side and hurriedly explained the situation. The young man nodded, beaming with the responsibility Jorl placed in him, and set off in pursuit of Rina. She didn't have much of a head start and he knew the routes up from the harbor better than anyone. His longer legs would let him catch up and shadow her all the way back, or "accidentally" encounter her and guide her home if she lost her way. Satisfied as he could be at the moment, Jorl took a different route, giving his family their space, and headed to the familiar comforts of his own home.

INSTEAD of answers to the problems before him, he had more questions. The abstract points and principles he'd discussed with Welv had been made concrete by Abenaki's proposal. But her premise: that in order for the Fant to flourish they required reintegration with other races had been turned on its head by the accomplishments of the Caudex. Six unknown colonies? Another five million Fant out there in the galaxy? His people were already thriving. Even if the Raccoon's theories promised still more, did he have the right to threaten the safety and stability of entire worlds?

He sat in the hammock at his desk, a blank sheet before him and a fresh stick of ink bamboo in his trunk. He'd been sitting like that, poised to produce a list of pros and cons as he worked through the contents of a large bowl of salad. He was nearing the bottom of the bowl and still hadn't written a thing. And then he felt a tug.

He set everything down and pushed himself deeper into the hammock and opened himself to what he assumed was Pizlo reaching out to him. The boy's name was on his lips when he realized the mental space that formed around him belonged to Klarce.

"I hope I'm not disturbing you," she said.

He smiled. There was much to admire about this councilor of the Caudex, not least of which was her conviction to her ideas and commitment to the survival of all Fant.

"Not at all," he replied. "In fact, I was just thinking about our conversation. I respect your caution and concern when it comes to the Alliance. No one alive on Barsk has any direct experience of them, only eight-hundred-year-old stories of disenfranchisement and oppression passed down from grandmothers."

"No one but you, you mean?"

He bowed his head in acknowledgment.

"And you would have me believe that those many grandmother tales are inaccurate, or grown out of proportion over the many years of their retelling?"

"Perhaps, in part. But no, there's certainly no shortage of truth in them. The real problem is they've become monolithic, rather than actual. There are trillions of people in the Alliance, and though they may share similarities, just like the Fant they are individuals. Yes, there are regional biases, planetary biases, racial biases. I served in the Patrol and I experienced all of that firsthand, but there are also sociological and educational variables that can transcend those, bring people closer together, create common cause and shared interests. I've seen that working alongside my fellow senators in the Committee of Information."

"You would tell me that the Caudex is painting with too wide a brush?"

"I'd ask that you consider that as a possibility."

"And if I tell you that we have? That for us these tales haven't passed down through so many generations and grown distorted because we have ready access to the original grandmothers who experienced the oppression directly? And yes, when you go back to these victims, Speak to the men and women who were displaced from Marbalarma and Dramblys and the many other worlds where they had lived and worked only to find themselves relocated to the wilds of Barsk—there's a reason we call our cities the Civilized Wood—you find personal descriptions of the individuals who sent them here. The accounts blurred over the years, I'll grant you that, but the eyewitnesses, that zero-generation that predates Margda's, they did not experience the Alliance as faceless, interchangeable figures. They saw them as individuals who actively destroyed their lives, separated kith from kin, stripped away all possessions, and cast them away with no concern as to whether they lived or died so long as the Fant were gone from their own daily experience."

Jorl frowned at her. "And in response? Margda and her generation—which includes your own founders—preoccupied themselves with survival. They took this planet that the Alliance had neither use nor love for and transformed it into an essential world to every stage of their economy and commerce. They sought niches and methods, drafted the Compact in a demand to have a voice and be heard again."

"I've told you before, the Compact doesn't guarantee our survival, it only delays the inevitable."

Jorl shook his head. "You're missing the larger point. When she helped draft the treaty, Margda knew that it was imperfect. You can see that when you study her life. It's there in between the lines of her writing. She saw the future and planned for it. And those plans *included* the Compact to buy us all time."

"No, you're making my point for me, Jorl. If Margda relied on her visions to keep us all safe until we reached some critical future point, the Caudex created that future. We've spent our time actually *doing* something. I would say we did so in case she was proved wrong and the Compact failed, but to embrace your explanation I could as easily say we were part of her vision. From that perspective, is it so hard to realize we're on the same side, sharing a common goal?"

Klarce escorted Jorl from her office and together they strolled along a promenade. Her control of the mindscape was perfect but strange. He knew himself beyond Barsk. The foliage in this city looked familiar yet slightly off, and were Arlo still alive he'd no doubt explain it all away as an effect of a different gravity, a different world. He'd walked on other worlds of the Alliance while in the Patrol, but to see a Fant city that did not exist on Barsk was a wonder all its own and moved him deeply.

He tried to keep any of it from showing on his face.

They arrived at a pavilion and stepped within until coming to a balcony that opened onto the largest chimney he'd ever seen. The degree of detail in this mindspace spoke of actual experience and not simply fanciful imagination. Klarce had stood here in the flesh, felt these breezes, smelled these fragrances.

"Where is this place?" He leaned over the balcony railing. Birds, far larger than any that existed on Barsk, flew past him, gleaming jewels of fruit clutched in their claws.

"This is the newsest of our havens. We call it Wella."

He didn't even try to hide the smile that pulled from his lips. "What a coincidence. We have a moon we call by that name."

"Don't be droll, Senator. We gave the first of our hidden worlds the name of one of our moons as a security precaution. We were overly cautious as it turned out, but on the off chance that some

Alliance senator or Patrol officer intercepted any correspondence, their confusion would be limited to our home system. As we expanded even more, the pattern stuck."

Jorl refrained from reminding her that *he* was an Alliance senator as well as a retired officer of the Patrol and instead asked, "I suppose you'll need to find a new naming scheme now?"

"No doubt, but we're still pushing a portal to the star system of what will likely meet the requirements to house our seventh colony."

He waved his trunk in a broad arch. "What sort of requirements applied here?"

"This is the sixth hidden world built and colonized by the Caudex. It's nestled inside a dead moon in a solar system that the Patrol surveyed and wrote off three and a half centuries ago."

"But the Alliance knows of this place? They've been here?"

"Been and gone. There's nothing here that can't be acquired more cheaply elsewhere. So they came and went, pushing their portals from one end of the system's plane to the other and beyond. It would take the nearest Alliance vessel more than two hundred years to get here. They have no portals in this system. Why would they?"

"But you do?" He reached out with his trunk, snagged some leaves and brought them to his mouth. Again a blend of familiar and strange, but also all part of the illusion Klarce provided.

"When the founders of the Caudex hit upon this plan, to potentially colonize systems where the Alliance would never return, they focused their best minds on the science and engineering of portals. The basics haven't changed much in several millennia. The Alliance builds them large, to accommodate multiple ships coming through at once. They build them to never close. We didn't have those constraints. Our portals only remain open when

330 LAWRENCE M. SCHOEN

we need to use them. Otherwise, we disassemble both sides so no one can slip through."

"And you think that keeps you safe?"

"Our enemies don't know we exist. And if they did, they can't find us. And supposing they somehow learned where we are, they still couldn't reach us in time to do us any harm. Once we established each of the hidden worlds, we began pushing new portals of our own outward from each of them. We have sufficient vessels and protected backdoors to allow us to remove the entire population of any of them with a hundred years to spare before even an unmanned attack could reach us."

Jorl pushed away from the railing, passing Klarce and pacing back into the pavilion. "That's a strategy of hiding and running away, not safety."

"And what would you have us do instead, *Senator*?"

He winced at the scorn she poured into his title. "Invite them in," he said.

"What?"

"You've done an incredible thing here, perfected a technique which would serve the Alliance's goal, its hunger, to expand to new worlds. Invite them to share in what you've created. Bring the other races to each of your new worlds and let them learn to live with us again."

"Have you heard anything I've said? Why would we want to live with them? They've shunned us, exiled our ancestors, turned us into monsters in their own folklore. We don't need them in our lives."

"You do," insisted Jorl. "And they need you. Everything the Alliance accomplished prior to moving the Fant to Barsk, the art and science, technology and mathematics, envisioned and developed and perfected over tens of millennia, all of that stems from diversity. When they forced our people onto Barsk, they cut us off from all of that. They stole an entitlement from us."

Klarce laughed. "And yet look what we've done, unhampered by their 'diversity.' If anything, we've excelled without it."

"For now. But you're mistaking stagnation for utopia. Look at history, Klarce. People need to struggle. We need differing opinions. We need argument and disagreement. It's the way we advance. If you lock all the Fant away in these hidden worlds, how will we grow?"

The balcony vanished without warning, replaced by the walls and furniture of a simple office. Klarce sat across from him on a long couch that faced a work desk.

"I hear you, Jorl. I really do. But what you're describing is theory, unsupported by any data. You might be right, or then again maybe not. If we take a bite out of that fruit and are wrong, well, we can't go back and have a whole, unblemished fruit again."

"Actually, you could," said Jorl. "Allow just one of these worlds you've created to become a mixed world. Integrate it however you like, and you'll see what I'm talking about."

She shook her head. "What you're talking about is using upwards of a million people, Fant like you and me, as unwitting participants in a social experiment. And even if I thought it was a good idea—and let's be clear, I do not—how would you keep knowledge of the existence and location of our other Hidden Worlds from non-Fant when your experiment goes horribly wrong?"

"You're making assumptions again—"

"And you're being a naïve academician. Let me be frank with you, the Full Council decided to tell you about Ulmazh and the colonies we've named for Barsk's other moons because after some debate it seemed clear that we all agree more than we disagree. You understand that there are forces in the Alliance—not everyone, of course, not even most, but some—who would see our entire race, wiped out. This is not a burden we wish to place on all Fant, and so the Caudex remains a secret on Barsk. Likewise, the knowledge of much of what we do is limited even on those worlds we've colonized."

"Is that why you gave the order to have me killed?"

Klarce stared, speechless a moment, then nodded as she thought it through. "Dabni told you this?"

"She did. But she didn't know why."

"You summoned Fisco, and the damn fool mentioned the Caudex. From what we already knew about you, it was obvious you'd try to track that down. So Sind activated a team to disrupt the consolidation of your memories of that conversation, only they failed. As did a second team. We still don't know how you managed that. But the point was, whether deliberately or accidentally, you'd breached our security and then proved uncontainable. We knew you to be engaged in regular communication with the Alliance senate. And as Margda's chosen you were already under suspicion. A difficult decision was made, and not lightly."

"What changed that led you to not only rescind my death sentence but also share your secrets of Ulmazh and six other colonies?"

"Your efficiency and your nature."

"Excuse me?"

"You went from knowledge of Fisco to locating the Caudex in a matter of days. You didn't attempt to transmit this information to the Alliance. You didn't see it as a threat or a danger. You personally went to investigate it, to explain it. You sat down with me—with a degree of antagonism on either side it's fair to say—and you sought understanding. The Caudex seeks the safety of our people, not conflict. We believe you do as well and that the best way to ensure we would not be at cross purposes—to ensure you would not *become* a liability—was to show you just how much was at stake and recruit you instead."

He considered this a while before responding. "So you're saying you trust me now?"

"Not so completely as that. We have common cause though. We're not philosophically opposed to the ideas of Fant living side by side with other races, but not if pursuing it brings Alliance scrutiny to Barsk. Find another way, and you'll have our support."

"What would you have me do?"

"Return to your books, Jorl. Write your articles. Give seminars. Study the past as is your preference and let others chart the future. Above all, do not threaten our security—"

"Or you'll have me killed?"

Klarce's sighed like a character in a play. "You can paint me as the villain if you like, but we seek to preserve our people. Part of who we are is a tradition of isolating and culling aberration. You're already exceptional, Jorl. Rein in your aberrance, for your own sake."

"Some would say that aberration is what keeps a society from stagnation," said Jorl.

"You're the historian. How often is that the story that survives the passage of time and the rigor of events?"

And with that, the audience ended. The nefshon connection had been severed and he was back in his own office, left to ponder Klarce's advice regarding the aberrations in his life. Understandably, he reached out for Pizlo.

TWENTY-EIGHT

REFUSAL

~~~~~~

THERE were times when Pizlo knew he thought too much, and other times when he thought he knew too much. This was neither of those. He felt betrayed by the moons and clouds and trees that should have been more forthcoming with information. And because all of these were just the metaphorical masks worn by his own precognitive abilities, he'd managed to betray himself.

His intention to puzzle it all out when he left the harbor had failed. Logic and reason didn't yield any insight and the whispered revelations he usually relied upon had produced the problem in the first place. If he possessed an answer in him, he hadn't stored it in his head. Pizlo kept his body moving, determined to climb up and down and across and back through the Civilized Wood as many times as needed for something to fall into place or until he dropped from exhaustion and might have a chance to find what he sought in sleep.

~~~~~~

HE'D climbed up and across the Civilized Wood and halfway back down the other side when a shiver ran through him. He stopped his descent to the Shadow Dwell, pausing on a meta-tree's broad branch. Closing his eyes, he opened himself to the sensation. The scene of Jorl's study flowed into his mind. "Where are you, Pizlo?"

"It doesn't matter."

"Everyone was upset earlier, though you seemed to have some knowledge of things beforehand."

"Some," he admitted. "But not all."

Jorl nodded. "I was hoping you'd be with Rina. You have a special connection to her and I know she'd be comforted by your presence."

"I had some things I needed to work out . . . still working out." Pizlo paused for just a moment, listened to the branch near to hand, and said, "She's fine. Chisulo caught up with her and they found a soup vendor near the park closest to Tolta's house.

"Thank you for that," said Jorl. "So, are you more upset about being surprised than by the content of the surprise?"

"I've been thinking about how we know what we know, and when we know that we know it," he said. "I knew that Dabni might hurt you, but then I knew she wouldn't."

"It's all going to be fine, Pizlo, I promise."

"No, it's not. Your wife changed her future, but not yours. That woman, Klarce, she's at the crux of everything. I see that. Once I heard she had tried to hurt you, every moon in the sky told me it all ran back to her."

"Maybe that was so, then. But after you ran off, after Dabni left, I came home and spoke with Klarce. We've reached an agreement. That's a very new development. Maybe you were right, maybe I was in danger before, but not now. Things can change, Pizlo. They can change for the better. They have."

He reached out, sought out the answer rather than waiting

passively for knowledge to come to him. And found, in this moment, Jorl was safe. Welcome news, but it wouldn't last."

"Maybe. For now, but like you said, things change, and that includes the change you're describing. What you're talking about's only temporary."

"It doesn't have to endure forever. It only needs to last until the next thing. And there's always a next thing."

"Okay, but . . . why is everything always in flux? Maybe if people really knew one another, it would be different, stable, and everyone would get along."

Jorl smiled. "It's a nice idea, Pizlo, but it's not possible."

"It is. I made a meme." The construct of Pizlo closed his eyes in Jorl's office, blocking out the illusion of vision there. In the real world he resumed his downward climb, blind but hardly slower, his hands and trunk finding grips as they always did.

"A meme?"

"Well, sort of. An echo, really. It's a different way to use nefshons. I saw Dabni do something, and it was kind of like waking up and realizing there was another color in the world or a new way to cook butterleaf that no one had imagined before. That started me thinking about how every Speaker does what every other Speaker does. Nobody questions it. Everyone just re-creates what was done before, retelling the same story."

"You're not making sense. Look, I can see you're still bothered by this. Why don't you come here, we'll talk. And we can join Rina and check in on her, too."

Pizlo shook his head and continued to drop. "I thought about giving it to her, but I didn't. Even though it would show her my life, I thought it might also make her sad, and that wasn't right. I mean, I'm not sad about being alone, but it's how I've always been. And since she hasn't, she'd see it differently, right?"

Jorl frowned at him. "You're talking about the meme you made?"

"You don't understand, and that's okay. I'm not like you or anyone and that's why it's my place to do things differently. I'm a contradiction. So I tried playing with nefshons in a fresh way and made my echo."

"But what does that mean, Pizlo?"

"I'll show you next time I take some koph," he said. "But you really need to talk to Dabni. I know you know she's a Speaker, but she's not like any you've known. She does things differently and she's not what you think she is."

"I know all about Dabni, Piz. Yes, she's a Speaker, and has kept that from me. And she works for a large group of other Speakers that are living apart from everyone else on Barsk."

"Apart, but not apart. Like me, but she gets to be a part which I don't. But that's not what I meant. Is that the same group that's living in Ulmazh or is there more than one group of Speakers that nobody knows about? Cuz that seems really unlikely."

"What? How do you know about that moon?"

"Maybe you don't know *all* about Dabni like you think you do."

"Pizlo, please. Just come home."

All around him the world whispered that he'd reached the last handhold. He let go and pushed off, dropping a short distance and landing lightly on a mossy patch at the bottom of the Shadow Dwell. Pizlo patted the pockets of his bandolier until his fingers found the right shape. He slipped the packet of koph into his mouth and opened his eyes, seeing the study again.

"Where is that, Jorl? Where's home? It's not Tolta's house. It's not yours. It's not any of the nooks and nests I've built throughout the Civilized Wood. It's certainly not on any other island on Barsk. Where do you imagine I'm supposed to feel at home?"

"With your family," said Jorl. "You're not a child like Rina. You know that running away won't solve your problems."

Pizlo sighed. The weight of the entire forest rested on his shoulders and he couldn't recall how it had landed there. "You talk like all problems have solutions."

"Because I believe they do."

"Maybe for you. But I'm not you. I could spend the rest of my life taking koph and walking up to frightened strangers and handing them my echo, and it wouldn't be enough time to solve my problems, not going one by one. But . . . oh."

"What?"

"I just realized, you could do it for me, Jorl. I've seen it; you're able to do things with nefshons that others can't. Like what you did to Bish." The golden swaths of his own particles began to shimmer around him as the koph took effect. Absently, he dismissed them.

"I don't talk about that."

"And I'm not asking you to, but you touched everyone. Can you do that with this?" Able to perceive and manipulate nefshons again, he locked down his end of the connection to Jorl and conjured up a copy of the meme he'd shared with Telko and with the Archetype. He held it out to his friend and former mentor, feeling himself reflected in its swirls. "Here. This is the echo I made. It's me. Will you take it?"

Jorl didn't hesitate. That's what Pizlo would remember, forever. The last thought that would flash through his mind in the instant before he died. Jorl accepted the meme at once. He *took* it. He drew the nefshons into himself, receiving the totality of what and who Pizlo was. Tears welled up in Jorl's eyes. He sighed and shook his head.

"That's . . . a lot to take in, but it doesn't change anything. It might have, a long time ago, but I came to know and accept you for who you are around the last time I spoke with your father. I've known you most of your life, and I've seen you learn and grow despite what the rest of the planet has thrown at or withheld from you."

"But others haven't. If I gave that meme to other Fant, to people who hated and feared me, who can't see past the label of abomination, it might change them."

Jorl nodded. "It would. I have no doubt of that. You'd go from being a thing, some abstract exemplar, to being a person, frail and flawed as anyone else. You'd be more real to them than they are to themselves."

"So do it. Please."

"Do what?"

"Spread my echo, Jorl. You can, right? You can make yourself big like you did, enough of you to circle all of Keslo, and the legion of you can pass my meme to everyone on Barsk."

"I never told you I could that."

"You didn't have to. I saw you do it before it even happened. I told you so, back when I was a kid, back before any of that stuff with Bish."

"Pizlo, your father once said to me, that just because a thing can be done, doesn't mean it should be done."

"But you *could* do it? You could give everyone an understanding of me."

"But if I did, what would I take away?"

Comprehension crashed into him and though he stayed upright in Jorl's study he fell to his knees in the Shadow Dwell. He cried out in both places, not as loudly as he had when the infant had died in his arms on Fintz, but with the same finality.

"You're talking about knowledge without choice."

Jorl nodded and Pizlo imagined the Archetype of Man would have looked the same had it been there wearing the body he'd made for it.

"But that's not fair!" He trumpeted, startling the tiny creatures within range. "Why is it more important to allow people their free will? Why do they get to be brutal and ignorant and hurtful?"

"If you can ask that, you already know the answer."

He curled his trunk back, letting his nubs wipe away his tears. "It's wrong to force understanding on them, because before they have it they wouldn't want it."

"Something like that," said Jorl. In the mindspace of his office he knelt and folded both his arms and ears around Pizlo. "I'm saying it's not my place—not anyone's place—to make that choice for someone else. Sometimes people do anyway, but it's wrong. Margda did that."

"Margda, the woman who prophesied about you?"

Jorl's ears flapped and he smiled. "That's the one."

"But she was a Speaker, and wrote the edict that says . . . oh. I get it. Her rules to break?"

"Pretty much. Margda believed that everyone in the galaxy fell into one of two groups in the never-ending game of our lives. Either you were someone playing the game full out, or you were just a piece on the board existing to be used and expended by need or whim."

"Those are the only choices?"

"She thought that. I don't. If there's more than one way to do a thing, then there's surely more than two. And what I did to Bish all those years ago . . . I never intended to do that. I didn't know I *could* do that. Like Arlo said, it should never have been done."

Pizlo pulled away and Jorl let him. Deep in the Shadow Dwell he got to his feet. "Arlo was pretty smart, wasn't he?"

"Your father was the wisest man I knew, both living and dead. I see a lot of him in you. Even more now that you've shared your meme."

"Yeah . . . but only because you accepted it."

Jorl shrugged. "What can I say, Pizlo? I know you. Yes, there are nuances and details swimming in my head now that weren't there before. But no surprises."

"I'm not an abomination to you?"

"Not to me. Not to your mother. Not to Rina. Not even to Dabni."

"Maybe. Maybe three and a half out of four. Okay."

"So you'll come home?"

"Yeah, but not right now. I . . . I've still got to think a few things through. But thank you. This has helped. A lot."

As he'd been taught, Pizlo severed the connection to Jorl. It wouldn't stop his mentor from reestablishing it, if he chose, but that wasn't a concern. Opening his eyes again he set off through the Shadow Dwell at a run, knowing his destination at last.

PARADOX and contradiction gave him purpose now. He'd been unable to convince Jorl that Klarce would change and once again do him harm. Dabni hadn't been the source of the threat before, just its potential instrument. It had been Klarce all along. And if she'd closed one door and believed everything was fine again, he knew she could just as easily open some new one. Bad things were coming, all the moons said so. If no one else saw the possibilities looming ahead then he'd just have to deal with them himself. This, finally, was his real quest. Not to secure the ink for his tattoo, that had turned out to be just vanity. And not to save a child that couldn't be saved, that was just ego and wishful thinking.

But this, to help his friend and teacher, to risk himself to keep Jorl safe. And the one person who still had choice in the matter was Klarce. He had to persuade her not to open any other doors.

Back at the dock, Dabni had thought his intention to go to Klarce a joke. She didn't understand about quests. But . . . maybe he'd been too caught up in the journeying part of things. Did he really need to physically go to her? He'd asked the rain and been told no, that it wasn't the right time yet. Yet? What did that mean? But the rain hadn't offered any further explanation. It had taken all his ramblings and climbing to work the idea through. He'd been too literal. The traveling wasn't the important part of a quest, to achieve his goal he only had to talk to her. And as Dabni had shown him, Klarce already knew about using koph to reach out to someone no matter the distance.

He emerged from the forest at the same spit of beach where he'd last talked with Ulmazh. It had a nice resonance for the Speaking he needed to do. He lay down in the sand, closed his eyes, and crafted a mental space of himself floating high in the sky, above the rain, above the clouds themselves, with the naked sky shining down on him.

<hr />

HE summoned the index he'd gotten from Dabni. It glimmered in his hands as he focused on it. Tens of thousands of threads in the index responded with a resonating shimmer when he sought Klarce's name. Far too many for him to sort through to find the thread of someone he'd never actually met.

But Jorl had, and Dabni, too. Pizlo added their names to his search, Boolean variables like he'd learned from one of Jorl's books. He quickly found Jorl's thread within the index, and then

Dabni's, and an intersecting thread that responded to the name with identity and resonance. Having found it in the index, he could find it anywhere now. Pizlo reached for her nefshons and instead of sensing the scattered particles of the dead he latched onto a thread from the living woman. He looped it in his trunk and tugged. Her awareness opened to him and he used it to pull her toward him from high up in the sky.

"What? Who?" She flailed, arms and legs and trunk careening about. Though Klarce had doubtless traveled to many many places, she'd apparently never created an imaginary venue unburdened by a solid footing. With a thought he rotated the sky around them until Barsk's space station approached them, engulfed them, and left them inside one of its many warehouses surrounded by stacks of cargo pods.

Klarce's response was to stop flailing and fall onto the floor. He reached out and offered her a hand up.

"Hello, I'm sorry about that. My name is Pizlo. I'd like to talk to you about Jorl."

At first, she reached for his hand, but that must have been instinct rather than choice, because before his fingers had more than grazed her skin she pulled back and screamed at him.

"Abomination! Get out of my mind!"

He saw her reach out with trunk and both hands, gripping the unseen thread that connected them, and then she was gone.

He reached out for her again, found a thread and tugged, but the connection was severed from the other end before it could form. He tried a third time, but without success. "Damn." Pizlo closed his eyes on the space station and reopened them on the beach. Every choice created new possibilities and closed off others. Reaching out to Klarce from Keslo was one of the latter. He looked up into the falling rain, squinting at the clouds. "Well? That didn't work. Now what?" And the answer came as the drops pelted his face. Now it *was* time to go.

~~~~~

HE broke through the forest's edge within sight of the funicular that delivered people to the harbor, and adjusted his course for the pier where Jorl's boat waited in its sloop. He'd have to borrow it. Again. So, maybe, if this was going to be a regular or at least frequent thing, he could talk to him about acquiring a simpler vessel just for him. The events from Fintz were still fresh in his mind, but he could imagine a day, some time far from now, when he might want to go off on another imram.

With the harbormaster nowhere in sight, Pizlo cast off and eased Jorl's boat into the harbor. Not far off, Druz waited with a spacecraft. Doubtless she was monitoring any approaching boats, the better to move out of their way before any drew close enough to see her vessel through the rain. But likewise, she could surely detect that he wasn't any other Fant. She might wonder what he was doing, but she would not evade him.

Quite the opposite, as it turned out. With no warning, he detected the bulk of the spacecraft moving toward him on an intercept course. He immediately powered down and left the wheelhouse to stand along the starboard side as the yacht approached. It slowed, opened a hatch, and scooped the smaller boat into its cargo hold with evident practice. Pizlo leapt onto a railing parallel to the boat where a Raccoon stood waiting for him. He stopped. Not one of the moons had mentioned anything about a Procy, though clearly this was the one Rina had met.

"You must be Prince Pizlo," said the Raccoon.

"Just Pizlo," he said.

"Oh . . . I thought Druz said—"

"Yeah, I'm sure she did. Who are you?"

"Sorry, I'm Abenaki."

Dots connected in his mind. "From Caluma. Your mother, Santo, is a journalist. Denzi, your father, is a civil engineer specializing in waterworks. You want to bring other races to Barsk. It's an intriguing idea, but I can tell you now that it won't work. The Fant will never agree to it, and despite Jorl, several members of the Committee of Information will keep the proposal from ever reaching the senate floor. And that's actually the least of the reasons, but it's not my place to tell you the others. I'm sorry, but there you have it."

The Procy recoiled, the mask on her face making her widening eyes truly amazing to see.

"How could you possibly know any of that?"

"I don't have time for this, but . . . I have to make the time because I know this happens. Fine. Listen to me. This is prophecy. *Your* prophecy." He closed the distance to the Raccoon and wrapped his trunk around her arm, pulling her in close. "You're going to have a choice to make soon. I won't make it for you. I could, but I won't. That choice will put you on a path alongside my own. You want to make a difference, want to improve the life of all people in the Alliance. I have the best chance of doing that, better than anyone who's ever lived. Remember that when it's time for you to choose. But for now, tell me where Druz is."

Abenaki stepped back like she'd been struck. She pointed with delicate fingers toward the inward hatch. "Through there. Turn right and follow the blue line on the wall all the way to the bridge. She's there."

Pizlo was already moving. He didn't need any lines. In fact, he was surprised he'd had to ask after her location. Maybe the moons couldn't see inside the ship. But no, that was just his metaphor.

His own talent for knowing things for some reason hadn't served up that particular bit of information. No matter, he knew how to get to the bridge.

⁓⁓⁓⁓

HE slapped the door control with his trunk and pushed through before it had opened all the way. Druz sat at first board. A glance showed most of the vessel's controls and instruments were locked down. Just enough technology active to keep it steady and in place, and to scan and identify any approaching Fant.

"How quickly can you ready us for flight?" He nodded as he walked past her and slipped into the seat at second board. He stopped with his hands raised over the controls, poised. He turned to look at her, his gaze repeating the question.

"Why do we need to go? And more importantly, where?"

"I'll explain while I help you prep. Please unlock my board."

Druz did as he requested and his fingers began to fly. He left the Sloth to run through the checklists and safety precautions while he pulled coordinates and other numbers from his vision and locked them in by way of answering her in the specific. For the more general he turned to her when he was done.

"To the moon, to Ulmazh. We need to go there now. *I* need to go there. And as this is the only ship that can get me there in time to do any good, I need you to take me there."

The Sloth had moved much more slowly at the main board but nonetheless completed her protocols while he said his piece. Now she sighed, locking both boards again but not resetting them back to rest. She shook her head. "We cannot do that, Little Prince. While I'm very fond of you, and I'm well aware that Jorl holds you in the highest regard, only he can dictate to me where I take this vessel."

"We're doing this *for* Jorl. He's in trouble. But to save him, we need to go to Ulmazh. I need to get there."

"I'm sorry, but no."

"Druz, you know all about my precognitive talents. You're the one who said how good I was, how powerful. Believe me now when I tell you we have to do this thing to keep him safe."

"A moment then, and I'll contact Jorl. If he approves the destination, I'll happily take you there."

"No!" The syllable resonated along his trunk. "He won't believe me, and when he tells you so, you won't either."

"Is there some proof you can show me, something that triggered this dire vision?"

"I don't have any . . . no, wait, I do." He snatched at the amulet on his throat and fumbled the controls a moment.

A voice like a tiny version of Dabni rose from the disc. "They wanted me to kill him. They didn't give me a choice. They rescinded the order or he'd be dead by now. Do you understand? They asked me to murder my husband, the father of my child."

"Murder?" From her expression, Pizlo knew she'd recognized the voice.

"Yes."

"And you need to go to this moon?"

"I do."

"Because the person who gave Dabni that order is there. And even though she took it back, what's to stop her from commanding Dabni to do it again?"

"Me," said Pizlo. "I'm going to have a talk with her."

"Little Prince, with a notable handful of exceptions, no one on Barsk will speak with you."

"That's right, but we're leaving Barsk. Ulmazh is going to be different."

"How do you know?"

He smiled at her as she unlocked her board again and finished the last bit of preparation. A light on the board went out. Far below in the cargo hold a ramp retracted and a hatch sealed itself. The Brady activated the shipwide comm system. "Abenaki, get yourself secured. We're about to get under way."

"Thank you," he said, and strapped himself into the second board's seat.

"You didn't answer my question. How do you know?"

"I just do."

"This is something one of your moons told you?"

He shook his head. "Not quite. This is something I chose for myself. I'll explain to the moon when we get there."

TWENTY-NINE

CONTRITION AND RESOLUTION

~~~~~~~

"T . . . he . . . he was here." Klarce didn't bother—or possibly couldn't—locking down a mindspace before yanking Sind into a conversation. They floated in darkness until habit kicked in and her unconscious provided a familiar venue, the simple cafe where they had met each morning back when she had been his assistant.

"What? Where, on Ulmazh?"

"No, you fool. Think! It's not like he has access to spacecraft. Here, in my mind. That abomination, he was here."

"That's absurd." Sind projected displeasure at the insult. "You're just stressed. You're always complaining about being required to use koph so frequently, why are you doing so now? Especially given your condition."

Klarce waved away both his argument and his minor hurt with a swipe of her trunk. "I'll take a break. I'll even grab a brief nap and let Temmel medicate me. But in the meantime, I need you to call the Full Council together."

"You're being ridiculous. What you're describing could not have happened."

"I tell you—"

He interrupted her. "And if you pursue this . . . this . . . hallucination to the Full Council I will not be able to protect you. Not everyone is pleased with the amount of autonomy you've been showing, and they'll use this as a justification to remove you completely. If that happens, I won't be able to help."

"Damn it, Sind, will you listen to me? The abomination of Keslo reached out to me. Do you understand me? He summoned me. He's a Speaker."

He shook his head. "That's simply not possible and you know it. There has to be some other—"

"He had a copy of the index in his hands!"

"But—"

"The Full Council. Do it now. I . . . I was wrong. I wanted to believe we had common cause with Margda's chosen, that Jorl understood and shared, no, that he embraced our goals to secure the safety of our people. But I see now that was just wishful thinking. He's taught an abomination to Speak, to reach out to any of us at the most basic level. And for what? A whim? To see if he could?"

"Klarce—"

"No. You will not change my mind on this. You weren't there. Here. Feel it for yourself. The horror. The violation." With fading strength she isolated the recent experience in her own mind. The technique was much the same as disruption of a memory but instead of scattering the patterns during encoding she copied them and then spun that copy off into a small knot of nefshon threads. She shoved it at Sind through their connection.

"Summon the Full Council. Share that with them along with

my contrition. I want their authorization to end this once and for all."

"You want to *shred* the senator? They'll never agree, and you need unanimity for that."

"They will. You all will."

"And how do you know it will even work? This senator was immune to our attempts to scramble a fresh memory and we still don't know how that was possible. Even with eight councilors all working the shredding, he may be too strong."

"Leave that to me. But for now, please, do as I ask. I . . . I do need to rest."

She ended the conversation and called for Temmel.

SHE slept, a bit. Temmel had given her a cursory medical examination and supplied both an analgesic and the meds to keep her neuromuscular glitch at bay a while. She'd be fine, he assured her, provided she didn't take any koph for at least a day. She smiled at him—hoping he was being facetious rather than naïve—and asked for a report on the field test of the devices invented by the physicist that had come up with them on the shuttle.

"Bernath tells me they were an unqualified success. The constructs of the conversants summoned remained coherent for the duration of the test. The two Speakers who participated reported some small degree of fatigue, but no different than one might expect from a prolonged summoning."

"And how many did each manage?"

Temmel double-checked the report. "Ten, all told. Eight using the new technology."

"How many of the devices did Bernath bring with them?"

"Sixteen."

"Have them brought here. Give them whatever servicing they need to be in optimal condition first, but I want them set up and ready to use."

"I don't understand. If you need Speakers for some task, there're far more than sixteen available to you here on Ulmazh. Why would you need to maintain constructs of any others?"

"Because other than myself, none of the Speakers here are now or have ever been members of the council."

"Why does that matter?"

She waved him closer. He seemed so young. Or did she just feel old. "You already know that there are techniques of nefshon use that most Speakers—even those among the Caudex—don't know about. The disruption of memories, the creation of memes. The maintenance of the index. All of these can be learned, but none of them are the sort of thing you'll likely stumble across on your own. You've mastered them yourself."

"Yes, but—"

She held up a hand to stop him. "I've told you, I expect you to replace me one day. When that happens, you'll learn yet another technique, one that has only been used twice before in the entire history of the Caudex. One that is only known to councilors because it is too terrible."

"And you mean to use this today?"

"If I'm not already too late."

~~~~~~

SIND had assembled the Full Council more quickly than she'd imagined he would, which meant his experience of her memory had shaken him as thoroughly as it had her. She'd taken as small a dose of koph as she dared, enough to participate in the council for a short while and no more. Despite her meds, she could already feel tremors in both hands. She had to keep this quick, had to keep them focused. The dread on the faces of the other councilors—both living and dead—when she arrived among them gave her hope that they would achieve a swift consensus. Until Nirl all but lunged for her.

"This is all your fault!"

She ignored the dead woman and looked to Marsh, opening with what she saw as a simple truth.

"I now believe my previous judgment was in error. Although Jorl ben Tral's actions in seeking us out as he did would suggest he is not a thrall to the Alliance, I no longer believe his interests and actions will parallel those of the Caudex."

"Agreed," said Marsh.

Nirl slapped at the table with her trunk demanding attention. "How is this even possible? An abomination on the brink of adulthood? An abomination gaining access to koph, to Speaking, to the index? And on your watch, Klarce. How did you let it come to this?"

Klarce recalled Jorl's assessment of Nirl, and despite the source drew calm from it. "Councilor Nirl," she said, "all due respect to your greater powers of perception notwithstanding, you and the rest of the Full Council were privy to the same reports as myself. If I was blind to any warning signs, I regret that you did not bring them to my attention."

"Damn you, I have the memory of that creature in me now."

"As do we all," said Kissel. "And we can choose to remove that soon enough. That's not why we are here."

"Agreed," repeated Marsh. "And Klarce, while I find sharing your experience of the abomination deeply regrettable, I understand why you had Sind pass it to us. What you are asking has only been considered a handful of times, only performed twice."

She bowed her head. "Do I have the council's consensus that it is necessary in this instance? Will you name him rogue and commit yourselves to shredding his very being?"

"That he is rogue is beyond doubt," said Soosh, nodding to Marsh as she took the floor. "No amount of rationalization or justification can excuse his decision to empower a creature that should never have lived with the ability to force itself on every Eleph and Lox—"

Melko, Sind, and Genz murmured approval of the assessment, interrupting and stopping Soosh. She let the pause linger and when none of the others felt the need to further amplify her words she continued. "But can we shred him? Just as we possess insights into nefshons that the Matriarch never imagined, it would appear that she taught him some few abilities that were never made public. How else did he resist the two teams that sought to prevent the memory of his summoning of Fisco, the event that precipitated all of this? And, too, we have his ludicrous explanation of why none among the Caudex have been able to summon Margda for years."

Genz jumped in. "Soosh has the right of this. With respect to his abilities, we still don't know what we don't know." He waved his trunk toward Klarce. "I assume this is why you asked for this extreme measure, rather than a reissuing of the physicality cascade meme."

"It is," she said.

"We are eight to his one," said Kissel. "Surely he cannot stand against us all."

"Perhaps," said Marsh. "But I believe Soosh's point is that we all have expressed the same certainty about disrupting his memory. We need to consider contingencies in the event that the eight of us are not sufficient."

Klarce lifted her head and one by one captured the gaze of her fellow councilors. "As to that, I have a plan."

~~~~~

TEMMEL hovered close at hand, insisting she hydrate, checking her blood pressure, and generally being a nuisance. But he'd done as she asked. The floor of her office had been littered with sixteen discs. Technology that was supposed to provide backup to Speakers serving sentry positions at the Caudex's numerous portals would today be used to destroy a man. The misuse of such a breakthrough irked her, and it irked her that it irked her. Her thoughts on Jorl had been so volatile. His smugness had annoyed her. His simple brilliance had charmed her. His earnest desire to be of service to the people had convinced her. But his enabling the abomination wiped all of that away. She would end him.

"You should rest longer before you attempt this," said Temmel, as he ushered the last of the techs out of her office. "The combination of your meds and the koph creates an interactive effect that is more debilitating than just the sum of the two when taken separately. You're going to burn yourself out if you don't stop."

"Waiting isn't an option. I need to have sixteen past councilors here when I confront Jorl, which means I need them now. There won't be time or will to summon them once the Full Council arrives and begins the shredding."

He shook his head. "Then it's not going to happen. At best, you can manage one more session of koph in the next day. Anything more and your body is just going to shut down. The physicist's results are astounding, yes, but it still takes a full summoning to fill the discs. You can't do that and Speak to Jorl."

"Which is why I need you to not only summon the councilors for those discs, but to brief them as well."

"Me? I don't know what you're intending to have them do. How can I brief them?"

"Do you need to know how to cook the meal to order it in a restaurant? Just tell them they've been called to lend their assistance in a shredding and to follow my lead when I appear to them."

"Can you at least explain what's going to happen?"

Klarce gave her assistant her most put-upon look, but he didn't back down. Ill-timed, but good. The sooner he stopped backing down the sooner he'd be ready for a seat on the council. She sighed. "While someone is alive, they are surrounded by a coating of nefshons."

Temmel nodded.

"The threads of it are woven tightly together. The members of the Full Council will descend upon Jorl's nefshons and unravel that coating, thread by thread. It's a slow process. Left to their own resources, a living being will automatically repair the nefshon coating, much like reconstituting a shattered hologram from a single piece. But disrupt enough of it, and the entire tapestry falls away."

"But what will that do to the senator?"

"Physically, he'll be unharmed, but his mind will be gone. His will, some would say, his soul. The essential part of him that drives his being and makes him a unique individual. He'll possess the same knowledge he has now, but won't be able to add to it. Nor initiate new thoughts or ideas. He'll be a highly intelligent idiot, able to follow simple directions but little else."

Temmel shuddered. His ears had fallen back and limp. The horror on his face was palpable. "No one deserves that."

"Which is why it requires a unanimous decision of the Full Council to implement the process. They'll join me when I reach out to Jorl. But they may not be enough. Jorl has caught us by surprise before. I need you to load up those sixteen discs with past councilors. I've prepared a list for you. Use the index and get to work."

"But you—"

"Yes, Temmel, I'll rest. I'm going to lie down right here, close my eyes, and attempt to nap. But only if you promise to wake me as soon as you're done."

"Yes, ma'am."

She moved to the couch and settled back. She even closed her eyes before waving her trunk one time more to get her assistant's attention.

"None of us are proud to do what we're doing today. But as we feel it needs to happen, let's make sure we do it well."

THIRTY

CLOUDLESS

PIZLO leapt from the airlock the instant Druz opened the outer door. He scrambled from the yacht and bounced across the airless surface of Ulmazh, careening wildly as he tumbled over the regolith. He'd been above Barsk before and gazed upon the naked stars, but that had been through the view port of a space station. It was something else again to have all the lights of the galaxy gleaming in the sky above him. So many of those stars warmed worlds not unlike Barsk, worlds overflowing with lives, both sapient and not. Worlds and lives that wanted to speak to him, to share their stories, to argue about insects and heroes and determinism and agency. For a terrifying moment he thought of just pushing off, flying free into the empty fullness of space, to embrace an endless moment of life and light and learning.

Then he remembered the true quest he was on, the threat to Jorl, and the moment passed.

The ship's locker had offered gear for a wide variety of races. He'd opted for an environment suit designed for a Fant so he could use his trunk, but the one-size-fits-most design of the thing was intended for adults and he couldn't help sliding around inside it. But no matter; though his progress lacked grace, he knew precisely where he was going. The moon itself had told him. Despite discouraging that part of himself that offered up visions disguised as conversations with his surroundings, he didn't begrudge Ulmazh telling him where to find the hidden gate in the shadow of a crater. He'd have found it himself, eventually, either by walking every possible bit of surface or asking Druz to use the equipment onboard Jorl's ship. He'd have found it; he still had agency, still exercised choice.

The gate hadn't been locked, but it did require three hands close together to open, which no two people clad in bulky environment suits would be able to manage. But one person with two hands and a trunk could operate the mechanism with ease. The gate opened, revealing itself to be a small door built into a much larger one, providing access to a wide airlock. Pizlo entered, closed the gate behind him and studied the controls on the opposite wall. A few experimental taps later and the airlock filled with pressure and breathable air. The inner hatch opened. Pizlo stepped through, closed the door behind him, and climbed out of his suit. He left it in a corner by the door, the helmet stacked neatly on the rest of it, and glanced down the hallway that led away from this spot. He was inside the moon! He eased a packet of koph out of his bandolier and slipped it into his mouth.

Like the airlock's gate, the hall was wider than it needed to be if only people came this way. It didn't run long and stopped in front of a door with a button on the frame. It looked quite a bit like the entrance to the funicular on Keslo. Either that, or some kind of elevator. He pushed the button and entered the box revealed by the opening door. Moments later the door closed on its

own and the whole thing began to drop straight down. An elevator then. Pizlo felt the koph starting to work and he reached for
Klarce's nefshons again.

In an instant he had a thread of her, holding it lightly with his
trunk. He didn't tug it, but sent his awareness running the length
of it here in the physical world, tracing the distance between them
until he knew her location as unerringly as any spot the world below had ever whispered to him. He let go of the thread, confident
he could follow it back to its source, deeper into the moon. Klarce
was here, in Ulmazh, and the elevator was taking him closer.

The door opened onto the sight of a middle-aged Eleph aiming something that was surely a weapon in his direction. It made
sense of sorts. You wouldn't have a super secret hidden base and
not post a guard at the only entrance. But he still had to get to
Klarce and he'd hoped for few delays.

"Don't move. Keep your hands and trunk where I can see them.
Who are you and what's your business here? You're not on my list,
and there's no one scheduled to be here."

Pizlo pulled aside the strap of his bandolier to reveal his tattoos.
He took a deep breath, hating himself for playing into his people's
twisted beliefs. The guard would have worked it out himself quickly
enough, but he didn't have time to waste. "I am Pizlo, Bearer of the
Seven Moons, the Abomination of Keslo. You cannot see me, cannot impede me. I am the rain that goes unnoticed, the fallen leaf that
is unseen. Stand aside as if it were your own idea and not something
I suggested, because in truth you never heard me."

The weapon slipped from the sentry's hands, fell slowly to the
floor and clattered as it bounced before laying still. He tumbled
backward and nearly fell over the desk behind him. Shaking his
head, Pizlo walked past toward another door and let himself
through.

He found himself on a narrow walkway that ran straight a while and then rose up and turned in on itself as it struck off at a right angle, apparently running upside down. One hand on the railing, he set off and as he neared the upward curve his stomach lurched. He kept going, dizziness nearly causing him to stumble forward, both down and up. The negligible gravity of the moon was replaced by the normal pull of Barsk but from the opposite direction and then he was through and gazing back down at the path he'd walked and the door he'd entered through. Above him the platform branched into a series of endless gantries that rose up and connected massive boxes as far as he could see. He aimed for the nearest, climbed until he was level with its box and could peer in. He found dirt and stone, moss and mold, the whir of insects and smaller creatures, and all of it in service to the roots and bole of the meta-tree that rose up out of the box and launched itself up up up toward the core of the hollowed moon. Pizlo turned in place, and through the dimness could see that each of the surrounding gantries' boxes held their own trees, a more precise arrangement than existed in nature but nonetheless all one would need to build a Shadow Dwell, of sorts. He clambered down into the box and made his way to the meta-tree at its center. Pizlo began to climb.

It made sense that if someone wanted to build a Civilized Wood then they'd have to start with meta-trees. The ones on the islands of Barsk had been there when the Fant arrived, but to create new ones why not grow them in pots like in a nursery? Big pots. Really big pots. Brought to the moon. How long did it take a meta-tree to grow? How long ago had they started all of this, not just bringing all the soil and pots and meta-saplings, but building the gate in the surface of Ulmazh and digging the corridor and the elevator shaft and hollowing out all the space to build a city, and where did they even put all the moon rock and stuff? The questions danced in his head as he pulled himself up through branches not noticeably different from those he'd known all his life in Keslo. There was a slight bounce and tug to his movements, as if the gravity wasn't quite right, but otherwise once he'd lost sight of the potted Shadow Dwell he might as well have been back home. Ulmazh itself hadn't answered any of the questions he'd been pondering but it did whisper suggestions and directions for the best route to take as he climbed ever higher.

When he finally passed through into the Civilized Wood of Ulmazh, differences leapt out at him. For one thing, the scope of everything from the boardways to the buildings was bigger, as if to accommodate a larger population. And there were *devices* everywhere. Little machines that whirred softly to themselves on lintels and corners and balconies. And on people, too. As Pizlo hung back, concealed by the foliage border in a broad avenue—much as he might have done back in Keslo—he saw Eleph and Lox going about their day. They didn't seem the least bit concerned that they lived upside down inside of a moon. And except for the bits of metal and ceramic clipped to their ears or about their wrists—more machines doing who knew what—they could have been any people from anywhere on Barsk.

The effects of the koph he'd taken earlier had begun to fade during his climb, and he took another piece and popped it into his mouth. He'd never overlapped doses before, but it would probably be all right, and besides this was too important. Throwing a mental switch, he made the swaths of nefshons surrounding the people on the boardway visible to him, and summoned a strand from the nearest of them. Then he conjured up the index, compared it to the strand, and found the person already there. Not that he needed it, but the match was further confirmation that the people who had made the index knew that there were Fant living in the moon.

He let the strand go and refocused on the index and the bit he'd identified as belonging to Klarce. She was nearby. The sooner he found her and convinced her to talk to him, the sooner he could fix things for Jorl. He had a good feeling for direction and distance so he let his perception shift back to the ordinary world. He pushed through the green, somersaulted and rolled to his feet on the boardway and ignored the gasps and stares of other folk as he ran along toward his goal.

Now that he was out in the open, Pizlo noticed other differences. The air was . . . odd. Kind of like it had been when he'd been snugged up in that environment suit, only now it wasn't something he could blame on the helmet. It was drier. The omnipresent rain of Barsk that permeated every breath on every island had no place here. And the light was wrong. The diffuse illumination of Keslo that filtered through the Civilized Wood via cunning arrays of mirrors and lenses from the edges of the forest and the tops of the canopy didn't exist here. Glow strips lined the ceilings of avenues and archways, not unlike those he'd seen on the space station all those years ago, but subtler and more cleverly worked into the architecture.

There was something different about the people he passed, too, but he couldn't say what. They recoiled from him the way others back in Keslo did, reacting first to his paleness and the dirt and stains and cuts that covered him head to toe. And then, invariably, they made the connection, some cultural shared consciousness that let them label him as other, unclean, abomination. They moved out of his path and erased him from their perceptions like a Speaker would dismiss nefshons that were of no interest. That was fine. The fewer obstacles in his path, the sooner he would reach Klarce and fix everything.

Pizlo's earlier estimate that this Civilized Wood was bigger than the one he knew back home was born out by his having already traversed twice the length of the main boardway of Keslo that ran from one end of the island to the other. He was getting tired. He'd passed many different neighborhoods each with their own bookshops and apothecaries and spirit stores, numerous gymnasiums and performance balconies and parks. Several hundred pedestrians going about their own business had encountered their first abomination and would whisper of it that night. He'd lost track of how many municipal buildings he'd ticked off on his run, but paused at last in front of a modest one, little more than a simple office suite. The outer door had Klarce's name carved into it, along with the word "Councilor" and on a line below, "Ulmazh Office-Hours By Appointment."

Pizlo let himself in, his ears lifting as a faint beep accompanied him. The room held a small desk directly opposite the entrance, a young Eleph seated behind it, his head down as he worked through a tablet and made notations upon it with the stylus he held in his trunk. Framed projections on both side walls showed changing images of Fant smiling and waving as they stood in front of parks and libraries and orchestras, and always with the same middle-aged woman in the middle of them. Klarce. Seeing the images, he saw the calmer, happier version of her features than the horrified face he'd briefly connected with.

"I'll be right with you," said the man behind the desk, not yet looking up, his attention still focused on his work. "The councilor isn't available today, but I'll be happy to schedule an appointment for you in just a moment."

"I don't need an appointment," said Pizlo. "But I do need to speak with Councilor Klarce. It won't take long though."

"I'm sure you believe that's the case," replied the man, and the smile in his voice was warm and friendly. "Everyone does, but the reality is the councilor's time is—" He broke off as he finally looked up and stared at the latest visitor in the office. Pizlo gazed back, and waved.

"You're . . . Pizlo."

Pizlo grinned. He saw recognition on the face of the man looking back at him, seconds before he averted his gaze. And he'd actually spoken to him, called him by name. Remarkable.

"I am. But how do you know that? Who are you?"

The man stammered, his ears flapped furiously in distress. He fixed his gaze over Pizlo's shoulder and spoke to the door there. "You—You were in a report I prepared for the councilor. I'm T–Temmel. I'm Councilor Klarce's assistant. She's, ah, not in."

"Yes, she is. Just through there." Pizlo waved his trunk to indicate the door on the wall behind Temmel's desk.

"What I mean is, she's busy. In conference. Can't be disturbed." He swallowed hard and kept looking at anything and everything else in the room. But for all that, Temmel'd kept talking to him, only the eighth person in his life to ever do so. Neither Ulmazh nor any of the other moons had even hinted that such a thing would happen. Was it because he'd learned of him from some report, become someone real rather than an abstract idea? It was hard for the man, but he was managing, and Pizlo realized it would be so easy to turn away from his goal, to just stay and talk, make a connection to another person, expand the tiny universe of people whom he knew and who might come to know him. But this was just an obstacle, a trial on his quest albeit a very appealing one.

Heroes were always tempted from their true course. He shook his head, sniffling once as he let go of this brief addition to his constellation of people.

"Yeah, but—and you'll just have to trust me on this—this is more important. Thank you, Temmel, for seeing me, at least for a short while. I—I really hope we can talk again." He walked around the desk and stepped through the door, leaving the stunned Eleph behind.

~~~~

THE inner room wasn't much bigger but held considerably more furniture. A floor to ceiling cupboard filled most of the wall to Pizlo's left, while the one on the right held a wide and fluffy couch, a low table with a shallow bowl of nuts upon it. A scattering of brass discs lay on the floor. The far wall held a semi-circular desk with a cushioned hammock seat and a single occupant who appeared to be sleeping. Klarce.

Pizlo locked the door behind him even as the Eleph on the other side gathered his wits and tried to follow him through. It would hold for a while. He crossed the room, avoiding the discs, swinging his trunk low to help himself to a few nuts as he passed the table, and climbed onto Klarce's desk. He settled himself in front of her and opened his perceptions to the nefshons she'd presumably gathered and the mindspace she'd created with them.

And immediately fell to the ground, pushed back by the presence of tens of people. He rolled on his back in the midst of them until he managed to find enough space to stand, far to the side. Blinking back surprise he saw that most of the Fant in the room were Jorl. A few others stood in the room, each of them astride one of the discs he'd seen on the floor. And, back by her desk, Pizlo could just make out the figure of Klarce on the other side of at least a ten of Jorl. She held a looping whirl of a meme in one hand, and in the next moment sent it racing down a nefshon thread.

As one, all the Jorls around cried out, "Rina!"

Klarce said something after that, but Pizlo failed to make it out. And then all but one of Jorl vanished and the space between himself and Klarce was empty. This was his moment, the critical point where determinism could be overturned by agency. Paradox. Something that couldn't possibly happen needed to happen, and could because he embodied contradiction. It was the fulfillment of his quest, and as he stepped into the moment he realized he couldn't see the future. But that was fine, what he needed now was the past. Pizlo closed his eyes on the scene and got his bearings again in the physical office. In both realities he rushed forward, grasping Klarce's hand in his.

THIRTY-ONE
RE-EDUCATION

~~~~~~

ORL lay in his bed, sound asleep, the emotional strain of the day before having taken its toll. He could have easily slept through till noon—even with the sartha outside his window cut back—but Klarce took that option away. One moment he was lost in some dream involving a library full of books from the time Before and the next he was blinking himself into awareness, having been summoned to a mindspace of the same office Klarce had shown him before, somewhere inside Ulmazh.

It was on his lips to make some wry remark that surely she could manage a full day without seeing him but the words fell away unspoken. Klarce looked . . . haggard, like someone who had been working with nefshons for too long over too short a span. Even for those who had built up an immunity to its worst effects, koph was still a toxic drug. The Caudex councilor had clearly been pushing herself too hard. And something else. Koph toxicity could account for her wan complexion, the droop of her eyes, but Jorl saw a tremor in her fingers and nubs as well.

"Is something wrong? I didn't expect to hear from you again so soon."

"Jorl ben Tral, your actions betray all our people."

He blinked back his confusion. "Are we back to this again? Yes, I still think it's important for us to find a way to live alongside the other races of the Alliance, but I told you I won't pursue it personally or encourage any proposals for it in the senate. I won't jeopardize the worlds you've built. I won't do anything to endanger the many Eleph and Lox living there."

"And yet, you have."

"Excuse me?"

"You bear an aleph, a mark that has taken on great historical significance and dates back almost to the beginning of our exile on Barsk. But you flout an even older tradition. No, worse, you actively work to undermine it."

"Klarce, I honestly don't know what you're talking about."

Her face twisted with disgust. "Don't play at stupidity. I'm talking about your pet abomination."

Jorl scowled back at her. "If you mean Pizlo, what about him?"

"He's sensitive to koph."

"Well . . . yes."

"And when you discovered this, did you train him to be a Speaker?"

"I did. But mainly so I could stay in touch with him, much like I'm communicating with you. It's not as though he can summon any other Fant. He doesn't know anyone. Moreover, he knows that even if he did, it would make any conversant he reached profoundly uncomfortable."

"That no longer constrains him."

"What are you talking about?"

"Members of the Caudex here on Ulmazh have reported an abomination appearing to them as a nefshon construct and interfering with their work."

"Oh, please. When I was half Pizlo's age I tried to convince a teacher that an abomination had stolen my homework. Your reports are surely just more of the same folklore and rumor that's always existed."

"Spare me your anecdotes. This rumor was substantiated today when your creature forced himself into my mind," said Klarce.

"That's not possible. He doesn't know anything about you. How could he summon you?"

"He can summon any Fant on Barsk. He has a copy of the index!"

"Sorry? Index? I don't know what that is."

"And I don't believe you. You're cunning, Jorl. Too cunning by far. Too cunning to trust. I admit, you had me fooled. I believed you before. You convinced me we had the same goals. And the very fact that you could do that is why I have gone to the council and asked them to stop you. Now, and for all time. And after we've dealt with you, I will personally put an end to your pet abomination."

With no further warning, an additional member of the Caudex grasped for Jorl, connecting to him via a nefshon thread and pulling himself into the conversation and the mental space Klarce had crafted. Then another did the same, then more, until the other seven members of the Caudex Full Council were present and glaring at him. He'd done the inverse of this often enough, using his enhanced abilities to Speak with the entire Committee of Information at one time. Completing connections to the other senators allowed him to bring them all together in the same place in the manufactured mindspace and communicate in real time.

This was different. These Speakers had nothing to share. Rather, they sought to take.

"This is *not* our way, but you have left us no choice," said Klarce. She still stood in front of him in the mindspace, now with one hand outstretched and a writhing loop of self-sustaining particles swirling on her palm. He'd seen that kind of structure before. Pizlo's echo of himself existed independent of him, a thing made of knowledge; a meme.

Jorl ignored Klarce. Whatever rationalization she babbled now was some pathetic attempt to assuage her own conscience. He shifted his attention to the other seven council members.

Each held the same meme, sending its message to him through the links they'd forced. It was as if they were somehow whispering to his mind. He had a vague awareness that his body had stiffened, his heart rate increased, but otherwise he wasn't in any physical danger. Then, was this a mental attack? He focused on the meme being thrust upon him. It was simple, like a recipe. Do this, then this, then this other thing, and repeat. The actual actions were incomprehensible to him but the directions themselves were easy enough to follow. He cycled through the recipe, once, twice, and recoiled as the effect of it reached him at last. He reacquired the perception of his own nefshon fabric for confirmation and instead of a smooth tapestry of golden particles he saw innumerable threads trailing off. He was being plucked, unwound, shredded.

Like anyone else, he had a near infinite number of nefshons bound to his living body, but the councilors' meme worked impossibly fast, propagating the idea of his unraveling to his own particles, making them a partner in their own unbinding. He looked inward, trying to see his own nefshons in ways no non-Caudex Speaker had ever considered. He touched one of the unraveling threads and coaxed it back into the seamless pattern that was its default, repairing the damage. He moved on to the next and the next, picking up confidence and speed. He could do this. Soon enough he was restoring his threads easily twice as fast as a meme caused him harm.

But eight Speakers assaulted him with the memes, deliberately of course. They had guessed that he could restore what another Speaker sought to destroy. But not eight to one. He'd slowed the dissolution, but he couldn't stop it. That's why they had come like this, attacking him en masse. No matter how fast he repaired the damage, an ordinary Speaker could never survive the scenario.

But he'd stopped being ordinary years ago.

"You've made a mistake," he said, even as his focus phased in and out. He had to hurry, the meme didn't need to run its course to defeat him, just leave him muddled enough as not to be able to defend against it. He had time yet, but not much. "You've forgotten the third law of Margda's edict."

"Third law? That never made any sense," said Klarce. "You won't distract us into sparing you. We do what must be done."

He summoned himself, much as any Speaker might summon the dead. He called to his own nefshons and created a doppelgänger, his duplicate in ability and power. Together, both of him stood facing off against the eight councilors and applied themselves to restoring the unraveling caused by the Caudex meme.

Klarce gasped, but it was a sound of surprise not defeat. "I see. I don't know how you've done that, but it doesn't matter. Two of you working in unison is still insufficient to heal you. You're only prolonging your suffering."

"I hadn't planned on stopping at two."

"You're babbling. No Speaker can maintain more than one additional construct."

"You mean, none of your Speakers can," said both Jorls. They nodded to one another and suddenly there were four of him. The quartet smiled at Klarce's confusion and then there were eight of him. Enough that each quickly restored a different suffering piece of their shared threads, slowing the devastation of all eight copies of the deadly meme. Slowing, but not stopping. And it was getting harder to concentrate. That had to be part of the effect, the eventual goal of the meme. What would be left of his mind if all of his nefshons unraveled? Worse still, he'd summoned himself too late. None of him were whole, and every copy he'd made already contained the shredding meme.

"You amaze me, Jorl ben Tral. Clearly you have resources that would have been a boon to the Caudex, if only you were not corrupted and amoral beyond any redemption."

"Corrupted and amoral? Because I honored a friend's dying wish? Because I guided a boy toward adulthood? Because I saw strength and ability and helped him to channel his gifts?" Jorl wanted to laugh. He felt like he was drunk, and recognized it as evidence that he was losing ground. He shook his head, ears flapping wildly. He was losing. All of him was losing. He looked into the eyes of himself repeated all around, felt the power that rested within him to do impossible things, to reach back to Before, to invoke the Silence, to scatter the Matriarch. Except . . . the control he needed wasn't there. He tried to summon himself again, doubling to sixteen as surely that would be sufficient to his need, but shied back as the nefshons he drew to increase his number were ones that were unraveling already. If he doubled again he'd finish the task for the council.

He was holding on, but barely. But the councilors kept moving their memes from one of him to the next. He held them at bay, stopped them from spreading their contagion further through his nefshons, but those that had already been infected continued their slow unraveling. It was like a forest fire; he could contain and attempt to extinguish the existing fires or prevent new ones from starting, but not both.

Unaware of his struggle, Klarce babbled on. "Your protege isn't a boy, he's an abomination. Your inability to acknowledge this basic fact makes you a threat to our very existence. And your abilities, impressive as they are, are further argument that you must be ended."

He laughed anyway. It bubbled up out of him, and he couldn't call it back. The absurdity. No, it was him. Sobriety had slipped away. His mental acuity had vanished, compromised by the meme, by the tatters of his nefshons. It was becoming harder to think. Any complex subtle strategy he might once have come up with had fled. All he found in the laughter was bravado and bluster. He used what he had.

"My *abilities* are keeping you and your council of self-righteous puppet masters from accomplishing your goals. And believe me, when you've tired, when your koph has worn off and your weak grasp on me fails, I will come for you, the quick and the dead, and show you the full range of my abilities."

Several of the councilors gasped, flinching at the threat. But Klarce only glared at him.

"Then it's a good thing we have more of us at hand. This technique is known to every councilor going back centuries. And in place of your abilities we have technology." She looked to the side, to someone in the real office. "Temmel, bring them."

A small mob of additional Fant materialized. Long dead councilors if Klarce was to be believed. He thought he recognized a few of them from his studies. They outnumbered him again and as he watched each took up the damned meme that was destroying him.

Soon enough they would be on him, three to one, and his shredding would be assured.

It was wrong, so wrong. Klarce was using the dead against him. It was one thing to have them on a council, to seek their insight, their experience. But no, she had weaponized them. Turned them into an instrument against the living.

"Stop fighting, Jorl. You cannot prevail against so many."

"You're wrong. Your many, living or dead, are nothing but a group of individuals attempting to work in concert. Even weakened, regardless of my number, I am one person, one mind, unwavering and indefatigable."

He couldn't summon more duplicates, not before restoring more of his frayed and unraveling nefshons. But he still had resources. He just needed a moment or two without their memes pulling at him to recover, but it had to happen before the reinforcements began to attack. He needed reinforcements of his own.

The solution came to him through the fog of his mind. He didn't need to create more of himself, he could follow Klarce's own example and let each of him bring still other Speakers to the fray.

"You're not the only one who can summon other Speakers," he said, and the whole of him reached out for the nefshons of the twenty-eight Speakers he'd interviewed for his history. The illusion of Klarce's office shattered under the volume required by their sudden appearance. Several of them surrounded each of his doubles, distracting the Full Council. The meme they'd been pressing on the eight of him faltered and the additional members Klarce had introduced stood bewildered.

Confusion reigned. The Speakers from his interviews stared around themselves in consternation. Some recognized one or another of the Caudex's past councilors, realized they'd been summoned in the presence of other summoned Speakers and whatever rationale they'd accepted of an aleph being responsible clearly didn't apply now. They shouted. They trumpeted. They stomped.

Their disruption bought Jorl the reprieve he needed and the eight of him focused all his efforts on binding and restoring the many threads that had not only come loose but proceeded toward tatters. He could feel the results as his mind cleared, still less than he wanted, but when he reached for his own nefshons to again increase his numbers the particles that came to him didn't contribute to his further dissolution. And so he doubled, and again. For the moment, he didn't have to resist the continuing depredations of the Caudex meme. Each of him contributed to the repairs of not just themselves but to those around him. As the health of his nefshon pattern improved he expanded his number still more, gaining more strength with each iteration, on and on until he was legion. Before the combined might of him, the last of the damage done by the meme fell away.

Klarce quailed. "This is impossible."

Jorl allowed himself a smile. "No, this is why you cannot find a trace of the Matriarch. This is power beyond anything you've imagined."

The eight members of the Caudex Full Council and the additional sixteen past councilors Klarce had brought against him stared around them. Hundreds of Jorl stood before them, whole. With no sign of effort he dispersed his interviewees; they'd provided the distraction he'd needed. Now he would end this.

"We're done, Klarce."

Dozens of him disrupted the other seven members of the council. The living ones were likely back on Barsk, the dead had probably been summoned by Speakers back in their council room. In both cases, he effortlessly shattered the linkages they'd made to Klarce to participate in his demise. The sixteen others remained. They were present in the same physical space as her, and despite his efforts to disperse their nefshons as he might at the end of any normal summoning, they remained. No matter how many of him tried, he could not touch the nefshons of their constructs.

Jorl tore his attention from the mystery of the sixteen figures he couldn't disperse as Klarce trumpeted with rage.

"No!" She was screaming now. Her eyes had gone wild and her ears stood out from her head. Far from giving up, she looked more dangerous than before. "If I cannot shred your nefshons to destroy your mind, I will break it another way!"

"I don't want to hurt you," said Jorl. "And you can't harm me. Stand down."

"There are other ways to hurt you," she said, and all at once she held a coruscating lattice of light. She stared at it for a moment and as Jorl watched she found what she sought and summoned nefshons from afar. It took a moment, and then she had pulled another Fant onto the plane of her mindspace. The councilors he couldn't affect watched with as much confusion as he did. The construct of a child took shape. A very young Lox. Rina.

"Papa? What's happening? Where am I? Why are there so many of you?"

"I should have done this to you myself, in the beginning, instead of trusting the task to your wife. But from what I've seen here, you could probably have dealt with the effects before your body surrendered to organ failure. I doubt your daughter will fare so well."

Her hand contained a different meme now, a different shape, a different program of memories and rules. One moment she held it high above her head, and the next she sent it racing down the thread that connected her to Jorl's daughter.

Rina blinked. She staggered and fell. Her construct vanished as Klarce let the thread that had drawn her there fall away.

"Rina!"

He felt sick to his stomach. All around him on the faces of the sixteen inviolate Speakers he saw horror and shame. But Klarce hovered over him glowing with victory.

"Like I said, there are other ways to break you. Your daughter's own body is killing her, Jorl. And it's your fault."

The hundreds of him vanished, each of them reaching for his daughter's nefshons and pulling themselves to her, leaving only one behind.

She laughed to see him flee, likely guessing where most of him had gone. "This meme isn't like the shredding. It's delivered its message to her very cells, taught them new directives which they immediately began to carry out. Her nefshons aren't being affected and there's nothing for you to fix. She's dead before another day passes. You did this, Jorl. You and your abomination."

And as if invoked out of nothing, Pizlo appeared and took her hand.

THIRTY-TWO
A GENUINE ECHO

~~~~~~

S HE slapped his hand away, aware that in removing his touch she was touching him. But it didn't matter, it wasn't real, he'd obviously forged another contact with her and appeared in her mindspace, present only as a shared fiction that meant nothing. This abomination with his pallid and scabby flesh, his rheumy red eyes, had no place in her life let alone in Ulmazh, the site of so many of the Caudex's victories. Almost she was moved to personal violence, even as she wanted to retch at his imagined touch. Both were reasonable reactions.

The wrongness of him tore at her, and strengthened her justification for the meme she'd unleashed. Condemning a child to death violated everything she believed in, but it would break Jorl ben Tral. If she could end the perverse fool who willfully empowered this boy beyond any sanity then every Fant on Barsk would sigh with relief.

All that passed through her in the instant. The creature's hand pulled back, but a pulsing ball of light remained on her fingers, a meme. Somehow, he had not only learned to Speak but to craft ideas into stable shapes. Jorl hadn't known how, so who had taught the boy? It didn't matter. Klarce wanted nothing of him, certainly not any thoughts that had passed through his mind. She sent her intention into the nefshons of his creation intending to sunder it before it could taint her.

She failed.

It wasn't like any meme she'd encountered, not a simple memory or directive. It cycled upon itself, pulsed like a living thing. Not the idea of life, but life itself.

Klarce stumbled backwards, flailing her arms and trunk at Pizlo. She glared at Jorl. "Is there no limit to your offense, that you would tie an abomination's threads to this meeting?"

Surrounded by the hovering, gaping councilors trapped in place by the physicist's discs, only a single instance of Jorl remained, hunched over having folded in upon himself as the other versions presumably tried to save his daughter. He shook his head, ears lifting in surprise. "Pizlo? How . . . what are you doing here?"

"I came to help. To save you. This is my quest."

"You didn't bring him?" Klarce pulled further away from Pizlo. "No . . . I can see that now. No threads tie him to you. You didn't summon him. And I didn't. Then how . . . No! No, it's impossible!"

She fell back into the waking world and saw the abomination an ear's length away. She struck him across the face and sent him tumbling backwards on the desk. He opened his eyes and locked his gaze to hers.

"You're here!" She shrieked at him, extending one arm in a warding gesture.

Pizlo righted himself on the desk, scooted to the edge and pushed off to stand directly in front of her.

"I am. I came all this way to speak to you. To stop this before anyone is harmed. To save everyone and tell you to listen to Jorl. Please." He reached out his trunk and curled it around the wrist of her outstretched arm.

She collapsed back into her chair and fled to the mindscape where Jorl still remained. The boy followed her, too far away to touch but she felt his grasp in the real world.

"I WILL NOT BE TOUCHED BY AN ABOMINATION!"

"What? Pizlo, where are you?"

"I'm on Ulmazh. In it. In her office."

"Jorl ben Tral, is there no limit to your treason against our kind? To send this filth not merely beyond the confines of your island, but past the atmosphere of our world? You empower him to foul me with his touch?"

Pizlo nodded to Jorl. "I won't let her hurt you. I'll protect you."

"There's nothing to protect me from. I'm finc. It's Rina who's in danger."

She saw confusion on the abomination's pale face. "Rina?"

"Klarce, stop this." Jorl pleaded. "She's an innocent, and no part of any dispute you have with me."

She shook her hand again but the meme the boy had placed there would not fall free. She glared back at Jorl. "The same can be said of the millions of Fant your own actions put in jeopardy. Now, recall your creature. Or I'll send the same meme to another person you love."

"No!" Pizlo shouted and stepped between his mentor and the councilor. "It's not that actions have consequences. You have it wrong. It's that all reaction is predetermined. And that's all you're doing, reacting. That's why your future is set. But knowing that means you can change it. That's the real power you have, that everyone has. Dabni could do it. It's what Bish understood, indirectly."

What was this babble? "What is a Bish?"

"It doesn't matter. If you choose, you could act instead of re-act. That's the paradox. That's why I'm here."

Jorl wept openly. "Pizlo, no, you have to leave. Please, for Rina—"

Klarce stood taller, sick to her stomach at the price of her victory, but victorious all the same. "There's nothing on all of Barsk that can save her. Your daughter is beyond hope."

"She's not," insisted Pizlo. "Jorl, only you know what you can do. You're not limited to Barsk. You can fix her. Go."

"He can't leave. He may have control over the others of him he created, but this one I drew here and even were he to disperse the thread I'd summon another before it was gone. His awareness remains with me so I can see him suffer."

The boy looked at her with an expression that suggested she was the abomination.

"I'm sorry," he said, and vanished from the illusion of mental space. Remembering he was there in her office, she switched a portion of her awareness back to the real world in time to see and feel his trunk slap her across the face. Startled by the physical attack, she released the threads and Jorl vanished. It didn't matter, his child was doomed and when she died the father would shat-ter. Klarce dissolved and fled the mindspace she'd created and stared at Pizlo. The sixteen former councilors vanished from her awareness, the discs that kept their nefshons in place the only sign of them. As if from a dream she became aware of a pounding com-ing from the other side of her office door.

"Please, I understand. You're not thinking through any of this. You're just responding. But there's another path, one that leads to your goals, if you just choose to take it."

Klarce marshaled her courage and pushed up from her chair

to stand and face him. Her hands trembled, but not from anything of his doing.

"I am a member of the Full Council. I have responsibility for the posterity of our people in a galaxy that has shown itself to be inherently hostile to us. I've dedicated my life to this cause, and I am prepared to give everything in pursuit of it. And I will not be dictated to by a disgusting creature that threatens everything I hold dear. You should never have been born!"

Pizlo winced but held his ground. "That's more reaction. The culture. The stories. That's not me."

"You're all that's foul and base, our sins made manifest!"

"No," said Pizlo. "I'm just a young man, a little different, but with more in common with you than not. Please, let me show you."

With the last bits of koph in his system, he took the choice from her and pressed the echo he'd given to her into her mind.

"What have you done?" An instant later both versions of reality fell away.

~~~~~

SHE was falling. Leaves and vines, twigs and branches, brushed and scrapped and tore at her on all sides but she felt none of it. She tumbled through the air, reaching out with hand or foot or trunk to touch this spot or that branch or this other bough, each time as if by design that seemed wholly providence, slowed or altered her descent. She hit hard, but not critically, as she plunged into cold water, tumbling ears over ass until, with a sense of delight, one hand tapped a stony bottom and pushed her up up up until she broke the water's surface and inhaled with joy to be alive. That first simple breath after falling and immersion was like an exaltation. And all around her it seemed the world was more alive than she'd ever noticed before. The water shared her pleasure. She pulled herself to the edge of what turned out to be a very small pool—what if she'd missed it by even an ear's width in her fall?—and the rock and dirt there sung wordlessly. She pulled herself up and out of the water, acknowledged her body was young, male, pale, bleeding, and full of wonder.

In the next instant she was on a beach, rain pouring down upon her as she communed with the waves and clouds and the moons orbiting high above. There was unity to the world that she'd never heard before, and wisdom, and direction. She tried to frame a question, to engage in dialogue even as she understood this was a conversation long past, a memory. And then she was gone again.

She was in a boat, a pitiful coracle that she rowed with a paddle in each hand, numb from endless hours of it. Her hands weren't used to such work but had kept at it, not feeling the pain or ruin. Then she was sitting beside a bed telling a story to a child—Jorl's daughter?—describing impossible concepts for an adolescent to be expected to grapple with, let alone worry down to the understanding of her audience. She lay upon an examination table, groggy but alert, gazing at a younger version of Jorl but seeing someone else behind his eyes.

A bowl of the most delicious paella she'd ever smelled lay before her and she devoured it with spoons held in one hand and her trunk while a woman watched over her with a motherly but haunted gaze. Before she could eat her fill, she was elsewhere, in a room with the feel of generated gravity; she climbed an adult Bos like a tree, reaching within his robes to steal something and run away. She spoke for hours with an ancient machine that had never known a Fant but told tales that moved her at her very core. She ran along the boardways of a Civilized Wood, seeing people flinch and turn from her, feeling sad for her isolation and pity for their helpless reaction to her. She sat with an even younger Jorl, learning to read and to write, glorying at the realization of print and the worlds opening to her by the wall of books in his home.

Kneeling on a pier in a heavy downpour she held a malformed infant in her arms, knew it for an abomination, and trembled with an ache greater than any she had ever known that it had died and she had been powerless to save it. She stood in front of Dabni, a Caudex field agent who nonetheless spoke to her, and held the index and understood all that it contained. She stared out the observation port in the Alliance's space station in orbit above Barsk, saw the rising of Telko and felt several lifetimes of knowledge and wisdom pour from it into her every cell. She felt rejection and hate and loathing but never pain. And from a handful, a meager few, she felt love and understanding and acceptance.

———~~~———

KLARCE came back to herself. She was on the floor behind her desk. Pizlo stood over her, concern on his face, weak eyes strained with worry. She ached, and while she'd felt that soreness before it felt new and fresh and oddly exciting. Her hands trembled, spasmed, and a part of her wondered if Temmel might be near with her meds and, too, if she was beyond their ability to help. She opened her mouth to speak and paused, tasting the scent of urine on the air, feeling the wetness of her clothes. She'd pissed herself, but it didn't matter. She tried to sit up and discovered the left half of her body had stopped working. Had she had a stroke? It didn't matter. None of it did, she knew that now. She raised her trunk up to reach out to the young man before her, wronged by her and by so many others. A gentle and gifted spirit vilified by folklore and ignorance.

"I'm sorry, Pizlo. I . . . I didn't know. I couldn't . . . but no, no excuses."

"It's okay," he said, and his easy forgiveness burned her more than any epithet he might have righteously thrown at her.

"It's not, but it will be. I cannot change the past, but I will write you a new future."

"No, really. It's fine. Are you okay? You were having some kind of seizure. I've never given my echo to a stranger before. I didn't know it would do that to you. I'm really sorry. I just wanted you to understand me so you would maybe understand Jorl better and realize you're on the same side. So you could choose for yourself."

She pulled herself upright using her trunk and her right arm, ignoring her sodden clothes. "Yes, I suppose I see that, but Jorl doesn't matter. I have to fix the wrong I've done to you—"

"No, really, I'm fine. Don't—"

"—that we've all done to you."

Klarce slipped back into the mindspace of her office, and sent a call out to a former classmate who now held responsibility for the teams of Speakers distributing the Death meme throughout Barsk.

"I have a meme for you. In a moment, I will pass it to you, and after I have, I need you to pass it on. Share it with each of your assistants to pass on to each member of their squads. Spread it to everyone, every man, woman, and child on Barsk. Do it now. Nothing is more important."

She passed along the meme Pizlo had given her that he called his echo, and let her connection slip. Back in the real world she slumped back beyond exhaustion.

"What did you do?"

She rubbed at her eyes with the nubs of her trunk. Was he upset? No, no, she had to reassure him.

"I love you, Pizlo. I'm sorry about before. But I've fixed it. I've set it in motion. Your echo is going out to everyone. Before the day is done, everyone will know you as the person you are, not an abomination. I've set you free."

She slumped backwards. Her vision blurred and unconsciousness beckoned. Why did Pizlo still look unhappy, horrified even.

"Free," he said. "At the expense of everyone's choice."

That made no sense. He'd understand. She'd explain it, later, after she'd slept and recovered. Was someone pounding on her door?

THIRTY-THREE
HEALING RINA

~~~~~~~~

RINA opened her eyes and knew she must be dreaming. Why else were so many people there in her bedroom? She turned her head and there was Kokab right where he belonged, perched on her pillow above and to the right. So, that was fine, but why all these other people? Mama was there, talking to Papa in the corner of her bedroom room and they both looked so worried. Except, Papa was also standing, closer to her arguing with a short furry person, a Prairie Dog? And he was also over by the door angrily waving his trunk at . . . a Badger? That didn't make sense. She'd learned about the Compact in gymnasium; other races couldn't come to Barsk. Wasn't that why she'd had to go onto Papa's ship to meet the Sloth and Raccoon?

She smiled a bit as she remembered meeting Druz and Abenaki. So wonderful. But . . . back to her room, why was there three of Papa? Oh, right. Because she was dreaming. That was it.

Closest to her, the Cynomy glanced her way then looked back at her father. He looked old and kind of sad. Or, maybe not. Did Prairie Dogs look sad the way Fant did? She thought so, she'd studied, about how people were people and all showed sad and happy and scared and other things the same way. So, yeah, he looked sad.

"This is ludicrous, Jorl. I haven't practiced medicine since I joined the senate thirty years ago."

"I didn't bring you here to have you practice. Your speciality on the Committee of Information is medicine and related life sciences, Welv. You know every development, every experimental technique, every disease that's been written up in an article or a grant proposal. What's happening to her?"

"Look, I understand. You're hurting. You feel helpless. And she's getting worse. But it's not as though I can perform an examination. As you explained it, all I'm seeing is your unconscious mind's description of how she appears to you. I can't properly take her pulse, let alone draw blood or perform any kind of scan."

"But you think you know what's happening?"

"Yes, precisely because as you say I've seen all the articles. The imminent physicality cascade, that very phrase, appeared in a paper about a virus called Martinase-VI, written by Burkl there." He gestured toward the Badger. "While you were finding *her*, I instructed your wife to soak your daughter in cold water and administer a gastric lavage using warm saline. The differential between the submersion and the irrigation should slow the progress of onset, if it is this virus. But it doesn't make sense. There's no way your daughter could have contracted it."

The version of Papa arguing with the Badger looked back at the one talking to the Prairie Dog and both said the same thing at the same time.

"That's what he says, but that's not important. Go with the idea that she could be infected."

"And I'm telling you that's impossible," said the Badger, her head turning to look by turns at each of Jorl. "My seven times great-grandmother engineered the virus for the ill-conceived Taxi rebellion on the Martin colony. She crafted a designer disease profoundly narrow in scope. It wasn't just limited to the Taxi race, it targeted a specific family line with very little genetic generalizability. There is no possibility a Lox could have any of the necessary genetic markers. Do you understand? Not a one of them."

"Genetic markers don't matter," said Dabni. She looked up from Jorl and Rina saw her mother was crying. "There's a technique that takes the idea of the disease, the memory of it within the body. That memory can be duplicated and passed to anyone. The actual virus isn't needed, the memory is enough to teach the new victim what the virus *would* do, and the body responds."

"Even if such a thing was possible—and I don't believe it is— the last sample of Martinase-VI was destroyed a century and more ago."

Papa grabbed the Badger's chin with his trunk. "Were any of the targeted family members Speakers?"

"Maybe . . . ye—yes, now that I think of it. There was one. How did you know?"

He turned to Dabni. "If a Taxi Speaker had the disease, the Caudex could have retrieved the memory of it, secure in the knowledge no one would ever learn of it because no other Speaker would ever summon them."

She nodded. "That makes sense."

Jorl whirled back to the Badger. "So what's the cure?"

"What? There's no cure, because no one's contracted the disease in ages, and back then those who did didn't know they had it in time to do anything about it."

"But you said samples used to be kept."

"Well, yes, for study—"

"And, as part of that study, did someone develop a cure?"

"No, not per se. But a treatment. But it only worked if the disease was caught in its earliest stages."

Papa seemed to smile. "Which is where we are. So what is it?"

"Not something you're going to have on Barsk. It involves administering a complicated series of retroviruses in a precise order to convince the afflicted organs that they need to stop tearing themselves apart. The only place set up for that is on Haven."

"Your ship!" cried Mama. "You could take her there in your ship."

"My ship is on Ulmazh," said Papa. "And even if it were here, there're no direct routes between Barsk and Haven. The trip would take several seasons."

The Badger shook her head. "I don't know how long the seasons run where you are, but Martinase-VI runs its course in less than five days."

The room fell silent. The three of Papa all looked so sad. Mama was crying again. Even the Prairie Dog and the Badger looked unhappy. This was a bad, bad dream.

Rina coughed and her parents turned to her.

"Kokab says . . . ," she trailed off. It hurt to talk. And now that she realized that, it seemed like everything hurt and it occurred to her that despite the bits that made no sense, maybe this wasn't a dream at all. Except, she was so tired. It would be so easy to shut her eyes and then maybe she'd have real dreams. Better dreams. But her doll was being so bossy and insistent. That didn't seem fair, but sometimes he got that way and there was nothing for it but to give in or he'd go on and on and on. So she tried again.

"Kokab says, tell Pizlo to hurry."

"Who's Pizlo?" said the Prairie Dog.

Kokab stopped nagging her. Rina smiled as she imagined Pizlo getting to meet someone new. He'd love that. It was a nice thought to hold on to as she let her eyes close and drifted off to sleep.

THIRTY-FOUR
DEPARTURES AND RETREATS

~~~~~~~~~

PIZLO raced through Ulmazh's inverted city, bounding along the boardways of the underground Civilized Wood that were achingly familiar but completely new, as if they conspired to mislead his every step. He bowled over frightened Fant who could not remove themselves from his path fast enough. Their reaction to him had changed. Instead of fleeing at the first unconscious recognition of an abomination, each sensorium processed additional bits and pieces, recognized the feel of him from the fresh distribution of his nefshon echo. He saw it in their faces as he rushed past. Their fear and disgust had vanished. Instead their eyes welled up with adoration. They loved him and more, wanted him to know they did. With no hesitation they followed and flowed after him. The chorus of their voices called his name, praising him, apologizing for their blind, senseless disregard, begging forgiveness, urging him to see each of them as individuals, as they now saw him.

Pizlo ran faster.

Somewhere far ahead lay an elevator to an airlock to the shielded opening he'd used to enter this place. Everything around him murmured directions to him, precognitive whispers of the fastest way to return to Druz and Jorl's yacht. Trusting to the voices that had guided him all his life, he barreled toward a dead end, a blank wall of living green. He left the growing mob that trailed his heels and dove into the tight foliage that every resident of this city knew to be an impenetrable surface. Leaves and branches tore at him, slowed him slightly, broke before his insistence and gave way. Several Fant tried to follow him even here, cried out as their larger, adult bodies met more resistance, as wood lacerated their skin and blood flowed. One shouted after him, "Pizlo, we feel the pain you're denied!" And further behind that, a murmur of voices crying plaintively, "We love you!"

A route through the uncivilized portions of Ulmazh's much younger forest called to him and he left his followers behind.

He scrambled and climbed, desperation fueling his speed. Rina was hurt. Rina was dying. It was his fault, his doing, and he'd foreseen none of it. In hindsight though, the obviousness of it threatened to paralyze him. If he hadn't come here, hadn't confronted Klarce, hadn't been an abomination, his best friend would be fine. This was what all the moons had been warning him of, not danger to Jorl's person but to his daughter. This now was his damn hero's journey. Not the ink for tattoos, not traveling inside a moon, not meeting and transforming Klarce, not saving Jorl. *This.* The struggle to save the innocent girl his blindness had put in danger.

Already nauseated from ingesting so much koph in one day, Pizlo nonetheless pulled a last wafer from his bandolier as he headed ever outward to the airlock. At the first hint of his own nefshons he shunted that awareness aside and reached for familiar particles that he'd never summoned before. Calling to them brought him a living thread from Druz above him in the ship on the moon's surface. He pulled the sight and scent and feel of her surroundings from her recent memories and spun them into the mindspace. He didn't know if Jorl had ever spoken to her like this and needed to keep her distraction to a minimum.

"Druz! Druz! Prepare for launch. Hurry!"

"Little Prince? I didn't see you come onboard. How did you evade the sensors in the lock?"

"I didn't. I'm not there yet. But soon. Don't worry about it, I'll explain. But this is an emergency. We need to leave the very instant I'm onboard. You understand?"

"I don't, but I can comply. I trust your explanation will be detailed."

"Yes, when I'm there. For now, do what you need to do so we can get downworld as fast as possible. Get us as close to Keslo as you can. Do you have maps of the island?"

"Of course."

"Right, right. You're going to need to land closer to shore than you usually do. Right in the harbor. Find an open portion of a pier and snug up against it. Oh, and open the airlock for me."

"That's not prudent."

"Maybe not, but it will save time. None of the people following me can get there before I do."

"Following you? Why are people following? Are you in danger?"

"Druz, please, focus. Do what I ask. I promise I'll sort it all when I'm there and we're underway."

Pizlo severed the contact and focused on finding the path the moon was sharing. The infrastructure of its Civilized Wood had never been explored by Ulmazh's residents. The meta-trees here had grown strangely in the artificial and upside-down gravity, thicker but not denser. Wood shattered as he forced a path forward and in retaliation his flesh tore. It didn't hurt, but even so he'd slowed, which meant, pain or not, he'd done himself some real damage. His left arm had stopped working. Glancing down he saw a red gash in the skin and a jagged bit of living bone poking through. It didn't matter. Druz could probably fix that once he got to the ship. And he had to, so he could locate Jorl and then get Rina to the ship. He reached again for nefshons, Jorl's threads, and gasped as he connected not with just one but a trio of him. They spoke as one, their resonance murmured to him, each piece little more than a whisper.

"Not now, Pizlo—"

"I know, Rina's in danger. I'm coming to help."

"You can't—"

"No, *you* can't. Not by yourself, not completely. You need to trust me on this. All the moons are in agreement. You can't save her without me."

Unspoken emotions from past discussions and arguments rippled through his connection, triggered associations that would never have slipped through, revealing the strain on Jorl. "Precognition is probabilistic. You can't fully know the future."

"You say that because you're on the outside looking in. You're partly right and you're partly not. We can have this debate some other time. But if you want to talk probabilities, then I'm telling you the odds of you saving Rina on your own—regardless of how many of you are involved—are just short of infinite."

"I won't give up!"

"Don't!" Pizlo shouted through the link and rushed along an open branch ever nearer the edge of metal and artificial soil that existed here in lieu of a Shadow Dwell. "Keep doing what you're doing until we get there."

"We?"

"Druz and me. We're bringing your ship back."

"That won't help. Nothing on Barsk can and the ship can't get her to Haven in time."

"It can," said Pizlo. "It *will*. The ship's infirmary has a stasis bed. It will keep Rina stable, but only if you keep the cascade from progressing too far. Keep fighting, we're coming."

He felt a pause and then a change. Amidst the strain and fear and rawness, a piece of Jorl's mind reorganized and fell into place. In that moment, in a context of gratitude and weariness, his mentor stopped seeing him as a child.

"Pizlo . . . hurry!"

He ended the connection as he ran/fell down the massive bole of a meta-tree, its surface roots angling toward the horizontal. A moment later he was running over dense packed earth towards a metal rim and the scaffolding beyond. He vaulted the edge and landed without pause upon a gantry, knowing the route through the hexagonal pattern of giant pots to the maintenance gate. He climbed a loop and up became down as the artificial gravity fell away and the moon pulled him in its own direction. He stumbled, his injured arm flailing uselessly and ran on. Ahead, he saw the same bored sentry who had let him pass as if being an abomination carried the same weight as Jorl's aleph. The guard stood at his duty station. This time his face broke out in an expression of awe and delight. He rushed to meet him halfway, babbling the while.

"I'm so sorry. I didn't understand before. I didn't know. Please, let me help. Whatever you need. Oh my, your arm . . . is that a compound fracture? Sit, I'll call for a physician. And maybe my son, too. He's about your age. Meeting you would change his life. All you've been through. I can't wait to tell him I met you, before I mean, and that I got a chance to make up for it. But the doctor first, of course—"

Pizlo cut him off with a curt wave of his trunk and never broke stride. "You want to help? Open the gate."

The man leapt to the controls and a second later the maintenance gate opened, its halves receding into the surrounding walls. Pizlo sped through.

"Lock it behind me. If anyone comes after, keep them from following. I'm leaving and it won't be safe for them up top."

"No, of course. I don't understand how it's safe for you. Do you want me to come with?" He followed the teen through, pausing at the control station on the other side. "I can code-lock the gate from here just as well. That would keep anyone from following and maybe I can lend a hand when you get up top."

Pizlo flinched at the earnest need in the man's voice. "No, really. Stay here. I'm good. Um . . . thanks."

Lights came up in the corridor as he stepped beyond the maintenance gate, harsher and brighter, a clear demarcation that he was leaving a place for Fant. The unforgiving sterility of space lay ahead of him and whether the builders of this place had intended it as a reminding metaphor or not, there was nothing of life in this corridor. He pressed on and arrived at last at the elevator to the surface. His ill-fitting environment suit lay where he'd left it. Pizlo paused only long enough to shove his feet into the boots. He snatched up the helmet with his trunk and hauled the legs of the suit up with his good hand and then was moving again. He fell into the elevator, punched the button for the surface, and pulled himself into the clothing, not even attempting to slide his broken arm into its sleeve. He forced himself to slow down and perform the safety checks that his precognition had brought to him, visions of all the ways he could die if he ignored them dancing through his consciousness. He disregarded the stifling feel of the suit's sleeve on his trunk as the readout in his helmet read green. Soon after, the elevator's door opened onto the corridor leading back to the disguised airlock and the surface of Ulmazh.

Pizlo refrained from running—it would only cause him to leap and crash into the ceiling and risk damaging his environment suit—hurrying toward the far end of the corridor in a series of carefully controlled bounds. He cycled the lock, flung himself within and slapped at the close-button with the empty mitten of his trunk sleeve, gripping the handle by the outer door, preparing to fling himself over the surface of Ulmazh the instant the airlock allowed.

The moon's rotation had carried the city's entry point into a spot of relative darkness. The searing red light of Ekkja lay somewhere beyond the horizon. The soothing blue white of cloud-wrapped Barsk was nowhere in sight. There was an abundance of starlight, and the hurried arc of tiny Wella as it tore across the sky, confusing everything with faint and ever-shifting shadows.

After the brightness within the corridor and elevator, Pizlo couldn't see anything on the moon's surface. His eyes had always been weak, and he'd long since learned not to rely on them. Jorl's ship was where he knew it to be and he set off for it without hesitation.

~~~~~

DRUZ'S voice met him as he entered the airlock. "What is happening, Little Prince?"

"We're leaving," he said. He ignored the protocols that insisted he stay suited until past the next set of seals. He pounded on the intercom with his fist. "The outer hatch is sealed. Lift now, please. It will be fine."

"There is a not insignificant possibility of harm to you if we depart before the final lock cycles. It won't be long—"

"Druz, listen to me. I've seen the probabilities, and seen beyond them. I'm good. But Jorl and Rina are not. Time is everything right now. Go!"

The airlock fell silent save for the hiss of building pressure. A moment passed and a rumbling vibration knocked Pizlo off his feet. He bounced off the wall and crashed to the floor as Druz accelerated the ship and fought off Ulmazh's claims of gravity. The inside of his suit felt wet. He was bleeding. A lot. Possibilities fell away now that they were moving, but the outcome was still far from fixed. He understood that now. He kicked off the rest of his suit and removed his helmet as the inner hatch unsealed. Druz awaited him on the bridge. He'd promised her an explanation but doubted any of it would make sense.

~~~~~~

RISING up from the airless grip of relatively tiny Ulmazh was much quicker and easier than a controlled push through the atmosphere of the much larger planet it orbited, but he'd impressed upon Druz the need. Crossing the thin strip of space between the two hadn't taken long and after some emergency first aid, a sling, and an IV to replenish his blood, he and Abenaki had used the remaining time prepping the stasis bed in the infirmary. The Procy's intimate knowledge of it proved an unexpected boon.

The ship fell from the sky with a determination greater than all the rain of Barsk. It was late morning, and most of the boats from Keslo had long since set off. Those gone fishing were far enough out as to not notice a spacecraft aiming for the dock, and those traveling to other islands wouldn't return until Druz had taken off again. Other vessels getting in their way wouldn't be a problem. Jorl had called in some favors and island officials had declared a temporary medical emergency to clear pedestrian traffic from the Civilized Wood all the way down to the harbor.

That last had been a mistake.

"There are people on the dock, Little Prince," said Druz over the yacht's intercom. "Thousands of people. I doubt the structure is rated for so many. If even a portion of it fails, as seems likely, they're in serious danger."

Pizlo stood in the hold, one hand and his trunk over a control board that would extend and maneuver a gangway to the pier once the hatch opened so they could take Rina onboard.

"That makes no sense. No one should be there."

"I have the dock on the screen now," said Abenaki. "I'm looking at a whole lot of no one."

"They've seen the ship," added Druz.

"How can you be sure?"

"They were standing still before, but now many of them are jumping into the water and swimming toward us. Many of the others are singing. Well, chanting, really."

"Chanting? Can you make out the words?"

"Yes, we're close enough now, but . . . you should hear this for yourself. Patching the audio through to this channel . . ."

Their voices echoed through the hold, hundreds of voices repeating two syllables, over and over. Piz. Lo. Piz. Lo. Piz. Lo.

The sound cut off and Druz came back on. "I'm uncertain how to proceed. If Jorl and his daughter are down in that throng, I can't see them. What do you want to do?"

Pizlo shut down the control board. "Send Abenaki to the infirmary to get some koph. I'm on my way to the bridge."

"Why?"

"Because we have to find another way in, and you've never been there. Take us up. Maybe if the people down there see us fly away, they'll leave the dock before it collapses."

"Understood. But why are they calling your name? I thought because of the circumstances of your birth they couldn't so much as acknowledge you."

"Yeah," said Pizlo. "That's changed. They adore me now."

~~~~~~

HE sat at the second navigation board, transposing a location as he knew it in his head to coordinates that the ship would understand. The Procy had returned with the koph about the same time as he'd sat down. He locked in the last bits just as the first perception of nefshons came to him along with a nausea that might have been from whatever meds Druz had added to his IV, or the toxic effects of so much koph in such a short span. He passed control of the board to Druz. "Take us there. I have to talk to Jorl, and then I'm heading to the volar airlock."

He reached for Jorl's nefshons and they came to him in a rush. He didn't bother with a mindscape. Jorl was there, standing in front of him in emptiness.

"Pizlo, are you ready for us? We're at the top of the funicular but there's been a delay of some kind. The car's stuck at the bottom."

"Change of plans. Instead of staying out of your way, there's a mob of people crawling all over the dock. That's probably why your rail car is stuck. Doesn't matter. You'd never make it to the pier and it wouldn't be safe to try."

"We *have* to try! We need to get Rina into the stasis bed."

"We will. But we're going another route. Go to the balcony that opens on Arlo's Chimney. I'll meet you there."

He let go of the connection to Jorl and opened his eyes to the bridge. Druz and Abenaki both stared at him.

"Druz, as you come up on those coords you're going to see a big hole in the green. It's a shaft that cuts all the way down to the Shadow Dwell. Get as close to that opening as you can. I'll rappel down it until I reach Jorl and secure Rina. Abenaki, come with me. I'm going to need your help to rig a grapnel and harness." Without waiting for a reply he started running through the ship.

The Procy followed. "Why do your people have holes cutting top to bottom through your forests?"

"They're . . . monuments. Memorials. This one is called Arlo's Chimney."

"Oh. Who was Arlo?"

"My father."

~~~~

TOO quickly, but not quickly enough, they were braking through the air above Keslo. Pizlo waited in the airlock on the underside of the foot of the ship. The outer door was open. How many doses of koph had he taken recently? It was too much. He needed to sleep, needed to purge the poison of it from him. Both would have to wait.

Wind and rain howled through the hatch. He stood poised to leap through open air toward what seemed a tiny hole in the rainforest canopy. The straps of a support harness cut into his body and for once he wished he could feel the pain of it. He didn't know what kind of transportation Jorl had arranged for Rina, and a variety of hooks and cables lay wrapped around his waist. The ship had surely reached the chimney first, but they wouldn't be far behind.

The future was stupid.

In one version, they'd mistakenly landed in the harbor and hordes of desperate Fant had boarded the ship to force apologies on him, beg forgiveness, ask to learn from him how they could be better, more generous beings. They still loathed all other abominations, just not him. They knew him, loved him more than they loved themselves. And their love had kept him from reaching Rina and securing her into the ship's stasis bed in time to keep her body from destroying itself.

In another outcome, some other portion of Keslo's citizenry had decided to seek out Jorl. He had helped raise him, after all, and who better to share their new insights with? Again, they blocked Rina from him and prevented her access to safety. Then there was the version where despite all precautions the grapnel malfunctioned, or a knot slipped, or a cable snapped, on and on down ever decreasing probabilities that all resulted in Rina's death. Stupid stupid stupid. Like the universe wanted him to fail and wanted her to die.

Pizlo was having none of it.

He jumped from the airlock, determined to contradict the wishes of the universe.

~~~~~

ONCE he'd cleared the open air and actually entered the mouth of the chimney, the rest of his fall was familiar. The six-sided shaft opened up around him, turning in a slow helix as it dropped. He knew every handprint of it all the way down, what to touch to slow his descent, where to grab or push. He didn't need two good arms and could have done this part in his sleep.

He reached the top of the Civilized Wood, and midway through it one side of the chimney opened onto a public balcony. School groups came there sometimes, choral groups as well, to experience the weird acoustics such shafts made possible. And though this chimney was named for Arlo, his newly adoring public wouldn't know to seek him here. The balcony was empty. He broke his fall, and hung.

He didn't wait long. Jorl and Dabni raced toward him down the approaching boardway dragging a wheeled cart between them. Some sort of folding bathtub perched atop the cart, water sloshing from it as they reached the balcony's railing and brought it to a stop. Rina lay inside.

"Is the stasis bed ready?" Jorl was out of breath, his ears down and back, his eyes wild.

Even before answering, Pizlo was swinging to the railing and unwinding the grapnel from about his waist, working out the best way to secure it to the tub. "Yes, it's all primed."

"The settings differ by race," said Jorl.

"That's what Druz said. She's already searching databases for the proper calibration for a juvenile Lox. The generic setting will serve to start and we'll fine-tune it once we're underway."

"Yes, but—"

Pizlo waved him off. "This isn't going to work. I'll spend more time wrapping up the tub than we can spare. Give her to me."

Jorl lifted his daughter from the water and handed her to Pizlo who cradled her against himself with his trunk and one arm. It was awkward but he wouldn't have to hold her for long. Despite the cold water dripping from her, her skin was hot. As he held her close she whimpered.

"Wait," said Dabni. "Please, take her doll, too. She'll want it when she wakes up." She tucked Kokab under the strap of his bandolier.

From down the boardway came a cry. They all turned. Tens of people were rushing toward them.

Jorl gasped. "What is happening?"

"My fault," said Pizlo. "Klarce sent my echo down. I didn't think it would . . . well, I didn't think."

"It's no one's fault," said Jorl. "More importantly, it's in the past now. History. Go, look after Rina. We'll deal with this."

"It's not just these people, Jorl, it's the entire planet."

"I understand. And between Dabni and me, we know more about nefshons and memes than anyone alive in the galaxy. We'll fix it. Not today, but soon. I promise. Now go."

There was no future in which Pizlo was going to win that argument. He stood on the balcony railing, briefly gripped the loose cable with his trunk and pulled, two short, two long, two short. High above, Abenaki responded to the signal and activated the pulley in the airlock. Pizlo began the long ascent back up the chimney. By the time his adoring public reached the railing he was well out of sight.

THIRTY-FIVE
THREADS OF PERSONALITY

~~~~~~

A s part of being Klarce's assistant, Temmel had received basic medical training. Moments after the Abomination of Keslo had fled, he was at the councilor's side. Her breathing was labored and her pulse erratic. Moving her seemed unwise but he brought in cushions from the outer office and made her as comfortable as circumstances allowed. He swallowed some koph and reached out for help.

Bernath was his first thought. He didn't know her well, mostly from reports, but she dealt with innovation and he needed something miraculous. He briefed her as best he could, and to his relief she promised to join him quickly, accompanied by the physician and the physicist who had accompanied her to Ulmazh. He didn't know what use a physicist could be but he recognized Lotle's name from past reports and knew her to be an expert on life extension. Keeping Klarce alive surely qualified.

When the three of them arrived it was Ryne who took charge. He began by powering down the discs on the floor, releasing the long-dead councilors who had hovered helpless and confused, trapped by technology.

"Lolte, when you're sure she's stable, lay her across this disc."

She nodded. "Of course! That's . . . was that one of the applications you'd intended?"

Ryne shook his head, the nubs of his trunk delicately activating the manual settings of the disc before him.

"What good will that do?" said Temmel.

Lolte continued her inspection of Klarce as she answered. "The body goes where the mind leads. Klarce's mind has retreated, presumably to gather its resources and heal her. But in the meantime, her body isn't receiving direction. There's a school of thought that believes one's nefshons begin to destabilize under such conditions."

"Destabilize? As in dissipate? I thought that only happened with death."

She gave him a hard look. "Not if we move her to that disc. Grab her feet and lift when I tell you to."

Temmel complied. "I still don't understand. You say she's dying. How will this help?"

Ryne made way for them. "It will prevent diffusion. That may not prevent discorporation, but if her body insists on dying it won't be because her mind led the way."

"So you're saying there's a chance?"

Bernath laid a hand on Temmel's shoulder. "There's always a chance. Whether she takes it is up to her."

They moved Klarce in place and settled in to wait.

～～～～

ABENAKI had aided Pizlo in securing Jorl's daughter into the suspension bed. She lingered just long enough to confirm that the young Fant somehow demonstrated a mastery of the control system and was happy to depart. She'd gone to the guest quarters Druz had assigned her when they'd arrived on Barsk and for the last two days had mulled over the things the Fant had said when he'd first come aboard. They disturbed her, and at last she sought out Druz where she sat at the board on the yacht's bridge. She'd stopped in the ship's galley on the way and arrived with food for them both. While Druz ate, she shared her questions and concerns. The senator's assistant seemed in no hurry to reply, finished the meal at a gourmand's pace, and held up one hand to forestall any further questions while she checked their progress on her controls.

Their ship was on its way to the portal that would take them from Ekkja's system and move them lightyears away to the next stage of their trip. It was the irony of space travel that the massive span between stars happened in an instant, and crossing the gap between neighboring portals in the same system demanded days to go from one to the next.

"You need to understand that Pizlo is a precognitive," said Druz, after an excruciating delay.

"So, you're saying he knows my future?"

"I'm saying he may have insight into some piece of a probable future," Druz said.

"How high is the probability?"

"The predictive sciences are . . . imprecise. I can tell you that Pizlo is the most powerful of any precog ever recorded. Some of that strength may translate into greater accuracy, but there isn't a lot of data that's been studied."

"But you're saying the future is fixed?"

"To the extent that it can be seen and understood, yes. Or, so we've always thought."

"But?"

Druz shrugged, pushing back the long sleeves of her robes, black nails tapping on the glass of her control panel. "But I've been listening to the recordings Pizlo made, and he believes that destiny can be tempered by agency, at least for those who can see the future."

"What does that actually mean though?"

"To you and me? Very little. We plod along same as always."

"And for the likes of Pizlo?"

"He believes he can effect change in his fixed destiny, and the fate of those around him."

"How? How could he do such a thing?"

The Sloth repeated her slow shrug. "Because he chooses to."

~~~~~

A tenday after Pizlo had departed with Rina, the Fant had achieved an uneasy quiet. Every inhabitant of the planet—regardless of whether they'd ever visited Keslo or not—had realized they *knew* that island's Abomination better than they understood themselves. They loved him and they were ashamed of themselves at the way their races' deep-rooted feelings for abominations had brought the boy such a lifetime of neglect and loathing. Their feelings toward all abominations hadn't changed, only for Pizlo.

On Keslo, where the entire population had at one time or another seen and turned away from Pizlo at least once, the need to absolve themselves ran higher. The piers where so many residents had gathered to greet him upon his return from Ulmazh had miraculously survived. A couple people had been injured in the stampede back into the Civilized Wood when Pizlo's ship had flown away from the harbor, but nothing worse. Tolta had returned home from an estranged family that now valued her as no mother and household of aunts and sisters had ever favored a daughter before. Her tiny house had become a shrine, pilgrims camping out on her doorstep for a chance to speak to the mother of the young man whose life burned so brightly for them all. The council boat had arrived with a unanimous decision to award Pizlo an aleph, insisting that Jorl be the one to inscribe the tattoo on the forehead of his protégé. Already songs were being composed describing such a singular event though it hadn't happened and probably never would.

During that time, Jorl and Dabni had buried themselves in the common cause of finding a solution to Pizlo's echo as much to distract themselves over concern for Rina's fate as to give themselves time to heal over the wounds Dabni had inflicted on their relationship. They worked together in a mind space that Jorl had conjured, leaving their bodies behind in a quiet and undisturbed location. Tolta's home was out of the question, as was Jorl's. In the end, they'd snuck down into the Shadow Dwell, bringing supplies to one of Pizlo's hideaways. No one had thought to find them there.

At the end of the tenday, Jorl summoned the seven members of the Caudex's Full Council—Klarce's nefshons somehow being immune to his call. They stood together in a mindspace of the council's meeting room on the final island and offered their help. Unsurprisingly, there was some resistance.

"I don't understand," said Sind. "What gives you the right to take from us our love of Pizlo?"

"Are you insane?" said Nirl, the contempt dripping from her tone. "I know you're bitter after we failed to end this rogue's life, but you and Kissel and Melko have been acting like it was a mistake to try. Think of poor Klarce and what this abomination did to her!"

"Klarce's situation is not Pizlo's fault," said Kissel, setting his meekness aside. "He tried to help her. And without her sharing his echo, none of us would know how wrong we'd been."

"I rather think that's Nirl's point," said Mason. "That echo has colored your perceptions."

"But not yours," said Jorl.

Mason nodded and emphasized his answer with a wave of his trunk that encompassed the deceased members of the council. "The echo was only sent out to the living. Only the dead have not had their sensibilities rewritten by Pizlo's life story.

"The dead, and a few who already knew him," said Dabni.

Jorl stamped a foot. "The point is, with Dabni's help I've come up with a plan to remove the worst of the effects, but it will require ongoing support at an unconscious level. That's not a part of my skill set but I'm assured it falls well within the scope of the Caudex."

"And what if we're not willing to sacrifice our insights into Pizlo's life? Would you just strip them from us?" said Kissel.

"No one asked your permission before imposing them on you, why do you think you're entitled to a say as to whether you can keep them?" said Dabni.

Melko trumpeted. "I will not be lectured by a disgraced field operative!"

Jorl stomped again until he had silence. "The solution is simple. I'll remove what I can, and then, with a clearer head, if you still want that knowledge, I'll restore it."

"You can't remove it," said Soosh. "Memory disruption is only effective before the new knowledge has had time to consolidate. Our people have had days to absorb and reflect upon the teachings of your protégé."

"I'm not going to disrupt the memory, I'm going to pull it out entirely. I've had some experience doing this before."

Kissel rose from his seat, shouting. "What gives you the right to force even that on us if—"

The rest of his words fell away. Jorl had begun pulling out the nefshons of Pizlo's life from where they'd entangled themselves in the totality of Kissel's own particles. The work was infinitely more nuanced than when he'd unleashed the silence on Senator Bish. Time slowed. Jorl worked quickly but the threads of Pizlo's life had overpowered Kissel, tying themselves into his own sense of self. Unknotting took time, far more time than a Speaker could normally manage in a single summoning. Jorl had no such limitation. It required as long as it required, and his power was more than sufficient to keep himself, Dabni, and the members of the council there in the mindspace until he was finished.

He took only those memories that were part of the original echo and no piece of how it had been elaborated or enmeshed into other ideas. Nor did he remove any other knowledge Kissel had of Pizlo, nor any nefshons that were not tied specifically to Kissel. All other nefshons related to Pizlo that existed were untouched. And then, well into the next day, he was finally done.

Kissel sat back down. "Oh."

"Yes?" asked Joel.

"He's . . . a remarkable young man," said Kissel. "Notwithstanding all he's had to endure."

"But do you love him?" asked Dabni. The other councilors, both the living who still held Pizlo's echo and the dead who never had, focused their attention on their colleague.

"Love him? No, don't be foolish. I . . . have admiration for what he's accomplished, surely. And . . . I think I need to reconsider our views on abominations. Surely we've outgrown that kind of cultural culling."

"So you've *cured* him?" said Nirl.

"In part. Memory is resilient. In taking away Pizlo's echo, I've left a hole that reflects its shape. Pieces of it will spontaneously reconstruct over time. Think of it like weeds in a garden. Periodically they'll need to be dug up. That's why we're here. Dabni has told me you have means to deliver a simpler, 'weeding' meme to everyone on the planet without their awareness. I'll need you to do that, once I've stripped what Pizlo inadvertently shared with everyone."

"Ridiculous," said Nirl. "You just spent most of a day unraveling the abomination from Kissel. How do you propose to manage the same thing for every person on the planet?"

"The same way I bested you on Ulmazh, by multiplying myself. Once for every Eleph and Lox that carries Pizlo's echo."

~~~~~

BERNATH returned to Barsk with the comatose Klarce and accompanied by Ryne and Lolte, the latter two following the councilor to a private hospital suite while Bernath went to report to Sind. By the end of the second tenday after the events on Ulmazh, the Full Council was mollified, Jorl had miraculously reclaimed most of Pizlo's echo from all the Fant, and Speakers on Ulmazh had begun implanting Dabni's "weeding" meme on a routine basis right alongside the meme that ensured people thought it normal to sail away at the end of their lives. Pizlo no longer burned in the hearts and minds of the people of Barsk. His status had dropped to that of a folk hero, the object of stories that everyone knew and no one ever tired of hearing again and again.

Sind traveled to Keslo and met with Jorl in an attempt to rebuild a pact that he would continue to uphold the secret of the Caudex and not endanger their goals or threaten the safety of Fant on the Hidden Worlds. And, too, he reassigned Dabni to serve as the

Caudex's liaison to the senator, an acknowledged ambassador rather than a spy. All things considered, both meetings went well.

Nor had Sind come alone. He'd brought Bernath with him. Though both had been purged of the majority of Pizlo's echo, their direct knowledge of the events kept an awareness of much of him in their minds. They lingered on Keslo, walking its boardways while under the influence of koph, following trails of his castoff nefshons that revealed where he'd been. They could not travel through the inbetween spaces of his most common routes, but where those paths crossed more accessible spots—near Jorl's boat in its slip, several observation stations high in the canopy, near the door to an apothecary—they could immerse themselves in the spoor of his memory and felt themselves somehow closer to him.

It was in one of these spots, a cove too small and isolated to have any practical value, that they found other nefshons, anomalous particles unlike any either Speaker had encountered. It made no sense, not least because no Fant other than Pizlo had spent so much time in the Shadow Dwell. Nor did the dispersal patterns lead anywhere else, suggesting that they belonged to someone who had been summoned after death rather than someone who, like themselves and Pizlo, had walked to this place. Sind had consulted the archive and Bernath had doubled-checked his efforts. These strange nefshons belonged to no Fant. Who then had young Pizlo summoned, and why?

They stayed in that cove for the night, huddling against the end of flood in a tiny shelter they'd erected, letting the koph fade from their bodies through the twin gifts of time and sleep. In the morning, they prepared themselves. By unspoken agreement Sind began drawing together those scattering nefshons that troubled them while Bernath hung back as witness to whatever might transpire. The dispersion halted, reversed, and took on shape. At first it seemed as if an immense block was taking form before them, but it collapsed in upon itself before becoming solid. And then they were facing a young Lox on the edge of maturity. He was oddly translucent, as if he composed of living glass. Within his substance shadows swirled and colors flashed. He stood before them naked and aware, as if unsurprised at being summoned.

"I can never tell how much time elapses between one visit and the next, but it pleases me to encounter new faces. Hail, and well met!"

"I don't understand," said Sind. "You . . . you have Pizlo's shape and appearance, but your self-image is nothing of flesh and blood. What are you and what is your connection to him?"

"Second question first. It has been my privilege to have been Pizlo's advisor. As for myself, I am the Archetype of Man."

"What does that mean?" asked Bernath, drawing closer and standing alongside Sind in the mindspace he'd formed of their cove.

"I was created to preserve and curate stories from a time you call the Before. But now that you have come to me, perhaps it falls to me to add to my repertoire and tell a tale of your modern time. If you would hear it."

Bernath and Sind shared a look that was equal parts confusion, concern, and curiosity. It required a moment before Sind recalled he was the seniormost member of the Quick Council, the highest ranking member of the Caudex still drawing breath. He flapped his ears to regain his composure and nodded for the creature cast in Pizlo's image to go ahead.

"Space is vast," said the Archetype, "and since the time of my creation many many different races of sapients have spread across thousands of planets of this galaxy. One such planet is Barsk, a world of hundreds of islands. One of these is Keslo, and on this island lived a young man unlike any other. He was the Abomination of Keslo . . ."

~~~~~~

THREE and a half tendays out from Barsk and Pizlo continued his vigil in the yacht's infirmary. He gazed down at Rina in the medical suspension bed, her life functions slowed to a crawl. The slight fever that had plagued her since her infection had faded and he took that as a good sign, though it made no sense. The bed should only have been able to delay the effects of her disease, not cure any of them. And indeed, that was the only positive sign. All the tone had gone out of her muscles. Though she slept, she looked more tired than relaxed. But according to the readouts she wasn't getting any worse. Blue lights played across her skin, a constantly repeating diagnostic array that made minute adjustments to the machinery. Druz had been in communication with experts on Haven and over the days of their voyage she had fine-tuned the suspension bed to the needs of a Lox child. Rina's readings had stabilized. There was every reason to expect her to remain like that until they reached their destination.

Their route would take them through twelve different pairs of portals and across as many planetary systems. Traversing the space between exits and entrances would take tens and tens of days, but they'd completely skip the much vaster distances between stars. Abenaki had spent nearly as long in the same suspension bed and assured him it had felt like nothing but a longish nap. Haven, arguably the most developed and cosmopolitan world of the entire Alliance, awaited them. A world that hadn't seen a Fant in eight hundred years would now save one.

Druz had set aside quarters for Pizlo but he had no use for them. He preferred to make a simple cot for himself in the infirmary. The

Brady didn't need him to fly the ship and the Procy had enough common sense to leave him to his vigil. He kept watch at Rina's bedside, interrupted only occasionally by the need to eat and drink, tend to his ablutions, surrender to a bit of sleep, or respond to one of Jorl's frequent calls. He never had any news for his former mentor. He could only assure him nothing had changed, that the stasis bed continued to keep the physicality cascade in check, that he'd reach out if there was anything new.

They'd just passed through another set of portals and arrived on the edge of still another star system. It was late night by the ship's schedule and the need to sleep pulled at Pizlo. He'd just concluded telling Rina another story, uncertain if she could hear him, through the fields of the machinery, through the difference of time. Days ago he'd thought of using koph to reach out to her, but Jorl had advised against it, fearful that it might stir her to awaken from the sleep that kept her alive. And so he stayed by her side, waiting with her and telling her stories. There was little of nature in the ship, no trees or wind or rain to whisper to him. The portals they used, the planets and moons in each system they sped through, these had tried to catch his attention and tell him things, but he'd ignored them. Rina was his only focus. He'd watched her sleep so many nights before, her rag doll tucked in the crook of one arm. In many ways, this was little different.

Pizlo had stayed up longer than usual, and for the first time since they'd left Barsk, Jorl had allowed a day to pass without reaching out to him. He found himself drifting into that place between wakefulness and sleep and spared a glance to his cot in the corner, unsure if he'd still be awake by the time he reached it. He pressed his face to the edge of the suspension chamber's transparent cover, level with Rina's and her doll. Maybe she could hear him, maybe not, but he always offered some reassurance before he stepped away and surrendered to sleep.

"You're going to be okay," he told her. "We got you into suspension. The organ failure cascade is in check and when we get to Haven they can reverse it before bringing your body back to regular time. I promise, you're going to be fine."

The doll turned its head as if scanning the room. It looked back to Pizlo and nodded, the blue light making the buttons on its face gleam.

"Thank you for that," said Kokab. "I was quite concerned. But now, tired as I see you are, I really think it's time we talked."

APPENDIX ONE:
PEOPLE

Abenaki (Procy female)—representative of a consortium of Raccoons seeking to emigrate to Barsk.

Adolo (Eleph female)—Klarce's lover.

Ajax (Lox male)—Speaker and member of the Caudex, he is assigned to Councilor Sind's staff.

Bernath (Eleph female)—member of the Caudex, she oversees operations of new arrivals.

Burkl (Taxi female)—biologist whose expertise includes engineered and weaponized viruses.

Chisulo (Lox male)—son of Keslo's harbormaster and barely a year out of his mother's house.

Ciochon (Ailuros male)—Panda that babysat Pizlo when he was on the station.

Dabni (Lox female)—field agent of the Caudex, wife to Jorl, mother to Rina.

Damace (Eleph male)—ethernaut and a younger brother of Klarce.

Denzi (Procy male)—civil engineer specializing in waterworks; father of Abenaki.

Druz (Brady female)—personal assistant and majordomo to Jorl.

Fisco (Lox female)—deceased Speaker of great renown. Once a resident of Belp.

Frilbo (Lox genderless)—imaginary and magical friend Jorl had as a child.

Full Council—made up of eight members, four of whom are living (Klarce, Melko, Sind, and Kissel) and four deceased members who are summoned (Genz, Nirl, Marsh, and Soosh). The living members are also known as the Quick Council, and are responsible for day-to-day governance.

Gari (Lox female)—young graduate student, assigned as an assistant to Ryne on the nameless island.

Genz (Lox male)—deceased member of the Caudex Full Council and its seniormost member.

Jorl ben Tral (Lox male)—historian and member of the Alliance senate, Margda's chosen and the fifty-seventh Aleph, mentor to Pizlo, husband to Dabni, father to Rina.

Hearne (Lox male)—food vendor with a shop on the main dock on Keslo.

Kentl (Eleph female)—Jorl's landlady.

Kissel (Eleph male)—member of the Caudex Quick Council as well as a surgeon.

Klarce (Eleph female)—member of the Caudex Quick Council, Adolo's lover.

Kokab (Lox-shaped male)—Rina's rag doll.

Kolleen (Eleph female)—mother of Klarce.

Krokel (Eleph male)—middle-aged and part-time faculty on the nameless island; an assistant assigned to Ryne.

Layne (Eleph female)—mother of Bernath.

Lin (Ailuros female)—mentioned in passing, the child of Ciochon.

Lolte (Lox female)—physician and systems biologist on the nameless island.

Marsh (Eleph male)—famous and much-beloved politician in life, he is one of the deceased members of the Caudex Full Council.

Melko (Lox male)—member of the Caudex Quick Council.

Nestwhistle (Lox female)—code name of a Caudex ethernaut assigned to monitor the far side of the Alliance's portal into Barsk space.

Nirl (Lox female)—youngest and most brilliant of the deceased members of the Caudex Full Council. Revealed to be a liar and academic thief after her death.

Phloda (Lox male)—the provost at the university on Zlorka and friend to Jorl.

Pizlo (Lox male)—son of Arlo and Tolta, the Abomination of Keslo, protégé of Jorl, student of the Archetype of Man, best friend to Rina. A precognitivist.

Regina (Lox female)—Klarce's secondary assistant and Adolo's second cousin.

Rina (Lox female)—daughter of Jorl and Dabni, Pizlo's best friend.

Ryne (Eleph male)—physicist who sailed away from the island of Taylr only to arrive at the final island and discover things are not as he believed.

Santo (Procy female)—journalist and the mother of Abenaki.

Shelby (Eleph female)—Rina's rhetoric teacher at the gymnasium.

Sind (Eleph male)—seniormost member of the Caudex Quick Council, mentor to Klarce.

Soosh (Lox female)—deceased member of the Caudex Full Council.

Su (Ailuros female)—mentioned in passing, the child of Ciochon.

Suliv (Lox male)—proprietor of a grocery and sundry shop in Keslo of the same name.

Temmel (Eleph male)—Klarce's primary assistant.

Walto (Eleph male)—elderly field agent of the Caudex, assigned to the island of Keslo.

Welv (Cynomy male)—senior member of the Committee of Information.

APPENDIX TWO:
PLACES

BARSK'S MOONS:

The planet has seven natural moons, as well as an artificial satellite in geosynchronous orbit above the island of Zlorka. At the time of this writing, the names of only five of the moons have been revealed to the reader.

Pemma—the second smallest of Barsk's seven moons. It was the third one Pizlo saw, and the moon which (he claims) instructed him to stow away aboard a cargo pod and travel up to the orbiting space station.

Nita—larger than Ulmazh but smaller than Telko, this moon has a connotation of being lucky, though no one seems to recall why.

Telko—the largest of the moons. This was Pizlo's fourth moon, seen from the viewport of the orbiting station.

Ulmazh—middle-sized of all seven moons, a crater in its northern hemisphere serves as the opening to a hollowed out area in which the Caudex has built a massive city.

Wella—the smallest of the moons, it has a more oblate shape, heavier in its bottom half than its top. For reasons that are unknown to this author, Wella is always referred to as having a masculine aspect.

ISLANDS OF BARSK'S WESTERN ARCHIPELAGO:

Emmt—a popular destination for young bachelors traveling from Keslo.

Fintz—a wide but thin island east and south of Gerd where Pizlo encounters an infant abomination.

Gerd—a smallish, nearly circular island that is considered the central island of the western archipelago. Fant often refer to other islands in the chain with respect to their position relative to Gerd.

Gumti—a kidney-shaped island in the southwestern half of the western archipelago and recently famous for being the home of the newest (fifty-eighth) person to bear the aleph.

Kelpry—an island south and west of Gerd in the western archipelago.

Keslo—an island located near the northeastern portion of the western archipelago. It is home to Jorl ben Tral.

Peckl—an eastern island of the western archipelago.

Phran—an island north of Gerd but still a good ways south and west of Keslo. On an eastern beach of this island, Pizlo saw his fifth moon.

Senjo—an island on the middle southeastern edge of the western archipelago.

Telba—an island to the north of Keslo. A Speaker there published a book of imramha after interviewing various adventurers. They are also renowned for their tea.

Zlorka—a part of the western archipelago, it is considered the most cosmopolitan of islands. Zlorka is the only land mass on the planet to touch the equator. It is home to the premiere university on Barsk, as well as the anchor point for the space elevator that transports goods to an automated station in orbit.

ISLANDS OF BARSK'S EASTERN ARCHIPELAGO:

Belp—home to Fisco, a renowned sixth-century Speaker.

Maxx—a medium-sized island, once home to the wood carver Rüsul.

Morab—a popular site for higher learning in the eastern archipelago; the closest rival of Zlorka in the west.

Myer—south of Relfa, this western island is a popular meeting point for scholarly conferences.

Relfa—the westernmost island of the eastern archipelago, it is a popular destination for groups of young men crossing over from the other island chain.

Taylr—second easternmost of the islands of the eastern archipelago.

Yargo—a tiny island in the southeastern section of the eastern archipelago, it is famous as the birthplace of Margda, the Matriarch of Barsk. Her childhood dwelling, once home to nearly a hundred children, mothers, aunts, and female cousins, is now a vast museum, complete with research library and gift shop. Tours are given twice daily.

WORLDS OF THE ALLIANCE:

Caluma—a mixed world and home to Abenaki, a Procyon.

Dawn—a major world of the Alliance; home of the senate.

Dorrance—colony world where former senator Bish has been exiled.

Dramblys—a mixed world, and past home to Fant.

Gripta—a mixed world, and past home to Fant.

Haven—a major world of the Alliance.

Kitsu—presumably a mixed world, though it has never been home to any significant population of Vulp.

Marbalarma—a mixed world, and past home to Fant.

Scrothe—a mixed world, and past home to Fant.

Sleipnir—a mixed world with almost no Marmo or Myrm.

Sworrub—a mixed world with a predominantly Marmo population.

boardways—major walkways within any Civilized Wood, they are characterized by broad avenues paved with wooden boards formed from the living wood of the meta-trees that define the city. While not formally zoned, they tend toward commercial structures with residential buildings clustering on smaller avenues that feed into the boardway itself.

Caudex—originally, a group of Speakers contemporary to Margda who broke from her seemingly arbitrary rules for Speaking. As they discovered powerful uses of nefshons they relocated to a singular island roughly midway between the planet's two archipelagos and began shaping Barsk culture and society in ways they believed would keep the planet safe from the Alliance as they advanced programs that would set their people free

cribble—a non-citrus fruit that has a peelable rind like an orange.

dark—the second of Barsk's five seasons, it follows mist and precedes storm. During dark, the cloud cover is at its thickest, some days blotting out any difference between day and night.

flim—a data storage medium that may take its name from either film (which it resembles) or flimsy (which aptly describes it).

flood—the fourth of Barsk's five seasons. Rainfall is heavy but thunder and lightning are much less common.

handscreen—a small, tablet-like computer.

mindscape—(also "mindspace" and "mental space") the illusion of place created by a Speaker during a summoning, often drawing most of the sensory details from the Speaker's unconscious memory.

mist—the first season of the year and also the hottest.

nahlet—a type of nut.

plel—a twenty-third-century term for "apple" that completely replaced the traditional word when English was hardwired into Earth's raised mammals.

sartha—a decorative plant native to Barsk, popular in gardens as each morning it releases a soothing, sleep-inducing fragrance.

spiralmint—a characteristic aroma of most formulations of koph.

storm—Barsk's third season, it comes after dark and before flood. Rainfall greatly increases, as much as eight times the downpour of the previous season. Thunder is nearly continuous and lightning is everywhere.

tenday—a common way of grouping the passage of days.

tenyear—a common way of grouping the passage of years.

wind—Barsk's fifth and final season. Cloud cover and rainfall are at their lightest, making this season the most popular time for travel between islands.

A NOTE ABOUT ELEPHANTS

One hundred years ago, our planet held millions of African elephants and some 100,000 Asian elephants. A century later, and those numbers have dwindled: 450,000 to 700,000 African elephants and somewhere between 35,000 and 40,000 Asian elephants in the wild. It's not too late to turn this around. You can make a difference, through education and support of one or more of the many agencies throughout the world that are fighting for elephant conservation.

Closer to home, I recommend you check out The Elephant Sanctuary (https://www.elephants.com), the largest natural habit refuge in the U.S., which provides a safe haven, individualized care, and companionship for both African and Asian elephants that have been retired from public exhibition at zoos and circuses. Located on 2,700 acres in Hohenwald, Tennessee (some eighty-five miles southwest of Nashville), The Elephant Sanctuary also operates programs to educate the public on the needs of elephants in captivity as well as the crisis experienced by elephants in the wild. Please take the time to contact them today and make a difference in the lives of these magnificent beings before they only exist in fiction.